THE ACTOR

About the Author

CECIL ALLEN IS THE GRANDSON of the famous actor and writer Ira Allen. He is a graduate from Indiana University and the University of Minnesota. Cecil has been a professional actor, a broadcaster and a college lecturer with the Dublin Institute of Technology. Retired, he is the father of two sons and lives in Malahide, Co Dublin with his wife Julie.

THE ACTOR

A Novel

Cecil Allen

First published in 2014 by
Cecil Allan
www.cecilallan.com
email: theactor@cecilallen.com

All rights © 2014 Cecil Allan

Paperback ISBN: 978-1503190641

All rights reserved. No part of this book may be reproduced or utilised in any form or by any means electronic or mechanical, including photocopying, filming, recording, video recording, photography, or by any information storage and retrieval system, nor shall by way of trade or otherwise be lent, resold or otherwise circulated in any form of binding or cover other than that in which it is published without prior permission in writing from the publisher.

The right of the author of his work has been asserted by him in accordance with the Copyright, Designs and Patents Act 1988.

All characters and events featured in this publication, other than those clearly in the public domain, are entirely fictitious and any resemblance to any person living or dead, organisation or event, is purely coincidental.

Cover design by Brendan Bierne
Cover illustrations by Godfrey Smeaston
Typesetting by Chenile Keogh

For Paul and Mark

'And one man in his time plays many parts.'
As You Like It
WILLIAM SHAKESPEARE

Prologue

26 September 1955

THE BLACK LEATHER WIDE-BRIMMED hat, set at a slight angle on the young man's head, cast a shadow over his eyes. He removed his hat, unbuttoned his long black leather coat and listened to the whispering voices that whistled around the church. The mourners, 'the have-to-be-theres', the old friends and the curious were waiting for the funeral service to commence.

The young man ran his fingers through his thick black hair, fixed his intense blue eyes on the coffin and slowly walked down the centre aisle of the church. At first, only a few heads turned and glanced at him. Then they took a second look. An audible intake of breath rippled down the church, more heads turned, mouths dropped open and elbows poked into bodies. Halfway down the church, an old man gasped as if he had seen a ghost.

'Are you all right Mr Stanley?' asked the woman beside him.

The old man nodded and made the sign of the cross.

The young man's footsteps rang out loudly in the now silent church.

'He's the image of Jim,' whispered an overly made-up, aging actress to her shocked companion.

THE ACTOR

'By God, you're right! Who is he?'

There were only a few people in the church who knew the answer to that question and one of them was the deceased. As far as the rest of the people were concerned, the actor Jim Brevin had never fathered a son.

1

It was three o'clock in the morning on the 28 March 1898, when Jim Brevin entered the world. The gas-lights in the Brevins' well-appointed three-story Victorian house on Dublin's fashionable North Circular Road had been glowing for hours. Theo Brevin, the child's father, had been up and down the stairs a hundred times to his wife's bedroom.

'Are you sure I can't do anything?' he called once more through the closed bedroom door.

'I think you've done enough already,' the midwife called back.

'How is my wife?' Theo asked, magnanimously ignoring the midwife's rebuke.

'She's as well as can be expected.' The bedroom door opened. 'You can come in now.'

'I can?' He tiptoed into the room. 'How are you?' he asked his exhausted, pale-faced but happy wife.

'It's a boy, we have a second son.'

Theo's eyes travelled to the new-born child in Grainne's arms. 'Truly wonderful, Grainne! Well done.'

Later that day, when Michael, their three-year-old son, learned that he had a little brother, he leapt for joy.

THE ACTOR

The Brevin home was a cheerful, happy place of velvet curtains, primrose-striped wallpaper, Japonisme woodcut prints and fine furniture. On the evening of Jim's second birthday, Theo was reading in his study when baby Jim stumbled into the room, wrapped his arms around his father's right leg and called out, 'Spider! Spider!'.

Theo lifted his son on to his knee and, smiling at the child, asked 'Where's the spider, little man?'

'Spider out there,' Jim said, and pointed to the garden.

'He's a fine handsome little fellow,' Theo said to his wife Grainne, when she came into the study in search of the boy.

'Michael and James are the most handsome boys I've ever seen,' Grainne said cheerfully as he handed Jim up to her.

'Naturally, they are,' said Theo, serious as always. 'They are Brevins.'

Later that evening, sitting in the drawing room in front of a roaring fire, Theo stroked his chin and declared 'Grainne, we are very lucky, we have two fine healthy boys.'

'Indeed yes,' Grainne replied and cocking her head to one side, added, 'I wonder if our third child will be a daughter.'

A moment passed. Theo sat bolt upright in his chair.

'Third? Are you?'

'No Theo,' Grainne said playfully. 'We are.'

'Truly wonderful!' Theo replied, wondering what on earth Grainne meant by 'we'.

On the 17 November 1901, Líla was born and the Brevin family was complete.

The Dublin of the 1900s was the second city of the British Empire. Union Jacks flew from public buildings, post boxes were painted red and Edward VII's reign had just begun. But Dublin was really two cities; a prosperous city of plenty and a tenement city of slums.

The city of plenty was a place of well-appointed Georgian buildings and squares where young gentlemen in straw boaters, striped blazers and white trousers promenaded young ladies in long elegant dresses and huge broad-brimmed hats along the paths of the city's gardens. It was a city where men in top hats and morning suits strolled to their place of employment and well-dressed ladies shopped in fine stores while organ grinders pumped out ragtime music for their amusement.

In Dublin's tenement city, hundreds of thousands of people lived in abject poverty in some of the worst slums of Europe. This city was a dark, disease-ridden place where shoe-less, rag-wearing children played all day on derelict rat-infested sites. It was a place where hundreds of unemployed men gathered daily on the docks and waited for a day's work. It was a place where destitute women and children scavenged for discarded, overripe or damaged fruit and vegetables in the gutters of the city's markets. It was a place where every night, tens of thousands of malnourished men, women and children went to bed hungry and it was a place where sixteen hundred prostitutes plied their trade in the city's notorious red light district. The brutal cycle of daily life for the people of the tenement city was hunger, ill health, unemployment and early death.

The plight of the slum dwellers was largely ignored or unknown to those who lived in the city of plenty and Jim, like most middle class Dublin children, grew up completely unaware of the great poverty and deprivation that was a mere ten-minute walk from his home.

One of Jim's earliest memories was of his father standing in the hall beside the seven- foot longcase clock. Theo pulled his pocket watch from his waistcoat, flipped it open and checked it against the huge mahogany clock.

'Spot on,' said Theo and snapped his watch shut. 'Know what time it is son?' he said to the five-year-old Jim, who was staring at him. 'It's cricket time – time to go to the club.'

Jim, as ever, pulled a face.

Jim did not enjoy going to the cricket club or playing cricket or watching cricket. He thought the cricket club was a dreadful place, not only because he hated the sport with all its silly rules and ridiculous equipment but because he'd have to talk to people.

Jim's lack of social graces and disinterest in cricket – or indeed, any competitive sport – alarmed and confounded his father.

'How could any boy not enjoy sport?' Theo would say to his wife whenever they discussed Jim. 'It's not natural!'

'James is a bright boy, leave him alone Theo, he's developing nicely.'

'You mollycoddle that boy far too much. It will come to no good.'

Jim loved to read and most of the time he could be found sitting in his favourite winged wicker chair in the morning room with his head buried in a book. He thrived in his world of imagination, fantasy and wonder. At meals, when his father was not at table, Jim would play the fool until he had his mother, Michael and Líla shaking with laughter. Yet when his serious-minded father was at the table the small boy would sit, eat and say little.

For decades, the Brevin family business had imported fine wine and sherries from Europe. Under Theo's expert guidance, the company had grown to be the largest importer of wines into Ireland. Every July, Theo would visit the vineyards of France, Spain and Portugal and select wine and sherry for his company.

From an early age, Theo insisted that his boys earn their keep and much of the children's Christmas and summer holidays were spent working in the business. Jim and Michael were put to work in the company yard with the stable manager Mr Stanley, cleaning out the stables and tending to the dray horses that pulled the delivery carts.

'It may be menial work but it builds character,' Theo replied whenever Grainne complained about the work he had assigned to the boys.

Theo Brevin was a big impressive man whose black wavy hair was always carefully shaped and waxed. He was a gregarious person who dressed fashionably. A proper, conservative gentleman who disapproved greatly of 'lady suffragettes' and women cyclists.

'Women on bicycles, it's vulgar and definitely unladylike,' Theo said to Grainne whenever he saw a woman cycling.

'It's the modern way,' Grainne would reply. 'You can't stop progress.'

'Yes, that is true,' Theo would reply. 'But I don't have to approve of it.'

Theo was a man's man who loved sport, but his true passion was cricket. He was captain of the Phoenix Park's Cricket Club and was particularly proud of scoring a century against the Clontarf Cricket Club in 1905.

'A great day,' Theo said to Michael many times when he recalled his victory in Clontarf. 'It's something I remember with great pride.'

THE ACTOR

Grainne Brevin took great delight in life. She was an overweight, happy woman with an infectious, hearty laugh who adored her husband and three children. Grainne was an enchanting, vivacious person who, at parties, after she had sampled a little too much of her husband's fine wine, would sing until all hours in the morning.

Every evening when the children were in bed, Theo would open a bottle of wine and he and his wife would sit in the drawing room and talk. On the evenings when Theo opened a second bottle of wine, Grainne would get a little giddy and her laughter would echo through the house.

Grainne and Theo did not agree on everything. One area of conflict was the Catholic Church.

'I don't really mind God,' Grainne said one evening when she had had a little too much wine. 'But I certainly don't like the people working for him. Why, oh why, would he call the grumpiest, most boring and loveless men to be his clergy? Imagine having to spend eternity with such awful people.'

'The men you speak about are great men and great thinkers,' Theo scolded her.

'Don't you talk to me like that! They're not great men and they certainly are not great thinkers. They are sad bachelors who live on their own and make up religious rules to suit themselves.'

'Sometimes Grainne, you go too far.'

'I never went far enough,' snapped Grainne.

'Grainne, if you question everyone and everything, what is there to be sure of?'

'Theo, you can always be sure of me.'

'Thank God for that,' Theo replied and took another sip of wine.

The Brevins' eldest boy, Michael, was very much like his father; Michael loved sport and never opened a book. He was an active member of the junior cricket club and every Sunday, during cricket season, he and his father had a practice match or played a competitive game. When Theo took his daughter Líla to a game, Jim was pressed into minding her; he was not happy about this and was not slow to show his annoyance.

Líla Brevin was an adventurous, headstrong, fearless tomboy who was always the first to climb a tree, jump across a stream or fight with her brothers or with any boy who might assume she was just a defenceless girl. Michael disapproved greatly of the way Líla behaved but Jim adored her and envied her spirit and enthusiasm. Theo loved his daughter but she confused him and he wished she were a little more ladylike.

'Grainne, this afternoon at the cricket club Líla struck young Richard Clark,' Theo said solemnly one Saturday when they returned from the park.

'He took her sweets,' Jim interjected, defending his sister.

'That's no excuse for violence. Besides, Líla is a girl and she shouldn't be fighting. I'm very worried about her.'

'Well, don't worry,' Grainne replied. 'Perhaps you should be worried about young Richard Clark. I'll say something to his mother.'

'No, no, leave it to me, Grainne.' Theo replied, waving his hand in the air.

Grainne smiled. Mr Clark was one of Theo's best customers and she knew nothing would ever be said to Mrs Clark about her son's thieving habits.

The other inhabitant of the Brevin house was the mighty Mrs O'Neill, the housekeeper. She was a matronly woman whose family was reared and whose husband had died a year before she took up her duties in the Brevin household. In addition to being an excellent housekeeper, Mrs O'Neill was Grainne's friend and confidant.

Sunday was family day in the Brevin household. Dressed in their Sunday best, the five Brevins would attend Mass and then would walk to the Phoenix Park and stroll through the gardens or visit the Zoo. On other Sundays, the family might go to the Botanical Gardens and if the weather was inclement, visit one of the city's museums. After their Sunday evening meal, Mrs O'Neill would visit her grandchildren and the Brevins would entertain themselves. They played card games, board games, word games and once a month they put on a family show. Theo played the piano badly with no sense of rhythm and missed every fourth or fifth note. Their mother would sing beautifully. Then, each child would do a turn. Líla would jump around and their mother would call it a dance, Michael would juggle cricket balls or anything else that came to hand and Jim would perform magic tricks or recite a poem or a monologue.

These evenings were very important to Jim; when he was conjuring or reciting his poems he was transported to a very special place deep within himself. Jim's best audience was his mother. She would mouth the words of the recitation with him and whenever he stumbled, she would prompt him. When he finished she would applaud loudly and shout 'Bravo!'

Theo's appreciation was more muted. One evening after a family show, Theo said to Grainne 'Sometimes I think that boy would rather live in his world of magic and monologues than with his family.'

'That's a dreadful thing to say,' Grainne said, following her husband out of the room. 'What if James had heard you? Theo, you must be careful with what you say. You can be quite insensitive sometimes.'

But Jim had heard his father; he had been behind the sofa when his father said it. It shattered him; how could his father say such a thing? Jim loved his family more than anything in the world and for his father to think otherwise shocked him. Maybe father doesn't like me, Jim thought. Maybe he never liked me. And so the family home became a battleground of stolen glances, silent reproaches and hurt expressions. At table, Jim seldom directed conversation to his father and when Theo spoke to him, Jim often looked the other way. Jim hated the way he was treating his father but he didn't know how to stop doing it. Most of the time Theo pretended not to notice Jim's frowning glances and deliberate silences but they hurt him and, as the years passed, Theo drew the conclusion that his second son did not like him very much.

2

JIM WAS SEVEN YEARS OLD when he first experienced the magical tinsel and gauze world of the theatre. It was St Stephen's Day 1905, and Theo had taken his family to the Queen's Theatre annual Christmas pantomime. Jim loved everything about the theatre: the feeling of anticipation and excitement he experienced as he climbed the steps to the theatre, the buzz in the huge auditorium, the elegance of the enormous red curtain, the shimmering of the huge crystal chandelier that hung from the ornate ceiling and the chattering audience as they took their seats. As he waited for the performance to commence, his excitement soared to almost unbearable heights.

The lights faded, the auditorium went silent and the curtain rose. Jim was captivated by everything he saw and heard: the colour, the music, the lights, the costumes, the sets and the magic of it all. He looked in wonder at the pretty girls as they danced around a maypole that mysteriously disappeared into the theatre's flies. He fell in love with Cinderella, laughed heartily at the comedians and booed the Ugly Sisters when they were mean to Cinderella; but most of all he was enchanted by the actors, and that enchantment was to stay with him for the rest of his life.

'That was truly wonderful, mother,' Jim said, remembering the words his father used when he was extremely pleased with something. 'Truly wonderful.'

'I'm very glad you liked it,' Grainne replied, suppressing a wry smile.

For weeks afterwards Jim pestered his brother Michael to take him to another show. Finally, one wet Saturday afternoon when a cricket game was cancelled, Michael agreed and the two boys set off for the Queen's Theatre. Rain poured down as the tram clanked and shuddered to a stop at College Green. The boys jumped off the tram, side-stepped a puddle of water and dodged their way beneath a sea of umbrellas to the theatre.

Sheltering beneath the iron and glass awning, Jim and Michael read the enormous four-colour poster. '*The Face in the Window*, a *sensational thriller!*' it blazed. '*See Ira Allen as the villain and Val Vousden as the detective fight on the rooftops of Paris!*' Beneath the text, two figures were fighting; one figure had a knife and was about to stab the other. The two brothers stood and stared at the exciting if frightening poster.

'Do you think they kill each other?' Jim asked his brother.

'I don't know. Do you still want to go? I don't mind if we don't go,' Michael replied clearly a little alarmed at the images on the poster.

'No, I want to go,' Jim said, more determined than ever.

The boys walked slowly up the stairs to the upper circle box office. Michael spoke into a small hole in the glass, handed in a shilling, and two tickets and a few pence change appeared in the opening.

Swept along by the milling crowd, Michael and Jim entered the theatre and sat in their seats near the front of the balcony. As they waited for the play to begin, Jim looked around the theatre; there was not another child in sight. The lights dimmed, Jim hunched down in his seat; a hushed reverence fell on the auditorium and as the curtain rose he gripped his knees in an attempt to contain his excitement.

If Jim loved the pantomime, then he adored the melodrama. The action, the fighting, the costumes, the props, the sets and the music were so exciting that he could hardly contain himself. The booing and the hissing of the audience delighted him, the fighting thrilled him, the singing enthralled him and the comic actors made him guffaw with laughter. He loved everything except when the villain gazed in his direction; that was the only time he looked away from the stage.

THE ACTOR

All during the performance, the audience reacted openly and vocally to what was happening; they gasped loudly when treachery was visited upon the heroine, cheered on the hero, and when the villain had the heroine in his grip, they shouted at him to release the girl and to give up his dastardly ways. Some members of the public talked loudly to each other during the performance, others ate fruit and if they didn't like what was happening, threw their uneaten fruit at the stage. Some called out witty responses to the players and when the action on the stage got a little talky or dull, they got up and went for a drink.

When the lights dimmed at the end of the play there was a split second of silence then the audience jumped to their feet and cheered, applauded and foot-stomped. Jim had never experienced anything like it and all he wanted was to see another play like it.

One Saturday, Jim and Michael went to the Abbey Theatre but Jim didn't enjoy the experience. He found the acting lifeless and dreary – there was far too much talk and even though the audience was very quiet and respectful, the actors spoke so softly that Jim could hardly hear them. He thought the costumes were very dull and with no set changes, fights, music, pretty girls or humour, he got bored. No, Jim much preferred the magic of the melodramas.

In the spring, Michael told Jim that he had joined the rugby club and that he was no longer going to go to the theatre. Jim was unperturbed; he attended the theatre on his own.

He would wait at the box office for a family to came along, then follow them up the stairs and when they had entered the auditorium, go back to the box-office, place a shilling on the counter and announce 'my father forgot to buy a ticket for my cousin.' When a ticket appeared in the opening in the glass he would say 'thank you' and once again enter the magical world of theatre.

During the next two years, Jim went to the theatre as often as he could. His two favourite actors were PJ Bourke and Ira Allen and of these two, he preferred Ira Allen. The performance that impressed him the most was when Ira played the tragic farmer Ciaran O'Leary in the melodrama, *The Bailiff of Ballyfoyle*.

From the moment Ira walked on the stage, a poor but proud and happy farmer, until he exited in the final act a homeless but dignified man, Jim was completely absorbed in Ira's performance. When the bailiff's men with a battering ram demolished the O'Leary home and cast the farmer and his family onto the road, Ira Allen's transformation from weariness and despair to red-blooded passion was so convincing that a shiver ran down Jim's spine. When the actor held up his fist to heaven and uttered the words: 'This is my home, my land, my country, and as God is my witness, I will not rest until it is mine again!' Jim was so overcome with compassion for the man that tears rolled down his cheeks. The theatre's great red curtain fell, the audience jumped to their feet and cheered and hollered and that was the moment Jim knew that theatre was going to be his life.

Michael Brevin sat in front of his father's desk and waited anxiously for his father to speak to him. It was late June, and Theo had summoned his eldest son to his study. Theo dipped his pen in the inkwell, signed the document on the desk, placed the pen at rest and said to Michael 'It's time you learned something about wine. Next Saturday, I'm taking you with me to Europe and we will visit some vineyards where you will learn how wine is made and why some wines are considered superior to others.'

Michael was delighted, but when Jim heard the news of Michael's trip to Europe he felt slighted.

One rainy afternoon, while Jim and Líla were sitting in the drawing room awaiting their mother, Líla bounced out of her seat, stood in front of the oil portrait of her grandmother and asked 'Why isn't Granny Molly smiling?'

'Because smiling hadn't been invented when they painted that picture,' Jim replied making a stern face like Granny Molly.

'That's not true,' answered an unsure Líla.

'Jim, don't be teasing your sister,' said Grainne entering with the afternoon tea tray. 'Líla, your grandmother isn't smiling because people didn't smile when they were having their portrait painted.' Grainne poured the tea and sliced the cream cake. 'When I was about your age Líla my mother took me to London and brought me to a theatre in the West End.' Líla flopped back in her seat and tucked her legs under her. Jim sat up straight in his seat.

'Was the theatre exciting?' Líla asked.

'The theatre was wonderful, full of light, colour and music. And the actors – oh, those wonderful English actors. Líla, soon I'll take you to London and we'll go to a theatre in the West End. It's like no other theatre in the world, it's truly magical.'

'Will you bring me too?' Jim asked, looking into his mother's eyes.

'Yes of course I'll bring you. All three of us will go and we'll have a wonderful time.'

'Good, because Father wouldn't take me anywhere,' said Jim, in a voice so laced with hurt that Grainne's heart shuddered.

'That's not so,' Grainne replied, ever so softly. 'Jim, your father loves you very much and you mustn't think otherwise. Theo's parents were very serious, strict people and that's the way he thinks he should be, but he does love you.' She brushed his fringe away from his frowning eyes. 'Besides Jim you have me. I will always be here for you.'

Brian Ahern, Jim's best friend, lived in the house next to the Brevin home. Brian was an intelligent, happy, innovative child. The two boys were the same age and while Brian was not handsome, he possessed the most piercing blue eyes imaginable. Brian and Jim played together, went to school together and sometimes slept in each other's homes. Brian would think up new magic tricks for Jim to perform or devise new ways of performing old tricks. It was Brian's idea to use a biscuit tin filled with candles as footlights for Jim's recitations and magic shows.

The boys made lots of things together: they made a canoe out of old wine boxes; it sank. They made a trolley cart from discarded timber and pram wheels; it worked. They constructed a magic lantern show, which frightened Líla so much that she couldn't sleep for a week. Their most successful project was the B and J Newsletter. Using printing jelly, indelible ink and paper from Theo's desk, the boys wrote, edited and printed their own six- page magazine. The newsletter ran to four editions and they sold it to friends, neighbours and relatives.

If Brian was Jim's best friend, then Ann Ahern, Brian's younger sister, was Líla's veritable sister. Like Líla, Ann was a tomboy; the girls did everything together and were constantly called upon by their brothers whenever they needed an additional hand or body for one of their projects or experiments.

Grainne Brevin was never a particularly healthy woman; she was overweight, exercised too little and drank too much. She also suffered from what the family doctor, Dr Moore, called melancholia.

'She needs total bed-rest and quiet,' he would say whenever the darkness fell upon Grainne, and with those words the Brevin household would change dramatically.

During their mother's illnesses, Mrs O'Neill, the housekeeper, assumed all household duties and Ciara, Mrs O'Neill's stern-looking niece, was brought in to help with the kitchen and household chores. There were almost daily visits from Dr Moore; the house smelt of antiseptics and carbolic soap, and Grainne's bedroom drapes were drawn day and night. Grainne would remain in her bedroom and only Theo, Mrs O'Neill and Ciara were allowed to attend her. The children were allowed a daily five-minute visit and that was only if their mother felt up to it. For weeks there was no gaiety, joy and certainly no laughter in the Brevin house. During those long dark days, Jim longed for his father to put his arm around him and hug him and tell him all would be well, but Theo never did. Eventually, as dramatically as the cloud of darkness had descended on Grainne, it would lift and life in the Brevin household would return to its usual happier self.

In the autumn of 1906, when Theo and Michael returned from their wine-sourcing trip, Theo announced – to Grainne's consternation and the children's delight – that he had decided to grow a handlebar moustache. Every Saturday morning, while the moustache was growing, the children would sit their father down on one of the wicker chairs in the conservatory and measure his whiskers' progress.

'I'm going to grow a moustache when I grow up,' Líla announced, one morning during the measuring procedure.

'Girls can't grow moustaches,' Michael replied, chuckling into his hand.

'Mrs O'Neill has one,' Líla said, correcting her brother.

A disapproving Theo scowled at his daughter. 'It's very rude to comment on a lady's facial hair,' he said sternly, and that was the last time anyone ever mentioned Mrs O'Neill's moustache.

After three months, Theo's moustache was thick and shiny with a good natural shape. One of Líla's little delights was to stand in the bathroom doorway and watch her father wax and shape his whiskers. Theo's moustache found so much favour with family and friends that he decided to keep it and after a short time the children could not remember a time when father didn't have his very decorative handlebar moustache. The three months it took Theo to grow his moustache was a memorable time for Jim; it was the only time he allowed himself to get physically close to his father. He stood in front of Theo, touched his father's growing whiskers and looked into his father's bright blue eyes.

On the 3 May 1907, an animated Miss Bronagh McManus, an ardent royalist, arrived for her weekly afternoon tea visit with her closest friend, Grainne Brevin. Bronagh delighted in joining clubs and organisations and one of her proudest boasts was that she was a paid-up member of eighty-nine clubs and organisations.

'I joined the movement but I wouldn't take part in any of their marches,' she replied when Grainne asked her about her involvement with the suffragette movement. 'Good heavens, Grainne, if I went on one of their marches I might be seen and that would never do.'

But for all her silliness and hypocrisy, Bronagh was an entertaining companion and Grainne greatly enjoyed her company.

'It's so exciting – the Irish International Exhibition is opening tomorrow,' Bronagh twittered while Grainne poured the tea. 'Can you believe it? In July, Their Royal Highnesses King Edward VII, Queen Alexandra and Princess Victoria will be in Dublin to attend the exhibition.'

'Yes, I can believe it. Poor Theo has been run off his feet organising additional shipments of wine and sherries for the celebrations.'

'Don't talk to me about such mundane matters,' Miss McManus exclaimed dismissively. 'I have to get to my seamstress and order new outfits and then I have to go to my milliner. A new hat is essential and I must visit the shoemaker for new boots – I must have new boots! Grainne, how can you be so calm when there is so much to do?'

'I've been to my seamstress and milliner and everything is in hand.

THE ACTOR

I've even ordered new sailor suits for the boys and Miss Gertrude Finnie, my milliner, has kindly invited the family to view the royal procession from her first floor premises in Dame Street.'

Miss McManus's head jutted forward, her eyes bulged and she asked conspiratorially 'Would you mind if I joined your family party for the day?'

Grainne pondered the thought. Having Bronagh for a whole day, all that chatter and fussing ... But it would be a kind thing to do.

'It would be our pleasure,' Grainne replied, and had another cream cake to steady herself. How am I going to tell Theo and what is he going to say she wondered as she helped herself to yet another cake.

The preparations for the Irish International Exhibition of 1907 had been going on for a decade. To house the many national and international exhibits, a new city of pavilions, exhibition spaces and offices had been constructed on a fifty-two acre site in Herbert Park. The exhibition's main building consisted of a central octagonal domed court with four radiating wings. The domed central court was as big as a rugby pitch and as high as a cathedral. Two million visitors were expected to visit the exhibition from all parts of the Empire and a new tramline had been constructed to transport the people to and from the city.

Business for many Dublin traders and suppliers boomed during the time of the exhibition. Theo usually received one or two shipments of wine every month but during the spring of 1907 it was almost a daily occurrence. Theo would go to the excise offices on the Dublin docks, sign for the shipment and pay the excise duty. Then with the necessary forms in hand he would proceed to the enormous excise warehouse where Mr Stanley and his helper were waiting for him. Theo would then meticulously check the shipment and supervise as each crate was loaded onto the covered delivery cart.

On the last Wednesday of April, Mr Stanley's helper fell ill and an eager Michael volunteered to take his place. Theo reluctantly agreed but Grainne, who had just stopped by the company office with Jim, glared at Theo and flicked her eyes to Jim. Theo understood the unspoken message and said 'Jim, why don't you go along with Michael and Mr Stanley.'

Jim didn't have to be asked twice; in seconds he was up on the cart beside his brother.

'Boys, I want you to do exactly what Mr Stanley tells you to do and do not get off the cart until you get to the excise warehouse.'

The boys nodded. Mr Stanley clicked his tongue, flicked the reins and the cart pulled out of the company's cobblestoned yard.

Mr Stanley was a pleasant, quiet man who never used two words when one would suffice. He had a large head and wild hair on which sat his small battered bowler. Any sudden movement, Jim thought, and Mr Stanley's hat would fall off his head; but miraculously it never did.

The trio journeyed through the city's busy streets and down along the docks where boats of all sizes were being loaded or unloaded. Suddenly the road became crowded with frightened cattle and farmers waving sticks at the unfortunate animals. Mr Stanley halted the cart, blew his red-veined bulbous nose and the boys watched the farmers herd the cattle on to the boats. As they waited for the quays to clear, Jim's eyes travelled along a line of shabbily dressed, grey-faced men standing along the quayside. Many of the men were carrying battered suitcases tied with belts, or brown paper packages tied with string.

'Mr Stanley, why do those men look so sad?' asked Jim.

'They look sad because they have to leave their families and go to find work in mines in Wales or on building sites in England,' Mr Stanley replied in his deep Dublin drawl.

A rock clattered against the side of the cart, and Jim and Michael jumped. A crowd of men in moleskin trousers and cloth caps, standing behind a high fence, started to shout and wave their fists menacingly at them. Suddenly one man jumped up on another man's shoulders, leaped over the fence and ran towards the cart shouting 'Scabs, bloody, fucking scabs!'

A uniformed, helmeted policeman raced out of a sentry box, caught the running man by the shoulder and hit him on the head with a truncheon. Jim and Michael gasped in horror as blood spurted from the man's head. The man fell prone to the ground and Mr Stanley cracked the reins and the horse galloped off down the quay.

'What was that man shouting?' Michael asked as he peered around the side of the cart.

'Why were they shouting at us?' asked Jim clinging to the seat as the cart bounced along the cobblestoned road.

'Union dockers, troublemakers all of them,' Mr Stanley said flatly and from the tone of his voice the boys knew that was the end of that conversation.

On the morning that the Royal Party was to travel from Dublin Castle to the International Exhibition in Herbert Park, the city's streets were festooned with blue, white and red Union Jacks. Hundreds of fashionably-dressed ladies in trailing skirts, broad-brimmed hats and parasols, accompanied by gentlemen in formal morning dress and top hats, bustled along the city streets in search of a good vantage point to view the royal procession. The excitement in the city was palpable, the mood was joyous; people laughed and chatted to strangers and every time a mounted policemen trotted by, the crowds hollered and cheered.

One hour before the royal visitors were to journey down Dame Street, Theo Brevin parked the family carriage in Parnell Square and before they embarked on the walk to Miss Finnie's millinery premises on Dame Street, Theo assigned each child a chaperone: Michael was to stay with him, Líla was assigned to her mother and Jim was to journey with Miss McManus. The family walked together up Sackville Street, but when they got to Dame Street the path was so thick with people that they had to walk in single file, along the shop fronts.

To walk straight past interesting shop windows was something Miss McManus couldn't possibly do, and when she had stopped for the umpteenth time to look at yet another window display, a very bored Jim started to look around. He peered down a cobbled backstreet and saw just beyond a row of tenement houses, a small grocery shop. He fingered the coins in his pocket and imagined the regiment of sweet bottles on the grocery shop shelf and while Miss McManus was admiring her reflection in the shop window and busily adjusting her bonnet, he slipped quietly away.

Jim pushed hesitantly on the shop door and a small bell tinkled. He walked into the musty smelling shop and a dirty-faced, rag-wearing, red-haired boy, who was standing by a rack of biscuit tins, turned and stared at him.

'Hello sir,' the toothless grocer said, as he wiped his greasy hands on his brown, soiled apron. 'Don't get many young gentlemen like you in here. What can I do for you?'

'I'd like to buy some sweets.'

The grocer pointed to a row of glass containers filled with colourful boiled sweets. 'Which ones would you like?'

As Jim was deciding which to buy, the dirty-faced boy walked over to him, reached out his hand and felt the sleeve of Jim's new sailor suit.

Suddenly very conscious of the boy, Jim drew back; he had never been so close to a poor person.

'Red, leave the boy alone,' growled the grocer, as he leaned over the counter and swiped the air above the red-haired boy's head.

'You have shiny shoes,' the boy said.

'Where are your shoes?' Jim asked. The boy didn't respond. 'Don't your feet get cold?'

'Sometimes,' replied the boy, wiping his nose on the sleeve of his threadbare jacket.

The shop door crashed open and a flustered, out-of-breath Miss McManus thundered into the tiny shop.

'There you are! How dare you run away from me?' Miss McManus cried out. 'You put the heart cross-wise in me.' Then with all the disdain of a lifetime's indifference to poverty, she shooed the red-headed boy away. 'Keep your distance, boy!'

'The children are just talking,' said the shopkeeper.

'They have nothing in common,' snapped Miss McManus, as she held open the shop door.

Jim didn't move and looking at Miss McManus, said 'The boy has no shoes.'

'I can see that,' Miss McManus replied sharply.

'We could give him money and he could buy shoes.'

'Don't be ridiculous!' As she pulled Jim out of the shop, she snapped 'You can't just give poor people money! They have to earn it.'

Sometime later, the rousing boom of a brass band signalled the imminent approach of the royal party. The onlookers in Miss Finnie's window craned their necks. The 8th Royal Hussars, on horseback, led the procession of King Edward VII and the royal party down Dame Street.

THE ACTOR

When the open-topped carriage was directly outside the millinery shop, the King looked up and waved and Miss McManus was so overcome with excitement she almost fainted. But Jim didn't see the King or the thousands of clapping, cheering people that lined the street below; he was still thinking about the dirty-faced little boy that had no shoes.

*

On the first Saturday in August 1908, Theo called Jim into his study, sat him in front of his desk and told him that in September he would be joining his brother Michael as a full-time boarder in the Killucan Boarding School, County Kildare.

Jim was shocked; he hated the idea of going away to school, of leaving his home, his mother, his sister Líla, Mrs O'Neill and even Ciara. But, no matter how much he protested when September came, Jim was enrolled in the Killucan Boarding School for boys.

3

Killucan Boarding School wasn't the oldest or the largest boarding school in Ireland but it was Theo Brevin's alma mater. To Jim, the school was a dull, grey place that smelt of stale perspiration and damp. But to Theo, the school had charm and its conservative Catholic ethos appealed to him greatly.

Built on top of a hill, the school was a quadrangle of buildings. One hundred and fifty boarders lived in five dormitories in the west wing of the quad. The rest of the quadrangle housed a library, two dining rooms, ten classrooms, one infirmary, two churches and an assembly room – gloriously called the Aula Maxima. Lush green fields, dotted with sheep, sloped gently down from the quadrangle to school's playing fields and on to the banks of the River Liffey where the school's boathouse stood.

The autumn sun was burning the morning mist off the school's playing fields as Michael and Jim walked along the river, deep in a heated conversation.

'Listen slug, you have to play sports here,' Michael said impatiently to his younger brother.

'Don't call me slug,' snapped Jim.

'It's what they call all juniors at Killucan.'

'I'm not a slug, I'm a person.'

'Here you're a slug.' Michael's reply was sharp and abrupt. 'Jim, there's lot of sports clubs to join, rugby, canoeing, athletics …'

'I don't like sports,' Jim shot back, interrupting his brother mid-sentence.

'You have to play sports. It's how you make friends.'

'I don't want to be here and I don't want to make friends.'

'But you are here, so join a club. If you don't, you can forget that I'm your brother.'

Jim didn't join a sports club and Michael didn't acknowledge him as his brother.

Jim spent most of his time in boarding school avoiding being bullied. He developed many techniques; he always arrived late for meals and ate at the 'late table', sat in the back of the classrooms and never made eye contact with anyone but teachers. He always managed to be the last in any queue and if anyone ever spoke to him he would look away or pretend he was busy doing something.

But Jim's avoidance techniques were not completely successful. One morning after Mass, Rory Malone, a tall, willowy, greasy-haired senior, tripped while walking down the steps of the church. Jim laughed, Malone saw him laugh and from that moment Malone became the scourge of Jim's existence. Every opportunity he got, Malone slapped Jim, tripped him or jeered him.

One Saturday afternoon in early October, a small freckled-faced boy was pinning a poster to the library's notice board when Malone deliberately pushed the boy and sent him crashing into Jim's study carrel.

'Watch it, slug,' grunted Malone. 'You didn't learn last year, did you?'

Jim picked up the poster from the floor; before handing it to the boy, he read it.

Drama society meeting, Wednesday in room 7 at 7. Juniors only.

'It's going to be great fun,' the freckle-faced boy said, as he pinned it on the board. 'Why don't you come along?'

'No thank you,' Jim replied, sullenly.

'We'll be in room seven if you change your mind.'

Jim did not respond. Yet the idea of performing in a play with other like-minded boys interested him and after evening meal on the

THE ACTOR

Wednesday he found himself standing outside room seven, trying to summon up the courage to open the door. Suddenly the boy from the library was at his side. 'Glad you came along,' he said as he opened the door for the two of them. There were twelve would-be-thespians in the room, chattering. A few of them paused to glance at Jim and then resumed their conversations.

'I'm Ciaran O'Donovan,' the freckle-faced boy said, holding out his hand. Jim hesitated, then shook it and suddenly two other boys joined them. 'This is Baggy O'Driscoll,' Ciaran said. 'All you have to do is look at his pants and you'll know why we call him that.'

'They're comfortable and I like them like that,' Baggy interjected with a shrug.

'And this is Finn Murphy, he's a genius, he knows everything.'

The boys talked animatedly and for the first time since arriving at the school, Jim felt a part of something.

With a bang, the door crashed open and a six-foot, broad-shouldered senior stood in the doorway. The room fell silent. The boys looked fearfully at each other.

'Is this room seven?' asked the six-footer in a low gravelly voice.

'Yes it is, sir,' answered Ciaran.

'That's Robert McCarthy,' Finn whispered to Baggy. 'He's a forward on the senior rugby team.'

'I know,' Baggy whispered back.

'That's right, I'm on the rugby team,' the senior said as he strolled into the room. 'Everybody sit down.' He pointed at Jim. 'You, what's your name?'

Jim told him and the rugby player told him to close the door. The juniors continued to look anxiously at each other.

'I'm you're new drama coach,' the rugby player said, as he dumped his bag on a nearby chair. 'In this room you can call me Robert and I will call you by your first name. In this room you are people. But outside this room you are slugs. Outside this room you don't talk to me. You don't even look in my direction. Now boys, make a circle with your chairs.'

The boys let out a collective sigh of relief and with a lot of scraping of chair legs against the bare floorboards, they arranged the chairs in a circle. The new coach asked each boy to call out his name and tell what county he came from. When the last boy had spoken, Robert McCarthy rose to his full six foot and said, 'We have a lot of work to do and we are going to have fun doing it. Later I will break you into pairs and during the week each pair will pick a scene from a play, practice it – or, as they say in the theatre, rehearse it – and next week in this room each pair will perform their scene. I will then cast the end-of-term play and assign the stage crew. In June, you will perform the play in the Aula Maxima before the Dean, the Assistant Dean and all juniors. No senior boys, except me, will be allowed attend the show.'

A surge of exhilaration gushed around the room. Jim felt excited and astonished at how alive he felt.

'Everybody stand up,' the coach said. Everyone jumped to their feet. 'For the rest of this meeting, I'm going to show you how to stage fight.'

The boys cheered, and when they quietened down the coach demonstrated how to throw and pull a punch. He showed them ways to fake taking a punch and how to fall without injuring themselves. He taught them how to safely use a knife on stage, and at the end of the meeting he assigned Jim and Ciaran to work together on a scene.

On their way back to the dorm, they talked about what scene they might perform. When Jim told Ciaran about the fight scene in the play, *A Face in the Window,* Ciaran was impressed and they decided that was the scene for them. That night, before Jim went to bed, he wrote down as much of the scene as he could remember. What he couldn't remember, he made up. Each evening the boys met and rehearsed their scene.

On Tuesday morning, after eating another bland breakfast, Jim rushed up the stairs and smashed into the dreaded Rory Malone. The senior fell backwards, dropped his books; a shocked Jim watched in horror as the books tumbled down the stairs.

'Pick them up, slug,' Malone bellowed into Jim's face.

Jim scarpered down the stairs and gathered up the books. When he handed them back, Malone grabbed him by the collar and dragged him down the corridor and through the lavatory door, kicked open a cubicle, stuck Jim's head down the bowl and flushed the toilet.

'Let that be a lesson to you to watch where you're going,' Malone growled and exited the lavatory.

Left standing there, with his hair dripping wet, Jim felt completely humiliated. The lock clicked and he tensed, but when the door swung open it was Ciaran who walked in. 'He picked on me all last year,' Ciaran said, as he handed his friend a dry towel.

Wednesday evening came, and Jim and Ciaran performed their scene. To their coach's delight the boys had incorporated many of the stage-fighting techniques he had taught them the previous week. Ciaran threw Jim over his shoulder and Jim pretended to stab Ciaran with a wooden knife. The group clapped loudly, but it was when the drama coach stood up and applauded that Jim felt most elated.

At the end of the meeting, when Robert McCarthy announced that Jim was to play the lead part in the play, Jim was delighted – but concerned how Ciaran was going to take the news.

'I'd rather be backstage,' Ciaran whispered to Jim. 'I told Robert I wasn't interested in acting.'

A minute later, the coach announced that Ciaran was to be stage manager and both boys were happy.

Robert McCarthy was not only the boy's drama coach, he was their mentor. He was patient with them, answered their many questions and always spoke to them as equals. As instructed, outside of room seven, the boys did not speak to or even greet Robert. When he passed them in the quad, they looked the other way.

However, Jim, Ciaran, Baggy and Finn were so fascinated by Robert McCarthy that one afternoon they went to see their drama coach playing a rugby match. During the match, Jim's brother saw him but after the match as Michael crossed the playing fields towards him, Jim hurried away.

Ciaran and Jim grew close. The boys sat for hours talking about the books they had read, plays they had seen and adventures they'd had. Jim told Ciaran about the day he saw the policeman hit the docker with his truncheon. When Ciaran told Jim that his aunt Sorcha had a small theatre company that toured in Cork and Kerry, the boys spent many hours planning a secret visit to see one of his aunt's shows; they never did go but they never tired of planning to do so.

Two weeks before the end of term, the night of the 1 June, Jim and

Ciaran were sent to fetch a mop and a bucket of water. Happily chatting together, the boys didn't notice the lanky frame of Rory Malone stroll out of a lavatory cubicle.

'Well if it isn't the sissy slugs,' Malone said, as he buckled his belt.

The boys froze. Malone lunged at them, caught Jim by the collar and Ciaran by the hair and pulled both boys towards the cubicle. Jim clasped his hands over his head and plunged them down on his captor's arm. Malone lost his grip and Jim was free.

'Let my friend go!' Jim shouted at Malone.

'Well you're a spunky little slug! If Ciaran's such a good friend of yours, why don't you take his place?'

Jim took a step forward, Ciaran kicked Malone's leg and the lanky senior lost his balance but as he fell, he caught Jim by the arm and then dragged him kicking and screaming into the cubicle.

'I hope you don't mind that I haven't flushed,' Malone sneered as he pushed Jim's head towards the stinking bowl.

'Let the boy go,' growled a deep gravelly voice. Malone looked around. The six-foot, broad-shouldered Robert McCarthy was standing by the washbasins. 'Slugs get out of here,' Robert grunted, without taking his eyes off the lanky Malone.

Malone released Jim, and the boys scrambled out of the room.

'Why are you picking on them?' the coach asked, leaning against a sink.

'They're slugs and sissies too.'

'Sissies?'

'Yeah, they're in the drama group,' Malone replied with a snicker.

Robert strolled over to Malone.

'I coach the drama group. Does that make me a sissy too?' Before Malone could reply the rugby-playing drama coach pounded his huge fist into Malone's soft stomach. 'Answer up, Malone.'

'No!' came a gasping reply.

'No what?'

'No, you're not a sissy and please don't hit me again.'

'If you don't want me to hit you again, you'll have to do something for me.'

'Anything,' replied a still gasping Malone.

'I want you to stick your head down that toilet bowl.'
'What? I didn't flush ...'
'I know,' replied Robert laconically. 'Some people have terrible hygiene habits.'

Standing in the doorway of room seven, Jim and Ciaran heard a muffled moan in the lavatory, followed by a toilet flush. A few seconds later, Rory Malone, his head dripping wet, crashed out of the lavatory, ran down the corridor and disappeared up the stairs. Robert McCarthy strolled out of the washroom. As he passed Jim and Ciaran, he said 'He won't bother you again.' And he never did.

Jim's stomach churned as he crossed the quad to the Aula Maxima. It was the first night of the end-of-year play. I must be mad, he thought as he put on his costume. A cold sweat formed on his brow as he checked his props. He picked up his script for a final glimpse before going on stage and thought: *Why am I doing this?*

Robert McCarthy took the script from Jim's shaking hand, looked his lead actor in the face and said 'Jim you are a good actor and tonight you are going to be great. So stop worrying and enjoy yourself.'

Ciaran peeped through a hole in the curtain and gasped when he saw the bearded Dean Avery SJ, in his long flannel coat and black trousers talking to the stern faced Assistant Dean Carrol. Then he saw Robert McCarthy sitting in the middle of at least fifty junior boys and he half-smiled. The actors took their place on stage; Ciaran pulled on the rope and the curtain parted.

When the performance was over the audience leapt to their feet and applauded loudly. That night, for the first time in a week, Jim slept soundly.

Two weeks later, Jim said farewell to his boarding school friends and he and his brother returned to Dublin for the summer. Mother was delighted to have her sons home again. Líla too was overjoyed and never stopped asking Jim questions about boarding school life. That night at the dinner table, Theo announced that on the following Saturday he and Michael were leaving for their annual wine safari to Europe. Jim was not invited and it never crossed Theo's mind to invite him; Jim knew this, and it crushed him.

4

The Saturday that Theo and Michael left for their wine tour of Europe was sweltering and only the light cool breeze that blew from the Phoenix Park made the heat bearable. That afternoon sitting in the garden gazebo, Jim told Líla and his mother about the school's drama society and the play they had put on.

'And did you enjoy performing?' Grainne asked as she took a sip of white wine.

'I was nervous but once I was on stage I didn't want it to end.'

'James you are a natural actor,' Grainne said rising her glass and placing a kiss on Jim's forehead.

'I would love to have seen the play,' Líla said and flopped into the seat next to Jim. 'Tell me everything, every little detail.'

In July, Ciaran O'Donovan, Jim's best friend at boarding school, came to Dublin and spent a week in the Brevin household. Jim was chuffed to have his friend stay in his home. Grainne made a great fuss of the boy and had Mrs O'Neill make Jim's favourite meal of rabbit stew and dumplings. After lunch the two boys sat in matching winged chairs in the back drawing room and talked.

'What will we do this afternoon?' Ciaran asked.

THE ACTOR

Grinning broadly. Jim handed his friend a brown envelope.

'What's in it?'

'Open it.'

Ciaran flipped open the envelope and when he saw the two tickets for the matinee performance in the Queen's Theatre his eyes beamed with delight.

'What's on?' he asked.

'*Arrah-Na-Pogue*, a melodrama, and Ira Allen and P J Burke are in it.' Jim got to his feet. 'We better hurry. The show starts in an hour.'

The theatre was buzzing when the boys took their seats in the front row of the grand circle. A small man with a flushed, ruddy complexion and a large woman in a loose-fitting floral patterned dress lowered themselves into their seats next to Ciaran. The woman carefully removed her wide-brimmed hat, admired the white stuffed dove attached to its crown then carefully placed it on the balcony rail in front of Ciaran. The surprised boy was still staring at the dead bird when the huge chandelier dimmed and the play began.

Ciaran was enthralled by everything he saw and heard; the music, the singing, the hero rebels, the villainous villain and the love-struck lovers. When Ira Allen as Shaun the hero, gave a false confession to save his girlfriend from imprisonment, Ciaran applauded; when Shaun escaped from the prison by climbing down an ivy-covered tower, Ciaran cheered; but when P J Burke as the villain fell from a twenty-foot tower to his death, Ciaran got so excited that he jumped to his feet and accidently knocked the large lady's hat off the balcony rail.

'Oh my God,' screeched the woman as she shook the arm of her sleeping husband. 'Kingsley, do something!' she demanded, as her hat glided down into the auditorium and came to rest on the head of a bald man in the stalls.

'The blasted bird has flown the coop,' Kingsley said. He leaned over the balcony and shouted to the bald man 'Well saved, old boy, well saved.'

'Kingsley have you been drinking?' the large lady barked at her husband.

'Don't be ridiculous, woman,' slurred Kingsley. 'I never drink when I go to the theatre.'

THE ACTOR

The lady snorted haughtily then tapped Ciaran on the shoulder.

'The least you could do, young man, is go and retrieve my hat.'

After the show the boys took a tram to St Stephen's Green. They walked around the park's pond and watched children feed the ducks and swans. They stood in front of the bandstand and listened to the Metropolitan Police Brass Band play Irish melodies. Then Jim took Ciaran to Grafton Street to see and hear his favourite organ-grinder and his monkey pump out a set of Scott Joplin tunes. When the music stopped, Ciaran handed a farthing to the organ-grinder's monkey and watched in wonder as the animal placed the coin in a box that hung around the organ-grinder's neck.

On Sunday morning after Mass, Jim introduced Ciaran to his friend Brian, and that afternoon the three boys went to Dollymount for a swim. Annoyed at being left behind, Líla and Brian's sister Ann followed the boys and when they were in the water the girls stole along the beach and removed the boys' clothes.

'Are you sure this is the place we left our clothes?' a bewildered Brian asked when they returned from their swim.

'Yes I am,' Jim replied, pointing to a huge granite rock lying in the sand. 'Yes, we put them here. I remember that rock.'

'We better look around the other dunes just to make sure,' Brian said and ran up to the top of a large sandbank while Jim and Ciaran went from dune to dune in search of their belongings.

'Look, over there,' Brian shouted, pointing to the wooden bridge that connected the beach to the mainland. 'There are two girls running across the bridge carrying a pile of clothes. Jeepers, one of them is my sister. Come on, let's get them.'

Out of breath from running and laughing, Líla and Ann dropped the clothes on the grass and giggling hysterically flopped to the ground. When the girls saw the three shoeless, half-naked boys running across the wooden bridge they burst out in another fit of laughing and giggling.

'I don't think that was very funny,' a red-faced Ciaran grunted as he tied his towel around his waist.

'Well you shouldn't have left us behind,' Líla blurted through her giggles.

'Líla, you don't even like swimming,' Jim barked as he pulled his knee-length pants over his wet togs.

'That's no excuse for not inviting us,' chimed in Ann.

How could I ever have thought Ann Ahern was nice? Jim thought, as he laced up his boots. Her and her silly hair.

'Why don't we throw the girls into the water?' Brian said, flicking his towel at his sister.

Líla and Ann jumped to their feet.

'Good idea,' Jim added, eager to save some face.

The boys lunged and, screeching wildly, the girls ran down the green. Brian was the first to laugh, then Jim joined in, then Ciaran smiled and started laughing.

A few minutes later the girls returned with a peace offering of a bag of bull's-eye sweets and all was forgiven. Five minutes later the Dollymount tram clanked to a stop and the children raced noisily up the stairs to the front seats of the open-top tram. Ciaran sat beside Líla and never stopped talking, Jim sat beside Ann and wished he could think of something to say and Brian sat happily on his own, chomping on the hardboiled sweets.

The following day Ciaran asked Jim if Líla and Ann would be joining them on their trip to the zoo.

'I haven't asked them,' Jim replied. 'Do you want them to come along?'

'Well, I wouldn't like them to feel left out,' Ciaran said, and all five children went to the zoo.

At breakfast the following morning Jim noticed that Ciaran spent a lot of time talking to Líla and she spent a lot of time giggling at his jokes.

'Where's the mechanical music machine you said your father got at Christmas?' Ciaran asked Líla.

'It's called a gramophone,' Jim interjected petulantly. 'It's in the front drawing room.'

'No, father removed it to his study,' Líla said. 'He said we were not to play with it. It's a very expensive machine and it's easily broken.'

'I'd really like to see it,' Ciaran said, putting on a pleading smile.

Jim half-opened the door of his father's study and poked his head into the room. 'Come on,' he said as he opened the door fully and walked over to the gramophone.

'It's beautiful,' Ciaran said, gazing in wonder at the music machine.

The Victor V Gramophone was a beautiful object. It had a mahogany base and flannel-covered turntable, a shiny metal moveable arm and a huge silver horn. On the side of the box was a bronze cranking handle and behind the turntable was a small drawer filled with short thick needles. On the table beside the gramophone were ten black seven-inch discs in brown paper sleeves.

'How does it work?' Ciaran asked, touching the gramophone cabinet.

'You place a disc on the turntable, put a needle in the gramophone and crank the handle.'

'Play it,' Ciaran said, daring Jim to break the rules.

'No,' Líla interjected. 'Father said we weren't allowed to do that.'

'We'll just play one,' Jim said and removed a black shellac disc from its sleeve.

'Put that down, the discs are very brittle,' Líla interjected.

'You don't even know what that word means,' Jim said as he inserted a needle in the gramophone's arm, cranked the handle and placed the stylus on the disc.

Ciaran's eyes popped and his mouth fell open when the sound of a symphony orchestra boomed out of the silver horn.

'It's magic!' he said and placed his head in the silver horn.

When the music finished, Ciaran picked up another disc and asked 'Can I play this one?'

'No you can't,' Líla said and reached out to take the disc from Ciaran. But Ciaran pulled his hand away and the shiny disc slipped from its sleeve. In shocked silence, the children watched the disk fall through the air. Then Jim and Ciaran gasped, and Líla screeched as it shattered on the wooden parquet floor.

'Sorry,' said an ashen-faced Ciaran. 'What are we going to do?'

'Children, you know you are not allowed in here and you are certainly not allowed to play the gramophone,' Grainne said sternly from the study's doorway. 'What's going on?'

'It was my fault,' Líla volunteered.

'No, it was my fault,' Ciaran interjected. 'I dropped it. My father will replace it.'

This is not fair, Jim thought to himself. *They shouldn't take the blame for something I instigated.*

'It's my fault. I brought Ciaran into father's study and I played the gramophone for him,' Jim said, looking his mother straight in the eye.

'So you're all taking responsibility, that's very laudable. Ciaran, there is no need for your father to replace the disc, you are our guest. Jim, Líla and Ciaran I want you to give me your word you will not play the gramophone again.'

'We promise,' the children said in unison.

'Thank you Mrs Brevin, I'm really very sorry,' Ciaran said and bowed his head.

'That's the end of this matter. No more glum faces, off you all go and play.'

As Jim walked past his mother, she placed her hand on his shoulder and said 'I'll talk to you later and I'm taking the cost of the disc out of your allowance.'

Jim nodded and followed his friend and sister out of the study.

On Friday morning Jim and Ciaran were chatting in the garden gazebo when a chilling scream ripped through the house. The boys raced out of the garden, galloped through the drawing room and halted when they saw a shaking Líla standing over her mother who was lying at the bottom of the stairs, her face covered in blood. Jim dropped to his knees beside his mother as a startled and out-of-breath Mrs O'Neill came rushing out of the kitchen.

'Oh My God,' she cried, kneeling herself to place her ear next to Grainne's mouth.

'Is Mommy alright?' Líla asked, dreading the answer.

'She's still breathing,' Mrs O'Neill replied. 'Jim, run and get Ciara – she's in the herb garden.'

Grainne eyes fluttered slightly. 'What's happened?' Her voice was slurred. She made no attempt to move.

'There was an accident. Are you all right?'

Wiping her hands on her soiled apron, Ciara bustled into the hall and gasped when she saw Grainne on the floor. 'Should I get the priest?'

'Certainly not,' Mrs O'Neill replied, her voice devoid of emotion. 'Fetch Dr Moore. Tell him it's an emergency.'

Without a word, Ciara skittered down the hall and out the front door.

'Jim, go upstairs and get a blanket, Líla fetch a bowl of water and a washcloth,' Mrs O'Neill said as she took Grainne's hand. 'Don't worry, the doctor will be here shortly.'

Fifteen minutes later the polite but frail Dr Moore arrived and examined Grainne.

'I don't think any bones are broken,' the doctor said after an initial examination of his patient. 'We're going to take you to your room so you can rest.'

When Grainne was back in her room, the doctor suggested to Mrs O'Neill that a telegram be sent to Theo asking him to return home immediately. While the housekeeper went to the post office to send the telegram the doctor took Jim aside and said to him 'I don't want you to worry about your mother.'

'Is mother going to be all right?'

'Yes Jim, your mother is going to be all right. But her recovery is going to take time.' Jim's eyes filled with tears. 'Jim, until your father and your brother return home you are the head of the house, so you're going to have to be strong for your sister and your mother.' The doctor placed his hand on Jim's shoulder. 'I will visit every day. However if you see any change in her condition, contact me immediately.'

On Saturday morning Ciaran's father, an army officer, arrived to a very confused Brevin household and with as little fuss as possible took his son back to Cork.

Theo and Michael were having a late lunch in the garden restaurant in the Amboise Hotel in the Loire Valley when they received Mrs O'Neill's telegram. They immediately packed their bags. Within the hour they were on a train for Paris. But delays in Gare du Nord meant they were already behind schedule when they boarded the train to Calais. There they were forced to spend the night, fretting over what they would find when they got home. In the morning they boarded the first sailing to Dover. From Dover they travelled by train to London and then on to Holyhead. But stormy seas meant no sailings so again they were forced to wait. Eventually they got a cabin in an overnight ferry to Ireland. On arrival in Kingstown, they took a cab to Dublin. Between stormy seas, cancelled sailings and delayed trains it took

Theo and Michael four worry-filled days to get home.

Theo was shocked when he saw his Grainne. Her face was grey, her forehead was bruised and she could neither talk nor move.

'The head wound is not serious. There was a lot of blood but it's a superficial wound and it will heal quickly,' Dr Moore said to Theo when they talked in the conservatory that afternoon.

'Then what is it that is concerning you?' Theo asked, reading the look on Dr Moore's face.

'Two things. Your wife's bouts of melancholia seem to be lasting longer each time. Then there is her drinking. She must moderate her drinking. It's aggravating the melancholia.' Theo shook his head as the doctor continued. 'First we have to get Grainne well, she'll need lots of rest and her recovery will take time.'

'Longer than last time?' Theo asked gravely.

'Much longer,' replied the doctor.

During Grainne's illness, the Brevins' joyous, noisy, home once again became a sombre house of whispers and grim faces. The bedroom curtains were drawn and Theo spent most of his days and nights at his wife's bedside.

Grainne's recovery was achingly slow. It was four weeks after Jim and Líla found their mother at the bottom of the stairs that they were allowed visit her. A week later Jim and Michael returned to boarding school and that day was the first day Grainne was allowed sit in her beloved garden.

5

IN HIS SECOND YEAR AT Killucan Boarding School, Jim became a senior and Ciaran, Baggy, Finn and he moved residence to St Kevin's dormitory where the boys continued to build their close friendships. Ciaran helped Jim with his maths, Baggy helped Ciaran with his English and Finn helped everyone with everything. In early September Baggy and Finn joined the canoeing club and Jim and Ciaran joined the senior drama society.

On the evening of the drama society's first meeting, Jim and Ciaran were walking down the main school corridor when a door flew open and the lanky Rory Malone crashed into them. All three boys froze; Malone's eyes looked up and down the corridor, then mumbling an apology he slowly backed into the room. Grinning broadly, Jim and Ciaran resumed their walking.

Ciaran opened the door to the meeting and the din of forty boisterous seniors blasted into the corridor.

'I guess word got out that the girls from St Bridget's might be here,' Ciaran said as he pushed his way into the room.

The only person in the room that Jim recognised was Robert McCarthy, the drama coach from the previous year. Robert was standing beside the studious, rotund, bespectacled drama society chairman Myles

Keogh, who was calling for quiet. A pasty-face, pencil-thin boy pushed his way to the front and in a high-pitched voice yelled 'Where are the girls?'

'Do you think any girl would be interested in you, you sad sack?' Myles shouted back and got a punch in the face for his insulting remark. Robert grabbed the squeaky-voiced fighter, pushed him back into the crowd and bedlam broke out. Fists flew, bodies flung themselves at each other and the meeting turned into an affray.

Assistant Dean Carrol stood in the doorway and glared at the brawling boys. Like a wave rolling on to a beach, silence rippled across the room.

'What in God's name is going on here?' demanded the imposing Assistant Dean. 'Is this a pugilist society or a drama society? Who's in charge here?'

'I am, sir,' answered the dishevelled Myles Keogh.

'Then take charge. If I hear another sound from this room there will be no drama society this year.'

'Yes sir,' Myles murmured sheepishly, the Assistant Dean walked away from the door and quietness reigned.

'I have two pieces of information to give you,' Myles began, still a little shaken by the Assistant Dean's sudden appearance and pronouncement. 'First, the female roles in this year production will be played by students from St Bridget's.' The boys hooted and cheered; Myles called for quiet. 'Second, the two schools will rehearse separately.' A collective groan rose from the floor. 'We will rehearse twice with the girls and Sister Concepta will be at both rehearsals and at all performances.'

'The Black Beetle strikes again,' a voice shouted from the back of the room.

'When will we get to meet the girls?' squeaked the pasty-faced fighter.

'We won't,' Myles replied and like a herd of disappointed wildebeests the boys started to migrate out of the room. When Myles resumed speaking there were less than twenty boys in the room.

The play Myles announced, to the remaining boys, was an adaptation of Charles Dickens' *A Christmas Carol* and auditions would take place during the second half of the meeting. Then Myles introduced Robert

THE ACTOR

McCarthy as the drama coach and Jim smiled. The meeting continued for an hour and concluded with the chairman asking for volunteers to be part of the stage crew.

For three long anxious days after the auditions, Jim waited for the cast-list to be posted. On the fourth day a breathless Baggy ran into the dining room, plonked himself beside Jim and said 'The cast-list is up on the notice board in the dorm.'

'Am I on the list?'

'I don't know. I didn't look. Damn, I should have looked.'

Jim grabbed his tray, rattled it into the return rack and darted out the door. In minutes he was standing before the notice board and a grin slowly slid across his face. He was cast as Tiny Tim, son of Bob Cratchit, clerk to Ebenezer Scrooge. He looked for Ciaran's name; it was there. He was named as the assistant stage manager; he knew his friend would be happy about that.

For three weeks Robert McCarthy rehearsed the play without its female cast members. Then on a cold crisp mid-November evening, Assistant Dean Carrol marched Robert McCarthy, Jim, Ciaran and the rest of the male cast and crew to St Bridget's College. The boys' shoes crunched on the frost covered ground and the cold evening air bit at their ears as they walked to the hallowed, male-free, school for girls.

Seated in the freezing assembly hall, the boys waited anxiously for the female cast members to join them. At one end of the hall was a raised stage, a stack of chairs and a large wooden table on which sat twenty teacups, a jug of milk, a bowl of sugar and a large plate of biscuits. At the other end of the hall were two huge locked wooden doors. With his back against the bottle-green assembly hall wall, Jim's eyes traced the cracks in the yellow distempered ceiling. With a clatter the doors at the rear of the hall opened and Sr Concepta, the smallest nun Jim had ever seen, glided into the hall. Dressed completely in black, Sr Concepta was no-more than four feet tall; she had a round body, a small head and a withered troll-like face. She was followed by her six uniformed young charges. The boys jumped to their feet. The girls looked straight ahead, but one girl, the one who closed the door, looked directly at the boys, flicked her thick blonde hair to one side and smiled. Every male eye locked on her and followed her as she breezed up the hall and sat with the other girls on the opposite side of the hall.

The Black Beetle glided over to Assistant Dean Carrol, coughed and in a terse, cold voice proclaimed 'This is not a social gathering, it is a cultural endeavour. There will be no familiarity between boys or girls.'

Everyone nodded insincerely, and Assistant Dean Carrol instructed the boys to arrange the folding chairs into two lines, six feet apart, down the centre of the hall. The girls were then seated on one side and the boys on the other. Assistant Dean Carrol and the Black Beetle took seats on the raised stage and Robert was asked to begin the rehearsal. Positioning himself at the top of the two lines, Robert welcomed everyone, introduced each boy and identified what role he was playing. Then he asked the girl who closed the door to introduce the girls. She stood, fixed her deep blue eyes on Robert and said 'My name is Ciara Walsh.' The name was instantly burned into each boy's brain. When she announced that she was playing Mrs Cratchit, mother of Tiny Tim, Jim's eyes nearly popped out of his head.

The first part of the rehearsal was given over to a reading of the play. There were a few giggles when the first girl spoke but everyone quickly settled down. When the reading was over Assistant Dean Carol chatted with the boys while they took their tea and the Black Beetle guarded her charges.

After tea the chairs were moved to one side and Robert rehearsed the scenes which featured the girls. Jim and Ciara's scene was the first to be called. As nonchalantly as he could manage, Jim strolled to the top of the room. Ciara hardly noticed him; she was polite but she only had eyes for Robert McCarthy. Every time Robert looked for a prop she volunteered to get it; every time he spoke to her, her eyes sparkled and every time he looked in her direction she smiled at him. Walking back to the dorm, Ciaran teased Jim about liking Ciara but he laughed it off, saying 'Everyone fancies Ciara Walsh.'

On the day of the first performance of *A Christmas Carol*, Grainne and Líla arrived in Killucan and took a room at the newly refurbished Killucan Arms Hotel. Tired and pale after her train journey Grainne took a nap and at seven o'clock that evening they made their way to the Aula Maxima. Halfway to the hall, Grainne stopped and put her hand to her forehead and without saying a word Líla took her arm.

THE ACTOR

Seated near the back of the hall, Líla could hardly contain her excitement; she read and re-read the programme and each time she did, she pointed Jim's name out to Grainne. At twenty five minutes past seven, with the hall almost filled to capacity the pompous Dean Avery SJ, accompanied by the stiff-necked Assistant Dean Carrol marched down the centre aisle of the hall and took their seats in the front row. The gas lights dimmed, the curtains parted and the play began.

Standing in the wings waiting for his cue, Jim's skin tingled and his hands grew sweaty; he was alive with excitement. He was the second actor to come on stage and the moment Líla saw him she felt like cheering, but she contained herself and to her great surprise she soon forgot that Jim was playing Tiny Tim and got involved in the story.

When the first girl from St Bridget's walked on stage she was greeted with hoots and boisterous applause. A furious Assistant Dean Carrol jumped to his feet and glared contemptuously down the hall. A hush fell on the auditorium. When the second girl appeared she too was greeted with hooting and cheering. This time the bearded Dean Avery SJ stopped the play, stepped on stage and removed a small notebook from his pocket. He pointed at four of the leading hooters, Assistant Dean Carrol called out the boys' names and Dean Avery ceremoniously wrote them in his notebook. When the play resumed and the third and fourth young actress walked on stage they were greeted with a proper dignified silence.

At the end of the show the curtain closed and the audience erupted into applause. When Jim walked on stage to take his curtain call Líla jumped to her feet and cheered, Jim saw her and his face lit up. After the show, Grainne took Jim, Líla and Ciaran back to the Killucan Arms for a meal. The boys ate like they hadn't eaten in weeks and Líla announced that Jim was not only the best actor in Kildare, but the best actor in the whole world. Later, in the hotel foyer as Jim was putting on his overcoat, Grainne asked him why Michael hadn't attended the play.

'Michael doesn't talk to me when we're in Killucan.'

'Why ever not?' asked an astonished Grainne.

'Michael said if I didn't play sports he wasn't going to be my brother anymore.'

'That's ridiculous and most annoying.' Grainne put her hand on

Jim's shoulder. 'Michael is so very much like his father. He allows others to do his thinking for him. But you and I are alike, we are thinkers. You are a lucky boy to have found something you value in life, even if it is a mask.'

'What are you talking about mother?'

'Nothing, forgive me, I'm rambling.'

On the other side of the hotel foyer Ciaran and Líla were also deep in conversation. He was explaining to her the responsibilities of the assistant stage manager and she was listening with rapt attention to his every word.

Blades of white sunlight cut through the grey morning mist as Grainne, aided by a recently-acquired walking stick, limped across the quad to Michael's dorm. A greasy-haired boy wearing an ill-fitting blazer escorted Grainne to the visitors' drawing room. After two great snuffles, the boy informed Grainne he would fetch Michael and three minutes later a sleepy-eyed, half-dressed Michael bounded into the room.

'Mother, I didn't know you were coming. Is there something wrong?'

'Yes, there is something is wrong.' There was ice in Grainne voice. 'Why don't you speak to your brother?'

'Oh that,' Michael said and flopped down on a discoloured, well-worn couch. 'It's not the done thing, Mother. Anyway, why should I?'

'He's your flesh and blood, he's your brother, that's why.'

'He doesn't act like my brother.'

'Are you acting like his brother? Michael you have only one brother and just because you don't share the same likes as he does, it doesn't mean you shouldn't look after him. You are an intelligent young man and you should use that intelligence other than on the sports field.'

The church bells pealed ten as Jim and Ciaran left their dorm and set out for the Killucan Arms Hotel. Halfway across the quad Ciaran stopped, and after a little hesitation asked 'Does Líla have a boyfriend?'

Jim looked at him and burst out laughing. Ciaran remained stoically solemn. Realising that his friend had asked more than an idle question, Jim stifled his laughter and replied 'I don't know.'

'Good,' Ciaran said and resumed walking.

THE ACTOR

In the foyer of the Killucan Arms, Ciaran thanked Mrs Brevin for her kindness and generosity then, after a hesitant, awkward, goodbye handshake with Líla, he went to the bookshop for his usual Saturday morning rummage among the books. But no matter how hard he tried, he could not stop thinking about Líla.

At the railway station as Grainne rummaged in her enormous leather bag for the train tickets, Jim told Líla about Ciaran's enquiry. To his surprise, Líla smiled demurely and said 'You can tell your friend that I don't have a boyfriend and that I think he is very nice.'

'I will,' answered a surprised Jim.

The second night's performance of *A Christmas Carol* was reserved solely for the students, family and friends of St Bridget's College. The hall was packed to capacity and when it came time for Ciara Walsh to deliver her first line, the girl opened her mouth and nothing came out; she could not remember her words. She stood frozen in panic, alone, unable to speak. Then she felt a tapping on her hand, looked down and Jim whispered 'I know I'm being uncharitable but I don't like that Mr Scrooge.'

That was her line, her words came back to her and she delivered the rest of her lines flawlessly. As Jim walked off stage after the scene Ciara grabbed him, pulled him into the folds of the back curtain and said 'You are wonderful, I will love you, forever!' and kissed him on the lips. Then with a twirl, she slipped out of the curtains and – seeing the fast approaching Black Beetle – cried out 'Sister, I got caught in the curtains! It was very frightening!'

'Oh you poor girl, are you all right?'

Jim stayed hidden in the curtain until the nun had gone.

All through the play, at every opportunity she had, Ciara hugged her Tiny Tim and held his hand, and Jim loved it.

When the Black Beetle complained that she didn't remember the hugging and hand-holding from the rehearsals, Ciara said 'Sister, the boy is supposed to be sick and I am his mother.'

'You're a dark horse,' Robert said to Jim in the dressing room after the performance. 'You got the girl.'

'You don't mind do you?' Jim asked hesitantly.

'I don't mind,' Robert replied then whispered 'The truth is, I fancy the Black Beetle.'

THE ACTOR

For the next week Jim became not only the envy of every member of the cast but the envy of every boy at Killucan School. On the following Saturday night, after the final performance of the play, Jim said goodbye to Ciara and as he watched the St Bridget bus drive out of the quad, Michael walked up to him and said 'Well done, brother. You did a great job.'

The brothers shook hands, Jim introduced Michael to his friend Ciaran and the rest of the cast, and for the first time ever the two brothers walked back to their dormitories together.

In June, Theo, Grainne and Líla visited Killucan for the annual sports day celebrations. In the morning Theo had a private meeting with Dean Avery SJ. Theo handed the Dean his customary generous donation and asked about his sons' progress. A smile leaked across the Dean's face; he stroked his long grey beard and in his soft Donegal accent said 'Mr Brevin, you can be assured your boys' spiritual needs are being fully met. Daily Mass keeps them close to God.'

When Theo pointed out that he was talking about his sons' academic progress, the Dean frowned and promptly referred him to Assistant Dean Carrol 'who dealt with all matters temporal'.

In the afternoon in front of the assembled parents, teachers and students, the Assistant Dean presented the sports trophies to the worthy winners. The boating awards were the first to be awarded and when Baggy and Finn walked onto the rostrum to receive the Mooney Cup for the canoe sprint-race, Jim and Ciaran cheered. The last to receive their award was the rugby team who had won their league. When Michael lifted the Reid Cup over his head the crowd went wild. Theo Brevin stood with his wife and daughter in the front row and his face beamed with pride. His other son stood beside him wishing his father was as proud of his accomplishments as he was of his brother's.

6

Monday 17 April 1912 was one of the worst days of Jim's life. It started out as usual, an endless Mass, a bland breakfast and boring classes. Sometime around eleven, wearing his customary neatly-pressed, straight sack jacket and serge trousers, a solemn-faced Assistant Dean Carrol took a puzzled Jim from maths class and escorted him to Dean Avery's office. On entering the office Jim saw an ashen-faced Michael sitting in front of the Dean's desk and his muscles tensed.

'Why don't you sit beside your brother, Master Brevin?' Dean Avery said softly, nodding to the chair beside Michael. Jim sat. The creases in Dean Avery's brow deepened, he drew a deep breath and just as he was about to speak, Michael mumbled 'Mother is dead.'

The blood drained from Jim's head.

'What happened?' he whispered.

He wanted to know everything. No, he wanted his mother alive. He couldn't breathe, his eyes went out of focus, his head swirled and everything went black.

Jim awoke and tried to focus his eyes. All he could see was white and all he could hear was a great pounding. He blinked and looked around; he was in a white room and the pounding was inside his head. Then he heard Michael's words 'Mother's dead' and the pounding grew louder. Something moved in the room, Sr Margareta placed a cold compress on his forehead and said 'You fainted.'

The pounding in Jim's head eased and an intense cold crept over him. 'Your brother is packing a bag for you. He'll be along in a few minutes to take you home.'

A blanket of dark grey hung over the countryside as the two brothers made their way home. Jim remembered little of the trip except the awful feelings of sorrow, pain and loss he felt every second of that wretched, endless journey.

The curtains were drawn on every window in their North Circular Road home. Michael stood at the front door and read the small notice pinned to it. Numb with grief he ran his finger along the black rim of it.

'What are you doing?' Jim asked.

Michael looked at Jim as if he had forgotten he was there, fumbled in his pocket for the door key, placed it in the lock and pushed the door open.

Except for the faint light that flickered from the front drawing room, the house was a cavern of silent blackness. The brothers walked through the dark hall and when they reached the drawing room they stopped. A solitary candle on the mantelpiece flickered light on their father and on their mother's open coffin. Theo saw his boys and tears welled in his bloodshot eyes. Michael hurried to his father, wrapped his two arms around him and held him firmly. With his head buried in Michael's shoulder, Theo's body shook. Upset at the sight of his grieving father, Jim looked away and gazed into the face of his dead mother. He was still looking at his mother's face when a red-eyed, traumatised Líla burst into the room, raced to Jim, thrust herself at him and held him tightly. Jim felt his father's fingers intertwine with his and the Brevin family was united in grief.

Later that day, sitting in the dining room, Theo talked to his two boys.

'Your mother has been unwell for some weeks,' Theo said in a soft but unfamiliar voice which kept cracking and fracturing as the words poured from him. 'On Saturday she had a severe headache and decided to rest. Líla was staying the weekend with Grandmother Brevin in

Clontarf and Grainne suggested to Mrs O'Neill that she should take the opportunity to visit her family in Rathfarnam. I returned home about six o'clock and found your mother lying unconscious in the hall. I have no idea how long she'd been there.' Theo paused a moment and sobbed.

'There was no one in the house to help her. I went and fetched Dr Moore but it was too late. There was nothing that could be done.' He stopped, blew his nose and composed himself. 'Mother never regained consciousness and on Sunday evening at eight o'clock she passed away.'

For over an hour, Theo answered Jim and Michael's questions. Then he instructed Mrs O'Neill to lock the piano and explained that all music, singing and gaiety were prohibited; the Brevin family was in deepest mourning. He then returned to his vigil beside his wife's coffin. Mrs O'Neill continued to dress the house for mourning; she covered all mirrors with black cloths, pinned small black ribbons on the backs of chairs and around the legs of tables and on all interior doors.

Jim retreated to his winged wicker chair in the back drawing room and with his knees gathered up to his body sat in the dark while a torrent of emotions assailed him. He loved his mother and he hated her. He loved her for always being there and he hated her for leaving him. He loved her for the time he spent with her and he hated her for letting his father send him away to boarding school. He missed her and longed for her and he wanted her back. 'Why did you die? Why did you leave me? I love you. I want you back,' he whispered to himself and wept and wept and wept.

Early next morning, carrying three beautiful floral tributes, Grandmother Brevin and Theo's two brothers arrived. Grandmother Brevin embraced her son and, knowing only too well the inadequacy of words, simply said 'I'm so very sorry.'

Next to arrive were Grainne's brothers and sisters, then some neighbours and later a very distressed Miss Bronagh McManus who gave her tearful and sincere condolences to Theo and the children.

For the next thirty six hours, people from all over the city called to the house. At noon the driver, Mr Stanley and his helper Vincent arrived with a small wreath and at about four o'clock on Wednesday a hearse covered by an ornate canopy and drawn by four black plumed horses arrived at their home. The hearse driver, a dark slender man, and the undertaker, a gaunt, bony-faced creature, dismounted the carriage and entered the house.

The following morning, wearing full morning clothes, a black cravat and top hat, Theo stood with his children in the front drawing room and asked each of them to say a final farewell to their mother. With her eyes red from crying and skin blotchy from the constant stream of tears that trickled down her face, Líla, too overcome to speak, kissed her mother on the lips and sighed 'goodbye'. Jim touched his mother's hand and for the last time kissed her powdered cheek. Michael, choking back tears, whispered goodbye and kissed her hand. Theo said a prayer, leaned down, removed Grainne's engagement ring and gold wedding band and slipped them on the little finger of his left hand. The undertaker closed the polished elm coffin and he and the driver wheeled the casket out of the house, placed it in the hearse and covered it with wreaths and floral tributes.

The hearse left the North Circular Road and proceeded directly to St Peter's Church, Phibsboro. Theo, Michael, two of Grainne's brothers and two of Theo's brothers carried the coffin into the church. Cannon Walsh led the prayers and after the short service the sacristan moved the coffin into the mortuary chapel and locked the church.

The following morning Bishop O'Hara, Cannon Walsh and four curates concelebrated the solemn requiem Mass. All through the service Theo stood tall. Every now and again his hand would move discreetly to his face to wipe a tear from his eyes. Standing beside his father, Jim suddenly began to panic; the image of his mother's face was beginning to fade from his mind. Theo draped his arm around his youngest son and the panic passed.

Standing behind the casket in Glasnevin Cemetery, Líla was so overwhelmed with grief that she could not move. Theo reached out, gently took his daughter's hand and guided her along the gravel path to the burial plot. The coffin was lowered into the ground, the bishop mumbled some Latin words and Theo picked up a handful of clay and dropped it on to the coffin. When the clay bounced off the casket the children flinched and Theo wondered how he was going to live without his beloved Grainne.

THE ACTOR

The days following Grainne's funeral were gruelling days for the Brevin family. Theo closed the business and withdrew from all social events. He spent his days wondering what he had done, for his God to take from him the person he loved so much; he spent his sleepless nights praying for her immortal soul.

Every morning when Jim awoke he remembered anew that his mother was dead and he experienced again the shock and pain of losing her. During the day, grief would creep up on him; he would stop whatever he was doing and it would consume him.

Líla's grieving was equally profound; most of her days and nights were spent in tears and when she wasn't crying the emptiness inside her grew until she felt she was no more than a shell.

Michael didn't know what he was experiencing and had no idea how the void within him was ever going to be filled.

Two weeks after the funeral Michael and Jim returned to boarding school. Michael excused himself from rugby and other sports and Jim dropped out of the drama society. The weeks passed with agonising slowness until finally June arrived and the two boys returned to their home.

7

The summer of 1913 was the first summer the Brevin family was without Grainne; Theo grew more intense, Líla became introverted, Michael became moody and Jim got more and more angry. In July, still wearing mourning clothes, Michael and Theo went to France for their annual wine safari, Líla went to Grandmother Brevin in Clontarf and Jim went to Cork to visit his friends Ciaran, Finn and Baggy. The boys did everything to try to lift Jim's spirits; Finn and his father took Jim to the English Market, where they bought fruit and fish from the stallholders. Baggy and his mother took Jim to Blarney Castle where they made him kiss the Blarney Stone and Ciaran and his father took Jim to Mizen Head where they attended a theatrical production of Sorcha O'Donovan's Touring Company of Irish Players. Then it was back to Dublin, and sadness descended again.

When September arrived, it was back to Killucan Boarding School for Jim, but not for his older brother – Michael was university bound. He enrolled in University College Dublin and quickly adapted to college life. He joined the cricket and the rugby clubs and was immediately chosen to play on the university's rugby team.

In Killucan on the first day of term, Jim was called to Assistant Dean Carrol's office.

'Your end-of-term results were poor,' the Assistant Dean said imperiously as he removed his thick-lensed spectacles. 'However, under the circumstances it is understandable. But now, Master Brevin, it is time for you to apply yourself to your studies. You are in your final years here at Killucan and it is vital you do well. I advise that you forgo all extra-curricular activities and by that I mean your involvement in the drama society.'

'Yes sir,' Jim replied, hardly hearing the man.

In spite of the Assistant Dean's advice, when the drama society became active, Jim auditioned and was cast in the lead role in the Christmas play. Constantly angry, Jim became truculent and fought with the cast, crew and his friends; he lost all interest in his studies, missed many classes, skipped all formal and informal study groups and only exerted his mind when working with the drama society. Jim received much acclaim for his performance in the end-of-term play but even that triumph seemed hollow because he wasn't able to share it with his mother.

In mid-December Jim returned home for the Christmas holidays with a plan of how he would continue his theatrical activities. An icy cold northerly wind was blowing hard when he arrived at the stage door of the Queen's Theatre. It was thirty minutes before the matinee performance of Ira Allen's play *The Eviction* and Jim was hoping to talk to the great man. As he stood building up the courage to open the door, a tall, wild-haired man brushed past him, pulled open the door and asked curtly 'Are you going in?'

'I am, sir,' Jim replied and walked through the door into a small lobby. 'I have a letter for Mr Ira Allen, what should I do with it?'

'Give it to Archie,' the wild-haired man said, pointing to a counter behind him.

Jim knocked on the counter and a small wooden window shot upwards. A man in a well-worn, soiled jacket and collarless shirt glared at him; Archie had drink taken.

'What do you want?'

'I have a letter for Mr Allen,' Jim replied, fingering the letter that had taken him three days to write.

'Will you be wanting a reply?' grunted the stage doorman.

'Yes sir.'

Archie's eyes rolled upwards, his nicotine-stained fingers shot out of the hatch and he snatched the letter from Jim's hand. 'Wait there,' he growled and crashed the window shut.

The walls of the lobby were covered in posters of past Queen's Theatre productions: *The Colleen Bawn, The Croppy Boy, Lord Edward, The Redskin's Revenge and Fr Murphy*. Beside each poster was a newspaper review of the show and below each poster were photographs of actors. A gust of wind swept through the lobby as the door opened and two tipsy, middle-aged women came in with it.

'Its freezing out there, Concepta,' shivered the fatter of the two women.

'Will ya looka here, Maise,' Concepta said as she nodded at Jim and adjusted her woollen shawl for indoor conditions. 'Are you one of my admirers?'

Jim blushed. 'No, I'm here to talk to Mr Allen about becoming an actor.'

'Oh, you're a very handsome young man. You'd make a lovely actor.'

'Don't mind her, son, she's only teasing you,' interjected Maise. 'Concepta, he's only a child.'

'What do you mean, I know nothing?' Concepta snapped sharply. 'I know a hell of a lot more than you, at least my people didn't come up on the canal barge.'

'What are you insinuating ...'

The window rattled up and Archie glared at the women. 'Go on about your business, you two.'

'Ah Archie, are you in a bad mood?' jeered Concepta. 'Is the wife not looking after you?'

Archie grunted and, sniggering loudly, the two women disappeared into the theatre.

'Are they actresses?' Jim asked.

'No they're not, they're cleaners,' Archie replied with a shrug. 'Mr Allen said if you come back fifteen minutes after the matinee he'll talk to you.' He slid a ticket for the show across the counter and before Jim could thank him, crashed the window down.

*

THE ACTOR

Fourteen minutes after the matinee finished and with butterflies fluttering wildly in his stomach, Jim returned to the stage door. As he stood in the lobby, the actors Val Vousden and Leslie Lawrence opened the inner door to the theatre.

'Can I help you?' Leslie Lawrence asked.

'I have an appointment with Mr Allen and I don't know where to go,' Jim replied.

Leslie Lawrence held the door wide and said 'On the other side of the stage you'll find a small corridor, Mr Allen's dressing room is the first door on the left – you'll see his name on the door. Watch where you're walking in there, the stagehands are moving a lot of things around.'

Brimming with excitement, Jim entered the backstage area. He strolled past a peasant cottage set, then a section of a big house and then a gypsy campsite. Above him he heard a whirling sound and, craning his neck, he watched a large canvas backdrop disappear into the darkness of the theatre's flies. A stagehand called out 'Everyone off stage,' the man pulled on a rope and the backdrop for the first scene of the show floated down from above. Jim waited until all was quiet then started across the stage.

Listening to the echo of his own footsteps, Jim imagined the hundreds of actors that had trod the wooden boards beneath him. Suddenly the main curtain rose and Jim was staring into the huge empty theatre; it almost took his breath away. He gazed out across the vast, vacant auditorium and felt he had come home. He was still looking when a stage hand tapped him on the shoulder and said 'It's not safe to stand there, son.'

With his heart thumping, Jim knocked on Ira Allen's dressing room door. The door swung open and May Murnane, the actress he had just seen in the play, stood before him. Her face broke into a joyous smile and Jim nearly collapsed; he had never experienced anyone as beautiful or as welcoming as May Murnane.

'Hello, you must be Jim Brevin. Go on in, Ira is expecting you.' Then she called over her shoulder 'I'll be off darling. I'll bring back milk for the tea.'

'Okay love,' answered an unseen Ira. 'Say hello to the kids for me.'

THE ACTOR

The actress waved to her husband, slipped past Jim and disappeared down the short corridor.

Jim stood in the doorway and stared. The actor was taller and thinner then he looked on stage, but his deep brown eyes were just as expressive and charismatic.

'Come on in,' Ira said, holding out his hand to his young guest.

'I am extremely pleased to meet you, sir,' Jim replied and shook his idol's hand a little too enthusiastically.

The actor smiled. 'Would you like a cup of tea? I'm afraid it will have to be black.' He looked into the mirror and wiped the last of the stage make-up from his face.

'No thank you, sir.'

The dressing room was long and narrow. Two dressing tables with illuminated mirrors filled one side of the room and two clothes racks, filled with stage costumes, occupied the other side. At the top of the room beneath a window was a full-length mirror and beside it was a small table with a gas ring, teapot, cups and an open tin of biscuits. The dressing room's upper walls were plastered with yellowing playbills, posters and photos of long-forgotten Queen's Theatre productions.

'Why don't we sit?' the actor said, as he slipped a pullover on over his costume.

Jim sat, intoxicated by the smell of greasepaint, spirit glue, the racks of costumes, the lighted mirrors and the hundreds of posters that clung to the walls.

'So you want to become an actor?' Ira asked matter-of-factly, running his long thin fingers through his thick brown hair.

'Yes sir, I do,' Jim replied emphatically.

'And do you think you have the talent to be an actor?'

'Yes I do sir, lots of talent.'

'And you want me to tell you how to go about becoming an actor?'

Jim nodded and fixed his gaze on his idol.

'Let me ask you a question. Will you do as I recommend, even if you don't like what I say?'

Jim answered with hesitation. 'Yes sir, I will.'

'Good, I'm going to tell you what I've told every other young person that has ever asked me that question. First, finish your education.' Jim frowned; the actor ignored the frown. 'Bright educated people make the best actors. When you finish your education, if you still want to become an actor, then don't – do something else.' Jim nearly fell out of his seat. 'Only if you have to become an actor, only if you can't think of anything else you want to do, only then should you even consider becoming an actor – and even then, God knows, it's not a good idea.'

This was not the advice Jim wanted.

'But I want to become an actor right now. I've been in four school plays and ...'

'I thought you agreed to take my advice,' interrupted Ira.

'I want you to give me a job, now,' Jim shot back.

'Ah, so that's the real reason you're here. You want a job, not advice.'

Jim sat silently, his eyes fixed on the actor's face.

Ira sighed. 'Jim, actors aren't given jobs, they are cast in specific roles in particular plays. You are a very young man, and there are few roles for people your age. Take my advice, finish your education. You'll need an education, no matter what you choose to do in life.'

How could such a great actor give such rotten advice, wondered Jim as he lay in his bed that night. He wished his mother was alive; she would have known what he should do next.

One week before he was to return to Killucan Boarding School, a sullen-faced Jim walked into his father's study and stood in front of the desk.

'What can I do for you son?' Theo asked, lifting his eyes from the ledger on his desk.

'Father, I'd like to talk about my future.'

'You want to do that now?'

'Yes sir.'

'Well you better sit down.' Theo closed the ledger and fingered the end of his moustache. 'What exactly do you want to discuss?'

'Father, I have chosen a profession for myself.'

'You have done what?'

'I want to be an actor.'

Theo's face flushed with disbelief. 'You want to be an actor?' His voice was so filled with disdain that Jim wished the ground would open and swallow him up. 'That's the silliest idea I've ever heard.'

'No father, it is not. I have thought about it. It's what mother would have wanted.'

'Don't tell me what your mother would have wanted. You're not going to be an actor. Like your brother Michael, you are going to join the family business, that's what you're going to do.'

'Father, it may be your intention that I become a wine merchant but it's not mine. I'm going to be an actor, it's my chosen profession.'

Theo scowled. 'I am not a wine merchant, I am a wine importer. And acting is not a profession – it's not so long ago that actors were considered no better than vagabonds. I will not permit you to make a fool of yourself like this.' He pulled a single sheet of headed paper from the top drawer of his mahogany desk and slapped it on the desk top. 'What does it say on that letterhead?'

Jim didn't answer.

'It says Brevin and Sons – not son, but sons.' Theo pushed the paper across to Jim. 'My father started this company and I spent my life building it up and someday the business will belong to you and your brother and you both will run it.'

'I'm fifteen years old, father. I'm a man and I'll make my own decisions.'

'You're not fifteen, you are fourteen. You are not a man and you most certainly do not make your own decisions.'

Jim could not understand why he was being treated with such scorn. He rose to leave the room.

Theo saw the hurt in his son's eyes and, lowering his voice, said 'Jim, sit down, please.'

Jim hesitated, then sat.

'It wasn't my intention to hurt you. Believe me, I have only your best interests at heart. This past year, we have all been through so much. I know it has been hard on you, I know you miss your mother. I miss your mother too, every day. I'm trying to be both father and mother to you and Líla and Michael. I'm trying to hold our family together and I'm trying to run a business that's under great pressure. These are very difficult times.' Theo lowered his voice to a near whisper. 'Some would say even dangerous times. There's much unrest in the country. That Larkin man is stirring up the workers. There is political unrest and a growing nationalism in the country. The Irish Volunteers, Óglaigh na hÉireann, are drilling and marching in uniform. Last Saturday, I saw them in the park. Your friend Brian Ahern was one of them. Son, I plead with you to forget this nonsense about being an actor.'

'Father, it isn't nonsense and I can't forget about it.'

'You will forget it,' Theo snapped. 'This subject is closed and don't mention it to me again.'

Jim didn't forget about it and tried many times during the week to reopen the discussion with his father. Every time Theo heard the word 'actor', he threw his hands in the air and said 'I told you the matter is closed.'

On his return to Killucan Boarding School, Jim had an academic review with the stiff-necked Assistant Dean Carrol.

'Your end-of-term results were very poor again,' the Assistant Dean said, stroking his chin.

'But I nearly passed everything.'

'There's no such thing as nearly passing,' replied the Assistant Dean. 'You failed three subjects and were border-line in all the rest. If you don't apply yourself to your studies you are likely to fail your end-of-year exams. Then you would have to repeat the year. To ensure that doesn't happen, I am directing you to resign from the drama society.' Jim's mouth fell open. 'Master Brevin, there will be no more theatre for you until there is a great improvement in your marks.'

Jim tried to apply himself to his studies but he saw little relevance in learning about the inner workings of the electro-magnet, or tenses in Latin, or the laws of chemistry, or Irish grammar, geometry or algebra. What good would any of this be to an actor? Mid-way through the term, he began to make his own plans for his future; he wrote to Ciaran's aunt Sorcha O'Donovan and two weeks later he received a reply.

During the school's Easter break, Jim made a final attempt to talk to his father about his theatrical ambitions. But when Theo ordered him to 'leave the study and close the door behind you,' Jim knew he had to turn his plan into action.

On the Saturday before he was to return to school and while Theo and Michael were at a cricket match, Jim sat at his father's desk and on company-headed paper wrote a letter to Dean Avery informing him that Jim would not be returning to Killucan after the Easter break. Jim signed the letter 'Theo Brevin'. He next climbed into the attic, found his mother's old battered leather suitcase, returned to his room and stuffed as many of his non-school belongings as he could into the case. He went to the post office and withdrew all his savings. At home he folded a five-pound note, placed it in the small inside pocket of his jacket and carefully, if crudely, sewed up the pocket; his rainy-day money he called it, only to be used in a dire emergency.

Sitting in the front drawing room waiting on the hansom cab to take him to Kingsbridge railway station, Jim didn't notice the shafts of cold white light that were slicing through the morning mist or the sad look on Líla's face or the beautiful lunch Mrs O'Neill had packed for him.

'Father said he won't be able to take you to the station. There's an emergency in the storeroom,' Michael said when he bounded into the drawing room. 'You don't mind if I don't go with you? I have a rugby practice that I'd rather not miss.'

'I don't mind. You go to your practice,' Jim replied.

Earlier during breakfast Jim had wanted to tell Líla about his plan but he knew she would not be able to keep a secret of such magnitude, so he didn't confide in her. When the hansom cab arrived, he hugged his sister and whispered 'Don't worry about me, I'll be all right.'

He left his home with a heavy heart; he was ashamed of his deceit yet he was certain he was doing the right thing. At Kingsbridge railway station, the driver pulled hard on the reins and the cab shuddered to a halt. Jim entered the station but did not board the train for Killucan. Instead, filled with his dream of becoming an actor and confident in the knowledge that he was fulfilling his destiny, he boarded the train to Bantry, County Cork, to join Sorcha O'Donovan's Touring Company of Irish Players.

8

Clouds of billowing white steam pumped from the train as it chugged, clanked and rattled its way to Mallow, County Cork. Sitting uncomfortably in a third class compartment, clutching his battered suitcase, Jim hardly noticed the lush lands of Leinster flash past. To make himself look older, he was wearing some of his brother's clothes, but they were not a good fit. The below-the-knee pants were a little loose, the high-necked shirt kept scratching his neck and the jacket was too large. Jim sat in the rattling carriage thinking that he looked rather like a clown.

The journey was uneventful until the train stopped at Kildare station. A severe, square-faced woman carrying a lidded wicker basket boarded the train and took the seat next to him. She placed the basket on her lap and spent the entire journey staring straight ahead.

Jim heard a low clucking. A waft of foul air made his eyes smart and he felt a dart of pain in his right arm. A hen had popped her head out of the woman's basket and pecked him. He flicked at the bird's beak with his finger but this seemed only to encourage it and to the great amusement of the burly cattle dealer sitting across from him, he had to spend the next hour defending himself from the hen's persistent attentions.

THE ACTOR

When the woman left the train in Portlaoise, a much relieved Jim stood up to brush the feathers off his jacket. While he wasn't looking, an unkempt youth slid his arm into the carriage and surreptitiously lifted Jim's suitcase off the ground. The cattle dealer grabbed the youth's arm, twisted it until he dropped the suitcase, and then tossed the youth out on to the station platform.

Jim thanked him profusely, and for the rest of the journey learnt everything there was to know about cattle dealing in Ireland. After many stops and many changes of passengers, the train pulled into Mallow station sixty minutes late.

Entering the old Bianconi Coach Station, the smell of horse urine and soiled hay assailed Jim's nostrils. 'Sir, what time is the coach to Blarney?' he asked a stableman who was tying a nosebag on to a horse's head.

'You've missed today's coach, the next one won't be till Wednesday,' the man replied without looking at him.

'I have to get there today. I must get there today. Are you sure there's no coach?'

'Of course I'm sure, and getting all upset at me won't change anything.' The man continued tending to the horse.

'How far is it to walk there?' Jim asked him, as calmly as he could.

'Only twenty miles. If you got up early in the morning you could get there before nightfall.'

Jim sat on his case and rested his head in his hands. The Sorcha O'Donovan's Touring Company of Irish Players was only going to be in Blarney for one day and after that Jim had no idea where they were going. What to do? Twenty miles … If he started walking right away, he might just get there before they left. Jim sprang to his feet so swiftly that he startled the coachman. 'Sir, would you be as gracious as to point out to me the road to Blarney?'

'That I can do,' the stableman said and walked to the station door.

Jim picked up his suitcase; as he followed the man, he stumbled over a wooden chest that was jutting out of an alcove.

'Are you all right? Now, just wait a minute …' The corners of the stableman's mouth turned upwards into a smile. 'That was very a lucky trip you took there.'

THE ACTOR

'Lucky?' complained Jim, as he dusted off his clothes.

'Yes, that's Mick O's stuff, he has to take that wooden chest and that box of fruit and vegetables to the big house in Blarney. If you don't mind sitting on a delivery cart, he could take you there.'

'He's going there today?' Jim asked excitedly.

'That he is, if you go across to the Coachman's Inn you could talk to him.'

'How will I recognise him?'

'Arrah, you couldn't miss Mick O, the poor man has an enormous head on him like a giant cabbage and a crooked foot. But he's a Kerryman and if you want him to take you to Blarney you better make it worth his while. The man loves a pint of cider.'

The bar in the Coachman's Inn reeked of stale beer, damp clothes, tobacco and sour perspiration. Dull grey light streamed in through the tavern's dirty windows and the hazy smoke that hung in the air stung Jim's eyes. Loud blotchy-faced, cattle traders and leathery-skinned farmers traded loud insults with each other while barmaids scurried about carrying plates of bread and cheese and jugs of ale. Fearful but determined, Jim rambled around the tavern until he came upon a small little man with an enormous head sitting alone in a corner. The man's clothes were ill fitting and badly made, his twisted right leg was encased in a metal calliper and on his foot was a black boot with a thick wooden sole the size of a sod of turf.

'Are you Mr Mick O?' Jim asked, unable to take his eyes off the man's calliper and bulky boot.

'If you take your eyes off my foot for a moment I'll answer that question.'

Jim flushed red and lifted his gaze to the man's face.

'Mick O, that's what they call me.' The man massaged the calf of his leg with the top of a blackthorn stick. 'What do I call you and what do you want of me?'

'My name is Jim Brevin and the stableman in the coach station said that if I buy you a pint of cider, you might take me to Blarney today. And I'm sorry for staring at your foot.'

'If that's what the man said, that's what I'll do, for he's the boss. Now be off with you and get me that cider.'

THE ACTOR

When Jim returned from the bar he placed a pint of cloudy cider on the table and Mick O downed half of it in one swallow. Jim took the seat beside him; he still found it difficult not to look at the man's leg. After a few uncomfortable minutes, Mick O downed the rest of the pint, stood up and announced 'I have some business to conclude. I'll meet you out front in five minutes.'

While Jim stood outside the inn drinking in the clean fresh air, he began to wonder if he had just been cheated out of the price of a pint of cider. Where was Mick O? The road was crowded with pony and traps, donkeys and carts, open and closed horse-drawn coaches, bicycles and many horses and riders. To his right, a one-legged man, wearing a torn overcoat tied at the waist with a string, was begging; his face was gaunt and yellow. An unkempt woman was dragging a crying child after her along the street; she stopped to shake the child, shouted at her and – when the little girl still didn't stop crying – smacked her across the face. A young curate in long black clerical robes tut-tutted to himself as he rushed past the scene. Leaning against the stone wall of the Coachman's Inn was an old man smoking a clay pipe; every so often he spat on the ground. On the far pavement, an elegantly-dressed woman with a wide-brimmed hat was pushing a perambulator. A policeman rounded the corner into view, and the one-legged beggar hopped quickly away.

There was still no sign of Mick O. A small herd of cattle driven by a farmer and his two wild-looking red-headed children clattered past, and a messenger boy on a delivery bicycle, his wicker baskets filled with fresh bread, dodged around the piles of cow, donkey and horse dung that littered the thoroughfare.

A modern two-seater automobile, a Rover Six, turned into the street and two strolling gentlemen in sack coats and bowler hats stopped to admire the gleaming horseless carriage. A cow wandered in front of the automobile and the annoyed driver blared the horn. The frightened cow reared up and the impatient driver blared the horn again. The animal skittered on the cobble stones, rushed back into the herd and stampeded them. Suddenly six wide-eyed terrified cows were running amok. People scattered in all directions, the messenger boy darted up a lane, the young mother grabbed her crying daughter and rushed into a nearby shop, the two gentlemen dodged into a nearby tavern, and the old man ended up sitting in the pool of his own spittle. A stampeding cow was galloping down the pavement towards the woman with the perambulator; Jim raced over and threw himself between the baby and the cow, waving his arms frantically. The commotion came to a quick conclusion when the farmer and his children herded the frightened animals back on to the road. The relieved woman was still thanking Jim when he heard the tap of a walking stick and the thud of a wooden-soled boot on the path behind him.

Mick O's walk was an ungraceful dance of limps, coupled with body jerks and flailing arms. But in spite of his hobbling, twisting and flailing, the man carried himself with the dignity of a wounded veteran in a military parade. Children stared at his calliper and huge boot but Mick O greeted all onlookers like lost friends and in the short distance between the inn and the coach-station more than twenty people greeted him by name.

'Why don't you give Nelly a few of these,' Mick O said, handing Jim a bunch of withered carrots and pointing at the donkey. 'Nelly and I have been together more than twenty years.'

Jim fed the carrots to the donkey while Mick O, groaning loudly, hauled the wooden trunk out of the alcove and lifted it on to the cart.

'I would have done that for you,' Jim said, rushing to help.

'The Lord helps them that helps themselves and no offence to you Jim, but I would much prefer his help than yours. Throw your case up on the cart and take one of those old sacks and place it under you when you sit up front.'

Mick O placed the box of fruit and vegetables on the cart, then hobbled over to the cart's metal-rimmed wheel. He swung his callipered leg out and up and when it landed on the cart's axle, jerked his body upwards and with a thump landed in the driver's seat.

'How did you get up here so fast?' Jim asked, as he joined him.

'Every cripple has to find his own way of dancing,' the large-headed man replied. Then he flicked the reins, clicked his tongue and called 'Nelly, take us to Blarney!' and the cart rumbled out of the station and up Mallow's main street.

As they passed the red sandstone ruins of Mallow Castle, a ragged boy driving an approaching cart loaded with peat and vegetables yelled 'How are ya, big head?'

Mick O simply raised his hand and waved.

Jim felt somehow obligated to apologise for the boy. 'Sorry about that. He's just an ignorant child.'

'Sure, you've nothing to be sorry about. But I feel sorry for the lad. He didn't turn up when the good Lord was handing out sense. He's more to be pitied than reprimanded.'

During the journey to Blarney, Jim learned that although Mick O was unschooled he had gathered a vast compendium of proverbs, truisms, axioms and adages which he regarded as the collective wisdom of country folk and which he sprinkled liberally into his conversations. He answered questions with questions and on more than a few occasions turned Jim's questions back on Jim. But he was always polite and pleasant and he had an infinite understanding and compassion for his fellow man.

'What happened to your foot?' Jim asked as the cart passed through Blackrock village.

'Nothing happened to my foot. I was born with it like that. It's the way the good Lord made me and a cobbler man in Mallow made that fine boot for me.'

Jim glanced at Mick O's callipered leg and wondered how anyone could endure such a deformity.

'A crooked foot is not the worst thing in the world,' said Mick O, when he saw the look on Jim's face. 'Aren't I alive and aren't my two fine big brothers dead?' He tapped the wooden seat of the cart. 'Don't you think that my two brothers would much prefer to have a crooked foot than be dead?'

When they arrived in the hinterlands of Quartertown, a farmer moving cows from one field to another had blocked the road. While Mick O and the farmer shouted pleasantries at each other, two gaunt, wild-looking women crept up behind the cart, grabbed a few apples from the box of fruit and vegetables and ran off down a side road.

'Should I run after them?' Jim asked, jumping off the cart.

'Why would you want to break your shin on a stool that's not in your way?' Mick O replied, shaking his enormous head.

'But they stole your property.'

'It's not my property and do you really think the man in the big

THE ACTOR

house in Bantry will miss a few apples?' Mick O leaned back and placed a sack over the box of fruit and vegetables.

'But they broke the law,' Jim argued.

'Maybe so, but necessity knows no law.'

The cart resumed its journey and Jim sat in silence listened to the cheeping of the birds and the relentless grinding of the cart's iron-rimmed wheels on the hard dirt road.

'Why is it so important that you get to Blarney today? Are you going to the fair?' asked Mick O.

'No sir, I'm going to Blarney to join the Sorcha O'Donovan Touring Company of Irish Players. I'm an actor.' It was the first time Jim had said out loud that he was an actor and he felt proud.

'And your father, is he an actor?'

Jim frowned. 'No, my father does not approve of the profession.'

'And why is that?'

'He doesn't think much of actors and he thinks I'm a fool because I want to be one.'

'He said that, in those very words?'

'Not in those words. He wants me to go into the family business. He doesn't understand why I can't do that. He doesn't understand me at all.'

'And do you understand him?'

Jim went quiet and looked unseeingly across the fields. A silent minute passed.

'Your mother, what does she say of you being an actor?'

'My mother died last year.'

'So, your father is still in mourning?'

'I am too,' Jim blurted out defensively.

'That's true,' Mick O conceded, then added 'But he didn't leave you.'

Jim went quiet again. When Mick O didn't fill the silence, he asked 'Am I a bad son?'

Mick O rubbed his chin. 'No, you're not a bad son, you're just a son.'

'Then why did I run away and not tell him where I was going?'

'I can't answer that for you, but every man has to do his own growing up, there's no forcing the sea.'

Jim was still thinking about what Mick O had said when they came upon an old man carrying a wicker basket of turf on his back. The man's weary face was covered in damp soil and when he stood aside to let the cart pass he called out 'Dia dhuit Mick O.'

'Dia's Muire dhuit Sean,' Mick O replied and stopped the cart. 'Would you like to put your load on the cart, my good man?'

'I won't bother, sure I'm nearly home.' Then, lowering his voice, the man whispered 'I hear the O'Grady family are on the side of the road.'

'Oh God help them, now nobody will want to know them. I'll take my leave of you Sean. I have to be in Bantry before dark. Slán leat.'

'Slán.'

Just outside of Grenagh, the cart passed a derelict thatched farmhouse with five emaciated children playing around the outbuildings. Staring out of the window were two adult faces; their crushed despondent expressions frightened Jim. 'Why do they look like that?'

'They look like that because they're waiting on the bailiff.'

The cart turned a bend in the road and slowed down. A family of half-starved children and their parents were encamped on the roadside. When the man raised his head, he had the same broken expression on his face as the people in the derelict farmhouse. Shocked, Jim looked away.

'Poor creatures,' remarked Mick O.

'Why are they living on the roadside?'

'Because the bailiff put them there, they have lost their land and have nowhere to go, so they go nowhere. They're called the dispossessed.'

'They look so frightened.'

'That's not fear son, that's the look of shame, for shame is a terrible part of poverty.'

On the outskirts of the villages of Greenhill and Burnfort, the cart passed four other families living on the side of the road.

Close to the town of Blarney, they joined a procession of slow-moving vehicles.

'It's going to be slow from here,' Mick O announced with a chuckle. 'Blarney's fair attracts all sorts of traders and hawkers.'

The procession ground and rattled its way slowly along the rough road and when they were in sight of the five hundred-years-old castle, Mick O stopped the cart. 'You'll take your leave of me now, Jim Brevin, the town hall is a just a little way down there.' He held out his hand to Jim.

Jim shook it. 'It's been a privilege talking to you, sir.'

THE ACTOR

'May you live as long as you want and never want as long as you live.'
'Thank you, sir.' Jim jumped off the cart. It was five o'clock.

9

Jim stood at the top of Blarney's main street and listened to the clucking of chickens, the snorting of pigs and the bleating of sheep that rose from the coops, creels and temporary pens that were constructed for the fair. He watched farmers' wives replenish and arrange the cheese, butter and eggs on their stalls while their burly husbands shouted orders at their children or whistled to their dogs. Smoke curled from kindling fires that boiled water for the traders' porridge and tea while their children hunched around the fires and munched on great chunks of dry bread. Buyers and sellers haggled over prices and when a deal was struck palms were spat upon and hands were slapped. A quietly excited Jim walked along the stalls of basket makers, cobblers, nail makers and tinsmiths until he reached the town hall.

There, he removed his cap, pushed on the door and walked into the hall's small empty rubbish-littered vestibule. To his right was a cramped ticket office and on the door into the main hall was a hand-written sign: No Entry. Jim pushed opened the door and looked into the main hall. It stunk of mildew and paraffin. At the far end was a small elevated stage in poor repair and lining the left wall were stacks of dust-covered, chipped and broken benches. Cluttering up the back of the hall were six broken chairs, a tea chest filled with rubbish and an empty oak barrel.

THE ACTOR

The paint on the walls was blistered and curling and oddly the floor on one side of the hall was cleared of litter and sprinkled with fresh sawdust. As Jim walked up the hall, his hand brushed against the wall and a large curl of paint snapped and floated to the hard floor.

'What do you think you're doing? I've just put that sawdust on that floor,' barked an agitated voice.

'Sorry, I'm looking for Miss Sorcha O'Donovan.' He looked around for the owner of the voice.

'Are you Jim Brevin?'

'Yes I am.'

A tall, dark, floppy-haired young man with heavy-lidded blue eyes and a devil-may-care expression sauntered to the front of the stage. 'Welcome, Jim!' With great theatrical flair, he leapt off the stage and swaggered across the hall, wiping his hands on one of the three damp rags that dangled from his back pocket. 'Good to meet you. I'm Shamus McGovern and I hear you're the new apprentice.'

'I hope to be.'

Shamus McGovern was about five years older and a foot taller than Jim. He wore an open-necked shirt, a knitted pullover, thick coarse corduroy trousers and heavy boots yet somehow he managed to project an air of confidence, flair and panache.

'Are you an actor?'

'Yes, I play heroes and the odd time I get to play a villain.' Shamus pushed back a clump of thick black hair that had flopped across his forehead. 'I also sing, dance and play the piano. I hang the curtains and backdrops, set the lights, change the gels, look after props, man the box office, check tickets. I even have to clean the venues but soon that will all change.'

'Why is that?'

'Because, my friend, you are the new apprentice and that's what apprentices do. Miss Sorcha is out drumming up an audience for tonight's show. While you're waiting, do you want to help me get the hall ready for tonight's show?'

Jim could hardly believe his ears. 'Yes of course, what has to be done?'

'I've prepared the stage and filled the Tilley lamps, now I have to wipe all the benches and position them in front of the stage. Then I have to sweep and sawdust the other half of hall and arrange the seating.' Shamus pulled one of the rags from his back pocket and threw it at Jim. 'Let's get to work.'

'How many actors are there in the company?' Jim asked as they wiped a bench.

'Right now there are five of us. There is an actor to play heroes, that's me and there's an actress who plays heroines, that's Patricia, Sorcha O'Donovan's daughter. Best to keep your hands off her.'

Jim's face flushed red at the very thought of putting his hands on anyone.

Then we have Bartholomew Bradley, he plays old men, informers and comic characters.'

'You forgot to say that I am the most experienced – and the only truly professional – actor in the company,' a deep voice growled from the wings. Bartholomew Bradley marched nonchalantly across the stage and a line of smoke rose lazily from the cigarette that dangled from his lips.

'Pleased to meet you, sir,' Jim said and offered to shake his hand.

The ex-military, larger than life, bald actor glared at Jim as if he was an undesirable. 'Sorry I can't return the compliment.' Then, to emphasise his indifference, he snorted – and the cigarette that was affixed to his thick lips bounced and shed its arch of ash down the front of his worn, baggy tweed suit. 'Shite, now see what you've done,' he exclaimed angrily as he brushed the offending grey ash off his jacket.

'Can't you be civil for once in your life,' Shamus snapped and for a split second his blue eyes flashed with intense anger.

'Temper, temper, Shamus,' grunted the older actor as he walked off the stage.

Shamus fell silent and Jim continued to wipe down the benches.

'He's an old fart, but he's not the worst,' Shamus said after a while, as he positioned a bench in front of the stage. 'Did you notice his eye?' Jim looked questioningly at him. 'It's glass and don't mention it to him. It happened when he was in the army. He's sensitive about it.'

'Tell me about the other actors?'

'Our resident villain is the gentle giant Sebastian B Morrow III, he's

THE ACTOR

Miss Sorcha's husband and Miss Sorcha herself plays comical maids, widows and older women. Their daughter Patricia plays the ingénue leads.'

'What parts will I get to play?' Jim asked, and held his breath.

Shamus smiled and winked.

'Miss Sorcha will tell you that.'

Forty minutes later, dressed in their costumes for the night's melodrama, Miss Sorcha O'Donovan, Sebastian B Morrow III and their daughter Patricia clattered into the hall. Miss Sorcha looked along the uniform rows of freshly-wiped benches and exclaimed loudly 'Excellent Shamus, the place looks like a church. We're going up in the world.'

Miss Sorcha was short and heavy-set with a huge voice and an angelic face. Although small of stature she was a formidable woman who revelled in her role of actor-manager and was fiercely proud of 'bringing theatre to the plain people of Munster'.

'You must be Jim Brevin?' she asked in a grandiose voice.

Jim looked at the short, barrel-shaped woman who held his theatrical future in her stubby little fingers and suddenly he became tongue-tied.

'Can't you speak? You're of no use to a theatrical company if you can't speak.'

He continued to stare.

Coming to his rescue, Shamus said 'Jim's been helping me arrange the seating for tonight's performance.'

'Yes, I'm Jim Brevin,' Jim announced loudly, suddenly finding his voice.

'Good for you, but there's no need to shout. Now come with me and we'll have a little chat and remember I never promised you employment, just an interview.'

In the hall's cramped ticket office, Miss Sorcha removed her coat, perched herself on the tiny office's only seat and pulled from her handbag Jim's letter. While she was reading, Jim quickly adjusted his collar, pulled down his shirt cuffs, rubbed each shoe against the back of his long stockings and steeled himself for the most important interview of his life.

Miss Sorcha gently placed the letter on the counter.

'I do not wish to give offence Mr Brevin, but you don't look eighteen years of age.'

'No offence taken Miss Sorcha,' Jim replied, remembering the answers he had rehearsed. 'I do not look my age but that gives me the advantage when playing children's parts.' Jim hoped he sounded more mature than his years.

'Mr Brevin, tell me about your theatrical experience and your circumstances?'

What Jim told his prospective employer was an enhanced list of his own theatrical endeavours combined with a resume of Michael's sports and academic achievements and a liberal amount of lies. Miss Sorcha listened carefully and did not ask any probing questions or challenge anything Jim said. Two weeks ago, she had dismissed the previous theatrical apprentice when his indiscretion with a girl of little virtue had been abruptly brought to her attention, and in any case Shamus had been loudly complaining about the extra work that she had lately thrust upon him. For all his inexperience and lies, Jim was eager, available and the only candidate for the job.

'In your letter you said you are a magician and a singer.'

'Yes I am,' Jim replied. He thought it best to be unequivocal when he lied.

'A magician would fit right into the variety section of our productions. You could do a few magic tricks and then you and Shamus could sing a few traditional Irish songs. Yes, that's what the show needs.' Miss Sorcha nodded her head as if she was agreeing with herself. 'Jim, I think you are going to be a great asset to the company. Welcome.'

He beamed. 'Thank you, thank you so much. You won't regret this.'

'I sincerely hope not,' Miss Sorcha replied and rose, indicating that the little chat was over.

Jim didn't move.

'Is there something else, Mr Brevin?' inquired Miss Sorcha sharply.

There was a slight tremor in Jim's voice when he answered Miss Sorcha's question.

'We haven't talked about pay and what parts I'll be playing?'

Miss Sorcha's answer came swiftly.

'You will be paid five shillings and six pence a week, your digs will

THE ACTOR

be paid for you and there will be no thespian contributions from you for the foreseeable present.'

Miss Sorcha's reply was so decisive that Jim knew the matter was closed.

Jim became the Great Magico, Illusionist Extraordinaire and the younger half of the Murphy Brothers from Co. Clare, Murphy Brothers, Singers of Irish Ballads and Rebel Songs.

10

Sorcha O'Donovan's Touring Company of Irish Players was a small fit-up company that toured the Cork and Kerry hinterlands performing almost nightly in town halls, barns and occasionally in the open air. Each night's performance consisted of a variety show in which the actors performed songs, dances, conjuring and juggling turns. Then after a short intermission, the company performed a one-act Irish play or an abridged version of a three-act melodrama. The plays told stories of rural bravery and defiance and often featured evictions, crop burning and lynching. Sets were spartan, scenery consisted of a few shabby weather-beaten backdrops and flats, lighting was basic, an amber wash and the acting was of mixed quality, but audiences enjoyed the shows and applauded enthusiastically.

Like most of the fit-up companies of the day, Sorcha O'Donovan's Company would arrive in a small town in the late morning, fit up the venue as a theatre, perform that night and move on the next day. In larger towns the company might stay a second night and in places as large as Bantry they would stay three or four nights. Audiences were frequently unruly, noisy and talked constantly throughout performances. They hissed and heckled the actors and they never stopped smoking and spitting. On the occasions when it became all too much for Bartholomew

THE ACTOR

Bradley he would stop mid-performance and demand that the audience cease their filthy practices but the audiences paid little attention to him and continued to smoke, spit and talk.

As the Great Magico, Illusionist Extraordinaire, Jim wore an old black cloak and top hat which he rescued from one of the company's costume baskets. For his act he revived some slight-of-hand tricks he learned for his family's shows and he quickly learned to use the set of rings that were left behind by the last actor who had doubled as a magician. As the younger half of the Murphy Brothers from Co. Clare, Singers of Irish Ballads and Rebel Songs, Jim wore an ill-fitting waistcoat, tweed trousers and peaked cap. He didn't have a great singing voice, so Shamus did most of the singing while Jim joined in the choruses.

After three weeks with the company Jim was made the "early man". It was the early man's responsibility to arrive in a town ahead of the company, acquire the keys to the venue, purchase paraffin oil for the stage lamps, set up a stage area and then wait for the arrival of the rest of the company. Later when the company cart arrived, Jim would help hang the backdrops and the curtains then he would place a row of Tilley oil lamps around the front of the stage. Most of Jim's chores were mundane but to him he was working in the theatre and that was exactly what he wanted to do.

Publicising the arrival of the Sorcha O'Donovan Touring Company required improvisation. Using the glass globe of an oil lamp as a loudhailer, a member of the company would walk the streets, announcing with great enthusiasm and verve, the details of the evening's show.

For most small towns the arrival of a fit-up was a cause for great excitement. Word of the company's arrival would quickly spread to the town's hinterlands and people would come from miles on donkeys, horses and by the oddest means of conveyance to be present at the show.

'Jim, you're a good-looking young man but you have dreadful posture and you walk like a duck. When you learn to stand and walk like a gentleman I'll think about casting you,' was Miss Sorcha's curt reply when Jim asked her when he was likely to be used as an actor.

Jim was devastated. What was the woman talking about? *I don't have poor posture and I certainly don't walk like a duck?*

Shamus laughed loudly when Jim told him what Miss Sorcha had said. Then seeing the hurt and disappointment on his face, he put his arm around Jim and said 'She is right, you need to improve you posture and your walk. She means what she says, she won't give you a part until you learn to stand up straight.'

Jim flounced off in disgust, but two hours later he returned to Shamus and asked for help.

With steely determination, Jim went about correcting his posture and his walk. He started every morning with a look in a mirror. He turned sideways, pulled back his shoulders, stuck out his chest and remained rigid for five minutes. Then standing erect he walked about the room. Throughout the day whenever he passed a mirror or shop window, he glanced at his reflection and would immediately correct his posture.

Shamus also monitored Jim's posture and every time he saw Jim slouch he would tap him on the back and Jim would immediately jerk his body upright. Shamus enlisted Miss Sorcha's daughter Patricia to help. She taught Jim to waltz, foxtrot and tango while Shamus taught him the rudiments of fencing. Each week his posture and gait improved and after two months Jim again approached Miss Sorcha and asked her to consider him for a part.

'Let me see you walk,' she called out.

Jim instantly regretted that he made his request at the end of a company meal.

'Is that too difficult?' Miss Sorcha demanded.

He climbed up to the stage and self-consciously walked across it.

'Better – now march across the stage, like a soldier.'

Jim did as requested.

'Good. Now let me see you sit.'

Jim hadn't practiced sitting but he sat as carefully as he could.

'Your sitting is not very elegant but your posture and walk have improved considerably,' Miss Sorcha concluded. 'Mr Brevin, I do think you are ready for a walk-on role.'

'Thank you very much,' Jim replied and slouched off stage. Miss Sorcha looked to the sky and sighed.

What's a walk-on role?' Jim asked Shamus as they cleared the table.

THE ACTOR

'A cough and a spit,' replied Shamus. Jim looked askance at Shamus, who laughed and added 'It's a small role; a servant with a few lines, a policeman who arrests the hero, a messenger. Something like that.'

Progress, Jim thought, but not much progress.

A week later he was given two lines in the play *The Gentleman Thief*. His role was that of a man-servant who was sent to summon a tenant to the big house.

On the morning of the show they rehearsed the scene three times. The afternoon passed very slowly and every time Jim thought about his forthcoming professional debut he went pale with fear. The minutes crawled by and every hour on the hour he practiced his two lines. He wrote his words on the palm of his hands and one hour before show-time he started to feel very nervous. The audience started to arrive and butterflies fluttered wildly in Jim's stomach. The hall went dark and he broke out in a cold sweat as the curtain parted. The variety show went without a hitch. After an interminable intermission the play began. A pale-faced Jim stood in the wings and waited. He heard his cue, his stomach dropped and he had to fight the urge to run out of the hall and disappear into the night but he swallowed hard and walked on stage.

Panic started to climb within him. His mouth went dry and he wished he was anywhere but on stage. He opened his mouth and the words came out. He breathed easier and waited for his next cue. It came and affecting a pompous voice he delivered his second line.

'His lordship would like you to be in the big house at six o'clock this evening, sir.'

A calmness fell upon Jim and he wished he had more lines. When he walked off the stage he exhaled deeply. His hands were trembling, his body was soaked in perspiration but he was happy; now he was a real actor.

11

The Sorcha O'Donovan Touring Company of Irish Players' high-sided, ornately decorated, horse-drawn cart wobbled along the roads of the largest county in Ireland. During the touring season the cart and its occupants travelled from the lush lowlands and valleys of East Cork to the barren magnificence of the mountains and peninsulas of West Cork. The road rose and fell over hills, twisted around fields, crossed bridges and passed through many towns and villages. Sitting on the front seat of the cart were Miss Sorcha, Bartholomew and Sebastian and travelling in the back of the cart with the sets, costumes and props were Jim, Shamus and Patricia.

Town after town, night after night, the company performed in parish halls, town halls, GAA halls, barns and even vacant churches. If no suitable building could be found the actors built a stage outdoors and performed under the moon. But no matter where they performed, Jim enjoyed it and never tired of it. He loved the camaraderie of the company, he loved the dramas on and off stage but above all he loved the excitement and adventure of being part of theatre.

Jim could never understand where the people came from but come they did and the company performed to mostly full houses. As the colourful cart passed along the road, heads would appear in farmhouse windows, behind walls and bushes and all along the horizon. As they entered a town, cheering children ran in front of the cart and when it stopped outside the night's venue, children and adults clamoured for complimentary tickets. Walking down the streets of the small towns of County Cork, Jim and his fellow actors were hailed from doors and half-doors. People loved the excitement of a fit-up in their town and as Miss Sorcha proudly put it 'the visit of fit-up to a town brought culture, drama and magic to the people'.

No matter what play the company performed, audiences enjoyed it. Young women loved Shamus' style and charisma, young and old men loved Patricia's youth and beauty and the children loved Jim's magic tricks. After the show a stream of young, and not so young, women waited for a word with Shamus, young men waited on an autograph or a smile from Patricia and the children begged Jim to perform more tricks.

The fit-up's scenery and stage properties were designed and built to work in all types of venues. In Ballydehob the venue was an open barn on the outskirts of the town. Jim and Shamus raked the barn's clay floor and constructed a make-shift stage out of three trestle tables, a few rostrum steps and a make-shift curtain. Bartholomew and Sebastian hung the backdrops on posts and Shamus positioned eight oil-lamps around the front of the stage area. Patricia aired, repaired and hung the costumes and everyone helped arrange the bales of hay into seating.

That night under the light of the moon, the company performed their most controversial play *The Kerry Informer; the Story of a Most Infamous Man*. Two months later when the company performed the same play in Kerry it was billed as *The Cork Informer; the Story of a Most Infamous Man*.

On the road, the actors stayed in digs. Whether the accommodation was in a town or on a farm it was always basic. In towns it was usually a room or part of a room with a bed, a wash basin and jug of water. Houses were dark and dull and usually lit by candles or oil lamps, so digs always smelt of candle wax or paraffin oil. Clean sheets were a rarity. Breakfast was usually black pudding, stale bread and water. When the bread was very stale, milk was poured over it to moisten it.

If the digs were on a farm there might be buttermilk to drink and a little butter to spread on the bread. Farm houses were usually one room dwellings so the room had to serve as kitchen, living room and bedroom. There was never running water in the houses and all food was cooked on an open fire in the house. Evening meals consisted of a plate of potatoes and turnips and every so often a thin slice of ham or cured bacon might appear on the plate. If the family had children they were sent to a neighbour's house for the night or shared their parent's bed. Jim slept many nights in a make-shift flea-infested bed beneath a picture of the Sacred Heart with a family of six sleeping soundly not three feet from him.

Often when Jim saw the food he had to eat or the bed he was to sleep in, he longed to be back home to eat Mrs O'Neill's gorgeous food and to sleep in his own clean comfortable bed. Every night before he went to sleep he would open his battered suitcase and look at the small silver framed photograph of his mother and Líla.

As the months passed, and Jim grew more confident on stage, he introduced new and bigger tricks into his magic act and he learned new songs for his singing brother's act. In return Miss Sorcha graduated him from playing walk-on parts to minor roles.

To Jim, Shamus McGovern was the very embodiment of what an actor should be. On stage there was something magnificent about Shamus; his presence conveyed virility, confidence and glamour, his stance and frame communicated strength, his intense blue eyes conveyed intelligence and his roguish smile beamed mischief. There was also something dangerous about him that gave his performances an edge; Shamus on stage was a magnificent mystery.

Off stage, he was as colourful a character as any he portrayed on stage. In the evenings after the show he always wore a natty blue sports coat with grey pinstriped trousers, highly polished shoes and a fedora at a slight angle on his head. His sartorial elegance, carefree grin and confident manner won many a girl, and not so young girl's heart. Women were attracted to Shamus and the dark-haired charismatic actor couldn't keep his hands off them. He loved the pursuit of women and devoted much of his time to it. Like a hunter who had scented his prey, he would identify a possible conquest and pursue her until successful. If there was a girl in the audience that he was interested in, he would fix his intense

THE ACTOR

blue eyes on her and smile as if she was the most beautiful girl in the world. By the end of the play, she would be under his spell – but once the conquest was complete, Shamus had no further interest in his prey. On the odd occasion when a girl he had targeted resisted his charm, Shamus would sit backstage in the theatre or in a sheebeen, rest his right ankle on his left knee and with a Woodbine dangling from his lips would say 'I didn't really like her, she had upside down legs.'

Most of the time Shamus was a charming, gregarious person but occasionally he would fall quiet and go into a dark place. At these times, he would become quarrelsome, intolerant and petulant.

One day, while setting up a small hall for the evening show, Jim asked Shamus how he went about building a character.

'First, I read the play and I think about the character. I find the man's body, how he carries himself and how he walks.'

'Why is that important?' Jim asked, leaning against a wall.

'When you find a man's walk, you know what the character thinks of himself.'

As Jim and Shamus were talking, Bartholomew Bradley came into the hall.

'What are you two intellectuals discussing today?' asked Bartholomew in his imperial sarcastic way.

'Acting,' replied Jim brightly

'Really, you know a lot about acting? Do you?'

'I know a little,' Jim replied. 'Well, what do you think of my acting?'

'Are you sure you want me to answer that question?' Bartholomew replied, removing the cigarette from his lips and running his free hand over his bald scalp.

Shamus shook his head at Jim but Jim took no notice and with all the innocence of a child replied 'Yes, I do.'

The actor paused and as if conjuring up all his great wisdom of theatre replied 'Your acting is tedious and terribly affected. In short you're a dreadful actor.'

Jim crumbled visibly at the older actor's words.

'You're an awful shite,' Shamus barked. 'Don't mind him Jim. He's only happy when he's being a pig.'

Bartholomew stiffened and pulled himself to his full height.

'How dare you use such vulgarities in my presence? The boy asked for my opinion. I gave it, no point in lying.'

'He was looking for some pointers about his acting, not some mean-spirited self-serving sarcastic remark, you stupid shite.'

'Language, language please, if 'tis advice he wants, I'll say this. To be a successful actor in this company all you have to do is to keep the audience from coughing and spitting.'

Then Bartholomew guffawed loudly and swaggered off stage. Shamus sat beside Jim but no matter what he said he could not console him.

In the afternoon, still smarting from Bartholomew's remarks, Jim sat in front of the dressing room mirror and half-heartily practiced his facial expressions. He looked around when he saw the reflection of the broad shouldered Sebastian B Morrow III standing behind him.

Sebastian was a huge, thick-necked man whose face oozed compassion. He loved his tiny wife, the theatre and life. He sometimes gave the impression that he was a stern man, particularly when he looked at people over the top of his wire-rimmed glasses but to the people who knew him and particularly his daughter, he was a gentle, intelligent giant who loved nothing better than to sit, talk and tell stories from his inexhaustible repertoire of theatrical tales.

In his soft voice he said 'I heard what Bartholomew said to you. I don't agree with him, you're a good actor, an inexperienced actor true, but then we were all inexperienced at one time or another.'

'Then why did he say what he said?'

'Who knows? Jealousy, envy, mean-spiritedness. Bartholomew is a very disappointed man and actor. That's why he plays villains so well – he is one.' Sebastian chuckled to himself. 'Tell me what are you doing here all on your own?'

'I'm teaching myself about acting, I'm experimenting with expressions,' Jim replied, a little embarrassed about being caught peering at himself in the mirror.

'You mean you're making faces at yourself. That's not the way to learn to act. Acting is about finding the truth of the character within yourself.'

'The truth of a character,' Jim asked in genuine wonder. 'How would I go about finding that out?'

'Well, you won't do it by making faces at yourself. Read the play.

THE ACTOR

Learn about the character from the script.'

'Why don't women find me attractive?' Jim asked Shamus one night while having an after-show drink.

'Lots of reasons,' Shamus replied. 'Look at your clothes, you dress like a farmer. Women want glamour in their life.'

'I dress well! This is a new cap.'

'I'm talking about style – you're talking about a farmer's cap. When we get to Bantry I'll take you to meet my friend the outfitter Bart Gavin, he'll set you right.'

Three weeks later the sun was high in the sky when the company arrived in Bantry for a three-day residency. As the company cart pulled up to the back of the town hall, Jim watched men in heather-green uniforms marching and carrying out military training exercises in the field behind the hall.

'Who are they?' he asked Bartholomew as they opened the back of the cart.

'Óglaigh na hÉireann, Irish Volunteers,' Bartholomew said a little too loudly. 'Some say, they're a front for the IRB.'

Jim looked quizzically at Bartholomew.

'Don't you know anything? The Irish Republican Brotherhood, they want to fight for Ireland's freedom. They're rebels.'

'They're going to fight the British?' Jim asked in an excited whisper.

'No, they're going to fight the fairies,' grunted the bald actor. 'They're dreamers and fools.'

'You mean like us?'

'What are you talking about?'

'That's what some people call actors – dreamers and fools,' Jim replied with a smirk.

'Just unload the wretched cart,' growled the older actor.

When the preparations for the night's show were complete, Shamus handed Jim his cap and said 'I'm taking you to the outfitters.'

Thirty minutes later Jim and Shamus were standing in Gavin's Men's Outfitter in Bantry's town centre and the overly fussy shop owner Bart Gavin, a tall well-groomed man with a bad back and poor eyesight, was tending to Jim's sartorial needs.

THE ACTOR

After trying on almost every bit of merchandise in the shop, Shamus and Bart decided that Jim looked best in a pin-striped, three-piece charcoal grey suit. To finish the ensemble the outfitter suggested a black, fly-fronted overcoat with long silk-faced lapels. Shamus looked at Jim, rubbed his chin and said 'something is missing'. Then he draped a white scarf around Jim's neck and placed a wide brimmed hat on his head. 'Perfect, now you look like a proper actor.'

Jim stood in front of the store's long mirror and admired himself.

'How much would all this cost?' He held his breath.

'The ensemble will cost you five pounds and five shillings,' the outfitter replied nonchalantly while brushing some invisible dust off Jim's shoulder.

'That's nearly five month's pay,' he whispered to Shamus.

'Can you do a bit better than that?' Shamus asked the outfitter.

'I'll drop the five shillings,' the outfitter said, with a nod of his head.

Jim looked to his mentor and said weakly 'I'll take it.'

'Good decision,' Shamus declared. 'Now Bart, I'd like to look at your silk ties.'

While Shamus looked at the ties, Jim continued to admire himself in the shop's full-length mirror.

Wearing his new clothes, Jim and Shamus strutted down the town and up over the hills above Bantry Bay. There they watched British steam-powered warships dock and refuel. Every time a lady or gentleman passed, Jim lifted his hat and smiled.

The following afternoon a uniformed telegram boy hurriedly dismounted his bicycle and rushed into the town hall.

'Are you Shamus McGovern?' the out-of-breath boy gasped as he pulled a telegram from the small leather pouch that hung from the thick belt on his waist.

'No, Mr McGovern is feeding the horse out back,' Jim replied, indicating the open door.

Shamus signed the telegram boy's record book, took the small brown telegram and tore it open. A scowl darkened the actor's face, he stamped his foot and, rubbing his forehead, paced the yard. Then he barged back into the hall, knocked on the ticket office door and without waiting on a reply, entered the office. A few minutes later, a troubled-looking

Shamus hurried out of the office and departed the building.

Miss Sorcha stepped out of the ticket office and beckoned to Jim.

'Mr McGovern had received tragic news,' she said, solemn-faced, when he entered the room. 'His father had suddenly passed away and he has left to be with his bereaved mother and sister.'

'That's terrible!' It was only then that Jim realised how little he knew about his friend.

'How do you feel about taking over Shamus's role tonight?' Miss Sorcha asked as matter-of-factly as if she was asking him to have a cup of tea.

Stunned, Jim stared into Miss Sorcha's small round face.

'Mr Brevin? I have asked you a question.'

'You want me to take over Shamus' part, tonight?'

'You're always asking me for bigger parts. Now I'm offering you one. What do you say?'

'I don't know the role.'

'Of course you do. You've seen it often enough. I've heard you rehearsing Shamus' lines when you thought you were alone.'

'I was only reading the part out loud ... I never thought ...'

'Sometimes the unthinkable happens. Look on it as an opportunity. What do you say?'

'Well if you think I'm ready ... I'll give it a try,' he replied with great uncertainty.

'That's the spirit,' she exclaimed in a crisp, decisive voice. 'Wonderful.'

Jim's next few hours were frantic. He had to learn his new lines, familiarise himself with the props and costumes. Sebastian volunteered to stay in the wings and give Jim a prompt when necessary. He also placed scripts on either side of the stage so Jim could refer to them whenever he came off stage.

'Do you think I can do it?' Jim asked Sebastian after they had ran lines together.

'If you decide you can do it,' Sebastian replied, 'you can do it. I know you can do it, but it's what you think that matters.'

While Bartholomew sang his operatic aria, Jim gnawed his lips; while Patricia danced her jigs and reels, fears and insecurities bombarded his mind and all during the interval he sat and fretted. When he was at his most intense, Sebastian sat beside him and said 'If you need to, you could go on stage with the script in your hand. It's perfectly acceptable to do that; it's done in all the best theatres.'

'No, let me try it without the script.'

'Good for you. You can do it.'

The play commenced, Jim heard his cue, his muscles tensed but as he walked on stage his mind cleared and calmness descended on him.

He played the part as if he had played it a hundred times. The audience loved him, they listened carefully to his every word, smiled with him, cheered him on and then applauded loudly when he caught the villain. Every second Jim was on stage Sebastian stood in the wings, book in hand ready to give a prompt – but Jim only needed him twice.

At the end of the play, Jim stood in front of the applauding, cheering audience and beamed with pride. The curtain closed and Miss Sorcha grabbed him, hugged him and kissed him on the cheek. Then she told him he would continue in the role until Shamus returned. Jim walked over to Sebastian, held out his hand and said 'Thank you sir, for all your help. You are a gentleman. I could not have done it without you.'

'Yes you could. You are a very good and a very brave actor,' Sebastian replied, took Jim's hand and shook it heartily. Then Patricia hugged him and said with great admiration in her voice 'You were wonderful, you're going to be a great actor.'

Even Bartholomew begrudgingly grunted a word of congratulations.

That night as Jim lay in bed he wished his father and Líla and Michael had been at the show. He was still thinking about his father and his family when his eyelids closed and he drifted into sleep.

The following morning when Jim walked into the company's weekly meeting Bartholomew glared at Jim with a look that would freeze water.

'Mr Brevin, this meeting is for actors only,' Bartholomew said. 'You are still an apprentice.'

Jim looked around the hushed group. Miss Sorcha's chair shuddered backwards. The lady rose and looking Bartholomew in the face said loudly and clearly, 'You are incorrect, Mr Bradley. I asked Mr Brevin to join us. He is now an actor.'

12

Five towns and five days after Shamus left Bantry he re-joined the company in Farranfore and on his first night back he and Jim went to a sheebeen. Jim expected Shamus to talk about his father and how the family were dealing with their recent bereavement but to Jim's surprise the only thing Shamus wanted to talk about was the good-looking girl sitting in the corner behind them.

'How are your mother and your sister?' Jim asked, interrupting Shamus's wishful monologue.

'What about them?'

Jim blinked.

'I don't mean to intrude but I just wanted to know how your family has coped with your father's death.'

'My father isn't dead. I needed time off to go to an audition in Dublin.'

Jim was awe-struck and horrified. 'You lied about your father's dying just to go to an audition? How could you do that?'

Shamus' heavy-lidded eyes darkened and he descended into a brooding silence.

'I didn't mean to upset you,' Jim whispered, after a moment.

The actor glared at Jim and from the well of his deepest feeling said with suppressed rage 'You think all fathers are like your father. Well they're not. Your father never hit you in the face with his clenched fist, or pissed on you or left you in a coal house all night. My father is a bastard.' Then he bowed his head and stared intently at an ale stain on the shebeen's wooden table.

Jim sat uncomfortable in the silence. Slowly Shamus' silent rage abated and he transformed back into his old charismatic self.

'I hear you got to play one of my parts?' he asked, as if nothing had just happened.

'Yes,' Jim replied, not quite understanding what he had just experienced. He asked tentatively 'Did you get the part in Dublin?'

'No. It was a long shot.' Then lowering his voice, Shamus asked 'Did you hear about the company's money problems?'

'I didn't hear anything about that. What did you hear?'

'Just a rumour. Probably nothing to it.'

Two days later Jim was backstage preparing his magic tricks for the evening performance when he heard Bartholomew Bradley call out 'I'd like a word, Miss Sorcha.'

'About what, Mr Bradley?'

'It's a private matter.'

'Mr Bradley, we're alone,' Miss Sorcha said tersely. 'What do want to say to me?'

Bartholomew dropped his voice a little. 'Very well. I have run into some financial difficulties and I must respectfully request a pay increase.'

'A pay increase, Mr Bradley?' Miss Sorcha replied at full volume. 'You are aware we have not increased our admission charges for four years, yet, venue charges, cost of sets and costumes and not to mention lodgings for the company, all have increased?'

'My costs too have increased,' interjected Bartholomew.

'Mr Bradley, the financial circumstance the company finds itself in is very precarious. It was my intention at the next company meeting to explain this and to request that everyone take a voluntary cut in pay of ten per cent.'

'That's out of the question!' replied a shocked Bartholomew.

'If that is so, then I'll have to let Mr Brevin go and as a consequence you and Shamus will be obliged to take over his work.'

'Miss Sorcha, I am an experienced professional actor, it is an insult to even propose that I do the work of an apprentice.'

'Mr Bradley if you do not agree to a reduction in salary or to take over some new company responsibilities I'll have to ask you consider your position. Think about your answer, we'll talk again later.'

Jim flopped onto a prop chair and dread rippled through his body. His dream could end any moment. His fate was in the hands of the least sympathetic person in the company.

That night after the show as the hall emptied, a dejected Jim watched a young woman flirt with Shamus and a smiling Patricia explain to a little girl that she was not really going to marry Jim. As he exited the hall he saw an older man that somewhat resembled his father walk into the ticket office. Before he went asleep that night he looked at the photograph of his mother and thought long about his father Theo, his brother Michael and his sister Líla.

The following morning a clearly uncomfortable Miss Sorcha asked Jim if she could have a word with him in the ticket office. Crestfallen, the young actor entered the tiny office and closed the door.

'Mr Brevin, I have some bad news for you,' Miss Sorcha said without preamble. 'I'm sure you've heard the whisperings about the company's financial situation.' Her stubby fingers danced nervously on the counter top and Jim braced himself for the bad news. 'In order to keep the company on the road I'm afraid I'm going to have to ask you to take a ten per cent reduction in pay.'

For a moment Jim was unable to absorb Miss Sorcha's words. Then the consequences of what Miss Sorcha had said exploded in his mind – his dream was going to continue. Bartholomew had agreed to a cut in pay.

'I know this is unwelcome news, particularly in light of all you've done for the company. But I assure you it's only for a short time.' Miss Sorcha placed a hand on Jim's arm. 'I'll try and slip you a few extra shillings whenever I can.'

An hour later when Bartholomew returned from drumming up an audience for the night's show, Jim grabbed his hand, shook it and thanked him profusely. Bartholomew glared at him as if he had lost his mind.

'I know what you did. You're not the man you pretend to be,' Jim said excitedly. 'Behind that mask of sarcasm and grumpiness is a decent human being.'

'I can assure you, Mr Brevin, I am the man I always was.'

Jim reappraised how he felt about Bartholomew and although the man became more and more sarcastic with him, he knew it was Bartholomew's way of coping with his world.

In mid-July as the company cart wobbled along the Atlantic Ocean Road on the Dingle Peninsula, Jim watched local women gather seaweed from the rocks and place it in large baskets that were strapped to their backs.

'What do they do with the seaweed?' Jim asked Sebastian as a woman with a basket passed the cart.

'They use it to fertilise the land and feed their animals. Sometimes it's all the people have to feed the animals. Inside those snug, cosy-looking cottages up there on the mountains is very real poverty.'

A week later the cart rolled into the medieval town of Tralee and after Jim and Shamus had kitted out the venue and finished their preparations for the night's show, Shamus clapped Jim on the back and said with great joy in his voice 'Tonight we stay in the best theatrical digs in Ireland.'

Thirty minutes later Shamus knocked on the door of the Elsinore Guest House on the Moyderwell Road. Mrs Lynch, a well-endowed auburn-haired widow with long wispy hair and an infectious smile, answered the door.

'Shamus, how are you?' Mrs Lynch cried out and gave him a bear hug. 'Introduce me to your friend,' the buxom landlady said when she finally released Shamus from her grip.

'Mrs Lynch, I'd like you to meet Mr Jim Brevin.'

'James, you have a wonderful name, a royal name – the name of a true gentleman and you look every bit a gentleman with your fine suit and hat. You are a true theatrical personage and I love the company of such people.' Mrs Lynch then shook Jim's hand as if she was trying to

THE ACTOR

shake the life out of him. 'Come in, come in,' she said.

The hallway was clean and bright and well-maintained. The wooden floor was polished and featured an antique rug, a mahogany chair, a small cherry wood hall table and a vase of freshly-cut flowers. An oil painting of the great actor Edmund Keane hung on the stair landing and the house smelt of polish and cut flowers.

'And what do you do in the theatre?' Mrs Lynch asked without taking her eyes off Jim. 'Don't tell me, let me guess. You're an actor and a very good actor too, I suspect.'

'Yes, I'm an actor,' Jim replied and looked warily at Shamus.

'I think I should give this young actor the special room. What do you think Shamus? Everyone should experience true luxury while in the pursuit of their art.'

'You're right, Mrs Lynch,' Shamus replied and winked at Jim.

'I have a very lovely room for you too, Shamus, mustn't forget my old friends.'

'You always look after me beautifully Mrs Lynch,' Shamus replied with mock theatricality.

Mrs Lynch giggled like a schoolgirl, rummaged in the drawer in the hall table and handed a key to Shamus and a key to Jim.

'Mr Brevin, I'm putting you in the Henry Irving room and Shamus you'll be in the Richard Burbage room. Both rooms are on the first floor. In one hour come to the parlour and we'll have afternoon tea.'

Jim pushed open the door to the Henry Irving room. In the centre of the parquet floored room was a large four-poster bed. Beside the bed was a marble-topped wash-stand with running water. The wallpaper was fresh, clean and cheerful and above a small Victorian fireplace was a framed picture of Henry Irving. Jim placed his small battered suitcase beside the bed and looked around the most beautiful room he had been in since he left home. He sat on the bed, kicked off his shoes, slid between the clean sheets and dozed off.

He awoke an hour later to a muffled pounding on the wall. He sat up and all went quiet. A few minutes later there was a knock on the door.

'Are you ready to eat?' Shamus asked when Jim opened the door.

'Yes,' Jim replied, stepping into his shoes. 'Did you pound on the wall a few minutes ago?'

'Oh yes I did. I hope it didn't disturb?'

'I don't like the way Mrs Lynch looked at me,' Jim whispered to Shamus as they walked down the stairs to the parlour. 'I think she's up to something.'

'Mrs Lynch runs a clean house and serves the best food in Ireland – what more could you ask? Besides she's a good-looking woman.'

'She maybe good-looking but she's old.'

'Not that old,' Shamus replied. 'Come on, I'm hungry.'

On the parlour table sat a feast. A large plate of triangular, crustless ham and cheese sandwiches, a plate of hot buttered scones and a three-tiered cake stand filled with dainty cream cakes sat on the table before them.

'I never let myself go,' Mrs Lynch said as she poured Jim a cup of tea. 'I'm as fit as a fiddle and as agile as I was when I was a girl of eighteen.'

'Indeed you are Mrs Lynch,' Shamus said as he helped himself to another sandwich.

'Mr McGovern, you say the nicest things,' Mrs Lynch replied and giggled again.

The flirtatious landlady was one of the first people to arrive at St Mary's Hall for the show that evening. When Jim showed her to her seat in the front row she beamed at him. When Jim and Shamus sang their rebel songs, Mrs Lynch joined in the choruses and when Jim performed his magic tricks she kept saying very loudly 'Impossible!' and 'Marvellous!' Every time either of them entered or exited the stage, she applauded loudly and when the play was over she jumped to her feet and cheered wildly.

After the show, Jim and Shamus went for a drink and then back to Mrs Lynch's fine guest house. Jim slipped between the beautiful clean sheets of the bed and within minutes he was asleep. He awoke with a start; someone was in the room. Holding his breath he waited; then he saw a naked Mrs Lynch slide into the bed beside him. He bolted upright.

'What do you think you're doing?' Jim asked holding a sheet against his body.

'Oh, do you wish me to leave?'

Seconds passed and when Jim did not reply, Mrs Lynch began to slide out of the bed.

THE ACTOR

'Wait,' Jim stammered, staring at Mrs. Lynch's ample naked bosom. 'You are a good-looking woman.' He tried to sound like Shamus.

'Oh, you're the second person that said that to me today.' Mrs Lynch giggled in her schoolgirl fashion.

Lowering his voice, Jim whispered 'We have to be quiet. Shamus is in the next room.'

'Don't worry about Mr McGovern,' Mrs Lynch whispered back. 'I took care of him this afternoon.'

'Oh,' Jim replied still clutching the sheet close to his body.

'Might I ask Mr Brevin, is this your first time?' Mrs Lynch asked as she took the sheet from Jim's grip.

Jim nodded.

'Well then we'd better make it special,' Mrs Lynch said and vanished under the covers.

'Oh,' Jim groaned and his head fell back onto the pillow.

The next morning Shamus sat at the breakfast table opposite an unusually quiet but smirking Jim. The kitchen door crashed open and a humming Mrs Lynch entered.

'For my two big fine actor men,' she said as she placed the finest cooked breakfast Jim had seen in months in front of two very satisfied actors.

13

In 'The Kerry Informer' Jim played the role of the informer and had to have a stage fight with a character played by Bartholomew Bradley. On the afternoon of 13 August 1914, Bartholomew met an old friend and because the friend was buying the drink Bartholomew imbibed a little too much.

That night during the show Bartholomew's concentration lapsed and he failed to anticipate Jim's stage attack. Jim lunged at Bartholomew, the bald actor lost his balance, his head hit the side of table and flailing wildly he tumbled to the floor.

Jim steadied himself. Bartholomew got on his hands and knees, and started to pat the wooden boards of the stage. Something rolled down to the front of stage; it looked like a misshapen marble. Bartholomew's glass eye had popped out of its socket and was now wobbling down towards a petrified freckled-faced girl sitting in the front row. The eye plopped off the stage and into the girl's lap.

'Mother of God,' she screamed, jumped to her feet and the eye fell to the sawdust-covered floor.

'For God's sake don't move!' Bartholomew bellowed at the girl. 'Please don't step on the eye! It's a very expensive item!'

Traumatised, the girl froze. Bartholomew leaped off the stage, picked up the eye, wiped it on his sleeve and popped it back into its socket.

'Hope it didn't frighten you too much, my dear,' Bartholomew said and patted the still shaking girl on the shoulder. Then he nonchalantly leapt back on stage, repositioned the upturned table and chair, stepped back into character and delivered his line to Jim. But Jim did not step back into character – like the rest of the audience he continued to stare in silent disbelief at Bartholomew.

'My God, Sebastian, do something,' Miss Sorcha pleaded to her husband as they stood in the wings waiting on their cue.

The gentle giant strolled on stage, grasped Bartholomew by the arm, turned the actor up-stage, away from the gaze of the audience and said sternly 'You're drunk and your eye is in backwards!'

'Damn,' Bartholomew exclaimed and quickly reversed his eye. Sebastian exited stage right and Bartholomew with great panache turned to Jim and repeated his line for the second time. Jim stepped back into character and the performance resumed. However the red-headed, freckled-faced girl sitting in the front row continued to groan all through the performance.

'You did that on purpose to me,' an angry Bartholomew bellowed at Jim the moment the final curtain closed.

'I did not,' a surprised Jim, replied sharply. 'You …'

'That's enough,' Miss Sorcha interjected and gestured for Jim to leave. 'Bartholomew, you're drinking again. You were once a great actor but drink was your ruination. If you continue like this you'll destroy what little remains of your career.'

'Thank you for your words of wisdom, but I merely tripped,' Bartholomew snapped and brushed briskly past Miss Sorcha.

As he did so, her eyes filled with tears.

Later that night, dressed in their best, Jim and Shamus sat in a smoke-filled, yellow-walled sheebeen and laughed about Bartholomew's roaming eye. But Shamus's laughter was forced and hollow; for the past hour he had been residing in his dark place.

'I better get us a round,' Shamus said and snatched the two empty glasses off the table. Russell's sheebeen was almost full; two toothless old men wearing well-worn clothes and smoking identical yellowed clay pipes sat chatting by the turf fire and three dirty-faced farmhands were arguing good naturedly in a corner. On the other side of the sheebeen some boisterous townsmen were complaining loudly about farmers and a pair of wild-looking inebriated younger men were sitting at the bar. Shamus placed the empty glasses on the counter and ordered two drinks.

'Are you going to buy Ciaran Og and meself a drink?' inquired one of the younger men at the bar. His voice was hostile.

'Good on you, Taghg,' sniggered his thick-necked, pale-faced companion.

'And why would I buy you and your friend a drink?' Shamus asked.

'Because you and your stupid play bored the arse off us,' replied Taghg.

Ciaran Og guffawed again.

'Sorry you didn't like the play.'

'And is your little nancy boyfriend over there, is he sorry too?'

Shamus' body grew tense and Ciaran Og nearly choked with laughter at his friend's wit and insight.

'I came here for a quiet drink, why don't you just leave me alone?' said Shamus very softly, trying to contain his anger.

Taghg rose from his barstool, placed his hand on Shamus' shoulder and barked into Shamus' face 'Tough man, are you? What are you going to do if I don't keep quiet? Hit me with your handkerchief, nancy boy?'

Shamus turned to the man, leaned backwards and with incredible speed jerked his head forward and slammed his forehead into the man's nose. The crack of shattering bone silenced the sheebeen. Taghg grabbed his blood-spurting nose and staggered backwards. Then Shamus kneed him in the groin. The man collapsed to the floor. Then Shamus grabbed an empty glass, smashed it off the counter and lunged at Ciaran Og.

Jim rushed across the room, grabbed his arm mid-air and held it firmly. 'Stop it!' he barked. 'Let's just get out of here.'

'Let me at that bastard, I'll cut his fucking face off.'

'No, we have to leave now!'

Shamus broke free of his grip, placed the broken glass on the bar and stepped over the still groaning Taghg – but as he passed Ciaran Og, he lunged at the terrified man and said 'Tell your friend he's lucky to be alive.'

'What the hell is wrong with you?' Jim said to him outside the shebeen. 'You could have killed that man.'

'Are you going to start on me now?'

'I'm trying to be your friend.'

'I have no friends. I don't want friends,' Shamus said with disgust. 'I look after myself.'

At breakfast the following morning, a bleary eyed Shamus sat across from Jim and mumbled an apology.

'He rubbed me the wrong way,' Shamus said, to justify his brutal outburst.

Jim silently accepted his friend's half apology with a nod.

Later that morning Shamus and Jim were repainting flats. Jim lifted one of them off the floor and splinters of wood gouged into the soft flesh of his hand.

'I hate these old things,' he exclaimed, dropping the flat and sucked the tiny bubbles of blood that oozed from his wounds. 'Why do they have to use such cheap wood?'

'Because they're cheap,' Shamus replied. 'I'll get a tweezers to remove the splinters.'

Jim sat on the lip of the stage and pulled out the larger splinter with his finger nails. Lost in his pain, he jumped when a strange voice spoke to him.

'You better put a dab of iodine on that wound or it might get infected.'

Jim looked up; the local uniformed policeman was standing in front of him.

'I'm Sgt O'Sullivan. Could you tell me where I could find Shamus McGovern?'

Sgt O'Sullivan was a six-foot-three, rough-looking man who expected people to give one word answers to his questions. If someone had the impertinence to give a longer answer he would stare vacantly at them until they stopped talking, then he would ask his question again.

'Well sergeant, Shamus went to his digs to get something. He'll be back in an hour,' Jim replied.

'Why are you speaking so loudly? You wouldn't be trying to warn someone, would you?' the policeman asked with suspicion.

'No – I'm an actor – when I'm on stage I project my voice …'

'Is Mr McGovern staying with Mrs Crowley?' the sergeant interrupted him.

'Yes he is.'

'Mind if I look around back there?' The sergeant nodded towards the wings and without waiting for permission climbed up on the stage and walked backstage. 'Is Miss Sorcha O'Donovan about?' he asked when he returned from his inspection.

'She's in the office in the front of the hall.'

'She wasn't there when I came in?'

'If she's not there I have no idea where she might be.'

Before Jim had finished speaking the sergeant had walked down the hall and opened the tiny office door.

A startled Miss Sorcha looked up.

'What can I do for you, Sergeant?' she asked, all of a flutter.

'I'm looking for Shamus McGovern.' The sergeant pulled himself up to his intimidating height. 'There was a fight in the sheebeen last night and Shamus McGovern assaulted my sister's boys. It was a serious assault. He broke one boy's nose.'

'Sergeant there's some mistake. Mr McGovern is not that kind of person. He's an actor,' replied a shaken Miss Sorcha.

'There is no mistake.'

'I am very sorry for your nephew's injuries,' Miss Sorcha said with genuine concern. 'I'll speak to Mr McGovern.'

'You can do as you please but I intend to arrest that blackguard and put him in prison. What's more, Miss Sorcha, I want you and your troop out of here. Pack your bags. There will be no performance tonight.'

'You can't stop us performing. You have no right, to do that.'

'I can and I have. It's a matter of public safety. People are very angry about what happened. I couldn't be responsible for your safety or the safety of your troop if you stayed here. Pack up and move on and I don't mean to the next village – I mean get out of the county. Go back to Cork where you belong.'

'Sergeant we have bookings all over Kerry – people are expecting us.'

THE ACTOR

'Yes they may be, but my nephew is in hospital. You brought that McGovern man into my county and into my town; well now I'm telling you to leave. I have a warrant for Shamus McGovern's arrest and I intend to serve it to him.'

In mock politeness, Sergeant O'Sullivan touched his fingers to the brim of his helmet and left a dismayed Miss Sorcha standing alone in the tiny office.

Shamus peered out of the wings.

'Thanks Jim,' he whispered with a wink.

'How come the copper didn't see you?'

'I hid in the prop trunk; thank God he didn't look in it.'

'Shamus McGovern I have never been so humiliated in all my life,' boomed a furious Miss Sorcha. 'You have brought shame on the company and the theatre.'

'If this is about last night I can explain?'

'It is about last night and I don't want your explanation. Because of your actions, the Sorcha O'Donovan's Touring Company of Irish Players is no longer welcome in this county. A county we have been performing in for the last twenty five years.'

Miss Sorcha took a handkerchief from her pocket and wiped her eyes.

'I know I let the company down, let me talk to the policeman, I'm sure if I apologise ...'

'Mr McGovern, there is warrant out for your arrest.'

Shamus froze and the look of a terrified child danced in his eyes.

'Miss Sorcha I'm so very sorry.'

'Empty words, Mr McGovern. You are a disgrace to yourself and the acting profession.'

The frightened look on Shamus' face quickly disappeared, his eyes turned dark and he said coldly 'Give me my wages and I'll be off.'

'Wages, there are no wages for you sir, the company has no money and now because of your actions we have no way of earning it. I have a good mind to hand you over to the police.'

Shamus took a step backwards.

'Then I better go. I'm well out of here,' he said and rushed out of the hall.

'Don't go back to your digs,' Jim said when he caught up with Shamus on the street. 'Sgt O'Sullivan is waiting there for you.'

'Damn, my bag and clothes are there. I have no money.'

Jim saw the terror in his friend's eyes.

'I have money,' Jim tore open the sewn-up pocket in his jacket and pulled out his rainy-day five pound note. 'Here take this and don't tell me where you're going; then I won't have to lie when the Sergeant asks me where you went.'

'Why are you doing this?' Shamus asked suspiciously.

'Because I'm your friend.'

'And I told you I don't have friends.'

'Then you're lucky I do.'

Shamus took the money and the two shook hands.

'Thanks, I'll get this money back to you.'

Then Shamus walked up the street and was gone.

An hour later, Miss Sorcha called the company together, explained the situation and announced that they would return to Mallow for one week where they would rehearse a new play, revise the casting of the two plays in repertory and organise an alternative tour. When the meeting was over Miss Sorcha handed Jim two scripts and asked him if he would to take over Shamus' roles. Jim thanked her, took the manuscripts but didn't know what to feel.

14

'Why resurrect such an old war horse?' an exasperated Bartholomew exclaimed when Miss Sorcha announced that *East Lynne* was to be added to the company's repertoire of plays.

'*East Lynne* will fill houses every night and we dearly need the guaranteed revenue it will generate,' snapped a curt Miss Sorcha to the petulant Bartholomew.

'What is the play *East Lynne* about?' Jim asked Sebastian when he opened the cart at the mill and loaded the wood they had purchased.

Sebastian leaned against the cart and said '*East Lynne* is an implausible story that revolves around an infidelity and a double identity. It tells the story of the beautiful and refined young Lady Isabel Carlyle, who deserts her hard-working but cold-hearted husband and their infant children to elope with an unprincipled spendthrift Captain Francis Levison. When the Captain deserts her, a repentant Lady Isabel in disguise takes the position of governess to her own children in the household of her former husband and his new wife.'

Ten days were allocated to rehearse *East Lynne* and to re-rehearse the re-cast *The Kerry Informer* and *The Bishop's Dilemma*. Also in those precious ten days, new flats had to be built and painted, costumes and props had to be sourced and a revised tour organised.

Patricia, Miss Sorcha's daughter was cast in the demanding role of Lady Carlyle. The complex adult role placed great demands on the young actress and she was nervous and fearful of the challenge. Jim too was concerned about playing a neglectful, somewhat cruel, high-minded husband. On the morning of the first rehearsal Patricia and Jim were awkward with each other. After the first reading Miss Sorcha halted the rehearsals and decided to work privately with Patricia.

Alone in the rehearsal room Jim wondered if he could play the role. He paced back and forth and when no answer revealed itself to him he threw the script on the floor.

'That won't solve anything,' Sebastian said as he sat on one of the rehearsal chairs. 'What's wrong?'

Jim didn't respond.

'If you're not going to talk to me I might as well get on with my own work.'

'I don't know if I can play the part,' Jim blurted out. 'I don't like the man.'

Sebastian took a moment and when he spoke, he spoke with the calm deliberation of a man who fervently believed in what he was saying.

'Jim, you are an actor playing a part, it is of no consequence whether you approve or disapprove of your character's behaviour; that is not your concern. It is not your job to judge him, leave that to the audience.' Sebastian picked up Jim's script and handed it to him. 'Why don't you read the text and find out about your character, learn what he values, and then you'll know why he behaves the way he does? After lunch we can talk again.'

Jim spent the next three hours reading the text and when Sebastian returned he told him what he had discovered. Sebastian listened carefully and when Jim finished speaking he said 'Good work – but there is something else bothering you. What is it?'

Jim lowered his head and mumbled 'I think I look too young to play the part.'

'Then we'll have to make you look older,' Sebastian replied and left the hall.

Five minutes later Sebastian returned, placed a well-worn wooden box on a chair, opened it and announced 'The actor's toolbox.'

THE ACTOR

The box was filled with sticks of greasepaint, spirit gum, brushes, eyeliners, mascara, rouge, powder, hair grease, wigs, plaits of hair and things Jim had never seen before.

'The trick is not to overdo it,' Sebastian said, peering closely at Jim's face.

Sebastian's first suggestion was that Jim should change the way he combed his hair. Jim parted his hair in the middle and with the help of some hair grease, combed the sides back. His second suggestion was that he darken around his eyes. 'It will give the effect of the deeper eye sockets that come with age.' Sebastian applied dark greasepaint and Jim approved. Sebastian's final suggestion was that he should wear a moustache; Jim agreed. From the make-up box Sebastian removed a grease-proof sachet filled with moustaches; he picked a narrow, thin one, smeared some spirit gum on it and pressed it on to Jim's face. The young actor looked in the make-up box's mirror; he looked older, he was happier.

Over the next four days Sebastian helped Jim discover more about the character of Sir Robert Carlyle. Whenever Jim would overact or 'ham it up' Sebastian would bellow 'you get ham at the pork butchers not in the theatre.' When Jim adopted a 'bogus mellifluousness' to his voice Sebastian called out 'anchor what you're saying in your soul not your throat.' And whenever Jim mumbled, Sebastian howled, 'diction and articulation are the actor's two best friends, use them.'

Patricia and he became comfortable acting together and as their confidence grew the quality of their performances improved.

'You must have a great love for the theatre,' Jim said to Sebastian one day during a break in rehearsals.

'You might think that. But I often wonder why I go hawking myself around the country like a gypsy, performing in one damp, disagreeable hall after another. The truth is, my wife believes what we are doing is worthwhile.'

'And do you not agree with her?'

'I know an actor on a stage can communicate more wisdom and truth in one hour than a university professor can do in a term.'

'So you think what we're doing is important?'

'Yes, I think it's important. I also think everyone lies to themselves about the importance of what they do and the theatre lie is as good as any other lie.'

'I don't understand, what you mean?'

'Oh I'm rambling,' Sebastian replied with a shrug. 'Let's run some lines.'

The other two roles that were assigned to Jim were parts previously performed by Shamus. Jim had mixed feelings about taking over the roles; he was delighted to play more substantial parts but the circumstances in which he came by them still troubled him. Another change he had to get used to was the change in the singing act; Bartholomew was Shamus' replacement. The actor had a good baritone voice and was a beautiful melodeon player, so some traditional songs were dropped and sea shanties were added. The duo also underwent a name change, they were now called The Singing Sailors.

'Not a dry eye in the house,' was Sebastian's comment when the curtain closed after the opening night's performance of *East Lynne*. Jim was pleased with his own work but he knew the night belonged to Patricia; she was magnificent in her role. The moment she walked on stage she captivated the audience and held them until the final curtain. There was a restrained intensity in her performance that moved audiences and every night during the play's final tragic act people could be heard sobbing. *East Lynne* quickly became the company's most requested and performed play.

On the first day of every month Jim wrote a letter to his sister informing her that he was well and happy. He always posted his letter as the company was leaving a town and never gave a return address. Consequently Líla was unable to tell him that in July, Theo had a massive stroke and that Michael had to take over the running of the family business. She also was unable to tell him that in August while she was tending to her father she had had a fall and had broken her leg in three places.

In early September the company had a four-day residency in Kinsale. The first night's show had been poorly attended, so the following morning Miss Sorcha instructed Jim to go to the market square and let the people of Kinsale know that Sorcha O'Donovan's Touring

THE ACTOR

Company of Irish Players was in town.

Gusts of cold autumn wind tore down the street and whipped around him as he carried a small wooden box and a glass globe to the town's market place. It was fair day and the square was filled with stalls selling new and used clothing, pots and pans, household goods, nails, leather goods and fruit and vegetables. Outside the post office Jim stepped on to his wooden box, raised the glass globe to his lips and bellowed into it 'Hear ye, hear ye, tonight's play is *East Lynne*, the tragic story of a beautiful woman who made a tragic mistake.'

Taking a breath before launching into the details of the play, Jim's eyes fell upon a petite, freckle-faced girl buying vegetables at a nearby stall. The girl had a pixie face with large, dark, doe-like eyes, a snub nose and naturally curly, light brown hair. The girl smiled at Jim and her smile was so intriguing and bright that he was instantly smitten by her. While Jim was returning the girl's smile the tall, thin postmistress, Miss Sheehan, thundered out of the post office.

'The theatre is a place of evil!' the hair-netted woman shrieked as she marched up to Jim. 'It is an occasion of sin!' She turned to the people that had gathered to listen to him, pointed a finger at them and said 'The parish priest will hear if any of you dare attend the theatre tonight.' The post mistress swirled on her heels and faced a surprised Jim. 'Tonight I'm going to my women's sodality meeting and I'll pray to God for your immortal soul. Now be off with you.'

Then Miss Sheehan promptly marched back into her shop and pulled the half-door behind her. The people dispersed and as Jim stepped off his wooden box he collided with the curly-haired girl. The glass globe slid through his fingers and he and the girl watched in horror as it shattered into countless pieces.

'Oh dear, I'm sorry,' cried the girl.

'It's all right.' He couldn't take his eyes off the young girl's face.

'Will you get into much trouble?' she asked, touching his hand.

His face turned crimson and he swallowed hard. 'No, it's a spare globe.' He pushed the broken glass off the footpath with the side of his boot.

Her face broke into an incandescent smile. 'I saw you in the play last night, you were wonderful.'

Jim stopped what he was doing.

'You were at the show?'

'Yes, I thought the play was really good and you were wonderful in it.'

'Thank you.' Again, he flushed bright red.

'I have to go. I only came out to fetch these vegetables. They're waiting in the kitchen for them.'

'What's your name?' he blurted out as the girl turned away from him.

'Sarah. Bye!'

In a daze, Jim watched the girl walk away. Halfway down the street she looked back and waved to him, and then was swallowed by the crowd.

'What are you standing there for like an amadán?' Miss Sheehan screeched, poking her head out over the post office's half-door. 'Go away, boy!'

With his wooden box under his arm, Jim walked back to the town hall and tried to remember every detail of every second he shared with Sarah.

When he told Miss Sorcha about the post-mistress's public admonishment of him and the theatre her reaction was annoyance coupled with righteous indignation. 'Jim, Bartholomew, Sebastian don your ecclesiastical costumes from *The Bishop's Dilemma* and follow me.'

Dressed in fake gold-trimmed archbishop vestments, mitre and crozier, Sebastian strutted behind the tiny Miss Sorcha; Bartholomew in his bishop's costume was next in the procession and Jim, dressed in curate black, completed the pageant. The sight of three men in full religious regalia marching through the streets of Kinsale caused a mild commotion. People stopped their hawking, bartering and trading and stared in disbelief at the spectacle of men in flowing church robes. But when they realised that the procession was not of clerics but of actors they hooted and hollered and cheered them up the street.

The procession stopped in front of the post office. Flanked on his right by Bishop Bartholomew and on his left by Fr Jim, Archbishop Sebastian raised his crozier and knocked on the door of the post office. For a moment nothing happened then a befuddled, disorientated Miss

THE ACTOR

Sheehan sprinted out of her shop and when she saw the three clerics she fell to her knees.

'Welcome your holiness,' she cried out and blessed herself three times.

The crowd giggled and laughed. Miss Sheehan looked up and when she recognised Jim, she jumped to her feet and shouted at all three thespians to go away. Sebastian raised his crozier, the crowd fell silent and in his best Shakespearian voice Archbishop Sebastian excommunicated all who had not attended the theatrical performance the previous night, then with his voice rising to a crescendo the huge man assured the crowd that 'if they attended to-night's show their excommunication would be lifted.'

That night the hall was filled to capacity.

15

In the interval between the variety show and the play, Sarah arrived at the town hall. When she asked the people in the front row to squeeze up and make room, they glanced disdainfully at her and then begrudgingly moved up. The play started, Jim strolled on stage and for the rest of the evening Sarah never took her eyes off him.

Seconds after the final curtain and still in his costume, Jim hurried into the hall, touched the exiting Sarah on the elbow and said tentatively 'Hello.'

She turned to him with a gentle gasp and her eyes shone.

'Hello Jim.'

'How do you know my name?'

'I asked that big actor in the ticket office,' Sarah whispered and flicked her eyes to Sebastian who was wishing the patrons goodnight. 'I really liked the play.'

'I'm glad you did.' He ran a finger nervously inside the collar of his starched shirt, gathered his courage and asked the question he'd wanted to ask from the moment he first saw her. 'Can I ... walk you home?'

'Oh yes, I'd like that,' she replied and flashed her eyes.

Their private moment together was terminated when the curtains parted and Bartholomew thundered on to the stage brandishing the

THE ACTOR

backcloths for the following night's show.

'Jim, you haven't even started your work,' he grumbled as he placed the backcloths on the stage floor. Then he glanced up at Sarah and his disposition changed from mild annoyance to outright hostility.

'Are you from Pike House?' he growled.

'Yes I am,' Sarah replied meekly.

'Who sent you?' Bartholomew demanded. 'What are you doing here?'

'Nobody sent me,' replied a startled Sarah.

'Don't you speak to my friend like that,' Jim said.

Glaring at Sarah, Bartholomew lit a cigarette and as he retreated into the shadows of the wings he barked 'Let me know when you've completed your chores.'

'Sorry, that man can be really rude,' Jim said.

'You don't have to apologise for him.' Sarah rubbed her hands together. 'He's not the only one who resents people from the big house.' Then she asked 'What kind of chores do you have to do?'

'I'll show you. You can help if you like.'

'I'd like that.'

Jim took Sarah backstage and introduced her to Patricia, Sebastian and Miss Sorcha. When he went to get a ladder Sarah wandered across the stage, ran her hand across the dusty curtains and, pretending she was an actress, took a bow to the now empty hall.

'I thought you were wonderful tonight,' she said when Jim leaned a paint-splattered ladder against the back wall of the stage. 'I think you're the best actor I've ever seen.'

'Thank you,' Jim replied and, beaming with pride, climbed the ladder. 'If you stand on the bottom rung it will keep the ladder steady.'

Sarah perched on the bottom rung and with a tug and a jolt Jim freed the backcloth from its mount. As she helped him roll it up, their hands touched and she smiled shyly. They stored the backcloth, collected all the costumes and props and as they were leaving Jim called out to Bartholomew 'Everything is done, I'm off.'

The late autumn air was cool and crisp and the moon was full; silvery light was filtering through the trees as they stepped out of the hall. Sarah shuddered and Jim removed his overcoat and carefully draped

– 115 –

it around the girl's tiny shoulders. He took her hand and together they walked through the narrow, pretty streets of Kinsale. A little way out of the town, Sarah stopped at the gates of a big country house.

'This is where I live,' she said as she leaned against the granite gatepost with the words Pike House carved into it.

'Is this where you work?' Jim asked, peering up the long dark driveway.

Sarah hesitated a moment, before saying 'Yes.'

'Is there something wrong?'

'No, it's as I was saying before, a lot of people don't like people from the big house.'

'I do.'

'Oh do you?' she asked, looking at him from under her eyelashes.

'What kind of work do you do in the house?'

'Whatever needs doing, whatever Major Pike instructs me to do.' A shadow flickered across the young girl's eyes. 'Let's not talk about the Major.' Sarah leaned boldly into Jim, placed her hand on his shoulder and kissed him gently on the lips. 'I'd like to bring you in but they don't let me have visitors this late at night.'

With a twirl Sarah slipped Jim's overcoat from her shoulders, handed it to him, cocked her head playfully to one side, opened the gate and skipped off into the night.

'Come to the show tomorrow night,' Jim called after her. 'I'll leave a ticket for you in the box office.'

'I'll be there,' came a whispered reply from the darkness.

All through the night Jim could not stop thinking of Sarah; she fired his imagination and she filled his dreams. When he awoke, she was the first person he thought about.

The autumn sun shone a cold white light on Jim as he opened the door to the stables at the rear of the town hall. He was filling the horse's nose bag with fresh oats when Bartholomew strolled into the yard.

'That girl, last night, she is from the big house, isn't she?' Bartholomew asked.

'It's none of your business where she works. You were very rude to her.'

Jim tied the bag of oats around the hungry animal's head.

'Never mind my rudeness. Jim, I've never given you advice before but

I have some advice for you now. Major Pike is not a man to be trifled with.'

'You know the Major?'

'Good God, no. We both served in the British Army in India at the same time but I never knew him. Pike was a commissioned officer, I was an enlisted man. I knew his batman, Oscar Brimicombe.' The stout actor removed a cigarette from the breast pocket of his well-worn suit and lit it. 'We were very good friends, Oscar and I; best bloke I ever met.' Jim sat on a tea chest and waited for Bartholomew to continue. 'Oliver Wolseley Pike, the man you call the Major, was very much disliked by his men and his fellow officers. He was in charge of the scouts' troop.'

'Was that an important job?'

Bartholomew snorted.

'Scouts in friendly territories always travel at the rear of marching columns and the swirling dust that the column kicks up makes the rear of it the worst place to be.' Bartholomew exhaled a lungful of smoke. 'Pike was a grossly incompetent officer and was forced to resign his commission.' He paused and then for the first time spoke unguardedly. 'He's quite insane and a nasty piece of work. Stay away from him and all he owns. I didn't and it cost me my eye.'

'What ...?' Jim blurted, nearly falling off the tea chest.

'Enough talk, I have said what I wanted to say.'

Bartholomew threw his unfinished cigarette on the ground, squashed it with his boot and left a perplexed Jim sitting on the tea chest.

That afternoon, Jim walked along the west bank of the Bandon River until he came to the elegant limestone mansion that was Pike House. The river-facing house had a four-column entrance portico, a massive central block and a beautiful walled terraced garden. Peering across the river, he looked for Sarah but the only person he saw was a uniformed chauffeur polishing a blue open-topped Addison automobile.

The rest of his day passed slowly and as the afternoon shadows transformed into evening darkness he went to the box office and arranged a ticket for Sarah. When the variety show started there was no Sarah, when the melodrama started there was no Sarah and when the final curtain closed Sarah's ticket was still uncollected.

In the yard behind the hall, a tired Sebastian and a dejected Jim loaded the sets, costumes and prop baskets into the company cart for their move the following morning. Then a gentle voice spoke from the darkness: 'Hello Jim, I'm sorry I missed the show.' Sarah walked into the light. 'I had to work late. You're not annoyed at me, are you?'

'No I'm not.' He slipped his arms around Sarah's slim waist and held her. 'I'll just finish loading the cart and then I'll walk you home.'

'You'll do no such thing,' Sebastian said, waving hello to Sarah. 'I'll finish the loading, you'll take the girl home.'

Hand in hand, Jim and Sarah again strolled through the streets of Kinsale. They talked about the show, how she had spent her day and anything else that came into their heads. When Jim told Sarah what Bartholomew had said about Major Pike, she let go of his hand and her face lost its constant half smile.

'That's a terrible thing to say, that man doesn't know the Major. He's not like that.'

'Sorry, I didn't mean to upset you.'

'I'm not upset but that man doesn't know what he's talking about.'

'You're right; he doesn't know the Major. Let's not talk about him anymore.' He cupped Sarah's upset face in his hands. 'Let's talk about happy things, it's our last night together.' They walked in contented silence for a while and when they were passing St John the Baptist Church on Friars Street, Jim spoke.

'The company isn't leaving tomorrow till the afternoon. Would you like to go for a walk to the dolmen in the morning?'

Sarah's eyes shone bright.

'Yes that would be lovely. I'll bring a picnic basket.'

When they arrived at the gates of Pike House, he slid his arm around her thin waist, pulled her close and kissed her. She put her arms around his neck, pressed her body firmly against his and kissed him again and again.

Autumn sunlight glinted off the shop windows, brightened the thatched roofs of the houses and warmed the people of Kinsale as Jim, wearing his best clothes, stood outside Pettigrew's Butter and Grain store waiting for Sarah. The street was almost deserted, a few late Mass goers hurried into church, and a soldier and his girl strolled arm in arm past the children playing hop-scotch close to a chestnut tree. At ten past eleven, wearing a demure pretty cotton dress and a white cardigan, Sarah arrived. Jim kissed her on the cheek, took the wicker picnic basket from her and, hand in hand, they walked over the stone bridge and out into the country. Lost in conversation, they didn't notice the lush woodlands, the meandering meadows, the fields of yellow gorse or the golden leaves of the trees twirl and twist in the light breeze that blew gently down the valley. Neither did they notice the blue-grey mist on the mountains or the dark clouds that were gathering. All they saw were each other and that was enough for them.

'What is a dolmen?' Sarah asked as Jim opened the gate to a field of knee-high grass.

'That,' he replied, pointing to four huge stones a hundred metres ahead. Three of the stones were upright and the fourth stone lay horizontally on top of the upright stones.

'Why did the people build them?' she asked as they reached it.

'A dolmen is an ancient religious monument. The three standing stones represent a trio of gods and the stone on top represents a ship that is taking the spirit of the dead to another place.'

'How do you know all that?'

'Sebastian told me.'

Sarah looked at him quizzically.

'The big actor in the box office.'

'Ah, I like him,' Sarah said and ran her finger around a spiralling circle that was carved in one of the upright stones.

'Don't do that,' Jim cried out in a voice filled with urgency. Sarah snatched her hand from the rock. 'Don't you know about the curse of the dolmen?'

'No,' she whispered like a frightened child. 'What is it?'

'If you run your fingers around the spiral circle, terrible things will happen to you.'

'I just did that.' Her hand went to her mouth. 'What should I do?'

A grin sneaked across Jim's face. Sarah eyed him, then lunged at him and in mock annoyance pounded his chest with her fists.

'I believed you. You made that up?'

As the sky darkened, Jim folded his arms around Sarah, held her tight and kissed her.

A blue open-topped automobile screeched to a halt and an angry-looking man wearing a tweed Norfolk jacket, tweed breeches and knee-length stockings jumped out of the automobile and raced angrily towards them through the long grass.

'Do you know that man?' Jim thrust Sarah behind him.

'It's Major Pike!' Her face was taut with fear.

When the galloping Major was a metre from Jim, he swung his silver-topped blackthorn walking stick through the air and struck Jim a terrible blow on the forehead, then, as Jim staggered back clutching his face, brought it down hard across the small of his back. Jim plunged to the ground. The furious Major raised his stick again but Sarah jumped in front of him.

'Stop it! Please! You're hurting him!'

'I intend to!' the Major shouted. 'When I'm finished with him he'll never walk again. Get out of my way, girl!'

Sarah stood her ground.

The Major dropped his stick, grabbed her by her shoulders and shouted into her face. 'You shameless strumpet, he's an actor, a bloody gypsy. You stupid, stupid girl you're just like your mother.'

He shoved her aside, but Sarah cupped her fingers into a claw, lunged at the Major and tore her nails into the soft flesh beneath the man's puffy eyes. Howling and flailing wildly, the Major grabbed his face. Jim stumbled to his feet, picked up the picnic basket, charged at the Major and slammed the basket into the man's chest. The Major fell backwards, struck his head on one of the standing stones and slithered to the ground. Jim threw the basket at the moaning man and limped back to Sarah.

'Come on, let's go.'

Sarah didn't move.

'Come on,' he said frantically.

'I can't,' she replied like a terrified child.

'Don't be silly, Bartholomew was right – the man is mad. Let's go.'

Sarah took a step backwards and tears welled in her eyes.

'I can't go with you,' she whispered. 'He's my father.'

THE ACTOR

'Your father?' repeated a stunned Jim.

Groaning, the Major tried to get to his feet. 'You blackguard, get away from my daughter!'

Sarah glanced fearfully at her father. 'Jim, please go or he'll kill you.'

'I can't leave you here with him.'

'Please go.' Tears rolled down her cheeks. 'I know my father; he won't hurt me.'

Low thunder rumbled, the wind began to howl and rain beat into Jim's face. He wiped away the blood that was trickling into his eyes from the wound on his forehead. 'Sarah, come with me.'

'No, just go,' she begged, her voice trembling with desperation. 'For my sake, go.'

He looked at her pale, rain-soaked face a long moment, then stumbled away from her; she pulled her cardigan around her slim tiny frame, as if doing so would protect her from her father's wrath.

As he lurched through the field, his foot caught in the root of a tree and his aching body crashed onto the ground. He remained lying flat in the long, rain-drenched grass. The Major was on his feet now and stumbling around looking for him. Failing to find Jim, he shouted some obscenities into the wind and returned to his daughter.

Jim heard the crack of a hand smacking against flesh and raised his head to peer through the grass; Sarah was holding her face and sobbing. He longed to run to her and help her, but he didn't; instead he watched the Major drag her across the field and fling her into the back seat of the automobile. The car engine roared and the car sped off. The wind whipped around him as he stood shivering in the rain, shame surged through every part of him. That was the last time he saw Sarah.

That night in Carrigaline, not twelve miles from Kinsale, a very bruised and sore Jim was unable to perform his magic act and because of his injuries the fight sequence in the play *The Kerry Informer* had to be dropped. Every night for a long time, Jim thought about Sarah and tried to imagine what she was enduring. Then he would bow his head in shame and vow that never again would he run and leave someone to suffer the consequences of his actions.

Jim spent his first Christmas away from home with Miss Sorcha,

Sebastian and Patricia in their family home in Mallow Co. Cork. On St Stephen's day he made a telephone call home but when Michael answered the phone, Jim replaced the receiver on its cradle and went for a walk.

One week after Christmas Day, the company resumed touring. In the cold winter of 1914 the O'Donovan Company performed in freezing halls in Mitchelstown, Glamworth, Ballyduff, Fermoy and other towns and villages in north County Cork. Seven weeks before Easter on the last night of the season, Miss Sorcha sat Jim in the ticket office and told him that she would not be inviting him back after Easter.

'Why?' Jim asked, staring disbelievingly into her face.

'Money, we lost a lot of money this year. I have to think of a new way of running the company. I have to shrink it. Jim you're a fine actor but even the best of us have rest periods. I'm sorry but there's nothing I can do. I wish you the best in your career.'

That night the newly unemployed, sixteen-year-old actor flopped heartbroken onto the flea-infested bed in his digs, put his head in his hands and wept. The following morning he said a tearful goodbye to Bartholomew, to his friend Patricia, to the kind and generous gentle giant Sebastian and to his former employer Miss Sorcha O'Donovan.

16

A COLD WIND SWIRLED AROUND Jim as he placed the key in the front door of the Victorian house he called home. This was the moment he dreaded and the reason he had spent last night in a guest house not three short streets away. He had approached the house many times but this was the first time he had got to the front door. He turned the key, pushed open the door and stepped into the hall.

Líla was walking down the stairs. She stared in disbelief, then lunged at him and threw her arms about him.

'Jim, you're home! This is wonderful! How are you? Father and Michael will be so delighted to see you. We were all so worried about you.'

Líla grabbed her brother's hand and pulled him down the hall into the back drawing room.

The wallpaper, the carpet, the curtains, the unsmiling portraits of his grandparents – all was exactly as he remembered. He sat in his favourite wicker chair and breathing in the smells of his childhood he talked to his sister. After a short while Líla's face grew serious and lowering her voice, she said 'A terrible thing happened to father.'

'What happened?' Jim asked. Líla's eyes went to the drawing room door and she placed a finger to her lips. A faint tapping and shuffling sound came from the hall, and a pale, grey-haired figure appeared in the doorway.

'Is that you, Michael?' the figure asked in a frail, slurred voice.

Jim suppressed a gasp. His father's face was lined and haggard, his eyes were dull and he had lost so much weight that his once dapper clothes swung loosely on him.

Jim swallowed and got to his feet. 'No, it's me, father – it's Jim.'

Theo shuffled across the room. His back was bent and he was leaning on a walking stick. When he saw his youngest son's face, thoughts of his late wife flooded into his mind. He wanted to, longed to, embrace his son but he didn't; instead he held out his hand and said 'Welcome home, son.'

'It's good to be home,' Jim replied as he shook his father's trembling hand. 'How are you sir?'

'Not very well. I've been ill. Líla will tell you all about it. It's time for my nap. Perhaps you'll come to my study later and we can talk.'

'Yes sir, I will,' Jim replied softly.

'Let me help you up the stairs, father,' Líla said as she took her father's arm and very slowly led him out of the drawing room.

'What happened to father?' Jim asked the moment Líla returned.

Líla sat in a chair and sighed deeply.

'Last July, father had a massive stroke – he nearly died. He spent a lot of time in hospital.' Líla's voice cracked but she continued talking. 'The doctors told him he had to retire from the company and he did. Michael is now in charge of the business.'

For the next hour Líla talked and Jim listened. She told him how close Theo had come to death, she explained that his recovery was going to be long, that his limp was probably permanent but his slurring of words would ease and become less pronounced with time. She told him that Theo tired easily and that every afternoon and some mornings he had to take a nap. She told him how Michael had dropped out of university and taken over the family business and that he was making a great success of it. She told him how Theo made Michael and herself members of the company board. Líla ended by telling Jim that in August she had broken her leg in three places, that her leg had been in plaster up to her hip and that she had had to use a wheelchair to get around.

Then she went silent and reached out for Jim's hand.

'Líla,' Jim said taking his sister's hand. 'You had to grow up quickly.'

'I did,' she said. 'And now I have a boyfriend,' she added brightly.

'You have a boyfriend? What's his name?'

'Don't sound so surprised and it's none of your business what his name is. Tell me about your adventure with the theatre company.'

'That's all so unimportant now. I'll tell you all about it some other time.'

'No, tell me now Jim. I need some happy news.'

'Very well,' Jim replied and he told her about the plays, the people and the places he visited. Líla laughed when he told her about Bartholomew's eye falling out on the stage, she snorted when he said he had been a magician and almost gagged when he told her he had been one half of a singing brothers' act. He told her about Shamus and what a wonderful actor he was but he didn't tell her how violent Shamus could be or why he left the company and, very deliberately, he did not mention Sarah.

When Theo woke from his nap, Jim joined him in the study. Theo sat on one side of the fire with a blanket over his knees and Jim sat opposite him.

'How are you feeling, father?' Jim spoke more formally than he intended.

'I get a little better every day. The doctors tell me if I take it easy and do as they say I will get back to near my old self, but it will take time.' It was difficult at first for Jim to make out what his father was saying but he listened carefully and by watching Theo's face he found he could understand almost everything.

'Michael is running the company and making a good fist of it too, but he needs help. Now that you're home you will be of great assistance to him.' Theo raised his handkerchief to his mouth and wiped some spittle from his lips. 'I'll make you a board member and Michael will organise a position for you in the company.' There was no anger, no reproach, in Theo's voice, just tiredness. 'I'm so glad you got the theatre out of your system.'

'Father, I'm sorry to hear about your bad health and I'm equally sorry I was not here to help. I'm here now and I intend to stay and do all I can to make things easy for everyone. But I think it best that we are honest with each other. I intend to continue my work in theatre – consequently I will not be taking up your kind offer of becoming part of the company.'

Theo's weak smile faded and the all-too-familiar silence fell between father and son. But then Theo placed his shaking hand on Jim's knee. 'Jim, I have no desire to fight you. I am not your enemy, I am your father. I do not approve of your choice of profession but it is your choice to make and you must live your life as you see fit.'

Jim was so relieved that his father was respecting his decision, he wanted to embrace him. But he couldn't, so he fidgeted in his chair and then turned the conversation to other things.

'I think you're a pillock, feckless and stupid,' Michael said angrily when they met later that day. 'I think your behaviour was abominable. If I had known where you were I would have dragged you back home and made you attend to your responsibilities. Your father was at death's door and your sister needed you and all you could do was gad about the country.'

'If you're trying to make me feel guilty there's no need. You can't make me feel any worse than I do already.'

'Am I supposed to care how you feel?' Michael shot back. 'How do you propose to make amends to father and Líla?'

'I intend to live at home and do all I can to help with father's recovery.'

'Father and Líla want to make you a member of the company board. I don't agree with their decision. I think they are making a mistake.'

'You need not concern yourself about that, if I am offered a seat on the board I intend to refuse it and I have no interest in working for the company.'

'How do you propose to earn a living? You're not going to scrounge off me.'

'I will support myself by my work in the theatre.'

'What?' replied a flabbergasted Michael.

'You heard.'

When Jim left the room, Michael sat back in his chair and realised he had no understanding whatsoever of his younger brother.

THE ACTOR

*

During the next six weeks, Jim contacted every theatre and production company in Dublin. He auditioned for particular roles in particular plays and possible roles in future productions but the result was always the same; lots of promises but no firm offers of work.

One evening as he sat in the back drawing room wondering what to do next, there was a knock on the front door. He answered it, and Ciaran O'Donovan, his old school friend, stood before him.

'Come in Ciaran, it's great to see you! What are you doing with yourself these days? How did you know I was home?'

'I'm studying law at the university, and it's great to see you too – but I'm not here to visit you.'

'Then why …?'

'He came to visit me,' Líla said, coming down the stairs in her walking-out clothes. 'I told you I had a boyfriend.'

'This is your boyfriend?' Jim's face broke out in a smile. 'Ciaran, my sister … how could you?'

'He could because I like him,' Líla said as she stood at Ciaran's side and took his arm.

'Well, little sister, you couldn't have picked a better person.'

'I know. Now if you don't mind, we're going out and you're not invited.'

'Ciaran, we'll get together tomorrow and I'll tell you what my sister is really like,' Jim said jokingly.

'Don't you listen to my brother – he's a dreadful person,' Líla said with mock annoyance as she and Ciaran strolled away.

To support Britain's involvement in the European war, the authorities in Ireland requisitioned all hay crops within a ten-mile radius of Dublin. This act resulted in a major shortage of fodder for the farms around the city. Affected also were the city's five hundred dairies. Most of the poor depended on milk as a cheap source of nourishment for their children but because the dairies could only source inferior fodder the milk quality deteriorated, children became malnourished and the infant mortality rate climbed to the highest in the UK.

The everyday sight of thousands of tons of high quality hay stored openly on the docks for shipment to the continent to feed the British army's horses, while Irish children, families and cattle starved, inflamed public opinion, increased the growing discontent against the military and nurtured the growing resentment of British rule in Ireland.

For three months Jim continued his search for theatre work. When his money ran out, Líla gave him money from her savings and he continued his search. But after another three months of rejections and vague promises of work, he asked Michael if he could work for the company as a paid employee.

When Michael replied his voice was scalding.

'I thought your life was in the theatre?' Michael laid a querulous emphasis on the word "theatre". 'It must be terrible for you being reduced to working for a living. My, my how awful life can be.'

'There's no need for sarcasm,' snapped Jim.

'Is there not?' Michael fixed a stare on him that cut through him like a knife. 'Am I supposed to just roll over and let you make a mockery of me and what I stand for and then give you a job?'

'I never said a derogatory word about you or the company. In fact I admire what you've done and how you've done it.'

'There's no need to plámás me. You know that if I don't give you work, it would break father's heart and I'm not going to do that; one of us doing that is enough.'

'I resent you saying that.'

'I don't give a dam what you resent. I'll give you a job but let there be no misunderstanding, I expect you to work and work hard. If you don't, I'll fire you and I'll do it with pleasure.'

'I don't expect any favours,' Jim muttered.

'Don't worry, you won't get any. I'm putting you in charge of the horses, their feed and all matters to do with transport. You will be the company's transport manager.'

'What? That's not a job! The company never had a transport manager – there's nothing to manage. We have two delivery horses and you know there is a shortage of fodder. What can I do about that?'

'You asked for a job. That's the job, take it or leave it,' Michael replied with a grin.

'I'll take it.'

THE ACTOR

When Michael told his father that Jim was joining the company as a paid employee, Theo was delighted and a little disappointed. He was happy that his two sons were finally working together in the family business but he would have liked Jim to be an equal partner.

To source better quality fodder for the horses, Jim went to the military and business authorities but with no success. He approached local farmers but the answer was always the same. 'The bloody military have requisitioned all the hay, they even oversee all the cutting. I can't get even as much as a blade of grass for my own horse. I can't help you out.'

Michael took great delight in Jim's lack of success and always made a point of mentioning it at board meetings.

Then Jim came up with the idea of retiring one of the delivery horse and carts and replacing it with an Albion 16 enclosed motorised van. Michael was appalled with the proposal.

'We have always used horses. We don't need one of those modern contraptions,' he declared vehemently at the board meeting. 'It is a childish ridiculous proposal and I am steadfastly against it.'

However, two members of the company board agreed with Jim and a month later an Albion 16 was purchased.

The Alb, as Jim affectionately nicknamed the van, was a beautiful machine, all metal and mahogany with a glass windscreen, brass lamps and high mudguards. When Theo saw the Alb with the words *Brevin and Sons, Wholesale Wine Merchants* painted on its side panels, he smiled proudly.

Jim quickly learned to operate the Alb and spent many hours driving it all over the city and the suburbs. It was his responsibility to maintain the new vehicle so he learned basic motor maintenance and became expert at servicing, waxing and polishing it. The new, swifter motorised delivery service was a huge success and business increased so dramatically that in January 1916 the company board authorised the acquisition of a second Albion 16.

Even though he enjoyed his new work in the family business, the theatre was never far from Jim's mind. Every week he attended a show in one of the city's many playhouses and every week he set aside a half day and sought theatre work. Many times he was close to being cast,

THE ACTOR

or at least he was told he was close to being cast; once for a small role in the Abbey Theatre, once for a show in the Gaiety Theatre and twice with independent production companies for the Queen's Theatre. But each time and at the last minute, he was told that another actor had got the part and so his theatrical resting continued.

17

During the first thirteen days of April 1916 it rained. Sitting alone in Doyle's Pub in Phibsboro after another unsuccessful audition with some self-important theatrical impresario, a down-hearted Jim stared vacantly into his empty half-pint beer glass. A shadow fell across him. A man dressed in a sharp tweed suit, new wool top coat and smart billycock hat reached into the inside pocket of his suit jacket, opened his wallet and placed a crisp new five-pound note on the table.

'Never let it be said I didn't pay my debts.'

Jim jumped to his feet.

'Shamus McGovern.'

'The one and only.'

'How are you Shamus?' Jim shook his friend's hand enthusiastically and then crammed the much needed money into his trouser pocket.

'Let me order a few drinks and I'll tell you how I've been.'

Shamus shook the rain off his billycock, placed it on the table and was removing his wet top coat when the bartender arrived.

'Two pints of your finest ale my good man,' Shamus said with a theatrical wave of his hand.

'I'm not your good man and we only have one kind of ale,' growled the scowling bartender.

'Then that's the one we'll have.'

'You're looking well,' Jim said eyeing Shamus's new suit and crisp white shirt.

'I dress to impress.' Shamus adjusted the pearl tie-pin in his colourful tie. 'I hear Miss Sorcha gave you the shove to make way for her nephew.'

'Who told you that?'

'I'm like the Special Branch; I have ears everywhere.'

The scowling barman plonked two foaming pints on the table. Shamus handed the man some coins and said 'Keep the change my good man.'

'You're too generous,' the bartender replied after he looked into his hand and saw there was no change.

Delighted to be in each other's company again the actors lifted their pints and clinked glasses.

'What happened to you after Kerry?' Jim asked, wiping the beer moustache from his upper lip.

'I went to London. I only returned yesterday.'

'Why did you come back?'

'Ira Allen invited me to be in his next production. I'm on my way to meet him now.'

'The Ira Allen?' Jim interjected excitedly. 'The Ira Allen who wrote Fr Murphy?'

'Yes.' Shamus took another mouthful of ale. 'Why don't you come along, I'll introduce you. There might be something in the play for you.'

'I don't know.' Jim shrugged. 'He might think I was being forward.'

Shamus chuckled.

'Jim, in this business you can't be too forward.'

Standing in the pub's porch, Shamus settled the billycock firmly on his head, looked at the rain bouncing off the ground and said 'Does it do anything else in this country but rain?' Turning to Jim he asked 'Is there a grocery shop nearby?'

'Moore's shop is down the road.'

'Right, Moore's it is then,' Shamus said, and walked out into the downpour.

'Why do you need a grocery shop?' Jim asked, hurrying along beside him, pulling his coat up over his head.

'We need to buy some mint sweets. Ira Allen doesn't like drinkers, especially afternoon drinkers. Bit old-fashioned like that.'

Jim stopped and the rain lashed into his face.

'I've had two pints; he'll think I'm a drunk.'

'Then we better get extra strong mints.'

With a handful of peppermint sweets in his mouth, Shamus pulled on the door of the Phibsboro scout hall and the three young actresses waiting in the foyer stopped talking.

'Good afternoon ladies,' Shamus said as he removed his billycock and smiled brightly at them. 'Are you all here to audition?'

'Well, I am,' said the young actress in a red and white-striped dress.

'I am too,' said the petite girl in a heavy woollen coat standing to Jim's right.

There was something vaguely familiar about the girl in the coat but Jim couldn't quite place her.

'We're all are here for the auditions,' added the tallest of the three young women.

'Then good luck to you all,' Shamus said looking directly at the actress in the striped dress. 'Nice to have met you … all.'

The interior of the scout hall was long, narrow and cold, its wooden floor was cracked and broken, the grey paint on the wall was peeling and the hall smelled of damp. At one end of the building a pale young man was playing the piano and a tall thin man was listening intently to him.

'I thought you might use this piece for your first entrance,' the pianist said to the standing man.

'Hello Mr Allen,' Shamus called out.

The tall man turned, adjusted the overcoat that was draped around his shoulders and said 'Shamus, good to see you. Glad you could come along.'

Ira Allen's presence filled the hall. He was taller than Jim had remembered him but his intense penetrating brown eyes were every bit as powerful as he remembered. Shamus and Ira shook hands like old friends; but they weren't old friends. They had met for the first time two months ago in London and worked together for six weeks in a play that neither wished to remember.

'I have the perfect role for you,' Ira said. 'He's the villain of the piece. I myself have always had a failing for playing villains; indeed some of my friends have the gall to tell me I don't have to act at all when I'm playing a villain, but I think this role is for you.'

'The villain in a major melodrama is something I always wanted to play,' Shamus said, twisting the ends of an invisible moustache. 'Heh, heh, heh.'

Ira Allen glared unblinkingly at Shamus and with mild annoyance but undisguised passion said 'Melodrama is not to be sneered at. It is great theatre. It is not intellectual theatre, it is theatrical theatre and audiences love it and I will not have it sneered at.'

'I wasn't – sneering,' Shamus replied, taken aback by Ira's intensity.

'I hope not. In the present prevailing dark mood of discontent, agitation and uncertainty in our country, the ironies, the inevitabilities and the comforting certainties of melodrama are very therapeutic and calming to audiences.'

'I can assure you, I meant no offence,' Shamus offered, but Ira talked over him.

'I take my work very seriously Mr McGovern, and I expect all members of my company to do the same.' Ira lifted a bound manuscript off the top of the piano and handed it to a still taken-aback Shamus. 'This is my new play *A Noble Brother*. It's the story of two brothers; one ne'er-do-well and one noble. Your part is the snake in the grass, Harry Travers. I have still to cast the ingénue lead and that's why we are here. I'd like you to read with a few actresses.'

'I'll be happy to oblige and again I'm sorry if I gave offence.'

'We'll say no more of that.' Ira opened the manuscript and pointed to a section of the text. 'Familiarise yourself with this scene, we'll use it for the auditions. If you'd take a seat over there, I'll fetch the actresses.'

'Certainly Mr Allen, and may I introduce my friend Jim Brevin. He spent a season with the O'Donovans in the southern provinces.'

Shamus winked at Jim and walked to the seat Ira had indicated.

Jim stood awkwardly in the centre of the hall and waited for the great actor to address him.

'So you are an actor yourself, Mr Brevin?'

'Yes sir, I am. At least I'm trying to be one, sir.'

THE ACTOR

'Aren't we all? If you're looking for work I'm afraid you're out of luck; all the male roles are cast.' Then the great actor's expression changed. 'Do I know you? Yes, I do. We met, about two years ago.' Ira's face lit up with amusement. 'So you didn't take my advice. Good for you. Would you care to help with the readings?'

A surge of adrenaline rushed through Jim so fast that it made him dizzy. He replied as calmly as he could.

'It would be a privilege, sir.'

'No privilege, just an opportunity for me to see what you can do. Go over to Shamus; you can share the script.'

Ira opened the door to the foyer and with great charm invited the three young actresses into the hall. The pianist had positioned three chairs opposite the piano and Ira escorted the actresses to them.

'I'd like to thank you for coming along today. I have seen you perform and I am sure that in time we will all work together. However I have but one part to cast and that's why you're here.' Ira handed each actress a single sheet of paper. 'Look over the scene and I'll call each of you in turn to read with one of my actors. Good luck ladies.'

'One of my actors, one of my actors!' Jim repeated Ira's description of himself over and over in his mind.

Ira called out the name 'Miss Catriona McLaughlin.'

Tall and pretty, Catriona McLaughlin was twenty-two and had been working with amateur companies in Dublin for the past eight years. She longed to be part of the professional theatre. Wearing her shiny chestnut hair piled high on her head and dressed in her younger sister's white broderie anglaise blouse, her older sister's long black dress and her own best boots she strolled confidently across the hall.

Ira shook the tall actresses' hand and said 'Mr McGovern will read with you, Miss McLaughlin.'

Shamus smiled, approached the young woman and shook her hand. Miss McLaughlin nodded to Shamus and he delivered his first line. When the young actress spoke she swallowed half her words and ran out of breath long before she had finished her first sentence. Miss McLaughlin stopped reading and her face went scarlet. Ira raised his hand, took the actress aside and said very quietly 'Miss McLaughlin, may I call you Catriona?' Catriona nodded and tears started to well in her eyes. 'Catriona I have seen you in the theatre, you're a very good actress but I sense you're a little nervous.' The girl's head nodded so quickly that Jim thought it might fall off. 'Catriona, you are among friends here. I want you to relax and enjoy yourself, take amoment and think about what you're saying.'

'Yes sir,' the young actress replied.'

'Mr McGovern, would you begin again please?'

Shamus gave Catriona her cue and this time when she spoke she spoke with great feeling. Her delivery was crisp and well-paced, each sentence was clear and the emotion rang true.

'Very good,' Ira said when the scene was over. 'Thank you Miss McLaughlin, you can resume your seat.' Ira looked in the direction of the two other actresses and said 'Miss Susan Duffy when you're ready?'

Susan Duffy removed her heavy woollen coat and as she walked across the hall her green silk dress swung gracefully around her ankles. Susan was a petite, refined, well-spoken young woman whose father was a regular investor in Ira Allen productions.

'In the interest of domestic tranquillity,' Mr Cillian Duffy had said to Ira as they sat in the Gresham Hotel the previous day 'audition the girl but please do not, under any circumstances cast her. I couldn't live with her mother if you did.'

'Certainly, Cillian, don't you worry about a thing,' Ira replied as he pocketed Mr Duffy's handsome cheque. 'I'll let her down gently.'

'Pleasure to meet you, Miss Duffy,' Ira said, taking the young girl's hand. 'Mr Brevin will read with you.'

Jim's great moment had arrived. He jumped to his feet, took the manuscript from Shamus and strolled as nonchalantly as he could to the centre of the hall.

'Begin when you're ready, Mr Brevin,' Ira said.

Jim delivered his first line; Miss Duffy glared at him as if he had slapped her face, turned to the actor-manager and declared 'I wasn't ready.'

Ira raised both his hands.

'Miss Duffy will you give Mr Brevin a nod when you're ready.'

'Thank you sir,' Miss Duffy replied and placed the tips of her fingers between her breasts, closed her eyes and took five long breaths. Jim

THE ACTOR

looked to Shamus, Shamus shrugged his shoulders, the pianist turned his head away and Ira patted the cheque in his breast pocket.

'I'm ready,' Miss Duffy said politely and waited on Jim to deliver his line.

Jim spoke his first line and when Miss Duffy spoke, her voice was so high that it was incomprehensible. Taken aback, Jim looked questioningly at the girl. Her face went red. Jim feigned a cough and then delivered his second line. Again Miss Duffy replied in an impossibly high-pitched voice.

This is dreadful Jim thought to himself. This is my only chance to impress Mr Allen and this girl is ruining it. Then he remembered why Miss Duffy looked familiar, he had seen her in a play in the parish hall a few weeks back and she could act. Jim turned to the play's author and said 'Mr Allen, may I take a moment with Miss Duffy?'

'Take all the time you want, Mr Brevin.'

Jim took Miss Duffy's hand, turned her away from the five onlookers and asked 'Do you normally speak in such a voice?'

'No, I don't,' Miss Duffy's replied. 'I'm so nervous – he's the great Ira Allen and Mr McGovern is so well known. I can't stop thinking they're going to laugh at me.'

'Nobody is going to laugh at you. Let me share with you a little technique I use whenever I feel the way you do. Every time I think there are important people in the audience I imagine them naked and then they don't seem so threatening. Do you want to give it a try?'

Miss Duffy giggled and said 'Oh yes.'

Jim turned to the five onlookers and said 'We're ready now.' Ira waved and Jim delivered his first line again. This time when Miss Duffy spoke her voice was an octave lower. It was full and sweet, her articulation and diction clear and she listened to and looked at her fellow actor. When the scene was over Ira, said 'Thank you Miss Duffy. That was excellent.'

Miss Duffy beamed a bright smile, leaned over to Jim, kissed him on the cheek, cupped her hand to his ear and whispered 'You really should give up drinking in the afternoon. You're a good actor, you don't need drink to perform.'

As she walked away, Jim quickly placed another strong mint in his mouth.

'Miss Fiona Whelan would you like to read for us?'

With her red and white dress clinging to her body, Miss Fiona Whelan strolled boldly across the hall. The confident young actress's willowy figure glided across the hall while her thick black hair bounced about her small face and highlighted the darkest, softest most vulnerable eyes imaginable.

'Miss Whelan, pleasure to meet you,' Ira said as he shook the self-assured actress' hand. 'Mr McGovern will you read with Miss Whelan?'

Certainly, my pleasure,' Shamus replied and smiled his best smile for Miss Whelan.

When the three actresses had left the hall Ira placed his hand on Shamus' shoulder, frowned and said sternly 'Mr McGovern, your drinking will have to cease. I don't want a repeat of what happened in London.'

'I can guarantee you there will be no repeat,' Shamus replied. 'This morning we attended the funeral of a dear friend and afterwards the family offered us a sherry; it would have been rude to refuse.'

Jim swallowed hard at Shamus's bare-faced lie.

'Funeral or otherwise I will not tolerate drinking either during rehearsals or during the run of the play – do I make myself absolutely clear?'

'Yes sir, very clear,' Shamus replied contritely. 'Should I keep this script?'

Ira turned to the pianist. 'George, have the rest of the scripts arrived?'

'My name is not George,' retorted the pianist sharply.

'Your theatrical name is George Harding. Have the scripts arrived?'

'No sir, I'm to pick them up in ten minutes.'

'Shamus, if you'd be so good as to wait in Sullivan's tearooms opposite St Peter's Church, I'll have a manuscript dropped over to you as soon as possible.'

'Certainly. And again, apologies about the sherry-breath.'

Ira's piercing eyes looked directly into Shamus's face.

'Odd that sherry should have the after-odour of ale.'

'Thank you for the opportunity to read Mr Allen,' Jim interjected in an attempt to break the ominous silence that had fallen on the hall.

'No need for thanks,' Ira replied. 'Sorry I don't have anything for

THE ACTOR

you in this play. That was extremely generous of you to help that young actress. You can act, keep at it. I'm sure we'll work together someday, that is if you can keep away from funerals.'

An elated Jim floated out of the rehearsal room. The great Ira Allen had just told him he could act. Some days could be simply wonderful.

'That chap Jim Brevin could play the part you want me to play,' the pianist said when they were alone together.

'But I wrote that role specifically for you,' Ira protested.

'You did not, it's not a role, it's a cough and spit; ten words in two scenes. Besides,' the young man smirked, 'I have a better offer – a paying job.'

'Young man, please don't refer to the role I created specifically for you as a cough and spit. And I do pay you, I feed you and I give you a place to live.'

'I'm your son, you're supposed to provide for your children.'

'You're not a child anymore, you're nineteen years of age.' Ira leaned playfully on the top of the piano and grinned broadly. 'This paying job, it's not for the Keogh Dancing School is it?' The pianist's fingers danced on the piano keys. 'I thought as much. That's not a proper job for a professional actor.'

'I'm not a professional actor.'

'How sharper than a serpent's tooth, to have a thankless child,' Ira declared, mimicking the style of a bad Shakespearian actor.

'Father it's a paying job …'

'I know about your girlfriend Alice Keogh. Your brother tells me everything,' Ira said, grinning like a child who was exposing a great secret. 'You're sweet on her.'

'What do you think of this piece of music for your exit in act one? I call it, exit of the ham.'

'Be careful son, Catholic girls are only after one thing.'

The young man stopped playing.

'And what is that, father?'

'A husband.'

'Mother's a Catholic.'

'My very point!'

The pianist laughed heartily, then suddenly the colour drained from his face, he slouched over the piano, his hands pressed hard against the piano keys and he coughed a hacking cough that shook his whole body. Ira Allen slipped the overcoat from his shoulders and draped it around his distressed son.

'Have you got your medicine?' All traces of playfulness were gone from Ira's voice.

'No, I've left it at home. I didn't think I'd need it. It will pass in a minute, Da. The hospital said this would happen every now and then. I'll go home after I collect the scripts.'

'You'll do nothing of the sort. We'll sit and when you're ready I'll take you home.'

Sitting in a cab Ira wiped cold sweat from his son's brow and as he listened to his son's hacking cough, he again experienced the helplessness and constant dread that he and his wife lived with every day of the many, many months their son had spent in hospital recovering from tuberculosis.

Forty minutes later Ira Allen strolled into Sullivan's tearooms and placed a bound, carbon-copy manuscript of *A Noble Brother* on the table.

'Sorry about the delay, there was something that needed my urgent attention,' he said quietly as he took a seat at the table. 'Shamus, because of the holiday we start rehearsals on Tuesday at nine thirty in the scout's hall. Now, might I be so bold as to ask you to excuse yourself. I'd like to have a word with your friend.'

'Certainly sir,' Shamus replied and as he rose he winked at Jim. 'I'll wait outside for you.'

It was then that Jim noticed the manuscript under Ira Allen's arm.

'It's a small but vital role,' Ira said and he placed the script on the table between them. The gold lettering of the play's cover gleamed in the light that bled through the cafe's windows.

'Let me tell you about the part, but first let me order some tea.'

'I've got a part in the play,' a delighted Jim announced to Shamus when he walked out of the tearooms.

'Congratulations, we have to celebrate,' Shamus said rubbing his hands together. 'Let's go back to Doyle's Pub?'

'You promised Mr Allen you weren't going to drink.'

THE ACTOR

'I said I wasn't going to drink during rehearsals but we haven't started rehearsals yet.'

Jim glanced at the clock on St Peter's Church steeple.

'I have to go. I promised my brother I'd make some last minute deliveries. How about we have that that drink on Saturday.'

'No, I'm meeting Fiona on Saturday.'

'The actress in the red striped dress?'

Shamus grinned.

Jim whistled. 'That was fast!'

'What about Sunday for that drink?'

'It's Easter, my family expect me to spend Sunday with them. How about Monday? By the way what happened in London?'

'Monday is good, twelve o'clock in Davy's of Portobello and I'll tell you all about what happened in London.'

'Sounds good.' With his script tucked safely under his arm, Jim ran up the North Circular Road.

After he finished his deliveries, he went to his bedroom, lay on his bed and looked at the cover of Ira Allen's latest play. In the warm glow of golden gaslight he opened the manuscript and entered the world of a wealthy merchant, a convicted villain, a dispossessed father, an eccentric country maid, a vile charlatan and a beautiful innocent young woman. Page after page mystified him, amused him, enraged him and finally comforted him. Good triumphed over evil and a father and a daughter were reunited. Jim closed the manuscript and lost himself in the thought that he was to be a member of the company of players that would have the privilege of being the first to bring Ira Allen's new play to life on the stage of the Queen's Theatre, Dublin.

18

On Easter Monday morning the grey skies of the past two weeks turned blue. Warm sunlight beamed brightly on the streets, on the parks and on the good citizens of Dublin. Walking along the banks of Grand Canal to Davy's Pub in Portobello, Jim skipped along the path like a happy child. Pausing a moment in the shade of a willow tree, he loosened his tie and observed the world around him. On the bank of the upper lock of the canal a father and his two daughters threw chunks of stale bread to the ducks and swans that were gliding effortlessly on the canal's still water. The girls shrieked giddily when the birds eagerly reached for and devoured the bread. Three noisy naked twelve-year-old boys jumped off the lock gate into the water of the lower lock. On the other side of the canal a troop of Irish Citizen Army volunteers marched along the road. As Jim crossed the road to Davy's pub, he found himself thinking there was something unusual about the marching men.

The floor of Davy's pub was covered in clean, fresh sawdust but the heady, musty smell of last night's cigarette smoke and drink still hung in the air. In the dark interior of the quiet pub an uninterested, unshaven bartender was leaning on the bar reading a newspaper in the gloom and sitting by the light of the window two cloth-capped older men were playing chess. In the unhurried silence of the pub, one of the chess players moved a piece and wiped his hand on the front of his collarless shirts. The second chess player lifted his cap, caressed his bald scalp and contemplated his next move. With a thud the pub's side door clattered open and a dapperly dressed Shamus sauntered in.

'There you are, Jim,' he called out. 'I'll get the drinks.'

A dull rattling of bottles disturbed the solemn silence of the pub. A slightly-built older man carrying a crate of beer bottles emerged from the cellar door and limped slowly along behind the counter. Shamus ordered two pints of porter from the bartender. The bartender burped and placed a glass under the tap and began to pull a pint. As the older man crossed behind him, the bartender slid back his foot and the old man tripped over it and nearly lost his balance.

'That invisible step, Jem, it will get you every time,' sniggered the bartender as he flicked a clump of greasy hair from his left eye.

Refusing to acknowledge his tormentor the older man kept on walking.

'Big man, aren't you,' Shamus said without looking at the bartender.

'What's it to you?' the bartender growled threateningly.

Shamus' forehead furrowed and his eyes darkened.

'If I ever see you do that again, I'll be over that counter and I'll put that grin on the other side of your bloody fat face.'

'Take it easy, it was only a little joke,' grunted the startled bartender. 'Sit with your friend and I'll have Jem bring you your porter.'

'That man is a right gobshite,' Shamus when he took his seat beside Jim.

The frail old man placed two pints of porter on the table, glanced back over his shoulder and whispered conspiratorially to Shamus 'Now you know why they call him an oul' blackguard.'

'Why do you take his guff?' Shamus asked as he put his pint to his lips.

'Where else will I get a job with this gammy knee?' Jem replied with a sigh of resignation.

'Here, have a drink on us,' Shamus said and handed the man a sixpence.

'Ah, you're a decent man and thanks for standing up for me, there's not many that would do that.'

The pub door crashed open and in a frenzy of noise and confusion four Irish Citizen Army volunteers in bottle-green uniforms stormed into the pub. They pointed their weapons at the pub's inhabitants as a fifth volunteer stepped into the pub.

'My name is Sergeant Joyce of the Irish Citizen Army,' barked the new entrant, looking around the room like a proud captain standing on the bridge of a mighty warship. 'Do as you're told and no harm will come to you.'

'Joyce, are you still playing soldiers?' growled the sweaty bartender. 'When I told you yesterday not to bunk off to go marching with your little friends, I meant it. Consider yourself fired, you're on a week's notice. Now get rid of the stupid uniform and get behind the bar.'

'My name is Sergeant Joyce and I'm telling you to go down to the cellar and stay there.'

'Who do you think you're talking to, you little runt?'

'That was an order I gave you, not an invitation to a debate,' the sergeant said and pointed his gun at the bartender. Jim tensed.

The bartender sneered, 'Is that supposed to frighten me?'

The rifle boomed and the mirror behind the bar exploded.

'Jesus!' screeched the bartender, dropping to the floor as shards of glass cut into the flesh of his back. 'I'm bleeding!' He scrambled about on the glass-strewn floor.

Sergeant Joyce lowered his rifle. 'You'll be dead if you don't shut your mouth.' He turned to his men. 'Jones, lock the doors, Mullin, sit those civilians against the back wall, Nolan close the window shutters and Ahern take that article of a bartender and lock him in the cellar.'

Jim caught the piercing blue eyes of the volunteer called Ahern and immediately recognised him; he was Brian Ahern, his childhood friend.

'How are you Brian?' he blurted out.

'I'm great, how are you Jim?'

'What's happening? What's going on?'

'The rebellion has started. Our lads have taken the GPO, Stephen's Green and City Hall.'

Jim stared at his childhood friend. 'Why?'

'We're fighting for our country's freedom, that's why.'

Brian was so filled with passion that his blue eyes almost glowed.

THE ACTOR

Electrified by this turn of events, Jim's awareness of everything around him suddenly heightened. He saw the high collar on his friend's thin serge uniform, the badge on the Cronje style slouch hat and the football-shaped leather buttons on his friend's jacket.

'Are you mad?' asked one of the chess players, when the rebel Mullin made him sit on the floor at the back of the pub.

'Don't think so,' replied the red-haired volunteer, in a heavy Dublin accent.

'Why does your revolution have to have to start in our pub?' grumbled the second chess player. 'It's very inconvenient.'

'We're here because this is the best place to stop the British soldiers crossing the bridge and getting into the city centre.'

'Are you Sean Mullin's son?' Jem asked as he sat on the floor beside the two chess players.

'Yes, I'm Red Mullin.'

'I knew it. You have your father's hair. Up the Republic.'

'You're an old rebel at heart,' Red replied with a laugh. 'When the shooting starts, it's best if you lie flat.'

The young soft-spoken volunteer Jones bolted the pub's front door and gestured with his rifle for Shamus and Jim to sit on the floor with the three older men.

'Let me just slip out of here?' Shamus whispered to Jones.

'No one leaves until Sgt Joyce says so.'

'For Jesus' sake, let me out of here. I'm not one of you bleedin' rebels. Once the British find out what you're doing, you'll all be goners.'

'Just do as you're told fella and nothing will happen to you,' the grim-faced rebel Nolan called out across the pub.

'Jesus!' Shamus exclaimed.

'Watch your language.' Nolan pointed his rifle at him.

'Sorry,' Shamus grunted insincerely.

For more than an hour, the pub and the street outside were silent. Suddenly artillery fire boomed in the distance.

'That'll be from the GPO,' Brian Ahearn whispered to Jim.

In the barracks across the canal an English voice barked an order and the sound of booted feet running across the barracks' cobblestoned parade ground boomed across the canal. Minutes later a platoon of armed British soldiers pounded across the bridge.

'Sgt Joyce, they're on the move,' murmured the quiet-spoken Jones.

'I see them – hold your fire, men.'

'Jesus, they're actually going to shoot at the soldiers,' Shamus said, crouching against the wall. 'We won't get out of here alive.'

'Don't fire until you can see the whites of their eyes,' ordered Sgt Joyce.

The pummelling of boots grew louder.

'I can see white, sir,' Red shouted nervously.

'They're really going to do it, they're going to kill someone,' Shamus moaned, holding on to the leg of the table.

'Pick a man and fire at him,' ordered Sgt Joyce.

In the pub four rifles cracked loudly and two soldiers crossing the bridge fell to the ground. A command was barked and the soldiers retreated and regrouped on the barracks side of the canal. For a few minutes nothing happened. Then the soldiers crept across the bridge again, hugging the parapet. Jones, Red and Nolan fired and another two soldiers fell, but the troop quickly formed two lines in front of the pub. One line lay on the ground and the other row knelt behind them. Jones, Nolan and Mullin reloaded. On command, the British soldiers on the ground opened fire and a hail of bullets ripped through the pub shattering windows, mirrors and walls. The kneeling soldiers then opened fire while another group of British soldiers pulled a machine gun on to the middle of the bridge.

'Fire at the machine gunners!' Sgt Joyce called out.

Brian Ahern and the soft-spoken Jones turned their rifles on the gunners but a hail of fire erupted from the machine gun. Windows exploded, doors shattered and the interior of the pub was engulfed in a hurricane of bullets, flying glass and splinters of masonry.

At the bottom of Rathmines Road, behind the British soldiers, a crowd of locals gathered. When the people started to cheer the rebels, two policemen forced the crowd back up the road. One defiant young man stood his ground and a very nervous British soldier pointed his handgun at the young man and yelled 'Get back, you!' The man quickly abandoned his defiance and joined the other observers.

After twenty minutes of machine gun fire an assault on the pub was ordered. Using their rifle butts the soldiers battered down the remains of the doors and windows but when they entered the pub all they found were the two chess players and the old bartender lying on the floor.

Heart pounding and high on adrenalin, Jim followed Sgt Joyce and the stern-faced volunteer Nolan down the twisting lanes behind the pub. When the lane emptied on to Upper Harcourt Street, he stopped; Shamus was nowhere to be seen. He turned and ran back up the lane.

'You're going the wrong way!' Red Mullin shouted when he met Jim running towards him.

'I can't find my friend!'

'He's not back there, come with us to Stephen's Green. The Brits won't be long figuring out where we went.'

Jones, Red and Jim were running towards St Stephen's Green when a Crossley open-topped lorry filled with soldiers thundered into Harcourt Street. The soldiers opened fire and within sight of the green the soft-spoken Jones staggered, fell against a railing and slid on to the ground.

'Help him!' Red shouted.

Jim grabbed Jones and dragged him into a doorway. Red dropped to one knee, crammed the last two bullets from his bandolier belt into the rifle and fired on the approaching lorry. He missed the driver and the lorry continued towards him.

At the bottom of Harcourt Street, a tall imposing woman in full Irish Citizen's Army uniform walked to the centre of the road, raised her Mauser rifle-pistol and fired three shots at the Crossley lorry. A bullet pumped into the driver's forehead, he slouched forward, the lorry swerved out of control and ploughed into the railing of a Georgian house. A disoriented Jones opened his eyes and asked 'What happened?'

'Never mind what happened, let's get out of here!' Red shouted.

Groaning British soldiers staggered from the crashed lorry. Red and Jim pulled Jones to his feet and they raced down the street. Six Irish Citizen Army Volunteers formed a line in front of the uniformed woman and opened fire on the dazed British soldiers. When Jim and the rebels reached St Stephen's Green, the woman in uniform ordered Sergeant Joyce to lock the gate. 'Who are you?' she asked Jim.

Jim stared at her; he had never seen a woman in trousers before, let alone anyone who had just shot a British soldier.

'He was in Davy's when we took over the pub,' interjected Red. 'He was a great help to us.'
'What's your name?'
'Jim Brevin, ma'am.'
'He saved my life,' volunteered the injured Jones.
'I saw what happened,' the woman said and holstered her Mauser rifle-pistol. 'Jones, let me look at that wound.' Jones stepped forward. 'You'll live. It's only a flesh wound. Find the medic and he'll dress it for you,' she snapped and with a salute she strode off across the green.

19

There were nearly two hundred and fifty rebels in St Stephen's Green. Some were wearing uniforms, some were wearing half uniforms and some wore civilian clothes. Their weapons were anything that could shoot: old rifles, shotguns, automatic pistols, even ancient revolvers. Some of the volunteers were digging shallow defensive trenches in the flower beds, others were climbing trees or cleaning weapons; most were young and some were women.

'A contingent of British soldiers is marching up Grafton Street and soon they'll commence firing on us,' the tall uniformed woman with the Mauser rifle-pistol called out. Take cover, don't do anything foolish and may God bless us all.'

All was quiet for fifteen minutes; then a rifle shot shattered the silence. Jones cocked his weapon as bullets rained down on the park, thunking into trees and skimming across the surface of the pond. Terrified, Jim crouched behind a tree, holding his head in his hands.

'You need to find better shelter,' Jones called to him. 'When there's a lull in the gunfire run to the groundsman's cottage.' Blood trickled from the bandage on Jones' head.

'You're still bleeding,' Jim shouted back.

'I'm fine, I'll survive.' He made a motion with his rifle and Jim raced to the small cottage on the south-west side of St Stephen's Green, crashed through the front door, upended a table and crouched on the floor behind it.

'What do you think you're doing?' demanded an angry voice.

Jim looked over the top of the upturned table; the tall woman in uniform was pointing her Mauser at him.

'I'm sheltering, Jones told me to come here.'

'Jones had no authority to tell anyone to do anything. Leave, this is an infirmary.'

The woman holstered her weapon. Jim got to his feet as Red Mullin and Brian Ahern clattered into the cottage. 'We're here for our orders!'

'I want you two men to build a blockade across the south side of the Green,' barked the woman. 'Commandeer every cart and automobile that comes along and block the road.'

They looked at each other, blankly.

'What's the matter?' asked the woman sharply.

'We can't drive, mam.'

'I can,' Jim said, although he immediately regretted having spoken.

'You aren't a volunteer,' snapped the woman.

'I know – but if I can help?'

'You can help.' The woman pointed to a ring of keys hanging on a rack on the wall. 'Ahearn get those keys and all of you, come with me.'

Bullets whipped along the grass as Jim, Brian and Red tried to keep up with the long strides of the tall woman. At the Green's Leeson Street entrance, Brian removed a heavy chain from the gate and Red pulled it open. Suddenly there was a great thundering of hooves and a huge blood-covered dray horse galloped towards the gate. Red threw himself to one side as the distressed animal reared up, screeching with pain, kicked the air then collapsed on the path. Lying on the ground, its muscles went into spasm and its body shuddered uncontrollably.

Transfixed by the creature's distress, Red, Brian and Jim stood and stared at the juddering animal. The woman pushed past Red, patted the distressed creature on the neck, placed her Mauser to its head and fired. The horse's nostrils flared, its eyes turned bloodshot and its head thudded on to the ground. Without taking a breath, the tall woman pointed down the street.

THE ACTOR

'Build the barricade about half way down the side of the Green – the trees will give you cover. The barricade will need to be at least two cars deep. Mullin, Ahern stop all vehicles, commandeer them and if the owners refuse to park them, do it for them; if it's an automobile, call Jim. Be quick, you don't have much time, once the British realise what you're doing they'll get a machine gun on to a roof and you won't be able to continue your work. Go, and be careful.'

Brian Ahern and Red Mullin ran into the middle of the road, stopped all carts and cars and ordered the drivers to park their vehicles across the road. Most drivers complied but when one furious automobile driver refused, Red grabbed him by the collar, pulled him out on the vehicle and pointed his rifle at the man's head.

'I've already killed two men today – do you want to be the third?' Red barked.

The driver backed away then broke into a run. Jim parked the car in the barricade.

When three young men in long coats and bowler hats attempted to remove their auto from the barricade Brian pointed his weapon at them and ordered them to stop. The men ignored his command, Brian fired over their heads and they quickly abandoned their plan. When another man attempted to retrieve his car from the barricade, Red shouted a warning, the man ignored the warning and Red fired at him. The man jerked sideways, toppled out of the automobile and limped up the road.

The barricade grew and was nearly complete when a sniper appeared in a nearby building. Brian, Jim and Red took cover behind a stone water fountain. Lying on the ground, Red shouted 'We need one more car to finish the barricade!'

'Leave it to me,' Brian said. 'Cover me.'

Red leaned around the fountain, fired on the sniper and a crouching Brian moved forwards. A bullet narrowly missed him. Red fired again and the sniper fell silent.

A Silver Ghost Rolls Royce flying a miniature white and gold flag on its bonnet turned down the south side of green. The chauffeur saw the barricade, stopped and was turning the car around when Brian kicked in one of the car's silver-plated front lamps, pointed his rifle at the chauffeur and said 'In the name of the Irish Republic I commandeer this vehicle.'

THE ACTOR

An annoyed portly cleric sitting in the back of the automobile poked his head out the car and said dismissively 'In the name of his Holiness the Pope I refuse your request. Now be a good Catholic boy and stand aside.'

Brian took aim at the cleric.

'Wrong on three counts, Padre. I am not a boy, I'm not a Catholic and it was a command I gave you, not a request.'

The cleric glared at the Brian, who cocked his weapon. The cleric sat stoically in the back and snorted.

Brian pulled the trigger.

The cleric felt the bullet breeze past his face and heard the thud as it hit the upholstery and then metal skin of the car.

'Out,' barked Brian.

The driver's door flew open and the chauffeur tumbled out. The terrified cleric scrambled awkwardly out of the car hissing 'You'll burn in hell for this,' and holding his bleeding ear ran as fast as he could up the street.

With much scraping of gears, Jim backed the Rolls Royce safely in beside the other cars, completing the roadblock. A burst of machine gunfire suddenly strafed the barricade; buckboards bent, glass shattered and upholstery ripped. As Jim jumped for cover his arm exploded in pain; he'd been hit in the shoulder.

With his hand pressed against his bleeding wound, Jim staggered up along the side of St Stephen's Green to where the dead horse was still lying. Brian, running in front of him, swung open the gate. Red leapt over the horse and into the park, and Jim followed him. Brian dragged the gate shut behind them, winding the heavy chain around the railings and inserting the key in the lock. A pinging noise rang out and he froze; the key fell from his hand and his fingers grabbed hold of the gate.

'Christ, I've been hit.'

A trickle of blood oozed from a small neat round hole in the back of his jacket; he groaned loudly and fell to the ground. Jim and Red ran to their injured comrade and dragged him into the bushes. With shaking hands, Brian unbuttoned his jacket and the three of them stared in horror as blood gushed from a large, fist-sized wound in his stomach.

THE ACTOR

Panic filled Brian's blue eyes; he tried to speak but couldn't. He reached out to take Jim's hand.

'I'll get the medic; keep Brian awake,' Red cried, as he ran to the groundsman's cottage.

Jim cradled his friend's head in his arms. Brian's body shivered violently, his teeth chattered and his face turned waxen.

'Talk to me, Brian!'

'I'm so cold.'

'Just hold on, the medic will be here in a minute. Wake up!'

Brian's eyes opened lazily.

'Brian, talk to me – do you remember when I used to put on the shows in my house? You put candles in biscuit tins and we used them as footlights?'

Brian looked at Jim in confusion as if he didn't know who he was. Then his eyes focused and he half smiled.

'Yes, I remember. That was a good idea, wasn't it?'

'It was a great idea.'

'I liked your magic tricks. Do you think you could magic me better?'

'I wish I could. But don't worry the medic is coming.'

'He'll make me better.' Brian's piercing blue eyes flickered, his head fell to one side and his body slumped in Jim's arms.

'Brian!'

Dazed and confused, Jim looked around for help; all about was quiet. In a stupor of shock and disbelief, he stroked his friend's white face and his own body started to shake.

He lifted Brian's head off his lap and placed it gently on the grass. He stood up and backed away from his dead friend. His injured shoulder ached, St Stephen's Green swirled around him and he emptied the contents of his stomach on to the ground. Leaning against a tree, he took deep breaths and waited for the nausea to subside. He saw Red and a blond-haired medic in an ill-fitting uniform approach. The medic checked Brian's pulse, then closed the dead boy's eyes. Jim leaned against the tree and wept.

'Jim, we have to lock that gate.'

Red's voice was barely audible to Jim. He tried to focus but everything was cloudy and sounded muffled. Red continued speaking and when Jim didn't answer, Red shook him.

'What's wrong with you? We have to lock the gate!'

Jim stared at him.

'My friend has just been killed and you're talking about a bloody gate?'

'I'm sorry for your friend but if we don't lock the gate, we'll all be dead.' Red pressed his rifle into Jim's hands. 'Cover me.'

'I don't know how to shoot a gun.' His head began to swirl again.

'Just do what you saw me do and for God's sake don't shoot me.'

Red ran towards the gate and a disorientated Jim stared wildly around, rifle in hand. Red grabbed the lock and chain off the ground. A bullet pinged off the bars of the gate. A sniper had positioned himself in a high window on the far side of the road. Jim lifted the rifle to his injured shoulder, finger on the trigger. Red looped the chain around the gate, clipped on the lock and hunted on the ground for the key. A second shot cracked from the window. Jim fired and the sniper jerked forward, plunged through the open window and with a dull thud hit the pavement and bounced. Jim dropped the weapon with a cry and pressed his hand to his shoulder – the recoil had slammed the rifle into his open wound, and he was racked with excruciating pain. Red found the key, fumbled it into the lock, turned it and raced back to Jim. 'That was a good shot.'

'That was a lucky shot.' Fresh blood was pouring down Jim's arm.

'Let's get that shoulder of yours looked after …'

In the temporary infirmary Jim clenched his teeth while the blond-haired medic cleaned and dressed his wound.

'The bullet passed through the flesh in your shoulder. I don't think any bones are broken but it will be sore. You need to have a doctor look at it as soon as possible,' the young medic said and quickly moved on to his next patient.

Throughout the day, sniper and machine-gunfire sporadically rained on rebel positions in Stephen's Green. The shallow trenches the volunteers had dug provided little protection and with every passing hour more men and women died. The carcasses of swans and ducks floated on the pond.

During a lull in the gunfire, a dishevelled drunk with a flowing beard appeared at the railing and said to Jones 'I want to join the fight for Ireland.' The man was so drunk he could hardly stand. 'Who's in charge here?'

'Commandant Mullin is in charge,' replied the tall woman in uniform who suddenly appeared from nowhere.

The drunken man blinked and staggered backwards.

'Jesus, where did you come from?'

'Never mind where I came from. Go home, sober up, come back tomorrow and then tell me you want to fight for Ireland.'

'Right ma'am. Good idea. I'll do that,' the drunk replied and staggered off.

At sunset the guns fell silent and the mood in the park became solemn. Some of the rebels began to pray, other whispered to each other while a few sang Irish rebel songs. An exhausted Jim slumped with his back against an oak tree and tried to forget the throbbing pain in his shoulder.

'Hey you, do you know Jonny Farrell?' whispered a female voice from outside the park.

A bent, grey-haired older woman in a faded print dress, clutching a brown paper bag, waved at him through the railings.

'Come here son,' the woman said as she adjusted the tight bun of hair on the top of her head.

'You shouldn't be here, it's very dangerous. Go home,' Jim whispered to the old woman.

'How can I go home, isn't my grandson in there? He's a bit of an eejit, he thinks he's fighting for his country, but he's harmless. His mother is very worried about him.'

'It's not safe to stand there, go home.'

'Listen son, I have a few cheese sandwiches for Jonny, will you give them to him? He must be starving.'

The woman pressed the brown bag through the railings.

'He's only a boy of sixteen – find him. Remember Jonny Farrell is his name. Make sure he gets them. You can have a sandwich for yourself for your trouble.'

An eerie silence was all about as Jim walked St Stephen's Green in search of Jonny Farrell. Many of the men looked frightened, their uniforms covered in dirt and blood, their eyes wide open and their minds confused. A few looked energised. Many were dead.

The first man Jim approached was asleep face down with his rifle pointing at the Shelbourne Hotel. The second man was dead and the third was in a high state of alert waiting nervously on the next burst of gunfire.

As Jim moved through the park he overheard snatches of whispered conversations.

'There were supposed to be five hundred of us here in Stephen's Green.'

'I don't think the men from Wicklow and Kildare are coming. They were supposed to move in and take over.'

'It's like fighting a steam roller. They just keep coming, they're endless, so many of them with so much equipment.'

'The priests and the bishops are against Sinn Fein because they have all their money in British War Bonds.'

When Jim located Jonny Farrell the young man had no need for sandwiches and he never would again.

It wasn't hard to find takers for the sandwiches. Everyone alive was hungry, they hadn't eaten for fifteen hours and hadn't stopped fighting for twelve. Exhausted and dirty, the rebels lay on the ground. Dirt had seeped into their skin, formed rings under their eyes and settled in their ears.

A wind rose and the cold damp night air seeped into the marrow of Jim's bones. Like stage lights at the end of a play, the sunlight faded but Jim knew that this was not a play and that tomorrow, when the light returned, the gunfire and the killing would resume.

20

THERE WAS A HINT OF orange in the dawn sky and as the early morning light began to filter through the trees the tall woman in uniform walked quietly among the volunteers, woke them and told them to abandon their positions and go quietly to the west side of the park. Within minutes the west side of the park was swarming with rebels. Across the street, Sergeant Beirne placed three sticks of dynamite at the base of the main door of the College of Surgeons, lit the fuse and ran for cover. The ground shook, a thunderous explosion rocked the square. When the smoke cleared the rebels en masse scurried across the road and rushed through the gaping hole that minutes ago was the building's main door. Moments later, British snipers were on nearby roofs and rifle fire was raining down on the escaping rebels.

Jones was halfway up the steps of the building when an arc of machine-gun fire ripped through him. His body shook and shuddered as the bullets pumped into him. Haemorrhaging, he crawled up the last steps of the building but a second burst of gunfire tore into his back and he stopped crawling.

Jim, Nolan and Red were among the last few rebels to leave St Stephen's Green. Red positioned himself at the gate and fired at the machine-gun while Jim and Nolan and the other two rebels dashed out of the park. The machine-gun rattled, Nolan and one of the other rebels made it into the College of Surgeons building. The other rebel was running across the street when he was hit by machine-gun fire, his right ankle burst open and he plunged to the ground. Squirming in pain he called for help. Jim grabbed him by the shoulders and pulled him behind a granite horse trough.

Crouched behind the trough they waited on the machine gun to stop firing, then Jim slipped his uninjured shoulder under Nolan's arm and pulled him to his feet. Jim's shoulder ached and burned with pain, he staggered, steadied himself and with bullets ricocheting and pinging all around, he and the injured rebel lurched across the road.

Red came running after them, the last man to leave St Stephen's Green alive that day.

In the college, they cleared a room of furniture and the injured were placed on blankets on the ground. With little medicine available, all the young blond medic could do was clean the wounds of the injured with water and dress them with field bandages. An exhausted Jim laid the injured rebel on the floor of the makeshift infirmary; he sat in a nearby chair and quickly fell asleep. He awoke when a skinny, wounded man with pink eyes tapped him on the arm.

'You wouldn't have anything to eat would you?' he asked. 'I'm nearly consumed with starvation.'

'I'll see if I can get you something,' Jim replied and staggered to his feet.

'Food supplies haven't arrived,' the sergeant in charge of the kitchen replied when Jim inquired about food for the injured. 'All we have is a box of Oxo cubes. I'm boiling some water. You wait a minute and you can take a few cups up to the infirmary.'

Jim handed a cup of steaming Oxo drink to the pink-eyed man and the man thanked Jim as if he had given him a feast.

All through the day, intermittent machine-gunfire rattled across the front of the College of Surgeons and long after every pane of glass in the Georgian building was shattered the gunfire continued. The day passed slowly. Jim helped out in the infirmary, brought hot drinks to the wounded and listened to the injured and the dying. As daylight faded Sgt Joyce ordered Red 'to close the shutters and to tell that sleeping volunteer to come away from the window.' Red shook the rebel sitting on the windowsill; he didn't move. Red pulled on the volunteer's overcoat, the body slid off the sill, thudded to the floor and rolled over on to its back. A young woman's face was revealed, riddled with bullets.

An eerie half-silence fell; gone was the pinging of bullets, the smashing of glass and crashing of masonry. Now all that could be heard were the cries and moans of the injured and the dying. Jim spent a cold night lying on the bare floor of the building with only a dead rebel's overcoat draped over him to keep him warm. His shoulder throbbed, his body ached.

Just before dawn, Red Mullin shook him and whispered urgently 'You're wanted on the roof.'

'Who wants me?'

'She does.'

The interior of the building was dark and brooding and the only illumination was the candle Red held in his hand. They climbed a mahogany staircase, Red opened a door and Jim stepped on to the roof. Silhouetted against the pink glowing sky, the tall woman stood looking out over Dublin.

'I didn't know it was dawn already,' Jim said as he buttoned up his jacket.

'That's not the sunrise,' the woman replied. 'That's our city and it's on fire. How is your shoulder?'

'It hurts.'

'Yesterday was a bad day.'

'It was the worst day of my life.'

'In many ways it was the worst day of all our lives. I have never before deliberately hurt another living creature. Yet yesterday I shot and killed two soldiers.' The woman sighed. 'That is something I have to live with for the rest of my life.'

'So what you did was wrong?'

'Good God, no. What we did was right. Our actions have changed the course of Irish history. We have woken the Irish nation from its slumber.' The woman turned her face to the city. 'Jim, you are a civilian and I cannot order you to do anything, but I can request something of you.' Her eyes travelled to his face. 'Will you transport two of our injured to Roundwood in Wicklow?'

Jim looked questioningly at her.

'The man you helped across the road is very important to the movement – he must live. And our youngest volunteer Michael Quigley must also survive. What do you say? Will you take them to a doctor in Roundwood?'

'How am I to get them there?'

'Go to the barricade, retrieve one of the larger automobiles and drive it to the side entrance of this building. I'll have the injured men waiting for you.' The woman handed Jim an envelope with the name Dr Malcolm Rosenblatt and an address written on it. 'Give the letter to the doctor and he'll look after the injured men. Jim, you need to leave the city immediately.'

'Why are you doing this? Why do you hate the British so much?' Jim asked as he folded the envelope and stuffed it in his pocket.

'I don't hate the British, but I do have contempt for their politicians. I loathe their evasions and lies and I am angry and horrified at how they have treated Ireland.'

Shaking off his fatigue, Jim slipped out the side door of the building and ducking low, ran along the green's railings to the barricade. He was about to open the door of the Rolls Royce when he glimpsed a miniature Union Jack mounted on the bonnet of an open-topped Wolseley-Siddeley Tourer. He carefully removed the flag from the Wolseley, tore the gold and white flag off the Rolls and replaced it with the Union Jack. Holding his breath he pulled out the choke, pulled on the starter and the car purred into life.

Inside the College of Surgeons, the two wounded rebels were wrapped in blankets and carried from the make-shift infirmary to the side door of the building. Red Mullin poked his head out the door and looked up and down the street; all was clear and quiet.

Jim drove down York Street, stopped the automobile at the half-open door and Red and two other rebels placed the injured men on the back seat. Red handed Jim a corduroy jacket and said 'Put that on, it will hide the blood on your shirt.' He eyed the Union Jack on the car. 'What's that doing there?'

THE ACTOR

'It's insurance; hope it works.'

Red chuckled and said goodbye, and Jim drove off into the rising dawn.

The one-eyed Roll Royce stole through the sleeping city. At Donnybrook the rain started to drizzle and by the time the automobile passed through Blackrock rain was teeming down in great sheets. When the car reached Bray they came upon a British Army checkpoint. Perspiration gathered at the back of Jim's neck and when his hands began to shake he grasped the steering wheel tightly and watched the rain dancing off the car's bonnet.

A lone soldier leaned out of his sentry box, looked through the pouring rain, saw the Union Jack and waved the car through. At Roundwood when the car chugged off the main road and on to the undulating pot-holed local road, the rain cleared. When the car bounced in and out of a huge pothole, Jim's shoulder wound screamed and the wounded men in the back groaned loudly. On the outskirts of Avoca when two grim-faced men in moleskin trousers and corduroy jackets walked past the car, neither of them gave a greeting but one of them glared at the Union Jack.

'Better get rid of that thing,' the older one said from the back seat of the car. 'It won't do us any good up here.'

Jim removed the flag and a few minutes later when a man and a boy driving a donkey-cart drew abreast of the automobile, the man smiled and the boy waved. A little while later Jim stopped the car.

'Do you know where you are?' the older rebel growled.

'We're in Roundwood but I don't know where the doctor lives.'

'Ask at the next house. Do you speak Gaeilge?'

'A little,' Jim replied.

'Use it when you talk to whoever answers the door. Say, Dia dhuit.'

A few minutes later when they came upon a row of six whitewashed cottages, Jim stopped the car and knocked on the first cottage. The door cracked open and a dark greasy-haired, heavy-jowled man of indeterminate age peered out at Jim.

'Dia dhuit,' Jim said self-consciously. 'I'm looking for Dr Rosenblatt's house.'

'Dia's Muire dhuit,' growled the man. 'We don't see many strangers here.'

'Two of my friends are injured. They need to see the doctor.'

The dour-faced man opened the door and Jim glimpsed a woman and a dirty-faced boy standing at the bedside of what was clearly a very sick young man. The man came out of the cottage, closed the door behind him and looked at the men in the back seat of the car.

'They're wearing uniforms?' muttered the man.

'That's right,' Jim replied.

With a furtive look the man said 'Go down the road a bit and take the first right turn. After half-a-mile you'll see a big oak tree. The doctor's house is the white house beyond it.'

Five minutes later Jim drove past an oak tree and up the driveway of a two-storey country house. He knocked on the door and waited. Thirty anxious seconds passed; he knocked again. Upstairs in the house he heard voices, then footsteps shuffled downstairs. The door opened and a short elderly man with sad grey eyes and a grey beard came into view.

'Good morning. What can I do for you?' asked the man sternly as he adjusted the cord on his dressing gown.

'Are you Dr Rosenblatt?'

'I am,' the man replied and cocked his head to the right to compensate for his left-ear deafness.

'I was told to give you this.'

The doctor read the letter, his body stiffened and he murmured to himself 'I never thought they'd really do it.'

'I have two injured men in the car, sir.'

Dr Rosenblatt leaned out of the door and looked left and right.

'Take the car to the back of the house and park it beside the barn.'

A few minutes later, dressed in a smart three-piece tweed suit, the doctor appeared bedside the car, handed Jim a set of keys and said abruptly 'Open the barn.' He glanced into the car. 'How long have the men been asleep?'

'The older man just fell asleep, the younger has been asleep for hours.'

He opened the barn door. Half the barn was given over to six stretcher beds and the other half was a make-shift operating room. A well-scrubbed wooded table sat in the centre of the operating area and beside it on a smaller table were some frightening looking medical instruments.

'Help me lift the young man on to the table,' Dr Rosenblatt said, as he donned a clean white coat.

Between them, they lifted the sleeping Quigley on to the table. Jim leaned on the side of the table, holding his own shoulder.

'Are you injured?' asked the doctor.

'Yes, I am.'

'Let me see.'

Jim removed his jacket.

'How bad are things in the city?'

'Very bad, many have died but a lot more are injured.'

'Well that's when happens when you pick a fight with the British Empire. Your shoulder needs a few stitches. I'll tend it after I examine the others. Go into the house, wash your face and hands; my wife will give you something to eat. Then come back and I'll attend to your shoulder.'

Jim watched the doctor cut open Quigley's trousers. When he removed the stomach bandage, blood gushed from the wound.

'Stop staring and go into the house,' the doctor said and his sad eyes returned to his patient's wound.

Forty minutes later a washed and fed Jim returned to the barn.

'You're lucky,' the doctor said as he stitched Jim's shoulder. 'The bullet passed right through, you've lost some blood but otherwise everything's fine. You need lots of rest. I have a house not far from here; spend the rest of day and tonight there and then leave early tomorrow. Ditch the car near the city and forget you ever came here. You need a change of clothes. Ask my wife to give you some of our late son's clothes.'

'How did your son die?' Jim asked gently.

'He was killed last year in France. He was a surgeon serving in the army.'

The following day at noon, Jim abandoned the Rolls Royce at Seapoint and cadged a lift on a donkey and cart going into the city. The cart driver, Sean Walsh, was a gaunt man with a pock-marked face and the hurt eyes of a man who had endured insults every day of his life. He wore patches on his trousers and his overcoat was tied with a piece of rope.

'I hear the city's burning,' Sean said and, without waiting on a reply, added 'Them dirty bowsies have destroyed the place, God forgive them.'

'Jesus Christ,' he screeched when they reached Baggot Street Bridge, which was littered with glass, rubble, a rotting horse carcass and the shattered remains of a checkpoint. Sean dismounted the cart and carefully guided his donkey around the rubble and the carcass. All was quiet as the donkey cantered down an eerily empty Baggot Street. A thunderous roar boomed from the city, the donkey reared up and Jim nearly fell off the cart.

'What in God's name was that?' Sean asked, as he adjusted his large peaked cap.

A few minutes later when the cart turned into Tara Street there was another thundering boom, this time accompanied by a great cloud of smoke, which billowed up the street towards them. Through the fog of dirt and smoke Sean guided the cart onto Burgh Quay. The thunder boomed again and again and in the smoke was a frightening flash of red. Then from the centre of the city there was a great thud, a rumble and in the sky a great plume of dirt and smoke rose up. A sudden gush of wind cleared the cloud of smoke and dirt and Jim beheld the British gunboat *The Helga* sitting on the river, its massive guns shelling the city. The big guns fell quiet, repositioned and then pounded cannon fire into Liberty Hall.

'Mother of God, my poor animal,' yelled Sean, jumping off the cart and patting his donkey on the neck. 'You poor thing.' He placed a black hood over the donkey's head and guided the frightened animal on foot along the quays. When they passed a blazing Sackville Street, Sean said a prayer but when they passed the occupied Four Courts he blessed himself. At Kingsbridge Railway Station, he thanked Jim for his company. Jim carefully dismounted the cart, bade farewell and continued on foot.

Holding his shoulder and stumbling like a drunken man he made his way home on the North Circular Road. He inserted the key in the lock, the door swung open and he collapsed into the hall. A startled Michael raced from the front drawing room and helped his brother to his feet.

'Look at the state of you! Are you drunk?' Michael saw the bloodstain on Jim's shirt. 'You're injured?' He called to Mrs O'Neill to fetch Dr Moore.

Líla came running. 'I think we should get him to bed!'

Lying in the bed awaiting the doctor, Jim told Michael and Líla a little of what had happened to him.

'Brian Ahern is missing,' Michael said when Jim stopped talking. 'It's rumoured that he's involved in the fighting. Like you, he hasn't been home.'

'Where's father?' Jim couldn't bring himself to answer Michael's implied question.

'He's taking a rest. He was very worried about you.'

Jim's eyes closed and for the next thirty six hours he slept.

During those thirty six hours, Dr Moore treated and dressed Jim's wound and Líla and Michael took turns sitting at his bedside. Theo prayed for his son's recovery.

When Jim awoke and found he was in his own bed, a great calm washed over him. Líla told him that he had two messages; one a note from Mr Ira Allen informing him that rehearsals were postponed for one week and one from Shamus who had called to the house. When he was feeling a little stronger, he asked Michael if he would ask Mr and Mrs Ahern and their daughter Ann to call on him.

'Can't it wait?'

'No,' Jim replied and bowed his head.

On Saturday morning, Michael, Líla and Jim went into the city. Most of the city centre was destroyed. All the buildings on Sackville Street including the Gresham Hotel and the General Post Office were in ruins; some were still smouldering. The street was littered with glass, rubble and the remains of burnt-out trams and cars. Rotting horse carcasses were everywhere and the dried blood of rebels, civilians and British soldiers marked the places where they had fallen.

At twelve noon the defeated rebels were marched down Thomas Street. Jim, Michael and Líla stood with their backs against a shop window and listened to the crowds taunt, curse, and throw rotten vegetable and fruit at the marching men. Jim bowed his head. A large woman standing next to him pulled her black woollen shawl tightly around her body and shouted angrily 'You dirty blackguards, look what you did to the city. How am I going to get food for my kids?'

'I hope they shoot the bastards,' shouted an elderly man with a grizzled moustache.

'They should be crucified,' corrected the large woman.

A large crowd of people rushed toward the rebels but the British soldiers with bayoneted rifles held the crowd back. Jim saw Red Mullin and tried to approach him but a soldier pushed him back on to the path. When the marching rebels turned into Dame Street the man beside Red asked 'Do you think the Brits might let us go?'

Red looked at the angry, baying crowd and muttered 'I hope not.'

On Sunday morning, on the 30 April 1916, four hundred tired, hungry, unwashed rebels were marched in formation down the quays, placed on cattle ships and transported to internment camps in Wales while their leaders, imprisoned in Kilmainham Jail, awaited court-martial and execution.

21

During the six days of the 1916 Rising, 1,350 people were killed or severely wounded and the centre of Dublin city was gutted. Martial law was declared and citizens needed written permits to go about their daily business, military checkpoints were set up and permits and identification papers were constantly checked. Day and night, British Army soldiers accompanied by members of the Dublin Metropolitan Police raided houses and dragged suspected nationalists or rebel sympathisers through the streets and incarcerated them in military jails.

On Friday 5 May 1916, three days before his forty eighth birthday, the rebel leader John MacBride was executed by firing squad in Kilmainham Jail. He was the eighth leader of the insurrection to have faced a firing squad and his court martial took less than five minutes. In the following weeks, eight other leaders of the Rising were court martialled and executed and 3,430 men and 79 women were arrested and incarcerated.

The newly unemployed workers of Jacob's Biscuit Factory, Gresham Hotel, Clery's Drapery Store and hundreds of other devastated business searched in vain for alternative employment. Thousands of people went without food: markets had few vegetables, butchers had little meat and rich and poor alike queued outside Johnston, Mooney and O'Brien and other bakeries for their ration of two loaves of bread a day.

A hundred times that week, Jim re-lived the violent death of his friend Brian Ahearn. His mind slipped into an ever-darkening pit. He walked about his home in silence; he said little, ate little and slept little. When Theo asked Dr Moore what to do, the doctor replied 'When his mind absorbs all that has happened to him he'll get some peace.'

On the 9 May, Jim opened the hall door of his home and white blinding sunlight assaulted his eyes. He turned his head sharply away from the blazing sun, adjusted the sling on his arm and started his walk to the scout's hall for first rehearsal of *A Noble Brother*.

The footpaths of the North Circular Road were filled with unemployed men beginning their search for a day's work, women walking children to school and many hungry beggars. At St Peter's Church, a young man in a shabby suit looked furtively left and right and limped across the road. Jim was still wondering where he had seen the limping man before when a British Army open-topped lorry filled with armed soldiers, screeched to a halt. Six soldiers jumped out of the lorry, grabbed the man and knocked him to the ground. One soldier placed his booted foot on his face and another soldier patted him down. Jim suddenly remembered where he had seen him before – he was one of the rebels from the College of Surgeons. Jim took a step backwards and blended into the growing crowd of onlookers.

A tall, severe looking officer carrying a riding crop slid out of the front of the lorry.

'Check his right leg?' The man's trousers leg was pulled up and a blood-soaked bandage was revealed. 'That's our man, take him away.' Then turning to his sergeant the officer said 'Check everyone's permit, there may be other rebels about.'

A young soldier pointed his rifle at Jim and shouted 'Permit.'

Jim handed over his papers and watched as the other soldiers pulled the captured man to his feet and threw him like a sack of potatoes into the back of the lorry.

'Spread your legs and raise your arms,' the solider barked.

Jim did as he was ordered. When the soldier patted Jim's shoulder, he winced.

'Open you shirt and jacket!' commanded the soldier.

THE ACTOR

Jim did as instructed.

The soldier called to his officer 'This man has an injury, sir, no visible blood.'

The officer strolled over to Jim. 'Are you a rebel?' he asked coldly.

'No, I am not.'

The officer's eyes searched Jim's face. 'How did you injure your shoulder?'

'I fell off a delivery lorry,' Jim replied, repeating the lie he and Líla had concocted the previous night.

The officer slapped the riding crop against Jim's injured shoulder. Pain tore through his body. After a few seconds the officer said 'No blood. You might be telling the truth. Where are you going?'

'I'm an actor, I'm on my way to rehearsal.'

'An actor? I thought you said you fell off a delivery lorry?'

'When I'm not working in the theatre I work in the family business.'

'And what business is that?'

'Wine importation.'

'Really? Tell me, was last year a good year for the Chablis grape?'

'Chablis is not a grape, it's a wine region in France. Chablis wine is made from the Chardonnay grape and last year was a good year for that grape variety.'

'You know your grapes,' the officer smiled wryly. 'Off you go and good luck with the play.'

Five minutes later a perspiring Jim, hugging his aching arm, pushed open the door of the scout's hall and stepped into the foyer.

'Are you all right?' asked a short pudgy man in a well-worn dark suit and steel rimmed glasses.

'Yes I'm fine.'

'Were you stopped by the soldiers? The army is everywhere; I was stopped three times on my way here. They're rounding up rebels.'

Jim looked puzzled at the man for he had difficulty understanding his thick Belfast accent.

The man suddenly stopped talking and looking suspiciously back at him. 'You're not a rebel are you?'

'No, I'm Jim Brevin. I'm here to rehearse with the Ira Allen Company.'

'Jim Brevin, I'm Mick Duffin the company's stage manager, pleased to meet you.' Jim took the man's outstretched hand and shook it. 'You're the actor that's going to be my assistant?'

'Yes I am, Mr Duffin,' Jim replied, only understanding half of the words the man had uttered.

'Well then I'm very pleased to meet you. Call me Mick. The last few weeks have been terrible, all that fighting and then the terrible news about Ira's son?'

'Ira's son? Was he injured in the fighting?'

'No.' Mick lowered his voice. 'His TB is back, he's in the hospital in the Phoenix Park. Ira and May are terribly worried.' The stage manager adjusted the steel-rimmed glasses on his nose and rooted in his bulging leather bag. 'Ah there it is,' he said and handed a sheet of paper to Jim. 'That's your contract.' He handed Jim a fountain pen. 'You need to sign it.' Jim scrawled a signature on the paper and handed it back to the stage manager. 'You should always read things before you sign them,' Mick said as he carefully filed the signed contract into his bulging bag. 'The contract you signed is for six weeks which includes a five-week national tour.'

'Yes, the tour starts in Belfast and ends in Cork.'

'That's right. What happened to your arm?'

Jim repeated his rehearsed lie and added 'I'm to take the sling off next week, so it won't affect the show. What does an assistant stage manager have to do?'

'Lots of things, but your main job is to be the company's prompter and you will have to help the stagehands with the set changes and stage machines. Why don't you go on into the hall? Young Fiona Whelan is in there on her own.' When Jim went to remove his overcoat, he added 'I wouldn't take your coat off yet, it's still a bit chilly in there. I lit a fire but it hasn't taken hold yet.'

The willowy Miss Fiona Whelan was sitting by a smouldering blackness that was supposed to be a fire. Jim wanted to engage the girl in sparkling conversation but, unable to think of a single interesting thing to say, he sat himself at the large well-worn wooden table that filled the centre of the room, opened his script and pretended to read. Every now and again he stole a glance at the actress. Once when she smiled back at him, his face burned red; he looked away and buried his eyes once again in his script.

'Ah you didn't poke the fire,' the stage manager called out from the doorway.

The actress looked at Mick like a child that didn't know why she was being reprimanded. Mick, in ten quick strides crossed the room, lifted the iron poker from its stand, plunged it into the base of the smouldering mass, jiggled it, and joyous bright yellow flames leapt up the chimney.

'There you are, a bit of heat.'

Fiona smiled meekly and the instant the stage manager left the hall she gathered her belongings and crossed the room to Jim.

'Do you understand that man?' Fiona said in a low voice. 'Is he speaking English at all?'

Relieved that he didn't have to instigate the conversation, Jim replied almost confidently 'I think he's from Belfast.'

'Do you mind if I sit beside you?' Without waiting on a reply, she sat. 'He gave me something to sign but when I asked him what it was, I didn't understand his reply.'

'That was your contract. Did you read it?'

'No.'

'Did you sign it?'

'Oh yes.'

'You should never sign anything without reading it first,' Jim said pompously.

'Did you read yours?' Fiona cocked her head to one side and fixed her dark fiery eyes on him.

'Oh yes.'

'What did it say?'

'Oh, the usual stuff.'

'What usual stuff?'

Jim coughed.

'Standard stuff – beginning dates, end dates, that sort of thing.'

'Oh my, I feel a bit of a fool, I should have read it.' Fiona paused then flashed her eyes at Jim. 'We never really met. My name is Fiona Whelan.'

'Hello Fiona, I'm Jim Brevin. Pleased to meet you.'
'Me too. I know who you are. You're Shamus's friend.'
'Yes, I know Shamus,' said Jim rather darkly.
'What happened to your shoulder?'
'I had a bit of an accident.'
'This is all so very exciting,' Fiona exclaimed suddenly and her excitement was so infectious that Jim felt the dark cloud in his head lift a little.
'Yes it is exciting, very exciting,' he replied.
Singing to himself, the stage manager strolled back into the hall, clattered his leather bag on the table and said to Fiona 'It's still cold in here, isn't it?'
Fiona glanced at Jim and flipped the palms of her hands upwards.
Jim waited a moment and then with a smirk said 'Yes it is still a little cold, Mick.'
The stage manager pulled a newspaper from his bag and began to read. Fiona leaned over to Jim and whispered 'Thank God you're here.'
'The incomprehensible Mick Duffin, they haven't found you out yet,' bellowed the dapperly dressed Leslie Lawrence as he swanned into the hall.
'Not yet Leslie,' the stage manager replied in a clear and precise accentless voice.
Fiona and Jim looked at each other in astonishment.
'He's pulled that old Belfast trick on you, hasn't he?' the jolly actor said, shaking his finger at Mick like a schoolteacher reprimanding a naughty student and Mick laughed loudly.
'I think he got us,' Jim replied with a smile. 'I'm Jim Brevin and this is Fiona Whelan.'
'Leslie Lawrence at your service, Miss Whelan,' the personable actor said taking Fiona's outstretched hand and placing a kiss on it.
Leslie Lawrence was an extremely versatile actor who specialised in playing comic church and army characters. Wearing a finely-tailored tweed suit and contrasting waistcoat, he looked every inch a gentleman. He adjusted his monocle, ran his fingers through his hair and said 'What dreadful times we're living in, I was stopped twice by army patrols.'
'We all were,' the stage manager said. 'What's the latest on Ira's son?'

THE ACTOR

'I haven't heard anything since Saturday.'

Leslie removed his monocle, his face broke into a broad smile and he said to Fiona 'I've seen you on stage young lady, you're very good.' Then turning to Jim he said 'And you sir, I've heard of "break a leg" but don't you think breaking a shoulder before we even go into a rehearsals is going a little too far?' And when Jim stared at him, puzzled, he added 'That's a little joke.'

'Very little,' interjected Mick. 'I heard you were at the Abbey Theatre the other night.' He handed Leslie his contract to sign. 'How was it?'

'Didn't like it, but then I saw it under adverse conditions. The curtain was up.'

'Come on, Leslie, it couldn't have been that bad.'

'Just because the critics said the play was numbingly boring, poorly acted with atrocious dialogue doesn't mean that I have to rate it that highly.'

Jim and Fiona snickered, Mick laughed but Leslie laughed loudest of all.

Leslie read his contract then pointed to the last paragraph and said 'What's this clause about the management reserves the right to cancel the show without notice?'

'Ira instructed me to insert it in all contracts.'

'So the show might not go on?'

'So it seems. There are problems, Ira is right now talking to the police about late permits and there was an emergency meeting with the theatre's management last night. Ira will fill us in when he arrives.'

Jim felt a surge of dread and Fiona's face went white. Leslie signed the contract and handed it back to Mick. With a clatter the door swung open and Shamus McGovern sauntered into the room.

Jim hurried over to Shamus. 'What happened to you?' he asked in an angry whisper.

'Hello Jim, I see you made it here all right,' Shamus said nonchalantly.

'Where did you disappear to?'

'I didn't disappear anywhere. I skipped over a wall into the backyard of a friend's house.'

'You did a bunk on me.'

Shamus's eyes darkened and Jim felt a chill that had nothing to do with the coldness of the room. 'I knew you'd be all right.'

'You knew nothing of the sort. How could you do that to a friend?'

'I told you a long time ago I don't have friends, I don't look after people and I don't expect others to look after me.' Shamus leaned into Jim face. 'Now grow up and fuck off.'

'Hello Jim Brevin.'

Jim turned and looked into the sad eyes of May Murnane. The actress was wearing a feathered stole around her neck, a coffee-coloured coat, kid gloves and sitting on her head was a straw hat which was trimmed with roses and feathers.

'Hello Mrs Allen, it's a great pleasure to meet you.'

'But this isn't our first meeting, is it Jim? I never forget a handsome young man.'

Jim smiled shyly.

'Yes, Mrs Allen. You are correct.'

'You've grown up, and by the way call me May. We are all actors here.'

'How is your son?'

The smile on May's face faded and for a second Jim glimpsed the face of a frightened, worried mother.

'Improving,' she replied but Jim knew it was a lie. 'It's very kind of you to ask. Ira is with him now.' The masking smile returned to May's face and she removed her kid gloves. 'Dear me, what happened to your arm?'

'I had an accident. The sling is only temporary.'

'Very good, let me introduce you to Maura Sweeney.' She turned to the cheerful looking, rose-cheeked woman by her side.

'Pleased to meet you Jim,' Maura said and shook Jim's hand.

Maura's bright eyes and long luxuriant hair made her look younger than her forty years. Possessing perfect comic timing and a beautiful singing voice, she was one of Ireland's finest comic actresses. She specialised in playing unruly maids and other comic domestics but behind her bright eyes there was a great sadness – two years ago she had buried her beloved husband.

'I'm going to make a cup of tea. Would you like a cup, Jim?' Maura asked.

'Why don't we make tea for everyone?' May interjected. 'I'll just have a quick word with the other two new members of the company and then I'll join you in the kitchen.'

'Right, May. You take your time.'

'Maura and I are making the tea today,' May cried out, after she had exchanged a few words with Fiona and Shamus. 'Tomorrow you men will make the tea.'

'That day will never come, madam,' Leslie Lawrence called out across the room. 'A man's got to have some principles.'

'You can have all the principles you like, but tomorrow you will make the tea,' May said with a casual wave of her hand.

Jim sat at the far end of the table. Shamus grinned at him, Jim twisted in his chair, the leg of his chair snapped through a rotting floorboard and Jim toppled to the floor. All eyes turned to him.

'It went through the floor,' Jim explained to everyone as he extracted the chair leg from the hole.

'Tea's ready,' Maura said, popping her head out of the hall's tiny kitchen. 'If you want tea you have to come and get it.'

Walking to the kitchen Leslie Lawrence pointed to Jim's shoulder and said 'What happened here?'

'I had a bit of an accident,' Jim replied. 'Fell off a lorry.'

'You seem to fall down a lot? Does it run in the family?'

Jim stared at Leslie.

'Leslie, leave the boy alone,' Maura Sweeney said as she poured the tea. 'He doesn't understand your sense of humour. Indeed half the time I have no idea what you're talking about.'

'Maura you're a beautiful woman, you don't have to understand anything,' said Leslie, then leaned over to Jim. 'Never argue with a woman. She'll drag you down to her level and then beat you with her experience.'

'I heard that, you long streak of misery,' Maura snapped warmly and continued pouring the tea. 'Leslie you are full of rubbish.'

'That was a nice thing to do,' Fiona said to Jim when she sat beside him at the table.

'What?' Jim replied a little more sharply than he'd intended.

'The way you helped that young actress during the audition, it was very nice thing to do.'

'Oh that, it was nothing.'

The door swung open and Ira Allen entered the hall. He crossed the room, placed a folder of papers on the table and said 'Hello everyone, where's May?'

'I'm in the kitchen dear,' May called out.

'We'll begin shortly.'

Ira disappeared into the kitchen. The hall went silent and then from the kitchen they heard 'Thank God, Ira. Oh thank God. When do they think he'll be able to come home?'

'One thing at a time,' Ira's voice replied. 'He's only beginning to improve. He still has a long way to go.'

A few minutes later Ira and May sat at the table and when all the cast were seated Ira said 'Welcome everyone. Sorry about the confusion of the start date for rehearsal but the last few weeks have been exceedingly turbulent and tragic.' He squeezed May's hand. 'I know everyone is not here but we must begin. I have spoken to …'

The door creaked open and the tall, wild-looking Richard O'Hare and the diminutive Francis P Dawson crept into the hall.

'Well if it isn't the long and short of it,' Leslie Lawrence commented loudly.

'You can always rely on Leslie for some smart or stupid remark,' snapped Richard, as he patted down his hair.

'And would you be able to tell the difference, Richard,' retorted Leslie.

'Enough gentlemen,' interjected Ira taking control of the situation. 'Richard, Francis please take a seat.'

As the two actors sat down at the table, Richard muttered 'Bloody British Army stopping me and searched me. I ask you, do I look like a rebel?'

'I don't know, Richard. What does a rebel look like?'

'Lawrence, if you say another word to me I'll plant one on you,' Richard snapped.

'Gentlemen that's no way to behave, there are ladies present,' Ira said sternly.

'Sorry, sorry,' mumbled Richard as he theatrically bowed to the ladies.

THE ACTOR

Richard O'Hare had a striking face and a large head that was topped with a mop of wild unkempt hair. He was a fussy man who had an air of self-importance about him that gave the holy men and historical figures he portrayed instant character. In real life he was a boisterous man who embraced victimhood with the zeal of a reformed drunk. Like most actors, Richard was profoundly superstitious. He would never mention the Scottish play by name or whistle in a dressing room and under no circumstances would he ever wish another actor good luck.

The second man was Francis P Dawson. Francis P was a short, clean-shaven, bald-headed man who specialised in playing corrupt politicians, wayward landlords and working men. He was an intense, severe looking person whose appearance belied his gentle personality; Francis P – as he was known – was a devoted husband and father and a most compassionate man.

'As I was about to say,' Ira said, casting a reprimanding glance at the two latecomers, 'I have spoken to the police authorities and have been informed that the system of permits will continue for the foreseeable future. The Queen's Theatre management estimates that audience size should at most decrease by twenty per cent. However as the theatre's management is eager to keep the theatre open, that figure should be taken with a grain of salt. But one has to ask the question – is this the right thing to do at this time of escalating unrest in our city and country? It is very difficult to know.' He paused and his words hung in the air. Jim gripped the side of his chair and Fiona glanced at him and then at Shamus, and Richard wondered what was going on. Leslie Lawrence was about to speak when Ira resumed talking. 'But I say people need to escape from what is going on all about them. They need to be entertained, they need a little respite from the horrors of everyday life. And that is what we will do, that is our work and it is important work.'

All around the table the actors relaxed and smiled at each other.

'To the new members of the company Shamus, Fiona and Jim I say welcome. I hope you will enjoy your time with us. Now let us proceed.'

Jim sat back in his chair and everyone at the table opened their scripts.

22

When the play reading was finished Ira closed the manuscript, the cast pushed back their chairs, stood and as one applauded loudly.

'Fine work,' commented Leslie. 'This one will fill houses.'

'Bravo, very moving,' said the wild-looking Richard.

'We have a very special play here,' Francis P said and shook Ira's hand vigorously.

'Audiences will love it,' agreed Maura.

May nodded approvingly. Shamus, Fiona and Jim applauded warmly and Jim felt he had been present at a very special moment of Irish theatre.

During the extended tea break that followed the reading, the wardrobe mistress Siobhan Brennan and her pretty daughter Angel measured each member of the cast for their costume.

'Is everything all right, Jim?' Fiona asked in her lilting voice.

'Did you see the people protesting outside Mountjoy Prison?'

'Yes, I saw them. They were carrying signs saying Mother of God Open the Prison Gates, Release our Fathers and Brothers. Mother of Mercy Pray for our Prisoners. I felt so sorry for them.'

'So did I, it's terrible. Someone should do something.'

'Jim, think about it the way Mr Allen does. We are doing something. This play will help lift the spirits of some of the people.'

THE ACTOR

'Perhaps he's right.'

'I think he is.' She was halfway across the room before Jim realised that his dark mood had pushed the girl away. Then his heart sank even further when Shamus placed his arm around Fiona's shoulder and gently pulled her closer to him.

'What about those rebels? Who asked them to revolt?' Richard O'Hare said to Francis P as they stood with their backs to the fire. 'They are just bowsies and mad for war.' Richard O'Hare kept his head and body perfectly still and he spoke as if he was weary and tired. 'I heard a woman on the tram refer to the rebels as "murderers, and starvers of the people". I don't mind telling you I agree with her.'

'Some people have sympathy with the rebels,' said the usually quiet Francis P.

'Aren't they entitled to their point of view?'

'I tell you they will ruin the country.'

'What country is that?' Leslie said stepping between the two men.

'Must you always be supercilious?' remarked Francis P. 'Some things are beyond a joke.'

'Wouldn't be Lord Leslie if he wasn't supercilious,' observed Richard O'Hare who chuckled with delight at his own witticism.

'Tell me, Richard?' Leslie asked. 'Do you even understand the word supercilious?'

'I'll bash you if you're not careful,' snapped Richard.

'Gentlemen please leave your bickering outside the rehearsal room,' May Murnane pleaded standing in front of the three of them. 'Leslie, you should have more sense than to goad Richard.'

'Are you suggesting that my reactions are predictable?' Richard asked indignantly.

'Richard, I am not suggesting anything. I was saying quite clearly and emphatically that you are as transparent as glass and that Leslie should not be taking advantage of that.'

As May walked away, Richard scratched his head. 'Was that a compliment?'

'You could say it was,' Leslie replied.

'I'm not at all happy with the way you speak to me, Leslie,' Richard said.

'Friendly banter, Richard – we are all friends here, aren't we?'

'I suppose so,' Richard replied gloomily.

After the break, Ira gave some script changes to the cast, the large table was moved to one side of the hall and Mick drew a chalk outline of the set for Act One on the floor. For the remainder of the day, Ira blocked out Act One. At the end of the rehearsal, he asked Jim to stay back 'for a little chat'.

'I know how you hurt your shoulder,' he said very softly, taking a seat and indicating for Jim to join him. 'You were in Stephen's Green on Easter Monday.'

'I am not a rebel.'

'That is not my concern. What concerns me is your health. Are you well enough to continue with the play?'

'Yes I am. My shoulder is improving every day. Mr Allen, I have been waiting on this opportunity for a long time. Please don't take it away from me.'

'I have no intention of taking anything away from you. I believe the best thing for you is to throw yourself into your work. I know it's how I cope with my difficulties.'

'Thank you, sir,' replied a much relieved Jim.

'There are two things I want to talk to you about. First I have been thinking about your role and I propose to write two scenes for you, scenes you can get your teeth into; scenes that will stretch you a little. What do you say?'

'That would be wonderful, sir,' said Jim.

Ira paused.

'What was the second thing you wanted to talk about?' Jim prompted.

'It's a little delicate, so discretion is called for. I want you to understudy Shamus but I don't want him to know you're doing it. More than likely you won't be called upon to play the role but I would like to give you the experience of being an understudy.'

Jim was so taken aback he could hardly speak and as he walked home it occurred to him that not once during the day had he thought about Brian Ahern and the terrible event that occurred in Stephen's Green.

Life for all citizens in the devastated capital grew harder by the day. One in every four men in Dublin's overcrowded tenements was unemployed. Hundreds of children sold wares on the streets and hundreds more begged for food or money. Many of the destitute children came from families where one or both parents had been imprisoned and others came from homes that were racked with illness, drunkenness or unemployment. Every night in Monto – Dublin's notorious red light district – fourteen hundred Irish prostitutes plied their trade to their regular customers and to the thousands of newly arrived British soldiers. Tens of thousands more Irishmen were away fighting in Europe in British khaki or with the Royal Navy.

A white spring sun shone on Jim as he walked down the North Circular Road to the rehearsal hall. It was his fourth day with the company and his first day without his shoulder sling. At St Peter's Church he came upon a British Army checkpoint and as he was waiting on a soldier to check his permit, a gunshot cracked in a nearby street. Jim flinched and the horrific image of a blood-drenched Brian Ahearn flashed in his mind. His head spun, he felt nauseous and he began to sway. The soldier grunted an order; in a daze Jim stepped forward and showed his permit. A second soldier patted him down and then waved him on. Then swaying like a drunken man Jim weaved his way down the street and when he reached the scout hall he stumbled through the door and fell against the wall.

'Are you all right?' said Ira. Jim was ashen faced.

'I was stopped by the soldiers; it's always upsetting.' Jim took several deep breaths and when he realised that Ira hadn't taken his eyes off him Jim asked softly 'How is your son, sir?'

Ira's eyes dulled.

'Like you, he has good days and bad days. Last night was not good. Thank you for asking.' Ira removed three sheets of paper from his bag and handed them to Jim. 'These are the scenes I promised you. One scene is comic, you'll share that scene with Maura, and the other one is dramatic, that you share with me. I've indicated where they are in the play. Learn your lines and we'll rehearse them on Monday.'

'Thank you sir,' he replied and colour began to return to his cheeks.

When Jim entered the hall the cast were sitting in ones and twos along the walls. Richard and Francis P were running lines, May Murnane and Maura Sweeney were chatting. Fiona was sitting alone reading her script. Jim decided to join her but as he crossed the hall Shamus called out to Fiona. Jim stopped, sat on the nearest chair and opened his script.

Looking over the top of his script, Jim gazed at Fiona. He watched the sunlight dance on her petite face, he admired the gentle movement of her delicate jaw and the contractions of her long throat and his eyes followed the line of the glossy black hair that framed her face. Fiona smiled at Shamus, his hand brushed a hair away from her eyes and Jim wished he was Shamus.

At the canal end of the hall in front of the chalk-marked performance area Mick positioned a small table and three chairs, placed the prompt script on the table and beckoned Jim to join him.

'First day off book is always a slow day,' Ira declared placing his bag on the floor beside Jim. Then addressing the cast he said 'We will no doubt all stumble a bit with our words but I ask you to be patient with each other. Jim is our prompter but he will only give you a prompt if you call for it. We'll begin at the top of the play.'

Francis P approached the table and said 'Ira, I haven't been able to learn my lines, pressure of work, you understand. So if you don't mind I'll carry my script for just a few more days.'

'Not the brightest thing to say,' Leslie whispered to Richard. 'Now we'll see a few sparks.'

'Pressure of work?' repeated Ira. 'I thought this was your work?' Francis P's face flushed red. 'I made it quite clear on day one that everyone was to be off book by day four. This is day four so you will be off book.'

'But I just told you ...'

'I heard what you said. But you will rehearse off book and if Jim has to give you every single line, so be it.'

Francis P sat on a chair by the wall and lifted his script to his eyes.

'Act One, Scene One,' Ira announced. 'Let's begin.'

Maura Sweeney mimed opening the door of the Leigh mansion, walked to the chair that represented the garden seat and delivered a short monologue. Maura then looked to Ira and said 'Mr Allen I have a song here, do you wish to rehearse it now?'

'No, Maura, we'll have a pianist on Wednesday, let's leave it till then. Shall we continue?'

THE ACTOR

Leslie Lawrence entered the performance area and played his first scene with Maura. Both actors were word perfect.

'Need to develop some stage business to bring that scene alive,' Ira commented. 'I have some ideas but I'll give them to you tomorrow.'

Shamus was next and he too was word perfect. To impress Ira, Shamus delivered his monologue using a stage technique he developed in the fit-ups. He stood completely still and staring at the back wall of the hall delivered his monologue with great intensity but in an almost hushed voice.

'I know this is our first day off book but as you are so solid with your lines I feel I can comment on your performance,' Ira said when Shamus finished his scene. 'What you're doing is very interesting. But in the Queen's Theatre you will be performing to anything up to two thousand people; the performance you just gave would not be heard beyond the front rows of the pit, let alone in the back seats of the gods. Another thing, I write red-fire melodramas that require big let-it-rip style of acting. So try it again, throw caution to the wind and let it rip.'

'Give me a moment,' Shamus said and a flicker of annoyance flashed in his eyes. He bent his head put his fingers to his eyes and delivered his lines with great energy, power and movement.

'Much better, now we have something to work with,' Ira commented and turned the page in his script.

'What does Mr Allen mean by let-it-rip?' Jim asked Mick at the tea break.

'It's an acting technique Mr Allen uses to ensure that he gives a big performance. It's more difficult to enlarge a performance than to shrink one – the way of ensuring that you give a big performance is to let it rip during rehearsals.'

'But that would result in uncontrolled shouting and an undisciplined performance.'

'That's true, if that was all there was to the technique,' Mick replied tapping his nose with his index finger. 'Watch Ira rehearse. In early rehearsals he does everything big and then he pares back his actions and vocal performance. He does it, bit by bit until he is only letting-it-rip during key moments of the play. Then he sets his performance and does not deviate from it. Audiences think his performance is spontaneous; but it only looks and feels spontaneous. Watch how his every performance is exactly the same, move for move, gesture for gesture and note for note. He is always in control and he never changes anything; even during his most vitriolic tirade, Ira is in total command of his voice and body.'

Richard O'Hare and May Murnane were the first to rehearse after the tea break. Word perfect, May's performance looked like a finished performance. However Ira made a few suggestions, she accepted them, assimilated them into her performance and to Jim's surprise her performance improved. Richard O'Hare too was word perfect but had little idea or understanding of the character he had to portray. Ira rose and demonstrated to Richard how the character walked and talked and how the character stood. Richard stood and every now and then nodded and when Ira had finished, Richard said 'Thank you Ira, most helpful.'

Ira smiled and resumed his seat happy in the knowledge that Richard would never deviate from his instructions.

At one o'clock Jim gathered his courage, sat beside Fiona and asked her to lunch.

'Thank you,' Fiona replied. 'But Shamus has already asked me to join him. Perhaps you'd come along? I'm sure Shamus wouldn't mind.'

'No thanks, I don't think that's a good idea,' Jim replied in a sulk.

'Perhaps some other time,' said Fiona, with a playful smile at Jim.

Encouraged, Jim asked 'How about going with me to the Theatre Royal on Friday?'

Fiona's playful smile changed to one of kindness and Jim knew his invitation was about to be rejected.

'Jim you are a very handsome young man but you are a little young for me. I'm sure there are many girls your own age who would love to go to the theatre with you.'

'Shamus is not the man you think he is,' Jim blurted out like a bold child.

'Jim, I'm a big girl. I know what Shamus is like.'

'No you don't.' Jim's eyes snapped with a burning intensity. 'He doesn't like people. I don't think he even likes himself.'

'That's a strange thing for a friend to say.'

'I don't know if he is my friend. I know he hurts people, people, like you.'

THE ACTOR

'Who hurts people?' Shamus asked, suddenly appearing at Fiona's side.

'Harry Travers,' Fiona interjected, raising her eyebrows at Jim.

'You're right Fiona, Harry Travers is an absolute cad,' replied Shamus. 'Jim how about joining us for lunch?'

'No thank you – Mick wants me to do some stage management work.'

'I'll get my coat,' Fiona said. 'I won't be a minute.'

The moment Fiona was out of earshot, Shamus said to Jim 'I'm sorry about the way I spoke to you the other day. Can we go somewhere after rehearsal and straighten things out between us?' And when Jim did not answer, he said 'We'll just go for one drink. I won't keep you long.'

'Very well, I'll see you in O'Sullivan's Tearooms after rehearsal.'

'O'Sullivan's Tearooms?' Shamus replied loudly but when he saw the stony-faced look on Jim's face, he added 'O'Sullivan's Tearooms it is then.'

During the lunch break Ira was sitting at the piano playing some of the show's incidental music when Leslie Lawrence sat down beside him.

'J M Kerrigan from the Abbey has formed a company called The Film Company of Ireland.'

'Really,' Ira replied as he played.

'They are going to make a moving picture called *O'Neil of the Glen* and have offered me a part in it.' Ira looked reproachfully at Leslie. 'No need to worry Ira, it won't start shooting until summer, so it won't interfere with your productions.'

'Shooting?'

'Yes, that's what they call photographing a motion picture show. They aim the camera at the actors and shoot the film.'

Ira thought a moment.

'What is it like acting in a moving picture?'

'Very odd, there's no talking so it's a lot of dumb show. It's all a bit disconcerting.'

Ira stopped playing and leaned towards Leslie.

'Keep this under your hat,' Ira said confidentially. 'I've been approached by Norman Whitten of Killester Films to adapt my play

Tara's Hall into something called a photoplay. What do you think?'
'Was there talk of money?'
'A little.'
'A little talk or a little money?'
'Both,' replied Ira and the two men smiled.

After lunch Richard and Francis P were the first to rehearse. Richard delivered his first line, Francis responded but when Richard delivered his second line Francis P paused and whispered 'line'.

'What's that?' asked Ira. 'I missed that word, Francis?'
'Line,' Francis P replied more loudly.

Jim gave Francis the line, Francis called for the next line and the next line and every line after that.

When the scene was over a dejected Francis P and a contented Richard resumed their seats. Richard leaned back in his chair, looked at Francis P in amusement and said 'Did you even read the play?'

'I read the play,' Francis P replied, but his mind was already miles away.

After rehearsal Francis P approached Ira and said softly 'Sorry about not knowing my lines.'

'Don't worry about it,' Ira replied. 'I'm sure you'll be off book tomorrow. We're rehearsing Acts Three and Four.'

Francis nodded but made no attempt to move.

'Are you all right, Francis?' Ira asked. 'Is something wrong?'

'Rory, my eldest lad, was in Jacob's factory on Easter Monday. He never returned home. Then early this morning we got word that he's in an internment camp in Wales.'

'Good God, man why on earth didn't you tell me?' replied an astonished Ira. 'If I'd known I would never … How is Maureen?'

'Dreadful, she spends most of the time sobbing and blaming herself for having talked so much about her nationalist sympathies.'

'How long will Rory be in the camp?'

'We don't know. Could be a year, could be five years.' The two men stood in silence. Then Francis asked 'How is your boy?'

'He's out of immediate danger but they tell me there is a likelihood of a relapse.'

'Do we ever stop worrying about our children?'

'No we don't,' Ira replied.

As daylight faded Jim sat in the back drawing room of his home and read and reread the new scenes Ira had given him.

'Are you going to invite father to see your show?' Líla asked Jim as she took the seat opposite him.

'No, he has no interest in me or in what I do.'

'You're wrong, father loves you and has a great interest in what you do.'

Jim snorted his disagreement.

'You are so blind, but then it probably suits you to be so.' There was anger and hurt in Líla's voice.

'What are you talking about?'

'You say father doesn't care about you. Then tell me why did he travel to Kerry to see how you were?'

'Father didn't know where I was,' Jim eyes leapt from the script to Líla's face.

'Sorcha O'Donovan is Ciaran's aunt.'

'Ciaran wouldn't tell anyone where I was …'

'Ciaran's my boyfriend, he told me.'

'And you told father?' Jim said accusingly.

'Of course, I told father and we both went to Kerry and saw you.'

'You and father went to Kerry?'

'Yes and after the show father talked to Miss O'Donovan.'

'I bet he tried to get me fired,' snapped an offended Jim.

'He did not. He did the opposite. When Miss O'Donovan told him she was going to have to let you go because of some money problems they were experiencing father agreed to pay your wages.' An astonished Jim sat up in his chair. 'One other thing, while we're clearing the air, where do you think I got the money I gave you?'

'You said you took it from your savings.'

'Jim, I never saved a penny in my life, and you know it. Father gave me the money so I could give it to you. So don't ever say he doesn't care about you.' Líla bowed her head and when she looked at Jim again her eyes were full of tears. 'Now I've broken my promise to father, I told him I'd never tell you those things.'

Jim put his arms around his sister, held her and said reassuringly

'Father will never know you told me. But thank you for doing so.'

After dinner as Jim drew the curtains in the back drawing room Theo shuffled into the doorway. Jim looked at his father. Theo's once dark wavy hair was limp and grey, his moustache was long and uncared for and the once impeccably dressed man now wore clothes that were creased and soiled.

'Where's Líla?' Theo said as he looked around the room. 'I need to go to my room.'

'Hello father,' Jim crossed the room. 'Would you like me to take you upstairs?'

'Thank you. That would be nice,' Theo said. 'You know Jim, you look so very much like your mother.'

'Thank you. I was wondering father, would you like to come to the theatre to see the show when it opens?'

'Yes I would. Perhaps Michael, Líla and Mrs O'Neill might come too?'

'Yes father that would be nice.'

During the following week, Jim watched Ira and the other actors develop their characters. Ira's role in the play was Jerry the Tramp, the *Noble Brother* who went to prison to save his brother. To convey Jerry the Tramp's acceptance of life's disgraces and defeats, Ira developed an intense sadness and softness in his voice, he stooped his body to convey the man's broken spirit and he gave him a warm smile to convey his still positive outlook on life. All the time Ira was developing his own performance he gave each member of the acting company advice and help with their roles; not as much advice and help as each actor craved but enough for them to find their character and to think it was all their own creation.

As assistant stage manager Jim sat at the table with Ira and Mick. Jim watched how each actor built his or her performance. He observed how Leslie transformed his character from a broad stereotype to a finely shaded multi-layered person. He watched May and Maura develop their performances through endless discussion with Ira. He watched Francis P who hardly ever spoke but listened quietly to Ira's comments and used them to improve his performance. He watched how Ira worked Richard like a giant puppet giving him every gesture and movement

THE ACTOR

and he watched how Ira helped Shamus put the quiet intensity of the first rehearsal into the bigger performance needed for the large theatre. But he paid most attention to how Ira worked with Fiona.

'Your gestures and movement are suitably large and graceful but you need to give Nana a heart and a soul,' Ira said when Fiona asked for guidance. 'If you as an actress feel Nana's pain then the audience will too. If you hate Harry Travers then the audience will hate him. Let me play you the music that will accompany the last scene in Act One.'

Ira sat at the piano and played the threatening music that concluded the act. Suddenly he jumped to his feet and said 'When Harry Travers tells you that if you don't marry him he will destroy your adopted father's reputation, you have to fill the moment with so much dread and fear that the entire audience is with you. When you tell Harry Travers that you will marry him but never love him, stand erect, put both hands to your forehead and look away from the dreadful human being. Then hold that position during the tableaux and more importantly hold the emotion until the music finishes and the stage goes dark.'

Encouraged by the way Ira directed Fiona, Jim approached Ira and asked for his opinion of his acting. Ira rubbed his chin 'You sure you're ready for this? I usually wait until an actor has a more substantial role before I comment.'

'Tell me, Mr Allen,' Jim replied and braced himself.

'You may not like to hear what I have to say.'

'Tell me.'

'Very well. Your acting is good, but it's dishonest. You have fixed your performance before you've found the character. Your characterisation is a stereotype, that's the lazy way of acting and the audience will see it as such. A performance should only be finalised after a relentless examination of the text and of your own imagination. Only when you have found your character's soul can you reveal it to an audience. Does that make sense to you?'

'Yes sir, it does. I have much work to do.'

'Indeed you do.'

23

It was a cold, windy morning and a grim-faced Francis P alighted from the tram at College Green and walked trance-like up Great Brunswick St. As he passed the front entrance of the Queen's Theatre, Ira opened the foyer door and called to him.

'Francis come this way, it'll save you walking down the lane.'

Without acknowledging Ira, Francis P walked into the theatre foyer.

'Francis are you all right?' Ira asked as he closed the door and guided the actor to a seat next to the box office. 'Did something happen?'

Francis P's eyes half-focused on Ira and with the weary intensity of a beaten man he said 'Last night, just as we sat down to dinner four soldiers and three detectives came to my house and ransacked my home. When they didn't find guns or explosive they arrested young Eamon. I stood helpless and watched seven grown men drag my boy out of my home and throw him, like a sack of potatoes, into the back of a lorry. The boy is barely sixteen years of age.'

'Where is your son now?' Ira asked.

'They took him to Richmond Barracks for fingerprinting and questioning.' Francis P rubbed his eyes. 'Richmond Barracks is a terrible place, there's no proper sanitation, one bucket for thirty men. Maureen and the girls are distraught. My two sons, gone; Ira what am I to do?'

'Would you like to go home and be with Maureen and the girls?'
'No, I'm better off here.'
'I'm really very sorry …' But knowing the inadequacy of words, Ira said no more and both fathers sat in silence.

The wind blew stray bits of newspaper along the base of the walls of Trinity College and holding his hat on his head Jim hurried to the theatre. When he turned down the lane to the theatre's stage door a gush of piercingly cold wind whipped around him.

Leslie Lawrence paid the hansom cab driver and stepped on to the path in front of the theatre. The impeccably dressed actor buttoned the top button of his coat, settled his trilby on his head and with silver-topped cane in hand, strolled down the lane to the theatre's stage entrance.

'Archie's not answering the door?' Leslie called out when he saw Jim knocking on the stage door.

'No,' Jim replied. 'I knocked several times.'

Leslie pounded hard on the door with his cane.

'The beggar's asleep.'

The door groaned open and a groggy-eyed, unshaven, very hung-over Archie pulled open the door. 'What's all the racket about? Oh it's you, you're early.'

'Yes it's me but I'm not early,' Leslie shot back and poked the stage doorman's enlarged stomach with his cane. 'Too much Arthur Guinness, Archie, you're losing your boyish figure.'

'Ah, you're worse than the wife,' grunted the doorman.

'Archie I know your quest to drink Dublin dry has caused you to make sacrifices of personal beauty and agility but you still need to do your job. A little lax in opening the door; need to move faster.'

'What are you talking about?' slurred Archie. 'You're not the first to arrive. Mr Allen is already here, he's talking to Mr Coyle, the theatre manager.'

'Splendid. Now be a good man and put on the stage work-light, please,' Leslie said as he pushed past him. 'Is this your first time backstage?' he asked as Jim gazed in wonder around the dark theatre.

'Sort of,' Jim replied as the free-standing stage work-lights burst into life.

'Would you like me to give you a quick tour of the place?'

'Yes I would.'

Leslie walked briskly onto the stage, pointed his cane at a high stool and high table tucked behind the proscenium arch and said, 'That's the prompter's corner where you will be spending a lot your of time.' He strolled over to the side wall, tapped the ropes attached to a series of pulleys and said 'These ropes rise and lower curtains, backcloths and other pieces of scenery to and from the flies above the stage.' Pointing upwards, Leslie then identified the different types of stage lights and explained their uses. He strolled to the lighting box and demonstrated how the faders on the control box dimmed and brightened the stage lights. In the scene dock next to the stage, he pointed out the sets for the show and in the paint dock he identified the old sets that were waiting to be repainted or touched up for re-use. In the prop room, Leslie introduced Jim to the prop room mistress, the happy-faced Freddy McGuire, and he ended his tour by taking Jim to an L-shaped room filled with sofas and armchairs.

'This is the green room,' Leslie declared with a big theatrical gesture. 'It is a sanctuary, a place where actors congregate before, during and after a performance. They come here before their entrances or after their exits, and then after the show, sans makeup and costume, they meet here and they invite their guests and friends.

'Why is it called the green room, there's nothing green here?'

'There are lots of answers to that question,' replied Leslie. 'The one I like best goes like this; many actors experience nervousness or are nauseous before a performance. A person who feels nauseous is often said to look green so the green room is the place where the nervous actors wait.'

'There you are Leslie, I was wondering where you were,' Ira called out. 'Jim, Mick is looking for you, he's in the dressing room area. Leslie, come with me I have to arrange a few tricky things with Mr Adrian Coyle, the house manager, and I need a little moral support.'

When Jim arrived at the dressing rooms Mick was pinning small white cards to each door.

'Have a look, see if you can find your name,' Mick said with a big grin.

THE ACTOR

On dressing room 1, the one closest to the stage, were the names Ira Allen and May Murnane. On the card attached to dressing room 2 were the names Fiona and Maura, on dressing room 3 were the names Richard and Francis P and on dressing room 4, were the names Leslie Lawrence, Shamus McGovern and Jim Brevin. Jim stared at his name and pride welled within him.

'Come on Jim. I want to show you how to operate some of the theatrical machines we'll be using in the show.'

'Certainly.' He took another quick glimpse at his name and followed Mick across the stage.

'These are three machines I want you to operate; two treadwheels, one for wind and the other for storm effects and the sheets of zinc for thunder. Mick was demonstrating how to ripple the zinc sheets when Liam, the theatre's chief stagehand arrived and told Mick he had assembled the ten foot stage-waterfall machine that had arrived from London.

'Keep practicing with the thunder sheet,' Mick said to Jim as he left with Liam.

When Jim got tired rippling the thunder sheet he replaced it on the wall, walked onto the empty stage and stared into the huge elegant auditorium. He imagined the theatre full of people; seven hundred and fifty people in the pit, two hundred in the two tiers of enclosed boxes, four hundred in the lower gallery and six hundred in the upper gallery. He felt happy; he felt he had come home.

'Jim, the great Henry Irving once stood on that exact spot where you are standing,' Ira Allen bellowed from the back of the auditorium. 'Why don't we run your scenes and get familiar with the size and feel of the place?'

'But Maura's not here ...' His voiced echoed around the empty auditorium.

'I'll feed you Maura's lines. Let's start.'

Jim looked anew at the vast empty theatre and his stomach churned.

'I know it's a little daunting but there's a first time for everything,' Ira called out. 'Go off-stage and come back in character.'

Jim exited, re-entered and gave his first line 'I have a message for your master ...'

'I can't hear you, a little more projection please,' Ira bellowed from the rear of the stalls.

'I'm sorry!'

'Don't be sorry, just project your voice,' came the gruff reply.

Jim bellowed his lines. Near the end of the scene, Mick rushed on stage and declared with child-like delight 'Ira, the waterfall is wonderful, it works like a charm. Come have a look.'

'I'd love to.' Ira jumped up on stage and said to Jim 'You need to learn to project your voice. Shouting is a poor way to convey character and emotion; it's far too limiting.' To Mick, he said 'I'm really looking forward to seeing this waterfall in action.'

Stunned and deflated, Jim remained on stage and watched his idol walk into the darkness of the wings. Ira's words had cut through him like a knife. He could not believe how casually Ira had said his voice didn't carry through the theatre. He felt like an imposter who had no place on the stage.

'You don't look like a happy man,' Leslie's voice boomed as he walked on stage.

'Mr Allen said my voice doesn't carry in the theatre.'

'That's not what he said,' Leslie replied and placed his monocle against his eye. 'He said you need to learn to project your voice.'

'It's the same thing.'

'No it's not, Ira was giving you sound advice, if you'll pardon the pun.'

'No jokes, Leslie. Why did he have to say it in front of Mick? He could have said it to me privately.'

'Ah, it's your pride that's hurt.' Leslie nodded and Jim looked away. 'Have you any idea of the pressure Ira is under? He is risking his money and his reputation on this production. If Ira thought for one moment you were not a good actor and that your voice wouldn't carry in the theatre he would have replaced you, but he hasn't. Instead he wrote additional scenes for you, took the time to help you and even gave you some good advice and what do you do in return? You should be thanking the man not moping around like an offended child.'

'I'm not moping like an offended child,' Jim replied angrily. 'How do I project my voice?'

THE ACTOR

'If you continue to speak to me in that tone you can go to blazes.'

'Sorry, I apologise.'

'I accept your apology. Projecting your voice is not a particularly difficult thing to do. Think about an opera singer, how does he fill a vast opera theatre with his voice?' When Jim didn't respond Leslie continued. 'He does it by breathing properly. When you breathe in, you fill the lungs with air, your ribs expand and your diaphragm goes down.' Leslie patted the lower part of his stomach. 'When you breathe out you empty the lungs and your diaphragm comes up. Now here's the technique; if you speak as you empty your lungs the sound will be supported and will project to the back of the theatre. Let's practice, take in a big long breath. Now release the air slowly; don't push it.' Jim did as instructed. 'Now take another breath but this time when you breathe out I want you to speak your lines.'

Jim inhaled deeply and as he exhaled he spoke his lines. To his amazement his voice sounded bigger and louder and it reverberated around the theatre.

'Now all you have to do is practice speaking like that, until it becomes so natural that you don't even know you're doing it. Now I have to leave you.' Leslie removed a sheet of paper from his pocket. 'Ira asked me to check with the prop mistress to see if all the bits and pieces have arrived. Keep practicing, I'll be back shortly.'

Jim was taking his sixth deep breath when in the darkness of the wings he caught a blur of movement. He cocked his head and listened; he heard the rustle of clothes, then quick footsteps and murmuring voices. He heard a sudden intake of breath then a loud slap. He leaned forward and thought he could make out a young woman with her head in her hands.

'Fiona is that you?' he called into the darkness. 'Are you all right?'

'I'm fine,' Fiona replied.

'What's wrong?'

'You heard what she said,' Shamus's voice growled from the darkness.

'She doesn't sound fine.'

Shamus's scowling face appeared in a shaft of light. 'It's none of your business.'

'I'm all right,' Fiona whispered and the two shadows faded into the backstage blackness.

A buoyant May Murnane rushed across the stage, hurried into her dressing room and told her husband that their son had a good night's rest.

'That's wonderful,' Ira said, embracing his wife. 'Let's hope it's the first of many.'

'I needed this good news,' said May, holding on to her husband's arm. 'It is good news isn't it, Ira?'

'Yes it is good news love, very good news.'

An hour before noon, Ira gathered the cast into the green room and told them that the technical rehearsal with costumes, lights, set changes, special effects, sound effects and an orchestra of a piano, two violins, a bass, two trumpets and a drum, would begin at twelve. 'Now I want you all to listen carefully to Mick. He has something very important to say.'

Mick rose and in his most authoritative, stage-manager voice, said 'During the interval between Acts Two and Three a ten-foot waterfall machine will be positioned about a third of the way downstage. It is a big machine and when it is in full flow, one hundred and fifty gallons of water will be cascading over it every thirty seconds. Now a warning: keep as far as away from the machine, particularly when it is in operation. We don't want any accidents.'

'Won't it be very loud?' asked the ever wild-looking Richard.

'Yes it will be, especially when it's in full flow. However, it will only be in full flow for a minute or two and during that time the orchestra will be playing, so most of the noise will be masked. Then before the action resumes, that is before Fiona delivers her first line, the flow of water will be reduced and with it the noise. At the end of Act Three while the interval act is performing on stage, the waterfall will be placed against the rear wall of the stage. Please don't interfere with, explore or even examine the machine. Leave it alone. Richard do you hear me?'

'I beg your pardon, sir. I take exception to being singled out.'

'Do you Richard?' replied Mick. 'Well, I remember when you explored the erupting volcano. I don't want a repeat of that incident.'

'Natural curiosity,' barked red-faced Richard.

'Then keep your natural curiosity in check, the waterfall is an expensive machine and we are responsible for any damage to it while it is in our hire.'

'What kind of fool does he think I am?' Richard muttered to Leslie.
'I don't know.' Leslie replied. 'What kind of fool are you?'
'Feck off Lawrence,' snapped a very annoyed Richard. 'Feck off.'
'Richard, what did you just say?' asked an astounded Ira.
'Oh nothing, I was just explaining something to Leslie,' replied a crimson-faced Richard.
'Please. Don't use such coarse language, remember there are ladies present.' Ira said. 'I have just a few things to say and then I'll let you all go. For the next few hours I ask for your indulgence and forbearance while we go about our technical rehearsal. It's a complex show with many lights, sets, special effects and music elements that require co-ordination. When we have completed the technical rehearsal we will take a break and at eight o'clock we'll commence a full dress rehearsal including the intermission acts. Go get something to eat and be ready in costume for noon. It's going to be a long day.'

On stage during the technical rehearsal Shamus's and Fiona's performances suffered little from the tempest that was raging between them. But off stage, they didn't look at each other and went to great lengths to avoid any and all contact. When they had to stand together waiting to make an entrance, a black silence stood between them.

It took Mick, Liam, Jim and two apprentice stage hands twenty minutes to position and stabilise the waterfall machine for use in Act Three. From a distance, an unseen Richard in full stage costume observed the men and the machine. When Mick dropped a black backdrop behind the waterfall Richard slipped through the wings and began his examination of the machine. Behind the curtain Mick having made some last minute checks said to Jim 'Let's test it out.'

Richard, unable to satisfy his curiosity as to how the machine worked, stepped into the waterfall's empty trough. Mick opened the machine's control box, switched on the power and nodded to Jim. Richard found a small opening in the back wall of the waterfall and leaned up to peer through it. Jim opened the water release valve. Mick activated the pump and water thundered through the machine. Startled, Richard looked around, realised what was happening and was trying desperately to scramble out of the machine when the torrent of water cascaded over him.

'Jesus, Mary and Joseph!' he shrieked as he toppled backwards into the machine's trough.

'Do you hear someone screaming?' Mick shouted to Jim over the roar of the cascading water.

'Yes, it's coming from the stage!'

'Close the valve!' He ran onstage.

'This infernal contraption is a bloody menace to the acting profession,' a soaking-wet Richard growled as he clambered out of the trough and staggered off to his dressing room.

'If there is the slightest damage to the machine, Mr O'Hare, you'll pay for its repair,' Mick yelled after the dripping actor.

When Richard was out of sight Mick grinned at Jim and they both exploded in laughter.

After four hours of stop-start rehearsing, Fiona stood grey-faced by the prompter's table, awaiting a stage entrance.

'How are you holding up?' Jim whispered to her.

'I'm well and I don't want to talk about what happened.' Fiona drew away from the prompter's table. 'Why are you looking at me like that?'

'He hit you, didn't he?' Jim whispered.

'No,' she said. 'I hit him.'

'You hit him?'

'Yes, I heard he was out with another girl last night and when I confronted him about it he laughed at me.'

Fiona's eyes welled with tears and Jim put his arms around her.

At the end of the technical rehearsal Mick called the cast and crew together. While he was talking, Archie, the stage doorman informed May that she had a phone call.

Ira glanced after his wife. 'Everyone, be back by half past seven, ready for an eight o'clock start. We will run the play from the top. I want everyone in full costume. We will only stop the rehearsal if absolutely necessary. Now go and get something to eat and be back on time.'

Ira and Leslie strolled to their dressing rooms. 'I had a little chat with Richard about the waterfall.' Ira paused a moment. 'It's very difficult to have a conversation with the man. He keeps changing the subject, he can be very confusing.'

'Talking to Richard is like been beaten over the head with a very large feather. It won't hurt you but it will drive you insane.' Leslie lowered his voice. 'Why do you continue to employ the man?'

'He's an old friend, he has a good singing voice and audiences love him.'

'And what does that say about their critical faculties?'

Ira took a long look at Leslie. 'I don't know which is worse, Richard or you.'

'At least I don't play in waterfalls.'

'I've often wondered what you do play at, particularly when you go to London.'

'Nothing mysterious. I visit my sister, Grace.'

'Your sister does not live in London, she lives in Midlands,' Ira said, closed his dressing room door and left Leslie standing in the corridor.

The instant Ira entered the dressing room he knew something was wrong. May was sitting in her street clothes trying hard not to cry.

'What's wrong?'

'He took a bad turn,' she replied. 'I have to go to the hospital, right away.'

Ira's hand went to his forehead. 'I'll go with you. I'll cancel the dress rehearsal. We'll open the show a day late.'

'No Ira, you'll do no such thing. All our money, every penny we have is invested in the show. You've even taken a loan against our home.' May got to her feet. 'If we open a day late we'll lose two performances. You must go ahead with the dress rehearsal; we cannot afford not to. I'll go to the hospital alone, join me after the rehearsal.'

'May, I don't have the heart for a dress rehearsal. I want to be with my son.'

'*Make* the heart for it,' May said harshly. 'I do it, all the time.'

Ira put his arm around his upset wife.

'May. You're such a strong woman. The moment the dress rehearsal is over I'll be on my way to the hospital.'

Ira kissed his wife, walked her to the front of the theatre, hailed a hansom cab and May set off alone to see her ailing son in the sanatorium in the Phoenix Park.

At eight sharp the dress rehearsal began. Maura read May's lines and whenever May and Maura's characters were on stage together Jim read May's lines. In the intermission between the first and second act, as the Lord Edward Brass Band was performing a selection of Irish melodies, Fiona approached Shamus and asked if they could talk.

'Go ahead, talk,' Shamus replied sharply.

'Shamus, I'm sorry I hit you but you were being awful to me.'

'I accept your apology,' Shamus said and began to walk away. Fiona touched his arm.

'Shamus, why are you breaking up with me?'

'Breaking up?' Shamus replied dismissively. 'I don't know what you're talking about, we were never together.'

'Now you're being a bastard.'

'C'est la vie,' Shamus replied with a shrug of his shoulders and walked away.

'Is your family coming to the show?' Leslie asked Jim in the dressing room after the dress rehearsal.

'Yes they are, on the second night. Do you think I could bring them backstage to meet the cast?'

'Take them to the green room, it's where all the best people meet.'

'I don't know what I did to annoy Shamus so much,' Fiona said to Jim as she fumbled with her gloves in the stage-door porch.

'It's not what you did. Shamus is the problem.' Jim placed his arm around Fiona and kissed her on the cheek. 'Come, I'll walk you home.'

Unseen dark clouds masked the stars as Jim walked Fiona across Sackville Bridge. The air was cold and damp and the ruins of the once glorious buildings of Sackville Street stood like giant tombstones in a desolate cemetery. In silence, Fiona and Jim walked past the burned out remains of Clery's building, the General Post Office and the Gresham Hotel. When they reached Fiona's home in Dorset Street, Jim took her hand and said 'Fiona, I …'

'I know you tried to warn me about Shamus,' Fiona interrupted. And as she let go his hand, she added 'I thought I could be someone special to him.'

'You're special to me,' Jim said.

'Jim, please don't. It's Shamus I want.'

THE ACTOR

Jim forced a smile. Fiona and he could never be anything more than friends.

24

Opening night and the nervous anticipation that suffused the dressing rooms and backstage areas of the Queen's Theatre created a quiet, forced calm. Richard O'Hare sat in his dressing room, head bowed, mouthing his lines, Leslie Lawrence paced and thought about the work ahead, Maura Sweeney performed vocal warm-up exercises in the green room and sitting alone in her dressing room Fiona Whelan read her script. Across the corridor May and Ira Allen talked about their son and a very nervous but excited Jim went about his stage management duties.

Half an hour before curtain time Ira stopped talking to his wife, manufactured a smile and visited each actor in the company. He personally thanked each of them for his or her hard work; to some he added a word of encouragement, to others he counselled calmness.

'How are you Francis?' Ira asked when he met his colleague in the corridor.

Francis P smiled and with the moist eyes of a happy man said 'Eamon came home this afternoon. The authorities released him without charge. He was tired and hungry but otherwise he was well. Maureen and the girls are ecstatic. I myself am ... beside myself.'

'Good, you deserved some good news.'

'How is your boy?' Francis P asked softly.

THE ACTOR

'Improving, every day is a little victory. Francis, have a good show.'

'How are you tonight?' Ira said to Richard when he greeted him in his dressing room.

'I hate opening nights,' Richard said with a sigh. 'I don't know why I continue to punish myself like this.'

Ira smiled, tapped Richard on the shoulder. 'Break a leg,' he said.

The street outside was thick with theatregoers. A queue of people spilled from the box office, down the theatre steps and out on to Brunswick Street. When the box office closed, one hundred and sixty people were disappointed. Inside, the audience excitement was palpable; people flooded into aisles, hurriedly removed their overcoats and hats and by curtain time the theatre was jammed to the rafters.

After making a last minute check on the three theatrical machines he had to operate, a nervous Jim took his place in the prompter's corner. Stagehands made final checks on the sets and lights. Jim opened the prompt script. Mick called for beginners and Maura and Leslie took their places on either side of the stage. Ira placed his hand on Jim's shoulder and said 'Jim, you are a great addition to the company. Have a good show.'

Mick gave a signal and the orchestra played the specially commissioned overture. The theatre lights dimmed, the stagehands pulled on the main curtain ropes, the curtain rose and row upon row of expectant faces in the auditorium were lit up by the light from the stage.

Maura Sweeney made her entrance, delivered her opening monologue and sang her first song. Sitting in the prompter's corner Jim's finger and mind followed every word Maura uttered or sang. The instant Ira Allen walked on stage the theatre went silent and the audience gave rapt attention to everything the actor said and did. When Ira lowered his voice the audience as one leaned forward not to miss a syllable. When he yearned for his long lost daughter, the audience sighed and when he laughed the audience joined him in laughter.

Shamus strolled confidently on stage, delivered his opening monologue and the audience immediately identified Travers as the dishonest, manipulative conniving villain of the night. When Travers slithered up to the distraught heroine Nana and tried to court her, the audience booed and hissed him. At the end of Act One when he gave

Nana the ultimatum, that she marry him or have her father exposed as a thief, a tall man in the pit jumped to his feet, waved his hat in the air and shouted 'You scoundrel! Nana alanna, my heart bleeds for you, he's a deceitful person do not believe him, he will betray you!'

'Yes he will,' shouted a scrawny man in the dress circle. 'The man is a cad, he's not good enough to lick your boots.'

Then the audience began to stomp and boo.

At end of the act, the cast formed a tableaux, the lights dimmed and the audience applauded loudly. Then in a blaze of light the Lord Edward Brass Band marched on stage and played the traditional air *Clare's Dragoons*. At the end of the song Richard O'Hare strolled on stage, a canvas cloth dropped down behind him with words of the *Wearing of the Green* written on it and standing in a bright beam of limelight Richard led the audience in a sing-along. At the end of the song a second canvas dropped from above, this time with the words of *It's a Long Way to Tipperary*, and again Richard led the audience in song.

The curtain rose for Act Two. Jim stood in the wings awaiting his first entrance; adrenaline surged through his body, his skin tingled, his mouth dried and his heart thumped. He heard his cue, walked on stage and eighteen hundred pairs of eyes locked on him. He stood in the bright glare of the lights, delivered his lines in a clear precise voice and the audience listened attentively to him. It was his comic scene and when Rose the maid, made an attempt to kiss him he bolted upstage and the audience howled with laughter. When he tripped, fell down the stairs and ended up at Rose's feet, the audience screeched in merriment but when Jim slid under the garden seat to avoid another of Rose's attempted kisses a large woman in a floral pattered dress called out 'Give her a kiss' and a gaunt toothless man in a bowler hat shouted 'I'll do it for you, if you like.'

After the scene, an exhilarated Jim resumed his seat in the prompter's corner. A passing Ira tipped him on the shoulder and whispered 'Jim, you have a natural stage technique and excellent comic timing. Well done. A bigger part in the next production is in order.'

Blushing with pride, Jim turned the page in the prompt book.

The play progressed and in the tableaux at the end of the Act Two, when Shamus as Travers attempted to kiss Nana the audience booed and hissed and shouted. Jim watched from his prompter's corner, aware that Fiona was experiencing the same emotion as that of her on-stage character. During the next intermission, Mick, Jim and the two stagehands moved the enormous waterfall into position. The moment the orchestra started the second-half overture, Mick started the water pump, Jim opened the valve and the curtain rose. When the audience saw the cascading waterfall, they gasped with delight and then to a person, rose from their seats and applauded loudly.

After the tableaux at the end of the next act, a trio of traditional musicians marched on stage and twenty four members of the Keogh School of Irish Dancing performed a selection of jigs and reels.

At the end of the play, when the villain received his just desserts, the audience applauded with delight. When father and daughter were reunited the ladies in the audience sobbed and when all threats to the central characters were removed the audience hollered and hooted.

The final curtain fell, the cast positioned themselves for their curtain call, the curtain rose and the audience jumped to their feet and applauded thunderously. Jim stood and listened to the rising applause that greeted Ira as he strolled on stage for his personal curtain call. Ira took May's hand, the two actors smiled at each other and then the entire company bowed to the cheering audience.

The following afternoon, sitting in the green room between performances, Leslie Lawrence read aloud the review from the morning newspaper.

> *Mr Allen's play A Noble Brother is a fine play full of comic invention and pithy dialogue with scenes that will make your throat dry and your eyes fill with sudden tears. As a playwright, Mr Allen draws his characters naturally and colours them with broad, bold brush strokes. His dialogue is witty and convincing and the audience followed the play's many twists and turns with deepest interest.*
>
> *The cast was uniformly excellent. The beautiful Miss May Murnane strikes the right note as the distraught mother, Miss Maura Sweeney's sweet voice thrills and the always reliable Mr Leslie Lawrence is right on form. The two newcomers to the company Miss Fiona Whelan and Mr Jim Brevin show great promise but the evening belongs to Mr Shamus McGovern and Mr Ira Allen.*

THE ACTOR

> *Mr McGovern's villain is beyond praise. Every time he made an entrance he caused such a pandemonium of discordant booing and hissing that one could scarcely hear one's thoughts. But it was Mr Ira Allen who dominated the evening; charismatic as ever, Mr Allen's performance was large yet intimate and full of believable emotion and feeling. Finally, the sets and the stage effects were first class, particularly the enormous waterfall. It is an astonishing machine and simply the best I have seen on the Dublin stage in years.*
> John Olive, critic in residence.

Theo, Michael, Líla and Mrs O'Neill attended the show on Tuesday night. When the final curtain fell Líla and Mrs O'Neill jumped to their feet and applauded enthusiastically and Theo and Michael remained seated and applauded politely. While Líla and Mrs O'Neill were putting on their coats, Michael leaned over to his father and said 'I don't understand why Jim wants to be an actor. It's all a mystery to me.'

'I don't understand either,' replied Theo. 'But then I didn't understand many things about your mother and to my eternal shame I never tried.' Michael looked quizzically at his father. 'Son, there are many ways of living life, just accept that Jim has chosen a different way than you. Not better nor worse, just different.'

In the porch of the stage door, a small nervous man in a beautifully tailored suit, a white-winged collared shirt, bright bow tie and a new bowler hat handed Archie a bouquet of flowers and asked that they be presented to 'the most beautiful actress in the play.'

'Would you be wanting a reply?' slurred the semi-inebriated Archie.

'Yes sir, I shall wait.'

Archie knocked on the dressing room door and handed the flowers to a delighted May.

'I'm to wait for a reply,' Archie announced trying to sound sober.

May opened the attached note, read it and smiled to herself.

'Archie, I'll send word out in a moment.'

May walked across the corridor to Fiona and Maura's dressing room, showed them the bouquet of flowers and read them the words on the card.

I would be delighted if you would consent to have tea with me in Bewley's

THE ACTOR

Oriental Cafe in Grafton Street tomorrow at 3pm.
   Yours in anticipation,
   Cedric O'Connor
'What do you think Maura?'
'What do I think, what does Ira think?' Maura replied her eyes almost exploding with devilment.
'It's nothing to do with Ira, the note's not addressed to him.' May winked at Fiona and added 'Should I go Maura?'
'I don't know. But if it were me I'd be tempted to have a look,' Maura replied and smiled at the thought of being so forward.
'Well then Maura, we know where you'll be tomorrow afternoon,' May said and presented Maura with the bouquet of flowers. 'The flowers are for you.'
'Let me see that card?' blustered Maura.
'I think you should go, Maura,' Fiona said and for the first time that day she smiled.
When the little man in the porch was informed that the reply was yes, he politely thanked Archie and as he walked out of the theatre he felt six foot tall.
Sitting in the green room after the show, Líla watched each actor as he or she walked into the room. When Shamus arrived, Líla stood erect hoping he might see her and talk to her but he walked straight past her and a disappointed Líla watched the tall, handsome actor shake hands with the actor-playwright J P Burke. Michael was perplexed by everything he saw and heard and secretly wished he was anywhere else. Mrs O'Neill was amused by all that was happening around her and Theo sat with his arms folded; the smell of the greasepaint and the exaggerated familiarity of the actors made him feel uneasy.
When Jim finally arrived, Líla ran to him, embraced him and congratulated him loudly. Theo and Michael were more restrained, they shook his hand politely. When Ira arrived, Jim introduced his family and while Ira talked to Theo, Michael touched Jim on the elbow and said 'You really like doing this play thing?'
'Yes I do.'
'But what about the family business?'
'Michael, I told you, the business is not for me but I hope you'll give

me a job whenever I'm not working in the theatre.'

'Yes of course I will,' Michael replied and scratched his head in wonder.

The following afternoon at a quarter to three, a nervous Maura Sweeney alighted from the tram at Nassau Street and walked to the bottom of Grafton Street. She felt a little guilty and unfaithful. Only two months ago, the childless Maura had removed the small black diamond cloth of mourning from the sleeve of her overcoat; on that day Derek her late husband had been dead for two long years.

Maura glanced at the clock above Weir's the jewellers and a voice in her head spoke to her. 'What in God's name are you doing, meeting a man at your age? Go home you silly woman.' But a second voice, a softer voice, Derek's voice, whispered to her 'Maura you've mourned long enough; it's time to start living again.'

The actress adjusted the fox fur that draped around her shoulders and wove her way through the shoppers, soldiers and street traders of Dublin's most fashionable street. Horse-drawn carriages and automobiles travelled its length. Elegant ladies with huge broad-brimmed hats walked with their formally dressed gentlemen along the footpaths while street musicians played Irish tunes for the entertainment of all.

A carriage pulled by two groomed and plumed white horses stopped outside Brown Thomas department store and while two uniformed servants placed large boxes in the carriage Maura glimpsed her reflection in the store's window. The mocking voice in her head chided her again 'Look at you, mutton dressed as lamb. Who do you think you are?' But Derek's comforting voice said 'You look lovely Maura, just lovely.'

Maura approached the Tutankhamen's Tomb inspired entrance to Bewley's Oriental Cafe and Archie, the stage doorman's description of her admirer flashed into her mind.

'He's a small twerp of a man, a dressed-up nothing, if you ask my opinion,' he had said.

'I didn't ask you for your opinion,' she remembered replying curtly. 'I merely asked you to describe the man.'

Maura pushed on the door, stepped into the cafe's exotic vestibule, removed her kid gloves and the dapperly dressed, diminutive Cedric O'Connor made himself known to her. The cafe manager escorted

Maura and her admirer to a table beneath the Harry Clark stained glass window in the main lounge. Smiling with delight, Cedric told Maura that he had seen her many times on stage and that it had taken him six months to pluck up the courage to send her the flowers. He also told her he was a master tailor and that he had a shop in Dame Street that employed five tailors and five apprentices. Maura sat and listened, happy to share an hour with a man who thought of her as a woman.

On Tuesday, Jim was sitting in his dressing room between performances when he saw Shamus slip into Fiona's dressing room and, through the open doorway, he overheard bits of their strained tense conversation.

'You've got to stop bothering me …'
'What are you talking about?'
'Our little fling.'
'It was never a little fling to me.'
'Whatever you call it, it's over.'
'But I love you.'
'Don't talk that rubbish to me.'
'Shamus, please …'
'I want you to leave me alone.'
'Shamus, I love you.'
'Just leave me alone.'

Fiona's dressing room door slammed. Shamus stormed into the dressing room, glared at Jim and said 'Let this be a warning to you, never shit on your own doorstep.'

During the rest of the week Shamus's outbursts became more frequent and unkind and Jim deliberately spent as little time as he could in his company.

25

As the day faded, an excited Jim arrived at the corner of Great Victoria Street and Glengall Street and gazed on the imposing oriental-style façade of Belfast's Grand Opera House. He watched a river of carts, automobiles and horse drawn trams flow past the theatre. He smiled when he saw eight bowler-hatted men in long coats, push eight, five-foot-high sandwich boards, mounted on what looked like bicycle wheels down the street. Each of the bouncing billboards carried the same message, *To-night and all this week at The Grand Opera House! Ira Allen's comic melodrama, A Noble Brother.*

The clattering of boots snapped Jim out of his thoughts. A nervous looking shop assistant in an ill-fitting suit opened the newspaper billboards outside the shop, slid a headlines poster into each of them and limped back into the newsagents. Jim read the posters *DUBLIN CITY QUIET, ALL REBELS SURRENDERED, SENSATIONAL CONNECTION FOUND BETWEEN GERMANY AND THE REBELS, GERMAN GOLD BACKED SEDITION MONGERS.*

Jim thought about his friend Brian Ahearn, bowed his head and walked across the street to the theatre.

On the first night of the company's residency in Belfast the theatre was only half full and the audience was unresponsive. However at the end of the first act, when the Belfast Firemen's Brass Band played a melody of Ulster songs, the audience warmed and applauded the music makers loudly. The audience then relaxed, forgot that the company was from Dublin and involved themselves in the play. When the final curtain fell, the happy audience applauded enthusiastically. The second night's audience was larger and applauded more loudly and longer and by the third night Booked Out signs hung on all entrances to the theatre.

The Wednesday night sky was pitch-black and rain was falling hard when Jim said goodnight to the stage doorman. Briskly walking along the rain-drenched footpath he stopped when he heard sobbing. Slouched in a shop doorway and lit by a harsh street light was a white-faced, weeping Fiona.

'What happened?' Jim asked as he slipped off his overcoat and placed it around Fiona's shaking shoulders.

'Shamus picked up a girl, right in front of me. She asked him for his autograph and he asked her to go with him for a drink.' Fiona shook her head frantically in disbelief. 'It was so insulting, he left me standing there like I was nothing. How could he do that?'

Jim placed his arms around his weeping friend. 'Come on, I'll walk you to your digs.'

'I don't want to go to my digs. I want to know what I did wrong.'

'You did nothing wrong.'

After the final curtain on Saturday night Jim, Mick and the stagehands dismantled the waterfall machine, crated it and prepared it for shipment back to London.

'Why aren't we taking the waterfall on the rest of the tour?' Jim asked as they packed the waterfall's pump into a separate protective crate.

'The machine was only available for two weeks and besides because of the troubles Belfast is one of the few ports in Ireland that can ship crates to London.' Mick nodded at the small bag in Jim's hand. 'What you got there?'

'Boiled sweets, I've got a bit of a sore throat, thought they might help,' Jim replied. He had become aware of the irritation in his throat a few days earlier and had started sucking on sweets but they were having little effect.

THE ACTOR

*

When the Ira Allen Company of Irish Players was on tour, Ira supervised everything. He organised the theatres, the get-ins and the get-outs and the transportation of the set, costumes and actors. He arranged the cleaning of the costumes, the booking of the interval acts and even the digs where the actors stayed. His attention to matters financial was even more meticulous. He kept detailed accounts of all monies spent and received. During each performance, a few minutes before the intermission, he would drape his overcoat over his costume, visit the box office and ask about the takings and why particular seats or rows of seats were vacant.

The second stop on the company's tour was in one of the oldest town in Ireland, Dundalk.

'I dislike Dundalk,' Leslie said as they checked into the guesthouse in Clanbrassil Street. 'It's a grey place, too much industry, too little culture.'

'I disagree,' Richard interjected as he scribbled his name in the guesthouse register. 'Dundalk is filled with history and culture. Its history goes back to 3,500 BC, nearby is the Proleek Dolmen and Dundalk is reputed to be birthplace of the mythical warrior Cu Chulainn.' Richard gave these facts as if he was a schoolteacher talking to wayward students.

But Jim wasn't thinking about Cu Chulainn, Proleek Dolmen or anything to do with Celtic Ireland; his mind was locked into the present. He was worried about Fiona, who had grown moody and quiet, and his throat was now causing him problems on stage.

When Francis P entered the theatre in Dundalk a few hours before ShowTime he heard Jim coughing and immediately approached him.

'Your cough, it's getting worse,' the diminutive actor stated. 'What are you doing about it?

'Richard suggested I gargle with hot tea and honey,' Jim replied. 'I think its helping.'

'Yes tea and honey, very soothing on the throat but it won't stop you straining your vocal cords.'

'Straining my vocal cords? I don't shout, I project my voice.'

'Come with me.'

Jim and Francis' heels echoed on the bare floorboards of the empty stage.

'I'm going into the auditorium and I want you to whisper your longest speech to me. I want to understand every word you say, so you'll need to over articulate.'

Francis P jumped off the stage, walked to the back of the auditorium and sat.

'Begin when you're ready,' Francis P called out.

Jim began whispering his longest speech but halfway through the speech he stopped; he had run out of breath. 'This doesn't usually happen,' Jim explained and started to cough.

'Yes it does usually happen,' bellowed Francis P from the back of the theatre. 'You just didn't notice it. Another thing you didn't notice, when you were running out of breath you gulped in air and then started to shout and that's where the problem lies. Breath control or rather the lack of it is your problem. When you were rehearsing your speeches did you break them into breaths?' Jim shook his head. 'You always need to plan your follow breaths, otherwise you'll damage your vocal cords. Before the next performance, sit down with your script and plan the precise places where you are going to take your follow breaths. In that way you won't run out of breath and you won't strain your vocal cords.'

'Why did you get me to whisper my speech?' Jim inquired when Francis P re-joined him on stage.

'Because stage whispering puts more demands on breath control than any amount of hollering or bellowing,' Francis replied and as he disappeared into the wings called out 'keep gargling with the tea and honey.'

Jim reviewed his speeches, planned where he would take follow breaths, practiced them and within a few days his throat was feeling a lot better.

In the second act of *A Noble Brother*, Richard's character Detective Furlong was required to write down an important piece of information. Because Richard refused to wear his spectacles on stage, he arranged for Jim to leave a red pencil on a sheet of white paper on the table, so that he could find it easily. On the Tuesday, Jim placed the red pencil on the paper as usual, but during the performance, Richard knocked against the corner of the table and, unseen by him, the pencil rolled to the floor. Searching for the pencil Richard patted the desk top and when he didn't find it he called out to Leslie 'Tell me again and I'll write it down later.'

THE ACTOR

Jim looked up from his prompter's script – that was a new line.

'Use the pencil, it's right there,' retorted Leslie.

Another new line? Jim jumped off his prompter's stool and looked on stage.

'There is no bloody pencil,' Richard snapped.

Leslie strolled over, picked the pencil off the floor and handed it to Richard. Jim sighed with relief. 'Need to get some glasses, dear boy,' Leslie remarked with a wink and the audience guffawed.

'You are a fool,' Richard roared at Jim in the wings immediately after the play. 'You're an idiot. I'll have your job for this, you incompetent amateur.'

'That's no way to speak to anyone,' cried Leslie, rushing to his defence. 'It's not his fault you're too vain to wear your glasses on stage.'

'The boy's not doing his job. I'm going to speak to Ira about this. I will not be embarrassed by an idiot.' Richard marched off towards Ira's dressing room.

'Leave this to me!' Leslie charged after him, with an anxious Jim at his heels.

'Gentlemen, we'll talk about this later,' Ira shouted over the two battling actors as they each simultaneously pleaded their case. 'Try to behave like professionals. Go to your dressing rooms and I'll talk to each of you tomorrow.' He pointed to his door and Richard and Leslie stormed out but as Jim went to follow them, Ira detained him and closed the door again. Seconds ticked by like hours. Ira placed his hand on Jim's shoulder and said 'Richard had no right to speak to you the way he did. I apologise for him. It won't happen again.'

'It doesn't matter sir,' replied a greatly relieved Jim.

'Oh but it does matter. It's a question of respect and respect always matters.'

The air was cool and the silence of the night was broken by the soft patter of Jim and Fiona's footsteps as he walked her home after the show.

'You don't have to walk me all the way,' Fiona said as they crossed Glengall Street.

Jim settled his wide-brimmed hat on his head and buttoned up his long coat.

– 214 –

THE ACTOR

'You were very quiet to-night,' he said.
'I never really knew Shamus, did I?'
'Nobody knows Shamus. I don't think he even knows himself.'
'You tried to warn me. But I didn't believe you.' Fiona took Jim's arm and said with great determination. 'I'm going to fight back. I'm not going to let him destroy me.'

The following afternoon, Jim put a small amount of spirit glue on one side of the pencil. He shook the table and the pencil remained stuck to the paper. Then he went to the green room to tell Richard about his inventive solution to their problem.

The moment he walked in, Richard jumped to his feet, coughed twice and said loudly and formally 'I would like to take this opportunity to publicly apologise to you for the way I spoke to you last night.' Everyone in the green room stopped talking and looked at Jim. 'You are certainly not an idiot. You are a fine young professional. I am sorry I lost the head. It won't happen again.'

'There's no need to apologise,' Jim replied, squirming with embarrassment and wishing he was back in his prompter's corner.

'There certainly is a need,' Richard replied loudly. 'The question is, do you accept it?'

'Yes I do,' muttered a red-faced Jim.

'Good, I hope we will become good friends.'

He extended his hand to a mortified Jim.

While Richard was making his public apology Leslie slipped out of the green room, went on stage, removed the sheet of paper with the pencil glued to it and stuffed it into the desk drawer. From his inside pocket, he took a sheet of paper on which was drawn a very realistic red pencil and left it on the desk.

During their scene together, when Richard attempted to pick up the pencil from the desk, his fingers slid over the image. He looked down, saw what he thought was the pencil and again tried to lift it. Again his fingers found nothing. Sweat oozed from the pores on his forehead. His hands became sweaty and his heart thumped in his chest. Was he going blind or mad? He patted the desk again but by this time Leslie was by his side, handing him a fountain pen and saying 'This might be of use to you, old boy.'

When the scene concluded, a baffled Richard left the stage and a smirking Leslie pocketed the illustration of the pencil, and replaced it with the actual pencil, still glued to the original paper. The moment the intermission arrived, Richard wearing his steel-rimmed glasses scurried on stage, checked the pencil and retired to his dressing room thinking he was going insane.

In the green room after the show Fiona tried to be her normal self. She had a talk with May about her son in hospital, she loaned Leslie her newspaper and was having a chat with Maura when Shamus walked past her and said a pointed 'Hello' to Maura. Maura nodded to Shamus and resumed her conversation with Fiona. Shamus dropped on to one of the sofas, picked up a magazine and called out 'Fiona, be a good girl and make me a cup of tea. I'm parched.'

'Can't you see I'm talking to Maura?' Fiona replied politely.

Shamus shot a look at Fiona, then smiled a fake smile.

'No need to be so touchy, I can make my own tea.'

'Good, be a good boy and make one for me and Maura too, will you?' replied Fiona.

Shamus' jaws went rigid.

'On second thoughts I don't need tea,' he snapped and stormed out of the room.

'Steady,' Maura said as she placed her hand on Fiona's trembling hand. 'Let him go.'

'Richard asked me if he could wear his glasses on stage,' Ira said to Leslie as they were leaving the theatre.

'Really?' Leslie replied with a smirk. 'What did you say to him?'

'I told him not to bother because you wouldn't be playing that pencil trick on him again.' Ira's voice was implacably cold.

Leslie looked taken aback, then recovered. 'He was very disrespectful to Jim. I thought I'd teach him a lesson.'

'How can you ask Richard to show respect for Jim if you don't show respect for Richard? Don't take matters into your own hands again. I manage this company.'

'Very well, you know best,' Leslie replied sarcastically.

'Yes Leslie,' Ira said. 'I *do* know best.'

THE ACTOR

Jim enjoyed talking to Francis P. He enjoyed Francis's encyclopaedic knowledge of the theatre, his intelligence, his quick mind and the perceptive and challenging way he thought about the theatre and the world around him.

'You shouldn't be wasting your time on that rubbish,' Francis P said to Jim when he saw him reading a penny novel. 'You should be reading the great plays of Shakespeare, Marlow and Johnson.'

'I studied them in school,' Jim replied without taking his eyes out of his penny novel. 'I didn't like them.'

'And that schoolboy was so wise that he still informs what you read and how you challenge yourself.' Francis P placed his hand over the page Jim was reading. 'How can you be great if you don't know what greatness is? You need to read modern plays. Chekhov, Ibsen and Strindberg have a lot of interesting things to say and they say it in new and innovative ways.'

'And why would that be of interest to me?' Jim asked petulantly.

'What will you do when melodrama goes out of fashion? Perform your penny novels?'

Francis P walked away and an astounded Jim looked after the actor as if he had just predicted the end of his world.

On the company's last night in Dundalk, after Leslie had delivered his witty monologue in Act Three, he went to open the stage door and the doorknob came off in his hand. Now he was stuck with no exit. The audience fell silent, waiting to see what he would do. He gave the door a quick bang to free it, but the door remained firmly closed. Improvising a monologue about poor workmanship, he strolled down to the prompt corner and whispered, 'For God's sake Jim go to a blackout, so I can get off stage.'

Nothing happened. Leslie stuck his head into the wings. The prompter's corner was empty – Jim had gone to change into costume for his next scene. The audience started to titter and a small fat bald man with a long black beard jumped to his feet and hollered 'You're in a bit of a pickle now sir, what are you going to do?'

The audience hooted. Leslie walked to the front of the stage, smiled broadly at the bearded man and said 'I always enter a room by the door but sometimes I enjoy leaving by the window.' He then turned upstage, opened the window and to wild cheering and applause, climbed out.

A few minutes later, Leslie sat before his dressing room mirror and exhaled deeply. On the table were two small screws and a white card on which was written '*Let's call it even*'.

Leslie burst out laughing.

26

On the morning Jim and the company arrived in the inland fishing town of Fermoy, it was crowded with hundreds and hundreds of people from Dublin, Cork and every county in Ireland. It was Fermoy's annual regatta week and the place was ablaze with colour and excitement. Every flower, plant and tree was dressed in its summer display of colour. Red and white bunting hung along the Blackwater River. Ruddy-faced rowers frowned in concentration as their boats skimmed along the river. Men in straw boaters and striped blazers and women in long pretty dresses holding lace-trimmed parasols cheered on the boating contestants. Behind the cheering spectators, young men with bottles of beer in hand ran along the path parallel to the river shouting and cheering their teams. Near the finishing line, houseboats laden with spectators bobbed up and down on the river and under an oak tree a banjo player played rousing tunes and melodies.

The streets of the town were festooned with red and white flags and the market place was alive with street entertainers, carnival rides and side-shows. An organ grinder ground out his music, fire-eaters, contortionists and sword swallowers performed their acts of skill and daring and excited children badgered their parents for coins to play on the carnival rides and games of chance.

Mick and his crew toiled all afternoon to prepare the town's theatre for the evening's show. The actors and musicians checked into their digs while Ira rehearsed with the local brass band and members of the Dillon Dance School. The afternoon dissolved into evening and when the boat races had concluded revellers went in search of places to eat or drink.

That night the theatre was crammed to the rafters.

After the show as Jim was attaching his shirt collar, Mick stuck his head around the door and said 'Two people have asked if you would join them in Grand Hotel for a little chat.'

'Did you get the name?'

'No, they said you'd know them when you see them,' Mick replied and his head disappeared from view.

Jim left the theatre and joined the last of the regatta revellers as they made their way to hotels and guesthouses. As he walked along the banks of the river, he buttoned up his overcoat and nodded to the rowers as they waxed their boats.

Jim opened the door of the not-so-Grand Hotel and stepped into its foyer. The bar was full and noisy. Traditional fiddle music rang out from one corner and when Jim entered the hotel's lounge, a merry, middle-aged woman in a feathered hat and floor-length dress approached him.

'I know you, you were in the play tonight,' the woman slurred. 'You were great.'

'Thank you,' Jim replied. He quickly looked around the lounge and, when he didn't see a familiar face, returned to the foyer.

A moment later an attractive, red-headed young woman, wearing an elegant floral silk dress that clung tightly to her sleek body, strolled over to Jim and said 'Hello Mr Brevin.'

Patricia O'Donovan stood in front of him and happy memories of his fit-up days flooded into his mind.

'Hello Patricia! It's wonderful to see you again.'

The two young people embraced each other warmly. Patricia kissed Jim on the cheek and holding on to his hand said 'You were fabulous tonight. I really enjoyed the show.'

'Why didn't you to come backstage? I could have introduced you to everyone.'

'That's exactly why we thought it better to meet you here,' Patricia's father Sebastian interjected. 'Shamus is not exactly one of our favourite people.'

'Sebastian, it's wonderful to see you, how are you?' Jim said and shook the gentle giant's outstretched oversized hand.

'Congratulations Jim that was wonderful work tonight.' Sebastian looked around the busy foyer. 'It's noisy here, there's a quiet residents' lounge on the first floor. Why don't we go there?'

'Tell me all about yourself and the company,' Jim asked excitedly as the trio of thespians sat in the comfortable upstairs lounge.

'I don't know where to start,' Patricia replied as she settled her dress about her knees.

'What shows are you performing this year?' Jim asked.

Patricia looked to her father.

'Shortly after you left Jim,' Sebastian said quietly. 'Sorcha fell ill and nine months ago she passed away.' Sebastian made the sign of the cross.

Jim was stunned by the sudden news. After a moment he composed himself. 'I'm so very sorry, I didn't know; she was a great lady of the theatre.'

'Yes she was,' Sebastian said with a forced smile. Then he ordered some drinks and said 'No more sad talk. The reason we asked you to come along tonight is that Patricia has something important to ask you.'

Patricia's face flushed a little and she began a short, prepared speech.

'Jim, we are about to form a new company, very much like the Ira Allen company. We will be based in the Opera House in Cork and we will tour to major theatres in Galway, Limerick, Kerry and Dublin.' Patricia sounded very much like her mother. 'We would like you to join the company as the young male lead. What do you say?'

'I would be delighted to join your company,' Jim replied, his face glowed with pride. 'What plays do you plan to produce?'

'We haven't finalised that yet, but we're very close,' Patricia said, delighted she had engaged her first actor. 'It's going to be very exciting. Welcome on board.'

Patricia held out her hand to Jim and he shook it.

'I'm already looking forward to it.'

'We are naming the company the Sorcha O'Donovan Company of Munster Players. I think she would have liked that,' Sebastian said as he ran his large hand over his great bald head.

'I think so too,' Jim said and the three friends lifted their glasses. They toasted the memory of Sorcha, they toasted each other and they toasted the future with the new touring company.

On the stroke of midnight, three uniformed members of the local constabulary entered the hotel, closed the bar and cleared the hotel's public areas.

'Why are they closing the place?' Jim asked Sebastian after a nervous-looking constable ordered them gruffly to vacate the lounge.

'I'll tell you in a minute, just leave your drink and let's go,' Sebastian replied and escorted Jim and Patricia down the stairs and out of the hotel. Once they were standing on the green outside the hotel, he said in hushed tone: 'We're lucky they let us have the regatta at all. A dreadful thing happened here a few weeks ago. Fermoy's head constable was shot dead by Sinn Feiners.'

'So it's not only in Dublin that there's trouble.' Jim tightened the belt on his coat.

'That's right, it's all over the country and it's still growing.'

'Did they catch the rebels?'

'Yes, they're in jail and they'll probably be shot.' Sebastian nodded to Patricia. 'It's best if we don't hang around here.' They said goodnight and as they parted Patricia said to Jim 'I'll be in touch.'

The following afternoon when Fiona arrived at the theatre Shamus was waiting for her.

'How dare you embarrass me like that?' he snapped belligerently. 'Get *you* a cup of tea? Who the hell do you think you bloody well are?'

'You asked me to get you a cup of tea; why shouldn't I ask the same of you?'

'If you ever try anything like that again I'll …'

'You'll what?' Fiona snapped.

Shamus's fist lashed into the air and Fiona flinched.

'If you lay a hand on her you'll have me to deal with,' Jim said, laying his hand on Shamus's shoulder.

Shamus gave a snort of derision; he grabbed Jim by the lapels and pulled him so close that Jim could smell the alcohol on his breath. 'This

THE ACTOR

is none of your damn business,' he growled into Jim's face. 'So stay out of it.' And with another grunt he shoved Jim against the wall and jostled his way past a pale-faced Fiona.

'Fancy a cup of cocoa,' Richard asked Leslie as they entered the parlour of the guest house on Kyle Street. 'Warm us up before we hit the hay.'

'Don't mind if I do,' Leslie replied and he sat in one of the shabby but comfortable armchairs.

In the small kitchenette that Mrs Linskey had made available to her cherished theatrical clients, Richard lit the single gas ring and placed a small saucepan of milk on it. He opened a tin of Fry's drinking cocoa and placed two teaspoons of cocoa power in each cup.

'What do you make of our young lovers?'

'Very sad, very disturbing,' replied an unusually quiet Leslie.

Noting Leslie's sober mood, Richard thought he'd risk asking a personal question.

'Ever been in love, Leslie?'

Leslie touched his fingertips to his lips and thought.

Martha Bulstrode was the girl's name and even after fifteen years to think of her caused Leslie pain. Martha was the loveliest, prettiest, most feminine creature he had ever met and the moment he met her, he fell in love with her. But his love was never reciprocated. Martha Bulstrode used Leslie's love to manipulate him and rule his life. She lied to him, deceived him and in the end betrayed him. Even her parting words, delivered in front of his sister and his closest friends were designed to hurt and humiliate him: 'I never loved you; you're a pathetic stupid man. I can do a lot better than you.'

The effect of it all was to turn Leslie from an open and outgoing young man into an insular man fearful of the world; a man who never allowed another person to get close and a man who used his considerable wit to keep people at arm's length.

Richard handed Leslie a steaming hot cup of cocoa and he jumped; he had forgotten he was not alone.

'You didn't answer my question.'

'What was your question?' Leslie asked in a voice so low that Richard could hardly hear.

'I said, have you ever been in love?'

'I have,' Leslie replied quietly. 'What about you, have you ever had a grand passion?'

'Oh yes,' Richard replied stoically as he dipped a Marietta biscuit in his cocoa. 'But he didn't love me. He just used me.'

The monocle dropped from Leslie's eye.

'I never knew you were …'

'You never asked. Besides it's none of your business.'

'You're so right,' Leslie replied. 'It is none my business.'

27

Wearing a high-waisted, silver lamé evening gown, a confident but nervous May Murnane walked onto the stage of the Cork Opera house and smiled at the audience of Cork's rank and fashion. It was opening night and a gala charity evening for the local branch of the National Association for the Prevention of the Spread of Tuberculosis. May Murnane and the committee of the NAPST had arranged and organised the evening and May had been asked to address the audience to explain the NAPST war against tuberculosis.

May smiled, the audience fell quiet and she spoke.

'I would like to congratulate the Cork branch of the NAPST on their fine work in the fight against the spread of tuberculosis.' May paused a moment. 'Last year tuberculosis caused twelve thousand deaths in Ireland, sadly most of them being young people between fifteen and twenty-five years of age.' May then went on to explain how unsanitary living conditions, poor nutrition and lack of hygiene were major factors in the spread of not only tuberculosis, but of typhoid, dysentery and the many other diseases that plagued the cities and towns of Ireland. She finished her speech with a heartfelt plea. 'The monies from tonight's performance will go to purchase two travelling wagons to be used to disseminate information throughout the greater Munster area. As a mother I know how devastating tuberculosis can be to a family; tonight my own son is in a convalescent home fighting this terrible disease.' Her voice cracked but she continued speaking. 'But he is winning his battle and so are we; in the last ten years the death toll in Ireland from tuberculosis has been reduced by a quarter. Your philanthropy and generosity greatly contributed to that victory, but it is only one victory in a war of many battles. A war that we will continue to fight and a war that, with your help, we will win. Thank you.'

The moment May stopped speaking the audience leapt to their feet and cheered and applauded loudly.

After they took the curtain call Richard remarked to Shamus 'Good audience, they really enjoyed the show.'

'Bloody country bumpkins, all they understand are puns and pratfalls,' Shamus replied dismissively.

'How dare you look down your nose at an audience,' Ira said to Shamus. 'You may think because the audience revelled in puns and quibbles that they are unsophisticated and uneducated people but you are wrong. Cork audiences and I'd say most Irish audiences, are discriminating listeners with well-developed imaginations and if you think otherwise you are mistaken.'

'If you say so,' Shamus mumbled and flounced off to his dressing room.

'Great turnout tonight,' May said to Ira when he entered their dressing room. 'I think we raised a lot of money for the association.'

'Yes, I'd say so my dear and might I say your speech before the show was first class; informative, clear and very heartfelt.'

'Thank you; it's kind of you to say so.' The tone of May's voice changed. 'This thing between Fiona and Shamus is getting pretty ugly. Maura told me, she heard them arguing again this morning. I think you should say something to Shamus?'

'I've already had words with him tonight.' Ira raked his fingers through his hair. 'He's a most disagreeable young man.' He sighed and shook his head. ' It's so close to the end of the tour, I think I'll leave the young people to themselves. But you are right May, it is very troubling. Casting Shamus was not one of my better decisions.'

'He's crass, tactless, and a graceless person. I don't like it. And Ira, I fear he was drinking before the show.'

'Yes I know dear, you've already mentioned that to me. It's a pity, he's such a very good actor and women love him – at least they like watching him on stage.'

'But does he care for them?' May's enormous brown eyes fixed on Ira. 'I don't think he likes anyone, including himself.'

'That is a very good observation.'

In the green room Jim introduced his school friend Ciaran O'Donovan and his parents, Major and Gwen O'Donovan, to Ira. The great actor was chatting happily to the Major when May joined them. Mrs O'Donovan complimented her on her speech and on her gown and when May returned the compliment and congratulated Mrs O'Donovan on her charity work, the Cork woman glowed with pride; now she would have something very special to tell the ladies at the bridge club.

The green room that night was a happy place but for the master-tailor Cedric O'Connor and the actress Maura Sweeney, it was an especially happy place. Cedric had taken the morning train from Dublin to be with Maura for the opening night and had just told Maura he was staying in Cork until the end of the week.

May walked across the lounge of the Metropole Hotel and the smell of French perfume mingling with clouds of cigarette smoke made her eyes smart. The lunch meeting with the association had gone well and May was now on her way to meet Fiona Weston. She had great sympathy for the girl and if Ira was going to do nothing about the situation she at least was going to offer the girl whatever moral support she could. May crossed the lounge and the brief snatches of conversations she overheard made her smile.

'Well Mr O'Sullivan, I haven't seen much of you lately,' said a smug ruddy-faced man standing at a table. 'Have you given up social life?'

'No,' replied the seated Mr O'Sullivan. 'I've taken up golf.'

'It was dreadful,' a stylishly dressed lady said in a poisonous Cork accent. 'I had to let an upstairs maid go, she was stealing from me.'

A lumpish effeminate man made the strangest noise in his nose and murmured to his weak-chinned companion 'O'Sullivan's son was involved in the fighting; they say the boy's a Shinner!'

May caught sight of Fiona sitting alone in an alcove. A waiter had placed an afternoon tea tray on the table in front of her and was standing waiting to be paid. May took the bill from Fiona's hand and said 'I asked you here so it's my treat.' She frowned at the waiter. 'Come back when we're finished and I'll settle up with up with you then. Away with you now.'

The disgruntled waiter frowned, bowed and walked away.

'Sorry I'm late, my meeting ran on.' May sat and removed her fur stole. 'How are you today?'

'I'm well, thank you.'

'I thought we girls should have a little time to ourselves,' May said conspiratorially.

'I know what you want to talk about,' said Fiona. 'I'm sorry that what happened between Shamus and I has been so unpleasant for everyone.'

'You are not responsible for Shamus's actions. I want you to know that you have my full support and that my door is always open to you if ever you feel the need to talk to someone.'

Fiona's eyes welled with tears. 'Thank you, that's very kind of you.'

May placed a tea strainer on a cup and poured. 'Maura said Shamus shouted at you yesterday.'

'Yes he did. He accused me of having an affair with Jim.'

'That's dreadful,' May replied and thought, that's what you have to expect from the likes of him.

'It is dreadful, for I have never given Shamus the slightest reason to believe anything like that,' Fiona said and momentarily lost herself in her unsettled world.

'Why don't you tell me everything?' asked May and handed Fiona the cup.

Ira gestured to Jim to sit on the chair beside his at the dressing table.

'You said you had a few questions about 'performance' you wanted to ask?'

'Mr Allen, every performance you give seems new, spontaneous and fresh.'

'Thank you, it's good of you to say so.'

THE ACTOR

'My question is how do you do it? I mean, how do you disappear inside the role? And how do you keep doing it for performance after performance?'

Ira thought for a moment.

'I don't really know how to answer your questions. What I do is instinctive. I learn my lines; think about the character and let ideas come to me. Where the ideas come from I don't know; but what I do know is I can't force them. When they finally arrive I play with them. I try different ways of delivering lines, different vocal patterns, different gestures and then when all that is done I let go.'

'You let go?'

Ira nodded.

'Let go of what?'

'I let go of everything and let my talent guide my performance.'

'Then you're not in control of your performance?'

'Of course I'm in control.' Ira rubbed his chin, thought for a minute and then continued. 'When I'm on stage it's like I'm able to split myself in two or even three. I am an actor, I'm the character and I can watch myself acting. The actor part of me is relaxed and calm, the character part of me can be out of control or experiencing the deepest emotions of love, happiness, revenge, pain, anger, or jealousy and the third part of me is guiding and shading my performance.'

'But isn't that exhausting? Experiencing all that emotion every time you give a performance?'

'A little tiring. But don't misunderstand me. Acting is not about experiencing emotion, it's about expressing emotion and that's a very different thing.'

'Then what you portray is not real?'

'Of course it's not real. It never should be real, but it should always look real. That's why it's called acting. The theatre is the world of illusion and imagination. The playwright, the production and the actors all provide the illusions, it's the audience that provides the reality.'

'Then how do you make your performance new and spontaneous every night?'

'I don't have to make it new and spontaneous every night – it only has to look like it's new and spontaneous.' He studied Jim's face. 'You don't understand what I'm saying. Am I not making sense to you?'

'No, you are making sense,' Jim insisted – not wanting to admit that he was still confused by the concept of 'letting go'.

That evening after the show Fiona came to Jim and Shamus's dressing room and asked to speak privately with Shamus.

Jim shot her a questioning look but she pointedly looked away. He pulled on his jacket and as he left whispered loud enough for Shamus to hear 'I'll be next door with Richard and Francis P if you need me.'

Alone with Shamus, Fiona stood with her back to the door like a child who was about to tell a parent that she had just broken a treasured family heirloom.

'I hope you've come to apologise,' Shamus said as he rubbed cold cream on to his face.

'No, I haven't,' she replied meekly.

'Then why are you here?' His voice was icy.

'Aren't you going to ask me to sit down?'

'No.'

Fiona sat.

'What do you want?'

'I think I might be pregnant.'

Without as much as flinching, Shamus continued to clean his face.

'Did you hear me?'

'I heard you.' Shamus still hadn't looked at Fiona. 'Are you saying it's my child?'

'Of course it's your child. It couldn't be anyone else's?'

'You slept with me, you probably slept with other men,' Shamus said with forced casualness.

'You're the only one I've ever slept with and you know that.'

'I have plans for my life and they don't include you or your child.' His voice was devoid of emotion.

Stunned, Fiona said 'But you said you loved me.'

'I say that to all the girls.' Shamus wiped the cold cream make-up mess from his face and met her eye in the mirror. 'It helps to get them into the sack.'

Wiping his hands carefully, he stood up, donned his jacket, picked up his overcoat and made for the door. 'When the play finishes I'm off to London and you won't be coming with me.' He opened the dressing-room door and was gone.

Fiona held her hand against her stomach as she started to tremble.

Jim yanked open the door of Slattery's snug, dropped down on to cracked leather upholstered bench and fixed his eyes on the glass of whiskey in Shamus's hand.

'You promised not to drink for the run of the play.'

'What are they going to do, fire me?' Shamus said contemptuously, flashing him a hostile look.

The service hatch slid open and a gaunt, bald bartender stuck his head through the hatch.

'Do you want something to drink or are you here for the air?'

'I'll have another Old Cromac, a large one' Shamus replied. 'My friend doesn't drink.'

When the bartender returned with his drink, Shamus raised his last glass and drained it into his newly delivered double.

'You haven't come in here to lecture me about drinking, have you?'

'No, what are you going to do about Fiona?'

'I knew it; she told you about her little problem,' Shamus exhaled a lungful of silvery smoke and watched it curl in the air.

'Fiona loves you.'

Shamus smirked.

'You know a part of me likes the girl. She's pretty; but now she is pregnant and that's not for me, no thank you.'

'But she's having your child.'

Shamus' face darkened and he glared derisively at Jim.

'How do I know it's my child? She did it with me; she'd do it with anyone. She might be doing it with you, for all I know. You love her, don't you, you silly bugger?'

Jim's face flushed with anger. 'She is having your child. For once in your life do the right thing.'

'Do the right thing?' Shamus spat the words at Jim. 'My mother tricked my father into marrying her when she was up the duff. But it won't work with me; I'm not going to be trapped like my father. You can have her. I hope you don't mind damaged goods.'

THE ACTOR

Jim exploded across the snug, grabbed Shamus by the lapels and pounded him against the wall.

'Shut your filthy mouth,' Jim bellowed into his face.

Shamus grinned and then flung his hands upwards, broke Jim's hold and crashed a fist into Jim stomach. Jim doubled over; Shamus raised and joined his fists and slammed them down on Jim's back. Jim dropped to the floor.

'You're some hero,' Shamus sniggered.

The hatch flew open and the bartender barked 'Keep it quiet in here. You're not in Dublin now.'

'Sorry.' Shamus helped Jim to his feet. 'Have a drink, Jim.'

'No thanks.' He pulled free of Shamus. 'I used to look up to you. I thought you were a great actor and a good friend.' He pulled open the snug door. 'Well you might be a good actor but you're nobody's friend and you're a lousy person.'

Jim walked out of the snug and Shamus shouted after him 'Fuck you and fuck Fiona.'

28

On Thursday evening Jim was standing in the wings repairing a broken prop lantern when he saw an animated Mick whispering to Ira. Then the actor waved his hand dismissively and walked away, saying loudly 'Mick, stop listening to gossip. Shamus is a professional – he'll be here in time.'

'He's already late,' Mick muttered to himself as he pulled on the curtain rope. Silently the theatre curtain rose and the clatter of Mick's big boots on the stage echoed around the empty auditorium. Still muttering to himself, the stage manager looked over the set, checked the show's large props and tested the stage machines.

Sixty minutes before show-time the actors were in their dressing rooms applying their make-up. The piano tuner in the orchestra pit stroked his long grey beard, placed his battered bowler on his head and called out in a heavy Cork city accent 'Mick, that's all I can do with it. I've tuned it and it may stay in tune for a few days but it needs to be restrung or replaced. Sometimes you just have to let get rid of a bad thing and this piano is a bad thing.'

'Thank you, I'll pass your comments on to the theatre manager,' Mick said and lowered the main curtain.

Forty minutes before performance, an increasingly concerned Mick checked the lights, the gels and the faders. Thirty minutes before the performance an uneasy Ira stepped into the green room and asked Francis P if he had seen Shamus?

'No. I haven't.' Frances P's eyes peered over the top of his newspaper. 'Is something the matter?'

'I'm concerned; if Shamus does not arrive in the next few minutes I'm going to have to consider cancelling the night's performance.' Then before he stepped out of the room Ira asked 'Any news of your son, Rory?'

'Yes, there certainly is. He's safe.' Francis P beamed as he lowered his newspaper. 'We got a letter from him yesterday. He's in an internment camp in Wales. Frongoch.'

'That's really good news. I'm happy for you.'

'Thank you. Maureen and the children are overjoyed.' Francis P's face became thoughtful. 'Ira, you won't believe this, but Rory and his comrades are forming a drama group in the internment camp.'

'A drama group in an internment camp, what an interesting concept.'

'Yes and Rory asked me for some play suggestions. Would you mind if I sent him some of your plays?'

'By all means, send them to him,' Ira said with a chuckle, and like a puff of smoke in a hurricane he was gone in search of his errant actor.

Thirty minutes before curtain up a concerned Ira and a worried Mick met in the actor's dressing room. Ira stood by the window and his eyes had a faraway look in them. A thin sheen of sweat glistened on his brow and he was grinding his teeth. A moment passed, Mick coughed, and Ira's thoughts returned to the present.

'Better inform the theatre management that we have to cancel the night's performance,' Ira's voice was grave but resolute. 'I'll make an announcement to the cast and audience when you return.'

'This is the first time we have ever cancelled a show.'

'There's a first time for everything, Mick,' Ira replied grimly.

Mick was on his way to the theatre manager's office when the stage door burst open and a glassy-eyed, dishevelled Shamus nearly crashed into him. The actor was inebriated.

'Nice to see you Mick, sorry I can't chat, I'm a bit late,' Shamus said and lurched past the now fuming stage manager.

THE ACTOR

Mick was about to explode when Leslie stepped in front of him.

'Mick, don't talk to the theatre management yet. Tell Ira that Shamus is here and that he's a bit under the weather. But don't let him see Shamus, tell him I said the situation is manageable.'

Mick grumbled 'I don't like it. But I'll talk to Ira and let him make the decision.'

'That's what I want you to do,' Leslie replied, taking Shamus's arm and guiding the actor to his dressing room.

'Where is he? I want to see him,' a seething Ira demanded of his stage manager.

Mick barred his way into the dressing room. 'I wouldn't advise a visit. If you say anything to him, you'll probably say too much.'

Ira glared at his stage manager. 'Did you cancel tonight's performance?' His voice was almost imperceptibly soft.

'No, not yet, I thought I'd give you the opportunity to reconsider now that Shamus is here.'

'Thank you Mick, that was the right thing to do,' a calm May Murnane said to the stage manager. 'Can you give Ira and me a moment?'

'Yes, but we have to inform the theatre management soon, they have to organise the box office to start refunding money.'

'Cancelling the show may not be the best thing to do,' May said the moment Mick closed the door. 'If Leslie says the situation is manageable, we have to listen to him. For the last fifteen years Leslie had been a loyal investor in your productions and when he speaks, particularly when it concerns finance, we have to listen. We simply can't afford to forgo a night's takings.'

Ira inhaled deeply. 'I don't like it, but you're right. But I am also right and if Shamus is not in command of himself I'll bring the curtain down on the show.'

'Very well; that's the way we'll handle it.'

The show began and to everyone's surprise Shamus missed very few lines. When he did stumble, Jim prompted him or another cast member covered for him. When he forgot to take a vital prop on stage, Leslie followed him and handed it to him. Throughout the show Shamus's voice remained clear and the only indication of his condition was that every now and then, he seemed a little confused. It didn't matter to the audience, who assumed it was the character and not the actor that was confused. When not theatrically interacting with Shamus, the actors did not speak to him or make eye contact with him, but every moment he spent on stage was nerve-racking for the whole company.

One minute before the interval, Mick joined Jim in the prompter's corner.

'Jim, stay with Shamus and make sure you pour coffee into him. I'll attend to your stage management duties.'

Sitting in his dressing room, a glum and intense Shamus sat and stared into the mirror.

'You better put this on,' Jim said as he handed Shamus his jacket for his next scene.

'Everybody hates me,' Shamus muttered. 'But you don't hate me, do you Jim? You're my best friend Jim, do you know that?'

Jim placed a cup of coffee in front of him. 'I'm your only friend. Drink the coffee.'

'It must be nice to be comfortable in your skin. You want to know why I don't let people get to know me.'

'I'm sure you're going to tell me.'

'I am, but it's a secret.' Shamus placed a finger to his lips and blew air around it. 'The reason I don't let people get to know me is because there is no me to get to know. I only exist when I'm on stage; the rest of me is an illusion. I don't exist; there is no me.' Shamus lifted the coffee to his lips and took a sip. 'Jim, Fiona is trying to trick me into marrying her but it won't work. I'll show her. Nobody messes with Shamus McGovern.'

'Shamus leave Fiona alone, you have to concentrate on your acting.'

'I'll show her.'

The dressing room door opened and Mick poked his head in and said 'Five minutes. Jim walk Shamus to his entrance and then go back on book.'

The show resumed and the scenes that Shamus shared with Fiona were the most difficult for Jim to watch and for Fiona to endure. Instead of charming Nana, Harry Travers sneered at her. Instead of gently taking Nana's arm and gliding her across the stage, Harry Travers grabbed her and shoved her across the stage and when he was supposed to kiss Nana gently on the cheek he grabbed her face and kissed her hard on the mouth.

As the scene continued the audience started to sense that what they were witnessing was not theatrical villainy but real cruelty and nastiness. They didn't enjoy or approve of this Harry Travers; they didn't boo or hiss as they usually did – rather they showed their disapproval with silence. However Shamus was untroubled by the audience's reaction and he carried on. When Ira saw Shamus kiss Fiona on the mouth he demanded Mick lower the curtain and end the show. Leslie took Ira aside and said forcefully to him 'This is their last scene alone together. Let the show continue and when it's over, do what you have to do.'

The instant the final curtain touched the stage floor, Ira grabbed Shamus by the arm, spun him around and said 'Shamus McGovern you are a disgrace. You are intoxicated and out of control.'

'No one noticed,' replied a disoriented Shamus.

'Everybody noticed.' A grin slid across Shamus's face; Ira lowered his voice. 'You think this is amusing? You have insulted our audience, belittled this company of professional players and have made a mockery of my play and you think it's amusing. You are a cipher, sir, and you will never again share a stage with me or my company of players. Pack your bags and leave.'

'What about the show tomorrow night?' Shamus asked, still grinning wildly.

'For you sir, there will be no show tomorrow night.'

The grin faded from Shamus's face, he looked from actor to actor and each one in turn glanced away, looked to their feet or shifted uneasily.

'I apologise for my behaviour,' Shamus said adopting his charm persona but when the look of steely determination on Ira's face didn't change, Shamus's face turned dark and he said 'You're jealous of me, all of you are jealous of me. The great Ira Allen is a bloody big ham. You're yesterday's man. Even drunk, I can act better then you.'

'This has nothing to do with acting,' Ira's voice was quiet but powerful. 'This has to do with decency, respect and character, none of which you possess.'

'To hell with you and fuck you all,' Shamus retorted loudly and stormed off stage.

No one moved, no one stirred and no one spoke. Ira broke the silence.

'I want everyone here at ten tomorrow morning; we have much work to do.'

In solemn silence the actors left the stage, the women returned to their dressing rooms and the men deliberately delayed returning to theirs. Richard and Francis P stood and talked, Leslie went to the green room and Jim tended to his stage management duties. Minutes later Shamus stormed out of the theatre and Mick approached Jim and told him Ira wished to talk to him.

'Come in,' Ira called out when Jim knocked somewhat hesitantly on the dressing room door. 'Take a seat.' Jim sat. 'I have something I want to ask you.' Ira removed his stage beard. 'Ah, I always feel better when I take that blasted thing off.' His deep brown eyes came to rest on Jim. 'I won't beat around the bush.'

Jim took a deep breath. He knew what Ira was going to ask and he had his answer ready.

'I'd like you to take over the role of Harry Travers. What do you say?'

'I'll do it sir,' Jim replied, gushing with confidence. 'And I have some ideas I'd like to try.'

At breakfast the following morning when Jim told Fiona that Shamus had already left the guest house she stared in disbelief at him and returned quietly to her room.

Ira started rehearsal at ten sharp. He announced that Jim was talking over the role of Harry Travers and that Mick was going to play Jim's role. Francis P, Leslie, Richard, May and Maura congratulated Jim, but when the company started rehearsing Fiona was not present. During the tea break, Ira asked Mick to take over the rehearsal while he paid a visit to his missing actress.

'You were expected at rehearsals at ten o'clock,' Ira said briskly to Fiona when she finally came down to meet him in the small guest house parlour.

'Mr Allen, I don't think I can rehearse today. Shamus has gone and I feel awful,' the actress sobbed, holding a damp white lace handkerchief to her red eyes.

Ignoring her tears, Ira stood tall and buttoning his long black coat said 'I expected you at the theatre at ten o'clock sharp, but you did not attend.'

'Mr Allen perhaps I didn't make myself clear, I can't ...'

'You made yourself perfectly clear, my dear.' Ira retorted. 'Now let me make myself perfectly clear. Miss Whelan you are not the only person with troubles. One of my sons is critically ill in hospital, Francis P's son is in an internment camp and the country had just experienced an insurrection. Thousands of people are near starving and thousands more are unemployed. Practically every family in the country has suffered the curse of emigration and you think because you have a broken heart it excuses you from participating in life.' His voice grew deeper. 'You are a professional actress; act like one. Be at the theatre at noon.'

At five minutes to twelve a composed if quiet Fiona arrived at the theatre. With eyes still red from weeping she apologised to Ira, to the company and in particular to Jim. During the rehearsal she was extremely kind and helpful to Jim; she prompted him, guided him and never stopped encouraging him. When he asked her to run a scene a second or third time she did so and when her interest waned and drifted towards thoughts of Shamus and her unborn child she forced herself to concentrate on the moment and on helping Jim.

That night as the audience took their seats, Jim stood tense and rigid in the near darkness of the wings. He hardly noticed when Leslie, Mick and the rest of the cast and crew wished him well. The orchestra played the opening music and Jim's skin tingled. Maura sang her song and Jim's hands grew sweaty. Richard exited the stage and Jim's stomach started to heave and just when he thought he was going to get sick he heard his cue.

Jim never missed an entrance, a cue, or a line. When he was off stage he buried his head in the script but on stage he remembered everything, he was always in the correct place and delivered his lines clearly and cleanly.

When the final curtain fell, a beaming Ira shook Jim's hand and said 'Good job.' May hugged him and whispered 'Thank you, Jim, it means so much more than you know.' Fiona embraced him warmly and Richard, Leslie, Maura, Francis P and the entire crew shook his hand vigorously.

THE ACTOR

That night a contented and still excited Jim Brevin found it difficult to sleep and when sleep did come he dreamt he was back on stage.

The following afternoon, ninety minutes before the matinee, a smiling Jim arrived at the theatre. Still basking in the glow of the previous night's success he sat in his dressing room applying his make-up and happily muttering his lines to himself. There was tap on his door and Ira slipped into the dressing room and sat beside Jim.

'Jim, last night your performance was good. A little forced but never the less it was good.'

'Thank you, sir,' Jim replied, somewhat taken aback.

'Why are you thanking me? It wasn't much of a compliment.'

'I was being polite.' He looked questioningly at his mentor.

'Jim, when you first came to see me a few years ago, I asked you if you had the talent to be an actor and you said you had.'

'Yes I remember that, sir.'

'And our conversation the other day, do you remember that too? Because that's what I want you to do this afternoon.'

Jim stared at Ira, trying to understand. 'You want me to … do what exactly?'

'I want you to trust your talent.' Ira leaned back in the chair. 'This afternoon when you walk out on that stage, I want you to let go. Don't force your performance, don't try to remember your lines or do what you did last night – just let it happen.' Ira jumped to his feet and as he left the room said with great relish 'I'm really looking forward to seeing what's going to happen.'

Jim looked into his dressing room mirror and two frightened eyes looked back at him.

Let go, he thought to himself as he stood waiting for the curtain to rise. Let go of what? The overture began. Maura sang her song. Adrenalin surged through him. Trust your talent. Jim heard his cue; he relaxed, let go and Jim's Harry Travers strolled on stage.

He didn't change a word of the text or a single direction, yet his performance was completely different from the previous night. His performance that afternoon was a combination of stillness and energy; it was skilful, it was powerful and it was adroit. He paced, he growled and he charmed his way through the play. He was completely immersed in his role, yet he was always aware of what he was doing and of everything that was happening on stage. He watched and listened to his fellow actors and his response to them was spontaneous, always matching, undercutting or topping their energy as the scenes demanded. His performance electrified the cast and Fiona, now free of Shamus's threatening presence, soared.

His performance energised the audience too. He gave them the time to laugh or boo or hiss. He read them and played to them and in turn they loved every moment of his Harry Travers. For Jim his performance that afternoon was special; it was a magical, transcendent performance and it became the benchmark for all his future performances.

Standing in the wings while the cast took their curtain call, a joyous Ira shook Jim's hand 'Well done Jim! You are a real actor and you possess great talent.' Then, leaning in to Jim, he whispered 'You let go, didn't you?'

'I did sir,' Jim replied grinning with delight. 'You were right.'

'Good, now go and take your curtain call.'

Jim walked onto the stage and the audience booed and hissed good-humouredly then rose to their feet and applauded loudly. Beaming a broad smile, Jim stood and basked in the applause.

After the final curtain as Fiona left the stage, Ira touched her on the shoulder and said 'Well done Fiona. I know it wasn't easy for you, but this is what we do.'

'Thank you Mr Allen,' Fiona replied. 'It is what we do.'

Fiona then went to her dressing room, closed the door behind her and wept silently.

The following Monday, Shamus boarded a cattle boat to Holyhead and two months later he appeared in a production of *East Lynne* at the Garrick Theatre, London.

On a wet rainy day in September a very pregnant Fiona Whelan tripped and fell while alighting from a tram in Rathmines. That night she lost her baby.

Jim knew nothing about it – he was on tour with the Sorcha O'Donovan Company and while in the Kingdom County it was rumoured that he and Patricia were romantically involved.

29

During 1917 and 1918 Ireland experienced great food and fuel shortages; meat, eggs, potatoes, vegetables, bread, milk, coal and even turf were in poor supply. The shortages caused prices to rise and in turn industrial unrest became widespread; bakers, coalmen, gas workers, dockers, railway men, even cemetery workers went on strike for higher wages. In an attempt to feed their families thousands of men enlisted in the British Armed Forces and quickly found themselves in Europe fighting in the trenches. In Ireland living conditions continued to deteriorate and even families with regular incomes began to suffer. In the tenements dry bread and tea became the main diet, the health of the nation declined, discontent grew and political unrest escalated. On November 11, 1918, the Great War ended.

In July 1919 in Drumcondra, Dublin, a member of the Royal Irish Constabulary was shot dead and before the year was out another sixteen policemen were killed. Retaliation by the army and the Metropolitan Police to each murder was instant and severe. During the autumn and winter of 1919, eight civilians were murdered by the police, fourteen thousand houses were raided, and the British authorities declared the rebel authority of Dáil Éireann illegal and many Irish leaders were imprisoned or deported.

But for 'the few', life in Dublin was still good, Grafton Street was still fashionable, the Gresham Hotel was rebuilt and every day ships docked in the harbour laden with luxury goods.

One night in November, Ira Allen slipped into Jim's dressing room in the Queen's Theatre. There was a spring in his step – his son had been released from hospital, and seemed to be doing well. He handed Jim a manuscript.

'That's the play you enquired about. Look after it, there are very few copies of it in existence. By the way, are you available for some work in the summer of next year?'

'I am sir.'

'Good, it's not exactly theatre work but it does pay well. We'll talk again when I have more details. In the meantime do look after that manuscript.'

Ira closed the dressing room door and Jim began to read the original handwritten manuscript of *Fr Murphy; the Hero of Tullow*.

'Time to lock up,' Mick said when he popped his head into the dressing room. 'Better hurry or you'll miss your last tram.'

Jim looked at his watch, found some brown paper, wrapped the manuscript in it and secured it firmly with a piece of string.

'What's next for Jim Brevin?' Leslie asked when they met at the stage door.

'Back working in the family business, Christmas is always a busy time,' Jim replied. 'Oh, Mr Allen asked if I was free next summer. Do you know what that's all about?'

'That'll be the film they're making of his play *Tara's Halls*. Ever been in a film? It's organised chaos and endless waiting for one thing or another, but it is fun.'

Searching for his gloves in his overcoat pockets Jim shifted the brown paper package from under one arm to the other.

'What you got there?' Leslie enquired.

'Mr Allen loaned me a copy of his play *Fr Murphy*.'

'Good play and a good read.'

'I know it's a famous play but who was Fr Murphy and what did he do that made him famous?'

Leslie held his monocle to his eye, and said 'You don't know your history, do you? Fr Murphy was the parish priest of Tullow, Co Carlow and he's famous because he was one of the leaders of the Wexford Rebellion of 1798. An unlikely hero, he started out as a pacifist, and in the end it took twenty thousand British troops to defeat him and his men at the Battle of Vinegar Hill. He was captured near Tullow and cruelly executed in the market place of his parish. To add further humiliation, the army impaled his head on a spike outside his church.'

'Sounds gruesome.'

'It's a very good play. It's Ira's best, full of rousing speeches and lots of spectacle.'

A cold wind bit into Jim when he stepped out of the theatre's stage door. The city was covered in winter's first fall of gleaming snow. With the manuscript tucked under his arm, he flipped up the collar of his heavy woollen overcoat, placed his trilby on his head and walked along the slippery path of Great Brunswick Street. It was ten thirty, ten minutes before the last tram to the Phoenix Park. He could cut down Moss Street and he quickened his pace on the snow-muffled street.

The swirling snow silently deposited itself on the derelict, gutted buildings of Moss Street. A homeless woman curled up in a doorway growled as the lamplighter lit a nearby streetlamp.

'Goodnight,' Jim muttered as he passed the lamplighter.

'Goodnight sir,' replied the lamplighter.

In the recess of a darkened doorway, Jim glimpsed the red glow of a cigarette – then heard footsteps behind him. He glanced over his shoulder. The lamplighter was gone and a man with a wide-brimmed cap pulled down over his eyes was running towards him. A sudden swish of bicycle wheels and five men in long coats and large-brimmed caps leapt off their bicycles and surrounded him. 'What do you want?' he cried, his eyes going from man to man. A rock shattered the snow covered streetlamp and the street was plunged into darkness.

The smoker stepped out of the doorway. He was a big man whose face was concealed by the soft rim of his fedora hat and the turned-up collar of his coat. He passed silently through the ring of men, tore the package from under Jim's arm and tossed it to the man standing behind him. Then he tilted his fedora back on his head and in a pronounced

Cork accent growled menacingly 'Who are you delivering the package to?'

Terrified, Jim couldn't speak. The big man took a step closer and with the toes of their shoes almost touching growled 'G-men are pigs that feed on their own young.'

'I'm not a G-man.' Jim stared at the tall smoker in fear. 'I'm not a detective. I have nothing to do with the Special Branch or anything like that.'

A fist ploughed into Jim's stomach. He gasped and the smoker blew a lungful of smoke in his face. One of the men slid a revolver from under his coat.

'I'm not a G-Man for God's sake I'm – an actor.'

The gunman nervously fingered the trigger of his gun; the smoker's impenetrable eyes fixed on Jim's face. He rasped 'Search him.'

Two of the men grabbed Jim and with their thumbs digging hard into his armpits held him while two other men ripped open his coat, rummaged in his pockets and tossed their contents on to the snow-covered street. The man behind the smoker leaned forward and whispered into the big man's ear.

'A what?' growled the smoker.

'A play, sir,' came the reply.

'A fucking play?' repeated the smoker incredulously.

'Yes it's *Fr Murphy*. It's a play about a priest …'

'I don't care what the fucking play's about!'

The man behind the smoker leaned forward, looked into Jim's face and said 'Are you Jim Brevin?'

'I am,' Jim said quickly.

'How're you Jim? It's Red, don't you remember me?'

'How do you know this man?' the smoker demanded of Red, who straightened up and resumed his position in the circle.

'He was with us in Stephen's Green during the Rising; he took two of the wounded to Roundwood.'

The smoker returned his gaze to Jim.

'Why are you out at this time of night?'

'I'm on my way home,' replied a still terrified Jim. 'I'm working in the Queen's Theatre.'

The smoker slammed the ripped package into Jim's chest and said 'If you value your life, go home and tell no one of what happened here.' He turned, walked away and was quickly swallowed by the darkness.

Four of the men surrounding Jim picked up their bikes and like ghosts followed their leader into the snowy night.

'Good to see you again, Jim …' The red-headed man lingered, as if reuniting with old friends at gunpoint was an everyday occurrence.

'Thank you … Thank you very much,' stuttered Jim.

'Red we have to go, the big fella will kill us if we hang around here!' the man who had followed Jim down the street whispered nervously to Red.

'Hold on to your hat Pat. Jim can you get me two free tickets for the matinee this Saturday?'

'You want tickets for the show?'

'Can you get two for me?'

'Yes, yes I can I'll leave them in the box office for you. What name should I put on them?'

He frowned, offended. 'Don't you remember me, I'm Red Mullin?'

'Yes I do, Red, of course, yes. I just wasn't sure it was your real name.'

The red-headed man leaned towards him and said 'By the way, I wouldn't hang around here if I were you; it's a bit dangerous.'

'Yes, thank you again, Red.'

Jim quickly buttoned his coat and walked briskly down the street.

'I never knew you went to the theatre?' Red's companion said to him.

'I've never been to the theatre but when I was in the internment camp in Wales the boys put on that play, *Fr Murphy*. It was good fun and it kept our spirits up. A chap called Rory played the lead role – his father is the actor, Francis P,' Red replied and cycled off into the snowy night.

Jim's heart pounded and cold sweat chilled his skin as he ran across Sackville Bridge and up Sackville Street. As he neared Nelson Pillar he saw the last tram for the Phoenix Park clank away from the stop. Slipping and sliding on the snowy street he raced after the tram, jumped on to the platform and heaving a sigh of relief flopped into a seat. The tram clattered through the darkness and Jim waited for his heart to stop pounding.

'I should put you off, you're not supposed to jump on a moving vehicle,' the gaunt conductor growled when Jim handed him the money for his ticket.

Two gunshots cracked the night. Jim's heart nearly jumped out of his chest.

'That's nothing to do with you, is it?' the conductor joked as he handed him his ticket. But when he saw the panic etched on Jim's sweating face, he backed away muttering 'Sorry it's none of my business, it was just a bad joke.'

The screeching tires of fast-moving cars made Jim's heart miss another beat. He wiped his hand across the tram's misted-up window. Two large black automobiles carrying armed men sped down Sackville Street, crossed the bridge and roared up the quays.

The following day when Jim learned that a special branch detective had been murdered near Moss Street, the blood drained from his face and he found it difficult to breathe.

30

Maebh Mullin sat in the stalls of the Queen's theatre and watched the noisy audience swarm into the cavernous auditorium. The overture began, the chattering dimmed, the curtain rose and the play commenced. Maebh was enjoying the madcap antics of Ira Allen's Myles na Coppaleen in the *Colleen Bawn* when halfway through Act One, Jim Brevin strolled on stage. Maebh sat bolt upright and for the rest of the play she couldn't take her eyes off the handsome young actor. He captivated her: she loved his good looks, his bright blue eyes, his resonant deep voice and his masculine charm. She clasped her hands to her mouth when his character was in danger, she sighed when he fell in love and her heart leapt every time he smiled. When the show was over Maebh sat back in her seat and thought, 'Jim Brevin I've never seen anyone like you and you have no idea how handsome you are.'

Jim stepped out of the stage-door and a ray of bright white sunlight blinded him. Shielding his eyes he turned from the sun and bumped into a group of excited middle-aged women swarming around Ira Allen. The fashionable women waved their autograph books in the air and screeched for Ira to acknowledge their presence even if only for a fleeting moment. Ira thrust both his hand in the air and affecting his most theatrical voice declaimed 'Ladies, be patient. I will sign every book; there is no need to crush and certainly no need to raise your voices.'

As Jim skirted the noisy, clambering ladies, he glimpsed a strikingly beautiful young woman across the lane. The girl was about five foot three with long black curly hair that gleamed in the late afternoon sun. A light breeze blew strands of hair across her face; she turned into the wind, and raised her hand to sweep away the offending hair. Jim's eyes were still locked on the girl when Red stepped in front of him and blocked his view.

'How're ya Jim? You was great in the play,' Red exclaimed loudly.

Jim looked at Red's face and he relived the menace of their last meeting.

'Hello – eh, you got the tickets?'

'Yeah, Jim this is me girlfriend Bridget.' Red put his arm protectively around the oddly dressed, chubby young woman standing by his side. 'See, Bridget, I told you I knew someone famous.'

'Hello Bridget, pleased to meet you. And I'm not really famous,' Jim said with his most disarming smile.

Bridget bowed her head, smiled shyly but did not take Jim's outstretched hand.

'Take the man's hand,' Red said curtly to his girlfriend. 'He won't bite you, just say hello.' While Red was trying to convince his girlfriend to shake hands, Jim craned sideways to get a look at the girl across the lane. 'Most of the time she's all right,' Red continued, but when he saw Jim was not paying attention to him he again moved into Jim's line of sight.

'Hello Mr Brevin,' Bridget said, after taking a deep breath.

'Pleased to meet you Bridget and please call me Jim.'

Bridget blushed scarlet and when she bowed her head, Jim's eyes drifted across the lane.

'Do you know that girl?' Red snapped, glancing over his shoulder. The girl gave a little wave. Red snorted. 'Is she annoying you?'

'No, no, I don't know her,' Jim replied, remembering the events of a few nights ago. 'Well she's annoying me,' Red grumbled and scowled at the girl.

Jim took a step towards Red and lowering his voice said 'You're not going to do anything to her, are you?'

'What are you talking about?' snapped Red. 'She's me sister, she wants to meet you, that's why she's waving.'

'She's your sister?'

'Why do you say it like that?'

Jim was still trying to reconcile the tough red-headed rebel and the fragile young girl as brother and sister when Red demanded 'Well? Do you want to meet her?'

'Yes, I would very much like to meet her,' Jim replied wondering where this was all going.

'You won't be saying that after you meet her; she's a bit of a handful.' Red gave a knowing laugh and waved his sister across the lane. 'Maebh is the brainy one in the family. You better be nice to her, she bought her own ticket for the play.'

As Maebh crossed the lane, a breeze fluttered open her coat and pressed her light linen dress against her slim body. Jim's eyes never left her, he guessed she might be about twenty but there was something ageless about her. She had a childlike face and luminous pale skin. When she reached the stage door she focused her brown eyes on Jim, smiled and took his breath away.

'Maebh this is Jim I was telling you about. Jim this is me sister Maebh.'

'Hello,' Jim said, his eyes locked onto Maebh's petite face.

'How'a ya Jimmy?'

Maebh's voice was husky with a soft Dublin accent.

'I'm well,' Jim replied grinning like a little boy on Christmas morning. 'Did you enjoy the show?'

'Yes I did and I thought you were good, but not as good as you thought you were.'

Startled, Jim stuttered 'I never said I was good.'

'I'm only teasing ya.' A smile flickered in Maebh's eyes. 'I really liked the show and you were very good.'

'You're right Red, your sister is a bit of a handful,' Jim said and quickly regained his composure.

'You should talk to me Da about her,' Red said and put his arm around his almost silent girlfriend. 'Right Bridget?'

'I might just do that,' Jim said without taking his eyes off Maebh.
'Might you now? And what would you say to him?'
Unaware of the playful but intimate drama that was happening Red said 'Where are you off to now Jim?'
'I have to get something to eat before the evening show.'
'Why don't you come to our house and have your tea with us?' Red said. 'We don't live too far from here.'
'That's very generous of you. But I really couldn't impose.'
'Why, where would you go if you didn't come with us?' Maebh asked.
'Karl's tearooms, serves an excellent early even meal, I usually …'
'Oh heavens Mr Brevin,' Maebh said affecting a posh accent. 'You better come with us; you need a proper home-cooked meal.'
'Maebh will you stop messing, it's Saturday and you know we only have salad for tea,' Red leaned into Jim. 'That's why she has no boyfriend; she's a real messer. Do you know how many times I've fixed her up with me pals?'
'I was never interested in any of your pals and I never needed to be fixed up,' Maebh snapped and flashed a look of mild annoyance at Red.
'Jim, if you think Maebh's a handful, wait until you meet me Da,' Red cast his eyes upwards. 'He's even worse.'
'Now I know where it comes from,' Jim said playfully to Maebh.
'Do you now?' Maebh replied and gently elbowed her way between Jim and her brother. 'You're coming home with us and we'll have no more talk about it, right Bridget?'
Bridget blushed and managed a slight giggle.
The last of the autograph hunters were leaving and Ira approached Jim and his new companions.
'Maebh, Red good to see you,' Ira said. 'Did I hear you say you were at the show?'
'Yes, it was great and you were great,' Red replied enthusiastically.
'And this young actor was excellent too,' Maebh interjected.
'Thank you for the compliment and you're right Maebh, Jim is certainly a good actor. If you don't mind I'll leave you young people to yourselves. I have a few things to attend to. Glad you enjoyed the show. Come again.'
'I thought I'd put a good word in for you with your boss,' Maebh

said as she tucked her arm under Jim's.

The partially rebuilt Sackville Street teemed with horses and carts, automobiles and hundreds of bicycles. A tram clanked past and presented its upper deck passengers with an unhindered view into the street's newly rebuilt offices and refurbished apartments. The paths of Sackville Street were busy too with people strolling casually, walking purposefully or rushing for trams or buses.

'Get your Herald, Mail or Telegraph,' a shoeless newspaper boy called out as the foursome passed Nelson's Pillar.

Maebh stopped walking and said to the boy 'How are ya Sean?'

'Hello Miss Mullin?' the boy said breaking into a smile. 'How're ya?'

'I'm well thank you, Maebh replied. 'How's business?'

'Miss, I only have ten newspapers left and then I can go home.'

'Then I better buy one so you'll get home that little bit sooner.' Maebh opened her handbag, found a penny and handed it to the boy. 'I'll have the Evening Telegraph please, young man.'

'Certainly Miss,' the boy said, and handed Maebh a pink newspaper and as he searched in his pocket for change Maebh winked conspiratorially at him and said 'Why don't you keep the change?'

'Thanks miss,' the boy replied beaming a big smile.

Maebh handed the newspaper to Red and as they continued up Sackville Street the boy resumed his sales call.

'He's one of Maebh's kids,' Red said. 'Did I tell you Maebh is a school teacher?

'Stop talking about me like I'm not here,' Maebh said repositioning herself between Jim and her brother. 'Can you make a living at acting?'

'Not really,' replied a bemused Jim and, glancing at Maebh's arm tucked into his, said 'Are you always so forward?'

'Blooming right I am. Why do you act if you can't make a living at it?'

'Because, I think it's a worthwhile thing to do.'

'I don't mean to be personal but how do you make a living?'

Jim shook his head.

'What?' Maebh asked with mock innocence.

'Just because you say you don't mean to be personal, doesn't give you the right to be personal.'

'You didn't answer my question,' Maebh replied completely ignoring Jim's last statement.

'And I'm not going to answer your question because it's none of your business.'

'Don't be so sensitive.'

'Very well, why don't you tell me something personal about yourself?'

'What do you want to know, Jimmy?'

'What did Red mean when he said you had trouble hanging on to boyfriends?'

Maebh flashed her eyes at Red as if he was a wayward pupil of hers.

'My brother Patrick talks a lot of rubbish. But for your information, Jimmy Brevin, I don't have trouble hanging on to boyfriends. Do you have trouble hanging on to girlfriends?'

'It would be impolite of me to talk about girlfriends.'

'But it's not impolite of you to ask about my boyfriends.'

'Touché.'

'Ask me something else?'

'What does your father do for a living?'

'What a question!' Maebh mocked and then in a perfect French accent added 'Mon père est boulanger.'

'Don't mind her. Da's a baker,' Red interjected as they passed the Gresham Hotel. 'I work in that hotel. I'm the maître d'hôtel.'

'Very impressive,' Jim replied.

'Patrick's not a maître d'hôtel; he's a rebel who pretends to be a waiter.'

'Keep you voice down Maebh,' Red said sharply. 'Streets have ears.'

'Sorry Red.'

'Jim, I think my sister is trying to impress you; she must fancy you.'

Red received an elbow in the ribs for his last comment.

'Well Red, I think I like your cheeky sister.'

'Do you, now?' Maebh replied playfully. 'And who asked you to?'

'I think it's your shyness I find so attractive,' Jim replied.

'You pig,' Maebh shot back. A stunned Jim stopped walking. 'Not used to hearing a woman speaking up for herself, are you Jimmy?'

0On the table was a plate of thinly sliced, tinned corned beef, a small bowl of lettuce, sliced tomatoes, two sliced hard-boiled eggs, a dish of margarine and a bottle of Chef Salad cream.

'Patrick, will you tell your brother Conor to stop messin' with his bike and come in and have his tea, and for heaven's sake make sure he washes his hands,' Mrs Mullin said as she circled the table with a large tea pot.

Red leaned back and shouted out the window 'Conor, tea's ready, hurry or there'll be none left for you. And Ma says to wash your hands!'

'Patrick, I could have shouted to Conor myself, you should have gone out to the boy and told him. What will your guest think of us?'

'Jim can think what he likes,' Red replied and poured milk into his tea.

Maebh placed a freshly cut turnover in the middle of the table and, taking a seat opposite Jim, took great care not look at him – but every now and again her eyes drifted towards him and then cut quickly away. Mrs Mullin observed her daughter and smiled.

Twelve-year-old Conor raced into the room and flopped down in the seat beside Jim. Mrs Mullin glared pointedly at her son's oily hands and the boy rose slowly and slouched into the kitchen.

'Where are Mary and Rose?' Red asked as he handed Jim the plate of corned beef.

'Your sisters are having their tea with Aunt Ann, they'll be home later.'

'Conor, say hello to Jim,' Red said to his brother when he returned to the table.

'How'ya Jim. How'd you know Red?' Conor asked as he reached for a slice of bread.

'I met your brother in Stephen's Green on Easter Monday two years ago.'

The mention of Easter silenced the table. Mr Mullin slowly put his knife and fork down, leaned forward and said very quietly but with the utmost seriousness 'You're not one of them so-called rebels, are you Jimmy?'

'No, I'm not,' Jim replied.

'Good, because I don't want any talk of them in this house.'

THE ACTOR

'Up the rebels!' Conor chimed in cheekily.

Mr Mullin shot his youngest son a withering scowl and the boy quickly lowered his head.

'Da you can't stop us talking about what's happening in the country,' Maebh said breaking the silence.

'War is not some silly game to be played at by fools,' Mr Mullin said, as Red sat in silent defiance. 'People die in wars, real people, not the toffs or the leaders but people like you and me. Maebh, how would you feel if Patrick or Conor was killed in this so-called fight for freedom or independence?' He looked sternly around the table but when his eyes fell upon Red, his son spoke.

'I know better than anyone, that it's not a silly game, Da. But I'm prepared to die for Ireland.'

'I'd prefer if you lived for Ireland,' Mr Mullin retorted sharply. 'I know you think highly of hotheads like Collins and de Valera but what concerns most people is not freedom or independence but having enough money to put food on the table and those real concerns are being trampled on by the bowsies you call rebels.'

'Da, we have a right to freedom,' Maebh said fixing her eyes on her father.

'Maebh, I'm talking to your brother. Patrick, I know your heart is in the right place but what he's doing is dangerous and foolish.'

'What are yis all talking about?' asked young Conor.

'Stop this talk, right now; you're frightening Conor.' Dorrie Mullin's voice was strong and filled with fear and anger. 'It would be nice to have one meal without any talk of Ireland and freedom.'

All conversation at the table ceased and after a minute the unlikely instigator of new conversation was the shy almost perpetually blushing Bridget.

'Jim, I thought you was very good in the play. You did your part well and I enjoyed seeing it.'

'Thank you Bridget,' Jim replied and conversation returned to the table.

When the dishes were cleared, Maebh placed a bowl of rhubarb and a bowl of custard in the centre of the table and as she resumed her seat, Jim looked at her and she held his gaze. Halfway through dessert, Red looked at his watch, jumped up from the table and said 'Have to go, Ma; I'm already late for the match. Thanks again for the tickets Jim, see ya.'

Red grabbed his overcoat and he and Bridget clattered out of the room.

'I don't mean to be rude but I have to go too,' Jim said when he had finished his dessert. 'I have an evening show. That was a lovely meal Mrs Mullin, thank you very much.'

'Ah sure it was only a bit of salad,' Mrs Mullin replied self-consciously. 'Nice to have met you Jim, and sorry about the family flare-up but that's the way of things in this house.'

'See you Jim,' Mr Mullin said as he lifted a pipe off the mantelpiece and grinned at his daughter. 'Maebh, why don't you show Jim out?'

Maebh made a face at him, followed Jim out of the living room, walked down the short hall and helped him on with his coat.

'Hope it wasn't too off-putting for you, but in our house everybody speaks their mind.'

'No, it was very interesting.'

'Interesting interesting or interesting boring?'

'Certainly not boring,' Jim smiled.

Maebh opened the door and as Jim brushed passed her in the narrow doorway he felt like taking her in his arms and kissing her, but he didn't. He stepped into the avenue and just as he was about to speak Maebh said 'Well, are you going to ask me?'

'I was going to, actually.'

'And what were you going to ask?' Maebh grinned.

'You don't make things easy for a fellow, do you?'

'Very well, I'll make it easy for you. If you did ask me out, my answer would be yes.'

'But I haven't asked you out, yet.'

'No, you haven't. But if you did ask me out, you know the answer.'

'Good. Would you like to go out with me Maebh?'

'I don't know.'

'I though you said the answer would be yes.'

'I don't know because you didn't say when you wanted to take me out.'

'Sunday?'

'Sunday would be lovely. I'll be ready at three.'
 'Then I'll pick you up here at three.'
'Good! And goodbye, Mr Brevin.'
'Goodbye now, Miss Mullin,' Jim replied and as walked down Primrose Avenue he was already looking forward to seeing the very pretty, mischievous Miss Mullin again.
Maebh closed the door and her face broke out in a huge smile.

31

The Royal Hibernian Hotel on Kildare Street was a place of ostentatious opulence. Decorated with huge gold leaf mirrors, Turner-inspired landscape paintings, heavy velvet drapes, crystal chandeliers and plush carpets, it was Leslie Lawrence's favourite place to dine. Every Sunday afternoon at twelve thirty sharp he would arrive formally dressed, sit at his regular window table and enjoy fine French cuisine.

'Wonderful show last night, Mr Allen,' the headwaiter said as he walked Ira to Leslie's table. 'My wife and I really enjoyed it; very humorous.'

'Thank you John, very nice of you to say so.'

Ira sat at Leslie's table and as he opened the menu he asked 'How was the Joseph Barne's play at the Royal?'

Leslie looked over the top of the menu and said 'The sooner Barnes gets his brushes out and paints his masterpiece the better, for he's certainly not going to write one.'

'A bit harsh there Leslie. Barnes is a good playwright and an excellent poet too.'

'Yes he is: I liked one of his two-line poems although there were dull stretches in it.'

'Very witty, I wish I'd said that.'

'Don't worry Ira, you will. I expect it will appear in one of your plays one of these days. Tell me about this meeting you have with Norman Whitten. Strange day to have a meeting, Sunday?'

'Yes it is. But apparently it's the only day he's available for meetings, the rest of the week he's off filming his *Irish Events* Newsreel.'

'How do you feel about him turning your play into a moving picture?'

'I don't know, it's just talk at the moment.'

'This is your third meeting. I know Norman, he doesn't waste his time. I'd say his plans are further along than you think.'

'We'll see.'

'Ira, do you go the motion picture palaces?'

'I have done. And I enjoy the flicker, lots of people do. I was surprised to learn that there are more moving picture palaces in Dublin than theatres.'

'Depressing isn't it? People would rather watch shadows on a screen rather than real human beings.'

'I have never seen such fussing about in all my life,' Dorrie Mullin said when her daughter asked her, for the third time, to comment on her clothes. 'If he's half as keen as you he won't notice what you're wearing.'

'Ma, I am not fussing. Just tell me, do I look all right?'

'You look beautiful. You looked beautiful in your blue rabbit-wool cardigan and cream dress, and you looked beautiful in your floral dress and white jacket, and you look beautiful now in your white blouse and plaid skirt. I tell you if the boy doesn't think you're beautiful, he's blind.'

The front door knocker thumped loudly against its brass base. Maebh's brown eyes shot to her mother.

'I'll get it,' Mrs Mullin said. 'You sit.' Maebh frowned. 'You don't want him to think you're eager, do ya?'

'Ma,' Maebh snapped, but Mrs Mullin was half way down the hall.

Maebh heard the front door open, she heard her mother say hello to Jim. The living room door opened and Jim entered the room with a bouquet of flowers. Maebh could not stop herself from smiling.

'Well, hello Jim,' she said, as though she was surprised to see him.

'Well, hello Maebh, these are for you,' Jim said, and he handed her the flowers.

'Thanks, they're lovely.' He's like a little boy, she thought, as she smelled the flowers.

'I'll put them in water,' Mrs Mullin said as she took the flowers from Maebh. 'You young people have better things to be doing then standing around here on a beautiful Sunday afternoon. Off with the both of ya.'

'Where are you taking me?' Maebh asked as she put on her coat.

'I thought we might go to the Phoenix Park and visit the Zoological Gardens.'

'I'd like that,' Maebh replied even though she hated the zoo.

Ira pushed open the door of 17 Great Brunswick Street and climbed a flight of creaky stairs to the office of the Central Film Supply Company.

'Come in, it's open,' a high-pitched voice called out when Ira knocked on the office door. He opened the door and a cloud of cigarette smoke billowed from the room. Sitting behind a small desk surrounded by cans of film, a camera, a tripod and two cases of lights was Norman Whitten, founder of Ireland's first moving picture newsreel *Irish Events*.

'Good that you could come along,' said the Englishman as he hung the handpiece of his phone back on its candlestick holder.

'My pleasure,' Ira replied.

Norman shook Ira's hand and as he moved cans of film stock off his desk and placed them carefully on top of a filing cabinet, he said 'Please take a seat.' He stubbed out his cigarette, tugged on the waistcoat of his tweed suit, rummaged in the cabinet and then placed a bound manuscript in front of the actor.

'Have a look at that,' he said, raising his eyebrows into his high forehead as he resumed his seat behind his desk.

'What is it?' asked Ira.

'Well it's what you theatre people call a play script and we film people call a photoplay.' Norman leaned back in his chair and lit a Golden Spangled cigarette. *Aimsir Padraig/In the Day of St Patrick* that's the title of the moving picture I intend to make,' he said through the smoke haze.

'You've changed the title,' Ira commented without picking up the photoplay.

'I've changed lots of things. Moving pictures are very different beasts from stage plays.'

'I can't help you with a photoplay. I know nothing of the mechanics of moving picture making.'

'Not here to do that, the photoplay is complete. I'd like to offer you the role of St Patrick.'

'I usually play King Laeghaire of Tara.'

'King Laeghaire is a minor role in the motion picture. This is St Patrick's story and I need someone with gravitas to play Patrick.'

Ira sat and made no effort to reply.

'I'll be straight with you Ira, my background is not in drama, it's in newsreel making, so I'd be relying on you to help me with actors, casting, and all that sort of thing.'

'When do you hope to start making your motion picture, Mr Whitten?'

'We've already begun pre-production, costumes are being designed, a slave market is under construction in Rush, chariots and pirate galleys are being built, props such as shields, lances and swords are made and most locations have been identified. We will shoot key sequences in the actual locations where the events took place: Tara, Slane, Slieve Mish, places like that. The picture will be widely distributed and shown all over Ireland, the UK and in many other territories. What do you say Mr Allen?' he asked earnestly. 'Will you join us?'

Ira picked up the photoplay, looked at the dapper Englishman who was going to tell the story of Ireland's most venerated saint and said 'I'll give you my answer on Monday morning.'

Maebh alighted from the tram at the Phoenix Park and a gush of wind billowed her plaid skirt against her legs. Smiling coyly she smoothed down her skirt, she took Jim's hand and as they walked in happy silence through the People's Gardens she curled her slender fingers in his hand.

'Get your monkey nuts, a ha'penny a bag,' shouted the black-shawled street traders outside the thatched entrance lodge to the zoo.

Jim bought a newspaper cone of nuts and gave it to Maebh. In the monkey enclosure as Maebh was opening the cone, a young chimpanzee reached out of the cage and snatched the cone from her hand. Maebh screamed, Jim wrapped his arm and around her shoulder; she giggled and they both laughed. When they visited the lion house,

Maebh impulsively stood close to Jim and when they took a ride on the elephants she gripped Jim's hand so tightly it hurt. Afterwards in the zoo's Victorian Tearooms they had fruit scones and cream and never stopped looking at each other. When Jim asked Maebh about her school, her eyes lit up from within.

'Jimmy, the children are wonderful, they are so intelligent and bright and they ask so many questions. They love me to read stories and they love Irish stories the best. When one of them learns the alphabet or recognises words I put their name on a special board and then when there are five names on the board I bring in a loaf of bread, jam and margarine and we have a little party.' Maebh's face became serious. 'Jimmy the children are often hungry. The tenements they live in are overcrowded; the poverty is shocking.'

Sitting in his living room Ira thought about how he would approach acting in a motion picture. During his visits to the picture palaces he had observed that many of the older actors used extravagant body language and exaggerated their facial expressions to convey emotion but that younger newer actors, like Lillian Gish, Charlie Chaplin and Greta Garbo showed more restraint in their acting. He also noted how the more minimalist acting style brought the audience into the creative process.

The church clock bells pealed seven as Maebh and Jim stepped off the tram on Berkley Road. They walked hand in hand up along the Georgian houses of Blessington Street and into the Blessington Basin. When they stopped, supposedly to admire a family of swans gliding on the still waters of the pond, Jim slipped his arm around Maebh's waist. Maebh turned to him, placed her hand on the back of his neck and guided his head down to her lips. Surprised by this, Jim didn't respond. Maebh tilted her head to one side and said 'It's better if you join in.'

Jim framed Maebh's face in his hands and kissed her. She rested her head on his shoulder and they stood looking at the swans and cygnets drift along the water.

Later, as they made their way out of the park, Maebh stopped under the arched gateway. Looking like a little girl who has been discovered playing with her mother's lipstick she said 'I don't usually kiss a boy the first time he takes me out.'

'Don't worry,' Jim replied and leaning towards Maebh said 'you're not the first girl that's found me irresistible.'

'You pig, you're a pig,' Maebh said and playfully pounded Jim with her fists.

Jim pulled her close and was about to kiss her when she pulled away.

'Stop, the neighbours might be looking.'

It was eleven o'clock on Monday morning and Norman Whitten was checking his camera and other film-making equipment when Ira knocked on the door of his office.

'It would be a pleasure to be in your motion picture, Norman,' Ira said when Norman asked him if he had come to a decision about taking the role of St Patrick.

'Great to have you on board,' Norman replied. 'Now do you think you could convince your wife to play the part of Patrick's mother?'

'I think I can do that,' Ira replied and added. 'I have some suggestions for other castings too.'

'Do tell,' Norman replied and for the next hour the two men discussed the motion picture they were about to make together.

'Michael has invited a girl to Sunday lunch,' an excited Líla said to Jim at breakfast. 'And he's instructed Mrs O'Neill to use our best china and glassware. Did you know he had a girl?'

'No, wait a minute, yes I do; he told me he met someone. I think he said she was a banker's daughter. She had a double-barrelled name – Clara Wright-Moran, something like that.'

'Is she nice?'

'How would I know? I never met her and don't ask me any more questions. I don't care who he brings home. I think we should respect Michael's privacy.'

Líla followed Jim into the drawing room. 'What are you talking about, privacy? You're usually as inquisitive as I am.' She scrutinised her brother's face. 'I know what it is.' Jim looked away. 'You have a girlfriend too.'

'Líla, could we be adults about this?'
'Do I know her, what's her name?'
'You don't know her and I'm not telling you her name.'
But Líla pestered him until he gave her Maebh's name.

At one o'clock a carriage pulled by two plumed, white horses stopped outside the Brevin's house and a beautifully dressed Clara Wright-Moran and Michael alighted from the carriage. Líla stood in the front drawing room looking out of the window.
'She's old,' she said, and her disappointment was obvious. 'I'd say she's thirty or more.'
'Don't be so rude,' Jim said, not looking up from the newspaper.
Clara Wright-Moran was slim and mousey-haired. She had high cheekbones and a natural toothy smile but her eyes lacked sparkle.
Michael opened the front door and Líla hurriedly took the armchair opposite Jim.
'Sometimes I think you're still a ten-year-old child,' Jim said, shaking his head.
'When am I going to meet Maebh?'
'You're never going to meet her.'
'We'll see.'
When Michael escorted his lady into the front drawing room Jim and Líla stood.
'Jim, Líla, I'd like you to meet Miss Clara Wright-Moran.'
'Call me Clara,' she said and flashed a toothy smile.
'Would you care for a sherry, Clara?' Jim asked.
'That would be lovely. An amontillado please.'
'Allow me,' Michael said and opened the drinks cabinets. 'Is father about?'
'He said he'd join us shortly,' Líla replied and took the seat beside Clara. 'Clara how did you and Michael meet? Tell me everything and leave nothing out.'
'Clara, tell Líla nothing,' Michael said as he poured the three sherries. 'No matter what you say, she'll turn it against you.'
'Michael, I've two sisters of my own. I know what interests us girls,' Clara said and smiled another toothy smile.

'I've met your sisters Victoria and Elizabeth and believe me they are nothing like Líla.'

'Pay no attention to my brother,' Líla said and curled her legs under her. 'He's just a man. Clara tell me how you met my brother?'

Half an hour later, wearing his new high-waisted, wide lapelled suit, Theo greeted Clara and had her sit next to him at the dining table. After Michael stood and said 'Father, Jim and Líla, I have great pleasure in informing you that I have spoken to Clara's father, the eminent banker, Augustine Wright-Moran and he has given us permission to marry. We are planning an autumn engagement.'

Theo murmured to Jim 'Why did he have to mention that her father was an eminent banker?'

'He must think that it's important,' Jim replied.

Theo sighed heavily, looked at Clara and wondered what sadness or regret caused her eyes to be so dull.

32

The sea was blue, the air was sweet and for Maebh and Jim, the world was an exquisite place to be. It was a sunny Sunday afternoon and Blackrock Park was filled with people. Couples lay on grass relaxing in the sun, while children chased each other or floated toy boats on the park's artificial lake. Jim and Maebh sat in deck chairs in front of the bandstand and listened to the St James's Brass and Reed Band play a series of joyous Phillip Susa marches. After the concert a dark cloud passed over the park and Maebh and Jim made their way to the nearby train station.

'Someone is waving at us,' Maebh said.

'It's Michael, my brother, and his fiancée Clara Wright-Moran. I wonder how long it will take Michael to mention that Clara's family is wealthy?'

'Oh, I've never met anyone really wealthy,' Maebh said a little nervously. 'Are her family aristocrats?'

'No, more like crooks, they're bankers.'

Maebh giggled.

'Hello Jim,' Michael said. 'You know Clara. And who may I ask is this pretty young lady?'

'Michael, Clara, I'd like you to meet Maebh Mullen.'

'How are ya Clara, glad to meet you Michael?' Maebh said and held out her hand.

Taken aback by Maebh's accent Michael blinked, smiled lamely and said over-politely 'Pleased to meet you Maebh.'

'Are you one of the Mullins of Sandycove?' Clara asked as she took Maebh's hand.

'No, I'm one of the Mullins of Primrose Avenue.'

'I don't know Primrose Avenue.'

'There's no reason why an eminent banker's daughter should know of Primrose Avenue,' interjected Michael with a smirk.

Jim's eyes darted to Maebh and the trace of a grin danced on his lips. Maebh glanced down before Michael realised that he and his fiancée were the butt of a private joke.

'Jim, I believe you know a distant cousin of mine,' Clara said filling the silence that had fallen on the foursome. 'He was at Killucan with you, Stewart Keogh?'

'Baggy is your cousin? What he's up to?'

'He's an accountant. He sends his regards and hopes you'll drop in on him when you're next in Cork.'

'I'll do that,' Jim replied delighted to hear about his friend.

'Clara it's getting a little chilly we should be moving along,' Michael said and even feigned a shiver. 'Nice to have met you – Maebh.' Michael tipped his hat, took Clara's arm and walked her briskly away.

'I think we were a bit rude to your brother,' Maebh said fingering the strap of her handbag.

'My brother's a snob. Besides he was rude to you. I hope he didn't upset you.'

'He didn't upset me. Some people don't know when they're being rude. The school principal does it all the time and he's a really nice man.'

The following evening, Jim was in his dressing room putting on his costume for the night's performance when Ira knocked on the door and slipped into the room.

'Good news, remember I said I might have some work for you this summer?' Jim nodded as he strapped on a belt and sword. 'I have been authorised to offer you a role in a motion picture *In the Days of Saint Patrick*. It's not a big part, but it would be a valuable experience. May,

Richard and Leslie are going to be in it. What do you say?'

'Tell me more?'

'You have two scenes: the first is in a slave galley. The boy Patrick, you and other boys are being transported to Ireland to be sold as slaves. When Niall of the Nine Hostages, that's Richard, whips the young Patrick, your character grabs the whip from him and gets whipped for his good deed. Your second scene takes place in a slave market where you and Patrick are sold to King Milcho, that's Leslie.'

'Is that it?'

'Yes, it should take about two days to film.'

'I'm game, count me in and thank you again for the opportunity.'

'Hope you'll still be saying that in the autumn,' he said.

'Have you met Jim's latest girlfriend?' a fuming Michael asked Líla when he stormed into the drawing room.

'No, what's she like?'

'She's as common as ditch water and she rides a bicycle. She had the audacity to wave to me today as she cycled up Sackville Street. I was with my friends, God knows what they thought! What is Jim doing with such a person?'

'What do you mean – such a person? What's wrong with her?'

'I've just told you she's common and she rides a bicycle.'

'Michael, sometimes you can be quite insufferable.'

'Better insufferable than common.'

It was the afternoon of Maebh's twenty-second birthday and when she opened the front door of her home, she came face to face with the unusual sight of a hansom cab parked outside. The cab door swung open, Jim stepped out and said 'Mademoiselle, your carriage awaits.'

'What's this?'

'It's a surprise,' Jim said and held open the cab door for her.

'Now there's style for ya,' Mrs Furlong, the next door neighbour shouted, from her bedroom window. 'You've got a live one there Maebh, hold on to him.'

'Thank you Mrs Furlong,' Maebh replied and stepped into the cab.

The horse trotted down the avenue and the cab rattled and swayed behind. Ten minutes later the cab pulled up outside the Queen's Theatre.

'What are we doing here?' Maebh asked Jim.

'I'm taking you to a show.'

'It's Sunday afternoon, the theatre is closed.'

'This is a special recital,' Jim replied; he removed a small wicker basket from the back of the cab and guided Maebh to the theatre's stage door.

'This is the tricky part,' he whispered to Maebh. 'Say nothing and do just as I do.'

He opened the stage door, walked into the foyer, waved to Archie, and walked Maebh to a caged metal ladder that was attached to the stage wall. Jim looked around and, when all the stage hands and backstage staff were out of sight, said 'Quick. Up the ladder.'

Maebh and Jim climbed twenty five feet up into the flies to a lighting gantry that stretched across the stage.

'We're going out there,' Jim said and pointed to the middle of the gantry.

'It's very high, I'm nervous,' Maebh said.

'It's safe. Hold on to the railings and don't look down.'

With two hands gripping the railings tightly, Maebh moved slowly out to into the middle of the gantry.

'Why are we up here?' she whispered as she sat down and dangled her legs in the air.

'Because these are the best seats in the house.'

'What's the show?' Maebh asked, as she nervously looked down.

'It's ballet,' Jim whispered, and pointed to four dancers stretching and limbering up in the wings. 'We have a bird's eye view.'

'You love your theatre, don't you, and it doesn't matter what kind of theatre it is?' Maebh said looking into Jim's face.

'Yes I do,' Jim replied. He kissed Maebh on the cheek and opened the wicker basket. 'Let's eat.'

Maebh greatly enjoyed the show. When the recital was over and all the dancers and the stagehands had left the stage, Jim and Maebh climbed down the ladder. As she stood on the bottom rung, Jim put his hands on her waist and as he lifted her off the ladder she deliberately brushed her body against his. When her feet reached the floor, Jim didn't remove his hands. He looked into her eyes, pulled her close, she raised herself on tiptoes and they kissed.

It was eight o'clock on a cold windy summer morning when the seven thirty from Amiens Street puffed its way into Rush Station. It was Jim, Richard and Leslie's first day of filming on the set of *In the Days of St Patrick*. The production manager, J W Mackey, greeted them and walked them through a small collection of tents that had been erected on a cordoned off section of the north beach. In the costume tent, a crowd of extras were getting dressed in ancient Irish clothes. Mr Mackey said, 'It's a little busy here, why don't I get one of the assistant directors to show you around, and explain what's happening? You're not needed until the afternoon so you can return here in an hour or so and get costumed.'

'Excellent idea,' replied Leslie.

Mr Mackey called over Brendan Delaney, the squat assistant director and instructed him to 'show the actors around.' Brendan Delaney possessed an encyclopaedic knowledge of film making. He walked the actors to the top of the beach, pointed to a boat bobbing on the water and said 'When the tide is fully out, we will shoot the slave galley sequences, tomorrow on this beach we will shoot the chariot race and the slave market sequence. Mr Lawrence you should go along and get some practice riding a chariot. The chariot master, the man over there with the bowler hat will teach you how to ride a chariot.'

'I don't have to drive one of those things, do I?' asked an astonished and startled Leslie.

'No, you're the king so you have a chariot driver but you do have to stand gracefully on the chariot as it races along the beach.

'My God what have I let myself in for?' Leslie groaned, as he walked towards the chariot master.

'How will they go about filming the chariot race?' asked Jim.

'The director wants to shoot the race using two different techniques,' answered Brendan. 'First a camera will be mounted on the rear of a flat-back lorry which will be driven in front of the charging chariots – that's called a tracking shot. When we have that shot in the can, he will shoot the race again, but this time it will be shot by three cameras placed in succession along the beach. The sequence will last about twenty seconds in the finished film.'

'Good God, that sounds like a lot work for such little reward,' Richard said.

'In some ways it is,' answered the assistant director. 'But it will look great.'

Richard and Jim sat and watched the chariots race up and down the beach. After a while Richard meandered over to the costume tent where he was given a burlap costume, a pair of sandals and a whip. He held up the whip and asked the wardrobe mistress 'What's this for?'

'It's for whipping slaves,' the costume designer replied. 'Didn't you read the photoplay?'

'No, couldn't make head or tail of it. Would you be so good as to get me a cup of tea?'

'I'm not a waitress. I'm the wardrobe mistress. Get your own tea.'

Richard was sitting in the catering tent drinking a cup of milky tea when Jim, wearing a similar costume but without the sandals and the whip, entered the tent. The two actors looked at each other and burst out laughing. Half an hour later a shaken Leslie limped into the catering tent and collapsed into a chair.

'Mr O'Hare, Mr Brevin,' the assistant director said on entering the tent. 'They are ready for you out at the boat.'

'Boat, what are you talking about?' Richard cried, his eyes nearly popping out of their sockets. 'I'm an actor not a seaman. I get sea sick.'

'The boat won't be moving. It will be in less than two feet of water,' the assistant director replied.

'I can't do it,' Richard insisted. 'I just can't do it.'

'Richard, if I can ride on a bone-shaking chariot that has no suspension, if I am to be shook and thrown about like a leaf in a force ten gale, you can stand in a motionless boat resting in two feet of water.'

Richard folded his arms and leaned back in his chair.

Jim leaned down to Richard and said very quietly 'You do realise that by not getting in the boat you are compromising Ira.'

'It's the principle of the thing, I'm not a seaman and refuse to become one.'

Leslie leaned over to Richard. 'If you don't get in the boat you won't be paid for today and you'll have to make your own way home.'

'Perhaps, I should give the boat a try,' Richard said and got up to go.

Aimsir Padraig/In the Day of St Patrick was released on the 15 March 1920, to coincide with the festivities for St Patrick's Day. Jim and Maebh sat in the Masterpiece Cinema and stared at the huge blank screen. The picture palace was crowded with eager people anxious to see one of Ireland's first feature-length motion pictures. Jim had booked a row of seats in the centre of the cinema. Líla and Ciaran sat on his right and Maebh was on his left. Beside Maebh sat Mary and Rose, her two younger sisters, and next to them were her two brothers, Conor and Red, and next to Red was Bridget, his girlfriend. Red handed Rose and Mary a bag of bull's eyes. A boy sitting behind the girls tapped Rose on the shoulder and said 'Gis a sweet.'

Rose held up the bag, the boy dived his hand in and Mary said to him 'Me sister's boyfriend is in this flick.'

'Is he?' asked the boy as he popped two sweets into his mouth.

'Yea, he's over there. He's got a real big part,' Mary pointed proudly at Jim. 'That's him there with me sister.'

Word quickly swept around the cinema that a movie star was in their midst. Some people leaned forward to get a better look, others stood and pointed at Jim, while Mary, Rose and Conor waved at everyone. When the film's director, Norman Whitten, and his lead actor, Ira Allen, walked down the central aisle of the picture palace, the audience stood and cheered. The two men took their seats, the applause subsided, the conductor raised his baton and the eight-piece orchestra played the Eimear Noone overture. The lights faded, the projector burst into light and the film's first title flickered on the screen.

"Killester Films present *Aimsir Padraig/In the Day of St Patrick.*"

Maebh took Jim's hand and held it tightly.

'How long before we see you?' she whispered.

'Not long, my part is in the beginning of the film.'

A second title card flickered on the screen and Jim felt the blood race through his veins.

"At the end of the fourth century in a land across the sea a child was

born – a child who was chosen to be the apostle of Ireland and to deliver its children from pagan darkness into the light of the one true faith."

The music swelled and a crystal clear image of an ancient galley appeared on the horizon. The second shot showed the boat's interior where slaves were being whipped mercilessly as they rowed.

'There you are Jim,' young Conor yelled out as he jumped to his feet. 'Jasus, you're wearing a dress.'

'Where is he?' shouted young Mary.

'Sit down!' yelled a man.

This is embarrassing, Jim thought as he crouched down in his seat. Conor resumed his seat and another image flickered on screen. The boat was now anchored in a small inlet and the slaves on board were being whipped off the boat.

'Jim, I thought you said you helped St Patrick on the boat?' Rose called down the row to Jim as the slaves were being marched on land.

'I'll be on in a minute!' Jim replied, but he wondered what had happened to his boat scene. They couldn't have left it out entirely, could they?

The next scene was to be in the slave market where Jim gave the boy Patrick, who was waiting to be sold, a cup of water, but the next scene was Patrick being sold. Jim slid down in his seat. His second scene had been cut too.

'You must have been dreaming about your part in the flick,' Red said loudly when the film moved on to Patrick tending sheep.

In spite of Jim's mortification the audience became engrossed in the story, and cheered and applauded many times during the screening. In the following days, weeks and months the film was shown in picture palaces, church halls, sports halls, school halls and in civic buildings in every county in Ireland. It was well received by critics, in the trade and by the public. Ira's performance was praised highly, critics used words like 'magnificent' and 'awe inspiring'. The *Connaught Catholic* called it 'saintly.'

For years afterwards people would come up to Ira in the street and ask him to bless their children, their houses or their farms. Ira always explained that he was not St Patrick but a mere actor who played the role of St Patrick. The people would listen patiently, nod in agreement and when he had finished talking, they would ask again if he would bless their children, their houses and their farms. He always obliged.

33

Immaculately dressed in his new Saville Row dinner jacket, Michael hurried along the freshly waxed hall and trotted downstairs.

'Is everything ready?' he called across the steam filled kitchen.

'No, everything is as it should be,' replied an edgy Mrs O'Neill.

Sheila, Mrs O'Neill's sister, lifted two tall steaming pots off the cooker, placed them in the sink, removed two baskets from the pots and placed two tied bunches of asparagus spears on a draining tray.

'When you're done there,' Mrs O'Neill said to her sister. 'Will you start on the cheese sauce?'

'Have you a menu for me?' Michael asked as Mrs O'Neill lifted a large pot of potatoes onto the stove.

'I put the menu on the sideboard in the dining room as you instructed,' the exasperated housekeeper replied.

'Oh, did you? Who did you say was looking after upstairs?'

'My granddaughters Eavan and Grace, will be serving in the drawing room and I will lead the service in the dining room. Michael shouldn't you be upstairs, looking after your guests? I see your grandmother has arrived.'

'What, they're here already?' Michael gasped, and he bounded up the stairs.

Mrs O'Neill's flicked her eyes upwards, 'men!'

The front door was open and a blast of piercingly cold air was blowing down the hall.

'Close the door out there, Grandmother Brevin will get her death of cold!' Grace was shouting from the drawing room.

'Don't shout at my guests,' Michael whispered crossly, beckoning to the young girl. 'Go close the hall door, take my uncle and aunt's cloaks and escort them into the drawing room.'

Miriam Brevin, the long-suffering wife of Theo's brother Gerry, stood in the hall and watched her husband slowly close the front door. When his mission was accomplished he removed his coat, shuddered and said without irony 'Cold as hell out there'.

'Go easy on the drinking tonight, darling,' Miriam said as she dusted dandruff from the shoulders of her husband's dinner jacket.

Gerry handed his coat to Grace. 'Has my mother arrived yet?'

'Yes sir, she's in the front drawing room.'

Gerry muttered to his wife, as he peered into the candlelit drawing room, 'Can you see her anywhere?'

'By the fire, darling,' Miriam replied.

Filled with the soft light of fifty candles and warmed by a blazing log fire, the room looked like something out of a fairy tale. Miriam's eyes danced around the room and lingered upon the beautiful flower arrangements that stood in each corner.

'Mater, lovely to see you,' Gerry said as he embraced his mother.

Mrs Brevin held her son at arm's length and said 'Gerry you've been drinking.'

'Just the one, very cold out there. Need something to battle the elements.' Gerry nodded at Theo. 'Where are you hiding the sherry?'

'Could you not at least say hello to your brother before you start to drink him out of house and home?' his mother said.

Gerry took a step backwards with the look of a hurt child. 'Mater, you can be quite caustic when you want to be.' He turned to his brother. 'Hello Theo, good to see you. Can I get you something?'

'No thank you, the sherry is on the drinks cabinet by the window. Paul is busy at it already.'

'Ah, Paul's here!' Relieved, Gerry strode over to greet his favourite brother.

Michael rushed to the front door, opened it and the entire Wright-Moran family bustled into the hall.

'Great news,' Clara said to Michael. 'Father is to be awarded an OBE for his services to the Irish War Hospital Supply Organisation.'

'Congratulations sir,' Michael said to Clara's corpulent father.

'Steady on there, it hasn't been formally announced. I can't accept your congratulations yet. Clara should not have told you about the proposed award. If word gets out before the formal announcement, they will withdraw the honour.'

Augustine Wright-Moran turned to his wife and his three daughters: 'Abigail, Clara, Victoria and Elizabeth! Protocol must be followed to the letter in this matter; not another word to anyone this evening.'

'And you can rely on my discretion sir,' Michael promised solemnly.

Augustine took his wife's arm and led his family into the drawing room. Across the room Gerry and his older brother Paul were standing at the drinks cabinet. Gerry sipped a glass of sherry and shuddered.

'Any idea where he keeps the whiskey?'

'Try there,' Paul said, nodding to another door in the cabinet. Gerry searched for whiskey and Paul slid a silver cigarette case from his pocket, eased one out with nicotine-stained fingers and popped it in his mouth. He flicked the lighter on the side of the cigarette case, a flame shot into the air and he sucked in a lungful of glorious smoke.

'Found it,' Gerry cried, as he placed a decanter of whiskey on the sideboard. 'Fancy one?'

'Pour away,' Paul replied and again sucked on his cigarette.

'How is Florence?'

'She's very well, I think. Very cold night out there tonight. On the way here I saw people walking on the frozen waters of the canal.'

'Not surprised,' Gerry replied and handed his brother a glass. 'When I got up this morning the sponges were frozen in the wash bowl on the nightstand.'

Michael introduced Clara and her family to his grandmother, who greeted Clara warmly, and when Abigail Wright-Moran shook Theo's hand, she asked 'Do you and your wife have many grandchildren?'

'I have no grandchildren,' Theo replied.

'But Michael is your grandchild.'

'Michael is my son and Mrs Brevin is my mother,' replied a miffed Theo.

'Your mother, I do beg your pardon.' Then, collecting her composure, she added 'An honest mistake. Your mother looks so young.'

'She thought I was old enough to be Michael's grandfather,' an astonished Theo said to Líla when she brought him a glass of sherry.

Líla chuckled and seeing the serious look on her father's face added 'Mrs Wright-Moran is not wearing her glasses.'

'You don't know if she wears glasses,' Theo said as he sipped the sherry.

Jim pushed opened the front door and Maebh hesitated before stepping into the hall.

'They won't bite,' Jim said as he helped Maebh remove her coat. 'They're quite civilised.'

'Yes we are,' Líla said as she crossed the hall and embraced Maebh. 'Welcome Maebh, I'm delighted to finally meet you. Oh, I love your hair; it's the new Bandeaux style, isn't it?'

'Yes it is. And you must be Líla?'

Jim put his arm around Líla and said 'This is my little sister, the bane of my life.'

'Pay no attention to my brother. Would you like to freshen up?' she said, taking Maebh's hand.

'Yes thank you,' and the two young women walked up the stairs chatting like old friends, and Jim, waiting in the hall for them to come back down, was delighted by Líla's kindness to his girl.

Michael was standing by the fire talking to Clara's father when Líla, Maebh and Jim entered the candle-lit drawing room. The instant Michael saw Maebh his back stiffened and he pointedly looked away from his new guests.

'I'd like you to meet Maebh,' Jim said to his father and grandmother.

'Nice to meet you Maebh,' Theo said. 'Jim tells me you cycle.'

'The girl cycles?' Grandmother Brevin said; she leaned back in her armchair and held her spectacles to her eyes. 'But you're so little.'

'Jimmy tells me you don't approve of women who cycle,' Maebh said mischievously to Theo.

'Oh, Jimmy is it?' Theo's eyes locked on Maebh's face. 'I may have

said something like that in the past but that was a long time ago.'
'Then perhaps we could go for a cycle together sometime?'
'I don't have a bicycle.'
'You could borrow my father's.'
'You're too generous.' Then, turning to Jim, Theo said 'I think this young lady is flirting with me!'
'And why wouldn't I flirt with you? Aren't ya a fine handsome man?'
Theo laughed.
'You're a very forward young woman,' Grandmother Brevin said. 'You're flirting with my son and walking out with my grandson, what's the world coming to?'
'I'm a modern woman,' replied Maebh.
'Good for you,' Grandmother Brevin said. 'I wish I was young again, I'd have a bicycle and perhaps even a motorcycle.'
Jim quietly revelled in how easily Maebh was conquering the room.
Mrs O'Neill's two granddaughters, Eavan and Grace stood in front of the large sideboard. Eavan rang a glass bell and, when the room had quietened, announced that dinner would be served in five minutes. Theo and Grandmother Brevin got to their feet. Gerry placed his precious glass of whiskey on the sideboard, saying 'I'll be back for you.' Then he trotted off looking for his wife. Theo took Líla's arm and said quietly to her 'Why don't you change places with Maebh? Your uncle Owen is on his own and you know how he enjoys talking to you.'
'Certainly father,' Líla said and as she passed Jim she whispered 'Father likes Maebh.'
'He has good taste,' Jim replied with a smirk.
Uncle Owen was an affable man whose dark-complexion, enormous bushy eyebrows and large moustache gave the impression that he was severe; in reality, he was a gentle man who greatly enjoyed family gatherings.
'How is Aunt Betty?' Líla asked as she walked her uncle to the table.
'Betty is unwell, it's her leg that's hurting her tonight. The truth is she simply does not like social occasions and her illnesses are very convenient excuses to avoid them. But that's old news. Look at you,

all grown up. Every time I see you I think of my dear, departed sister, Grainne. You are the image of your mother.'

'What a nice thing to say. No wonder you're my favourite uncle,' Líla said as Owen pulled out a chair for her.

'I bet you say that to all your uncles.'

'I do, but I only mean it when I say it to you.'

'What do you think of this spy mania that's sweeping the city?' Gerry Brevin said to his brother Paul as he placed his napkin on his knee.

'It's ridiculous,' replied Paul. 'My local policeman stopped me on the street and said "Sir, I am obliged to ask your name and to ask what you are doing in the area." You know me. I said to him. I'm Paul Brevin, I'm a lawyer and I work in that building over there and we both know that I have been working there for the past twenty years. Things are getting out of hand in this country.'

When everyone was seated Michael stood and said grace. Then, carrying a large silver salver on which sat a terrine of wild boar, Mrs O'Neill circled the table, stopped at Grandmother Brevin's side and served her. Grace offered the older lady some homemade chutney relish and Eavan placed a slice of rustic bread on her side plate.

'I believe Michael's brother Jim is an actor,' Victoria Wright-Moran whispered to her younger sister.

'Well he's certainly handsome enough to be one,' giggled Elizabeth as she looked across the table and smiled at Jim.

'I wouldn't do that if I were you,' Michael said, 'Jim's girl is a rather coarse person.'

Around the table the people chatted and talked and a feeling of great warmth and good cheer filled the room. When a lull came in the conversation Gerry Brevin said a little too loudly 'What do you young people think of those suffragettes who chained themselves to Government buildings last Wednesday?'

'I think they are a disgrace,' Michael said with great disdain. 'Women should never meddle in politics. A woman's place is in the home.'

'And would all you young ladies agree with that thought?' Gerry voice was becoming slurred.

'I wouldn't agree,' Maebh said. 'And Michael, would you dare say that if Countess Markievicz was here?'

When Clara's mother Mrs Abigail Wright-Moran heard Maebh's accent she gasped and glared at Maebh. A hush fell on the room. Jim placed his hand on Maebh's hand. Grandmother Brevin waved her hand in the air and said 'Michael, I think young Maebh has given you your answer.'

Michael's face reddened. 'Yes. Perhaps we should change the subject.'

Maebh's remark had humiliated and unsettled him and he tugged on his waistcoat and meddled with his cuffs to dispel his gloom.

In a cloud of steam and flurry of movement, Mrs O'Neill and her two granddaughters brought the main course to the table. The housekeeper held a salver of medallions of venison chasseur, her granddaughter Eavan had a shallow tray of asparagus tips au gratin and Grace carried a ceramic bowl of fluffy jacket potatoes. Waiting to be served Miriam turned to her brother in-law Paul and said 'how is that young nephew of mine doing in your office?'

'You mean young Tommy?' Miriam nodded. 'Not the sharpest knife in the drawer, is he?'

'What do you mean? He's my sister's boy.'

'He's an impertinent pup. Not a wet day in the place and already asked for a rise. He said he was doing the work of three men. Yes I said to him: two fools and an idiot. That put a stop to his gallop.'

Miriam's eyes widened and Paul's wife Florence nodded as if her husband's every word held the wisdom of Solomon.

Grandmother Brevin peered over the rim of her spectacles. 'Owen,' she said, 'are you still doing your work with the St Vincent de Paul Society?'

'Yes I am, and there are more people in need then we can cope with, so much more needs to be done.'

'That's nonsense; we do too much already,' interjected Gerry Brevin. 'Why don't these people get a job or stop having so many children?'

Holding her tongue, Maebh pressed the heels of her shoes into the parquet floor.

'I hope you don't mind me saying this, but you do-gooders do more harm than good. I say, if people can't provide for children, then they shouldn't have them.'

'But they do have children,' Maebh said unable to restrain herself. 'And they don't have jobs because there is no work for them. What are we to do, let them starve?'

Unaccustomed to being challenged directly by a woman, Gerry Brevin said 'Young lady. It may be an unfashionable thing to say, but the poor are almost a different species from us.'

Maebh was not cowed.

'The only difference between poor people and the people around this table is education and money.'

'I beg to differ with you,' Augustine Wright-Moran said condescendingly. 'There is such a thing as breeding and class.'

'Yes. And there are such things as stupidity and ignorance,' said Maebh.

The corpulent banker gasped, his jowls quivering with indignation.

'I apologise for Miss Mullin,' Michael said in the tension-filled silence. 'She has little understanding of what she is talking about.'

'What?' Maebh interjected, not quite believing her ears. '"She" is right here and "she" knows exactly what "she" is talking about. The question is, do you?'

Michael jumped to his feet. 'How dare you speak to me and to Mr Augustine Wright-Moran like that? He a guest in my home; and you are not aware of this but Mr Wright-Moran will soon be awarded an OBE.'

The banker nearly choked on the piece of venison he was chewing. 'You idiot, you blasted idiot,' he bellowed furiously.

'Did that person just call my grandson an idiot?' inquired Grandmother Brevin as she looked around the table of stunned guests.

Theo slapped his napkin on the table and said 'How dare you speak to my son like that? Apologise to him immediately, sir.'

A red-faced Augustine Wright-Moran lifted his massive body out of the chair, looked sheepishly at Michael and said very softly 'I apologise to you for my outburst. You are most certainly not an idiot.' Then looking around the table he said 'I beseech you all not to mention a word to anyone about the OBE, it could jeopardise everything.'

The banker resumed his seat and glared at Michael like a lion contemplating his next victim. Paul Brevin leaned over to Elizabeth

Wright-Moran and, speaking in a hushed voice asked 'Why has your father been awarded an OBE?'

'It's for his voluntary work with the Irish War Hospital Supply Organisation. He organises the gathering and shipping of sphagnum moss to the mainland.'

'Oh, how wonderful,' replied Paul having no understanding of what the girl was talking about.

'What is sphagnum moss?' Theo said quietly to Maebh.

'It's peat moss,' Maebh replied. 'It grows on bogs; they dry it and ship it to war hospitals in Britain.'

'What do they do with it?'

'It's used it as a surgical dressing. Because there's a shortage of cotton, they use it to dress the wounds of injured soldiers returning from the war in Europe.'

'How do you know all that?'

'I read it in the newspapers.'

'I see, not only pretty but bright. Jim's a lucky young man,' Theo replied and patted Maebh's hand.

'Yes he is,' Maebh replied and patted Theo's hand.

All through the serving and eating of dessert Michael ran his speech in his head. After coffee and liqueurs Michael rose and smiling nervously, addressed his assembled guests.

'The reason I invited you all here this evening is to inform you that I have asked Augustine Wright-Moran for his daughter's hand in matrimony and he has graciously consented to my request. And so it is with great pride that I announce that Clara and I are engaged. Victoria and Elizabeth, Clara's sisters, will be her bridesmaids and Jonathan Maloney will be my best man.'

Michael resumed his seat, Clara beamed and everyone congratulated the young couple.

'He should have asked you to be his best man,' Theo said to Jim amid the din of congratulations. 'You're his brother. He hardly knows that Jonathan Maloney.'

'It doesn't matter father,' Jim said and forced a smile.

'Congratulations,' Líla said as she embraced her brother after dinner.

'Thank you. But that common girl of Jim's nearly ruined the evening.'

'Maebh is not common,' Líla replied sharply. 'She is most uncommon. She has managed to do in one evening what we have been unable to do in years.'

'And what is that?'

'She has made father smile and laugh.'

'She's common and vulgar,' Michael snapped. 'She wears cheap clothes and cheap perfume.'

'I think she's wonderful. I like her. She's got fire and passion in her, just like mother.'

A weary Augustine Wright-Moran walked carefully on the mantle of white snow that covered the path outside the Brevin home. He climbed into his new carriage and said gruffly to his wife 'What an evening, there wasn't one political or social luminary at the dinner. Why is Clara associating herself with such people?'

'Clara is thirty two and not the prettiest rose in the bouquet,' Abigail replied. 'But at least Michael is the eldest son and he will inherit the family business.'

'That man's an idiot.'

The carriage door swung open and Victoria and her sister Elizabeth scrambled in.

'That was a jolly evening,' Victoria said with a giggle.

'That Maebh girl is a very a frank person,' Elizabeth said, settling in the seat.

'I don't like her,' grunted Augustine as he pulled his waistcoat over his plump stomach. 'She has far too much to say for herself.'

'I don't know how Michael thought she was suitable to be at table,' added his wife Abigail. 'The way that girl speaks she shouldn't be serving table, let alone sitting at it.'

Jim opened the door of the cab for Maebh, and said 'You were wonderful tonight.'

'They made me so angry, I had to say something.' She climbed in the cab, Jim called out to the top-hatted driver 'Primrose Avenue and back!'

THE ACTOR

Maebh laid her head on Jim's shoulder, looked at him and as the cab rattled away, said 'Was I wrong to say what I did to Michael?'
'No, but then I wouldn't dare argue with a woman like you.'
'Stop talking and kiss me.'

34

In 1919 the Dublin unit of the IRA began to wage an urban guerrilla war against the British Army and the police. The IRA formed special units; one unit was known simply as The Squad. Its sole purpose was to assassinate British intelligence officers and police detectives. The British authorities' response was to recruit, by coercion and intimidation, a network of spies and informers within the IRA. They also formed a new ten thousand-strong military unit. The unit was given a uniform of army khaki trousers with jackets and caps of such a dark green that they appeared black; the people nicknamed the unit the Black and Tans. Comprised mainly of brutalised, battle-hardened and demoralised British Army World War 1 veterans, the Black and Tans unleashed such a reign of terror, intimidation and death that the very sight of their uniform caused widespread panic and fear.

Ira arrived for the early show of *The Bailiff of Ballyfoyle* and an anxious Adrian Coyle, the Queen's house manager, was waiting for him. Adrian Coyle, an overly serious man who Leslie Lawrence once described as having the sartorial elegance of an unmade bed, asked Ira to accompany him to his office.

'The authorities in Dublin Castle have determined J P Bourke's new play *In the Dark and Evil Days* to be seditious. It is with regret the board of directors and I have cancelled its forthcoming production,' Coyle said once he and Ira were seated in his office.

'There is no theatre censorship in Ireland. The castle can't stop a stage production.'

'Strictly speaking you're right, Ira. But if we do not co-operate with the authorities, it would not be good for the theatre.'

'How did JP take the news?'

'He's angry, but he understands the theatre's position.'

No he doesn't, Ira thought, and you don't have the backbone to stand up for him.

'I would like to offer you Mr Bourke's slot. Do you have a production you could mount quickly?'

'Is there a chance that JP's ... ?'

'Ira, if you don't have a production the theatre will go dark.'

Ira ran his hand through his hair. Another two weeks of production would put his company in the black.

'Yes I have,' Ira said at last. 'But it will take more than three days to pull it together.'

Coyle picked up a document, pretended to read it, and said 'The numbers for *The Bailiff of Ballyfoyle* are good, we could extend the run for a week. What play are we thinking of bringing in?'

'*Father Murphy.*'

Coyle's moustache quivered and he glared at Ira with his small, dark eyes.

'*Father Murphy*? Isn't that about the 1798 rebellion? Don't you have something a little less political?'

'I have produced *Father Murphy* in this very theatre, every other year since 1909. The play is popular; the public love it and it was never remotely regarded as controversial.'

Coyle stroked his handlebar moustache.

'I'll put it to the board for their approval.'

'Should I wait or should I start rehearsals; delays cost time and money.'

Coyle shifted in his chair.

'No, that would defeat the purpose of this meeting. Go ahead with your preparations. In light of the play's history with the theatre I'm sure the board will agree with my decision.'

Minutes later Ira called a meeting with Mick and Leslie.

'You convinced Adrian Coyle that *Father Murphy* is not a political play?' Leslie said, the monocle dropping from his eye.

'I did, the man's an idiot,' Ira replied. 'But before you say anything, he's our idiot.'

Mick confirmed that the sets for *Father Murphy* could, with a little repainting, be ready in time. And after a few phone calls Leslie confirmed that most of the cast were available. Between performances Ira asked Jim to come to his dressing room. When Jim arrived, Ira handed him a manuscript of *Father Murphy* and offered him the role of John McNabb.

'McNabb? He is the villain of the piece,' Jim said.

'Yes he is, but he is not a traditional melodrama villain, he's a conflicted man. He does dreadful things but he does them for what he thinks are good reasons; think of him as a Judas Iscariot. Jim, we have a short rehearsal period, the production must be ready in ten days. Think you can be ready in time?'

'Yes sir, I'll be ready. And thank you as usual for the opportunity.'

Jim fizzed with excitement that night as he walked to his tram. The thought of playing the villain John McNabb to Ira Allen's Father Murphy excited him so much that he was blind to what was going on around him.

He didn't see the lorry load of Black and Tans race up the street and around the front of Trinity College.

He didn't notice the old woman swathed in heavy rags lying in the doorway in D'Olier Street.

Nor did he see the group of homeless drunks huddled around a small fire on the quayside, until one of them tugged at his coat. 'Spare a copper, me old son?' one of the men said.

Jim dug in his pocket and handed the man a few coins.

The man's cracked lips parted as he mumbled 'Thanks'.

On Sunday afternoon, a squad of Black and Tans staggered out of Connolly's Pub as Jim and Maebh alighted from the tram outside the main gates of the National Botanical Gardens. Seeing Maebh, the soldiers started to wolf whistle, leer and make obscene gestures. Jim hurried Maebh along the path. Two of the soldiers swayed across the busy street and followed them into the Botanical Gardens, nearly catching them up before their sergeant called after them and ordered them back to their lorry.

A troubled Jim and a pensive Maebh made for the warm interior of the enormous wrought iron Great Palm glasshouse.

'Sorry you had to go through that; they're just thugs.'

'It's not the first time I've heard such things,' Maebh replied and, preoccupied with her own thoughts, walked along the stone path between the exotic trees and plants.

'You're quiet today,' Jim said, taking her hand.

'Am I? Sorry.'

'Don't let those soldiers upset you.'

'They didn't.'

'This part I'm playing in *Father Murphy*, do you think Red might give me some help with it?' Maebh remained silent and her face grew grave. 'Did you hear me?'

'I heard you. What do you want to talk to Pat about?'

'I just told you. I thought Red might give me some help with this new part I've got. Are you all right?'

'I'm all right. I have more on my mind than your silly play.'

'It's not a silly play.'

'It is to me. You know, some people have real problems.'

'Oh yes I know: the poor,' Jim replied sarcastically.

Maebh let go of Jim's arm.

'Yes, the poor. And other people too.'

'Why do you always bring the poor into everything? It makes you sound like a socialist.'

'And what's so bad about being a socialist? You're so bourgeois – but I'm not allowed say that, am I?'

'You just have said it.' Jim looked out the windows of the glasshouse. 'You're just in bad form.'

Maebh's eyes filled with tears.

'I want to go home.'

Jim pulled open the glasshouse door and Maebh stepped out of the hothouse and walked briskly across the gardens. When she got to the main gate she crossed the street and stood at the tram stop.

'This is ridiculous,' Jim said when he caught up with her.

'Now I'm ridiculous, is that what you're saying?'

'That's not what I said.'

A tram clanked to a stop.

Maebh stepped on to the small platform but when Jim attempted to join her she stopped him and said 'Take the next tram. Maybe your brother was right, maybe we are too different.'

'Maebh what's wrong?' he pleaded. 'What did I do, what did I say?'

'It's not always about you,' Maebh said and the tram clattered down the road, tears trickled down Maebh's face and the rain that had been threatening all afternoon fell from the sky.

The air was crisp on the Monday morning that Jim walked down the Phibsboro Road to rehearsal. Suddenly two lines of Black and Tan soldiers advanced up the road. Automobiles jammed on their breaks, horses and carts halted, cyclists reversed and pedestrians fled into nearby shops. But three young brothers stood their ground and defied the advancing soldiers. The leader of the Black and Tans shouted 'Get out of the way. Quick time.'

The brothers didn't move. The squad leader levelled his rifle at the tallest of the young men and squeezed the trigger. A crack roared through the silence and the tallest of the young man collapsed to the ground.

'Jesus,' shouted the youngest of the brothers as he fell to his knees beside his brother.

The squad leader then turned his rifle on another of the brothers and the two boys backed up against a wall. Without even looking at the injured man the squad continued their manoeuvre up the road. When they had passed Jim dashed out of the chemist shop and ran to the injured man. A passing milkman stopped his cart and said 'Put him on the cart and I'll bring him down to the Mater Hospital.'

Jim and the two brothers lifted the injured man on to back of the cart, the milkman cracked his whip, the horse trotted off down the road and the two younger brothers ran alongside the cart.

THE ACTOR

Once in the rehearsal room Jim went straight to the kitchenette and washed the blood from his hands. As he was looking for something to dry his hands on, he started to tremble. He tried to calm himself but he kept seeing the young man lying in a pool of his own blood. He felt hot then cold. In a panic he left the rehearsal room and walked along the canal. When the air hit him his stomach churned and he vomited.

When he returned to the rehearsal room most of the cast had arrived. He sat quietly by himself and tried to think about the play but his thoughts keep returning to the wounded youth.

'Jim, I'd like you to meet a new member of the company,' Francis P said, breaking in on his reverie.

'Oh, hello? Francis P?' Jim was glad of the diversion.

'Are you all right Jim?' Francis P asked. 'You look very pale.'

'Just a bit under the weather.'

'Sorry to hear that. I'd like you to meet Geoffrey Myers, he'll be playing Fr Roche.'

Geoffrey Myers was not a handsome actor. He had a long jaw, wide gaps between his teeth and a nose that had been broken many times. Looking older than his forty years, he had the reputation of being an annoying windbag, argumentative and difficult to work with. But he had convinced Ira to employ him with his promise to be more friendly and respectful to colleagues; that and the unavailability of John Palmer the actor who usually played Fr Roche.

'Would you care for a cup of tea?' Leslie asked Geoffrey, after they had greeted each other.

'Yes thank you that would be lovely, milk no sugar,' replied the eager-to-please Geoffrey.

While Leslie was off fetching tea, Francis P introduced Geoffrey to Richard, Fiona and Maura. Leslie returned with a tray of steaming cups. The tea was gratefully received. Geoffrey took a sip, quietly placed his cup on the table and did not touch it again.

'I thought Geoffrey said he didn't take sugar,' May murmured to Leslie taking the tray to the kitchenette.

'Really,' Leslie replied. 'Did he?' Then, lowering his voice, asked 'Why did Ira employ him? He knows he's a trouble maker.'

'He's a good actor and he's been out of work for the best part of two years. Be nice Leslie, say something good about the man.'

'Very well. I believe that, while he was in Mountjoy Prison, he was voted January's inmate of the month.'

'For God's sake Leslie, don't say things like that. People might think you're serious.'

Ira strolled into the rehearsal room, rolled out a large poster on the table and took a step back.

'Have a look ladies and gentlemen; let me know what you think?'

The poster read:

> *Twice Nightly at 6:30 and 8:30*
> *Ira Allen's Great Irish Play*
> *Father Murphy or The Hero of Tullow.*

Beneath the play's title was:

> *Oh, Erin my country, how can you forget your sons that have bled in the fight*
> *And brave Father Murphy who laid down his life in the battle for Freedom and Right.*

Jim's eyes scanned the cast list and stopped when he read *John McNabb, a creature of Dublin Castle, will be played by Mr Jim Brevin.*

Leslie placed his monocle to his eye and said 'This is excellent; however you have misspelt my name.'

Ira lowered his large head to the poster.

'No I haven't. It's perfectly correct.'

'Sorry, my mistake, the lettering on my name is so small it is hard to see.'

'Leslie, reluctant as I am to say it, you are playing a supporting role.'

Both men smiled their stage smile. Each had made his point.

On Tuesday afternoon, Jim walked through the Blessington Basin and took a seat in the summerhouse. He had hoped he might see Maebh. But at five o'clock, with his head bowed, he strolled out and down Blessington Street to the theatre.

Between shows Jim was walking to Karl's Tea Rooms for something to eat when Red suddenly appeared at his side. As they walked, Red kept looking over his shoulder.

THE ACTOR

'Maebh said you wanted to talk to me.'
'How is Maebh?'
'You should know, you're her boyfriend.' Red again looked up and down the street. 'Did you have a fight with her?'
Jim nodded.
'That's what's wrong with her. She's like a bear with a sore bum. Can we get off the street?'
'Yes, do you want to get a cup of tea?'
'I'll have a pint if you're buying?' Red said and slapped Jim on the back. 'Come on.'

Sitting in the sawdust-covered lounge of the Trinity Bar, Jim ordered a pint for Red and an orange mineral for himself.
'Well? What do you want to talk to me about?' Red asked after downing half his pint in one swallow.
'Oh yes. I'm playing a part of a spy in *Fr Murphy* and I was wondering if you could answer a few questions for me?'
'Oh that, I thought it was something else.'
'Like what?'
'Jim, the Castle are on to us. There's a spy in our unit.'
'There is? What are they going to do about him?'
'It's already done. He's dead and the unit has been disbanded. I have to leave the country quickly before the Castle comes after me.'
'Does Maebh know?'
'Yes, I told the family on Sunday morning.'
Jim now understood what had been wrong with Maebh. But Red had exposed himself to real danger by meeting him. 'Why are you here?' Jim said. 'You shouldn't be seen in public.'
'I needed to talk to you. Can you lend me fifty pounds? I need the boat fare to America. I'll pay you back.'
Jim didn't hesitate. 'I'll have it for you tomorrow, come backstage before the first show.' He hesitated then added 'Why do it, I mean all the fighting and the killing?'
Red pulled a folded sheet of paper from his pocket.
'That's the letter every Black and Tan recruit is given when they arrive in Ireland.'
Jim opened the folded paper and stamped across the top of Dublin

THE ACTOR

Castle headed notepaper was the word "Confidential".

To all new Royal Irish Constabulary recruits,
Should the order "Hands Up" not be immediately obeyed, shoot and shoot with effect. If persons approaching a patrol have their hands in their pockets, or look in any way suspicious, shoot them down. You may make mistakes occasionally and innocent persons may be shot, but that cannot be helped as you are bound to get the right parties some of the time. The more you shoot, the better I will like you, and I assure you no soldier will get into trouble for shooting any man.
Lt. Col. Smyth.

When Jim had finished reading, Red said 'That's why I had to keep fighting.' He was pale and serious. 'This has got to end and it's fallen to us to finish it and that's what we will do.'

Jim knew then that Red had blood on his hands.

Twenty minutes later when Jim and Red left the pub, two armoured cars with swinging turrets and a green caged-in Crossley Tender thundered into the street and swerved on to the kerb.

'A round up, see ya,' Red said, and he ducked back into the pub.

With his heart pounding in his chest like a jackhammer, Jim walked up Great Brunswick Street towards the Queen's Theatre. A shabbily dressed young man in a bowler hurried past him. Suddenly a Black and Tan shoved the bowler-hatted man into a doorway and struck him with the butt of his rifle. The man fell backwards but never uttered a word. Jim's palms began to sweat.

In the cage on the back of the Crossley lorry, four nervous young men peered out at Jim. At the front of the lorry a young woman in a trench coat was being questioned by a soldier; suddenly the soldier slapped the woman across the face, grabbed her by the neck and flung her to the ground.

Two other soldiers jumped out of the Crossley and shouted 'You fucking Irish bitch, you Catholic ride.'

One of the soldiers stood over the woman, pointed his rifle at the woman's terrified face and shouted 'One more smart remark, bitch, and I'll put a hole in your fucking head.'

THE ACTOR

An iron hand grabbed Jim by the shoulder, pushed him against the wall and a soldier shouted into face 'You! Fucking Paddy! Show me your identification papers.' Jim groped in his pocket, found his papers and handed them to the soldier. The soldier glanced at the papers, swore again, lowered his rifle and as Jim walked away the soldier kicked him.

In the near darkness of the theatre, Jim leaned against the backstage wall and tried to calm his breathing. He closed his eyes but the image of the young woman being slapped and thrown to the ground repeated over and over in his mind. A shiver of dread quivered through him. What if that girl had been Maebh? What would she have said? What would he have done? And worse, what would the Tans have done?

35

With every passing day the war grew more vicious and pitiless. Gun battles, skirmishes and ambushes were commonplace. The rebels destroyed bridges, ambushed Black and Tans and police and caused as much mayhem as they could. Whole areas of Dublin city were regularly cordoned off for round-ups and house to house searches. If rebels or weapons were found, the house or business premises was burned to the ground.

It was the first day off-book for the cast of *Fr Murphy* and Leslie Lawrence as usual was struggling with his lines. Suddenly, the arrival of Adrian Coyle interrupted the rehearsal as he demanded a private word with Ira.

'Take a five minute break,' Ira said and he led Coyle to the small kitchenette.

'What is the reason for this intrusion?' Ira asked the theatre manager.

'Damn it man, you said it was not a political play.'

'I never said that. I said it was not a controversial play.'

'You played me for a fool. Well, we'll see who the fool is now. I'm cancelling the production.'

'For what reason?'

'*Father Murphy* is a political play and members of the board told me to close you down.'

'When did the board meeting take place?' Ira asked.

'It wasn't a formal board meeting.'

'And is the board aware that I have a contract for the production?'

'Of course,' Coyle replied and pulled nervously on the left side of his moustache.

'Then you're a man of principle. I congratulate you. It takes courage to do what you're doing.'

'Courage? What are you talking about?'

'Don't be so modest. You signed my contract, if you cancel it now, the theatre will have to compensate me and the board will be forced to ask for your resignation.'

'My resignation?' Adrian Coyle coughed and his neck jutted forward like a frightened bird. 'Ira, perhaps I was a bit hasty. Perhaps the show should go on – it would be a statement.'

'Are you sure of this Mr Coyle? What about the board?'

'Yes, I think so. Yes, the show should go on. I'll talk to the board.'

'Good, you're making the right decision,' Ira said as he walked the manager to the door and bade him farewell.

'Leslie, I think we are going to need your help on this one,' Ira said as the door closed. 'I need you to talk to your pals on the board …' He stopped talking when he realised the entire company of actors was looking at him.

'How real is the threat to the production?' asked a worried Richard.

'I think the production will go ahead,' Ira replied.

'What exactly is the situation?' demanded Geoffrey. 'Do we have a show or not?'

'Geoffrey, I can't give you a definitive answer.'

'Then what can you give me.'

'Raising your voice won't help, Geoffrey,' Leslie said. 'Don't get so worked up about things.'

'Don't get worked up about things! I'm not rich like you, Leslie. This is the first job I've had in two years and the now the bloody British authorities, or someone licking up to them, is trying to close the show. Whose bloody country is this?'

'Calm down,' Francis P said, and put his hand gently on Geoffrey's shoulder.

'Calm down? How can I calm down?' Geoffrey shook Francis P's hand off his shoulder. 'Everything is falling apart. Last week, my sister Eileen died trying to save her child when drunken Tans burned her street in Balbriggan. Twenty five homes destroyed.' Geoffrey's eyes were wild with panic. 'They burned the dairy co-op where Eileen's husband worked and now he's an out of work widower with two children – how do I help him if I don't have a job?' His eyes burned with anger and desperation. 'I'm delighted Collins and his men are taking on the British and their agents. I hope he kills every bloody one of them.'

Ira walked over to Geoffrey and said calmly 'This production will go on stage and we will take it on tour. Then we will put on a benefit performance in Balbriggan for your brother-in-law and his family.' Geoffrey collapsed into a chair and wept.

Ira continued calmly. 'Why don't we have a quiet cup of tea together and you can talk to me about possible venues in Balbriggan.'

Jim was pressing his stage moustache to his face when a breathless Red Mullin thundered into his dressing room.

'The Rozzers are after me. They came to me house but I escaped out through the bedroom window.'

Booted footsteps clattered in the corridor. Doors flung open, questions were barked. An anxious Red looked around the dressing room.

'Is there another way out of here?'

'No,' replied Jim. 'Do the police know what you look like?'

'I don't think so.'

Jim grabbed a blue military jacket, a pair of trousers and a shirt from the costume rail and pushed them into Red's hands.

'Walk with me to the stage. If anyone asks, tell them you're my dresser. Then wait in the wings and when I come off stage, help me change into those clothes – and keep calling me sir.' Red nodded.

Jim handed him an envelope. 'Put that in your pocket, there's a hundred pounds in it.'

'Thanks Jim. I will repay you.'

'That's the least of your problems. Now open the door and walk behind me.'

Red opened the door and a sturdy man in plain clothes blocked his way. Behind him stood two uniformed policemen.

'I'm Inspector Doyle and I'm looking for Patrick Mullin. Is he here?'

'I don't know anyone of that name,' Jim replied and went to walk past the inspector.

'Wait, I have questions for you,' growled the inspector.

'I'll answer all your questions after the play,' Jim replied. But the Inspector didn't move. 'The chief constable is in the audience tonight, are you ready to explain to him why you stopped the show?'

'We'll talk later,' Inspector Doyle said; he nodded to the uniformed policemen and they stood aside. 'How come you're not wearing make-up?' the inspector asked as Red brushed past him.

'He's my dresser; he doesn't need make-up,' Jim said haughtily.

Just then, Francis P came out of his dressing room. He stopped when he saw the police.

'You know this man?' the inspector asked Francis P as he pointed to Red.

Jim's back stiffened. Red braced himself to run.

'He's the company's dresser,' Francis P answered casually. 'Jim has a quick change in Act One and he needs some help. Now inspector, we have to go otherwise we'll all miss our cue.'

The inspector looked dubiously at Red.

Francis P leaned over to the inspector and said, as if he was imparting a state secret, 'The man's not the full shilling, it's a charity to employ him.'

'Ah, I see,' the inspector replied, 'I thought there was something odd looking about him.'

Before Red could say a word, Francis P glared at him and said, as if he was talking to a child 'Desmond, last night you forgot my hat. Make sure you bring it tonight.'

'Yes sir, sorry sir,' Red replied and lowered his head.

'Sorry I detained you all,' the inspector said almost apologetically. 'We'll be out of here as quickly as we can.'

'We all have our work to do, sergeant,' Francis P replied.

'Inspector,' snapped the policeman a little miffed.

'Of course, inspector,' Francis P said and as Jim, Red and Francis P walked away, the inspector knocked on Maura and Fiona's dressing room door.

All during the first act, a Dublin Metropolitan Policeman stood at the stage door and questioned everyone entering and leaving the theatre. The police were still searching the backstage area when Jim exited for his costume change.

'Mr Jim, sir,' Red said affecting what he thought was a theatrical voice. 'Allow me to dust your jacket.' Red pulled out his handkerchief and brushed imaginary dust off Jim's shoulders.

'Don't overdo it, Patrick,' Jim whispered, and pushed Red's hands off his shoulder.

'What's that, sir? Missed that, sir? Say again, sir?'

Jim eyes flicked to the policeman at the stage door.

'You're mad,' Jim said very softly.

'Stark raving mad sir, stark raving bleedin' mad.'

Jim returned to the stage. Ten minutes later the police left the theatre and five minutes after that Red left.

During the play's first intermission, Jim stopped Francis P backstage.

'Thanks for your help. How did you know I told the police that Red was a dresser?'

'The dressing rooms walls in this theatre are so thin you can hear people change their minds. Did your friend get away?'

'Yes, thanks to you. Why did you take such a risk?'

'I hope someday, someone might do the same for my sons.'

The rain was falling hard when Jim left the theatre. He was wondering where and how Red was, when he saw Maebh standing in a doorway across the lane. She was soaking wet, her thick black hair was plastered against her face and her huge eyes were red from crying. She saw Jim and walked slowly to him.

'I'm sorry Jimmy. I said some horrible things to you. I didn't mean them. I was so worried about Patrick.' Sheets of rain whipped across Maebh's face. 'Thank you for helping Pat.'

'It's the least I could do for my girlfriend's brother.'

'Am I still your girlfriend?' Maebh asked, her eyes welling with tears.

'You'll always be my girlfriend.' Jim took Maebh's face in his hands and he kissed her. 'Come on, I'll take you home.'

'Yes please,' she said, and curled her fingers into his hand.

The following morning Jim almost skipped into the breakfast room. Líla looked up from her food and said 'Someone is in a good mood.'

'Yes I am. I'm in a very good mood. Good morning father.'

'Morning son,' Theo called out from the window seat. 'Would this good mood have anything to do with a certain young lady?'

'I don't know what you're talking about father. I'm always in a good mood.'

Michael hurried into the breakfast room. He sat beside Jim and said 'I want you to go to Cork and oversee the installation of the new stocktaking system. It shouldn't take much longer than three days.'

'Morning, Michael.'

Michael sniffed. 'Good morning, Jim.'

'Sorry, I can't oblige, I'm in rehearsal for a production. If it can wait a few weeks, I'll be able to do it.'

'I'll go,' Líla interjected.

'No, the men would never take instruction from a girl,' said Michael.

'I'm a woman, not a girl, and the men most certainly will take instructions from me.'

'This is all very unsatisfactory,' Michael snorted. 'When I take over the company Jim, you better start looking for a new job.'

'And when do you expect to take over the company?' Theo asked from his window seat.

'I didn't see you there, father.' Theo folded his newspaper and waited on Michael's response. 'I don't want to be indelicate father, but you won't live forever.'

'I know that son, and I don't want to be indelicate either, but I have to tell you, I have left the company to all my children, equally.'

'You can't do that, I am the eldest son. The company is mine. It's my legal right.'

'Your legal right is what I leave to you in my will.'

Jim and Líla grinned, Theo resumed his reading and Michael flounced out of the breakfast room.

*

THE ACTOR

The normally bright and cheerful Maura Sweeney entered her dressing room and sat. But that afternoon her face was grey, her eyes dull and she looked lost. May Murnane sat beside her and asked very softly 'How is your sister Jean?'

'She died this morning,' Maura's voice was faint.

'Oh, I'm sorry, Maura.'

'Six months ago she and her husband Joe and their two lovely boys, Eamon and Philip, were looking forward to the new baby. Then diphtheria took Joe and the two boys. Then this morning, Jean died. A whole family … wiped out in less than six months.'

May placed her hand on Maura's hand.

'Oh God. I'm so sorry, Maura. I'm really sorry. How is the baby?'

'She's with the midwife.'

'What's going to happen to her?'

'I don't know. I suppose she'll be put into an orphanage.'

'Is that what you want for your niece?'

'No, but who else would look after her?'

May looked deep into Maura's eyes.

'I could look after her, couldn't I?'

'Yes you could. Do you think your husband, Cedric, would like that?'

'I don't know, we never talked about such things.'

'Then talk to him.'

'Yes I will.' Maura replied.

When May left the dressing room Maura mechanically put on her costume and her make-up. At six thirty the curtain rose, and not one person in the audience had the slightest indication of the pain and sorrow that the ever-smiling Maura Sweeney was enduring.

36

On Friday, after the second performance of *The Bailiff of Ballyfoyle,* Adrian Coyle approached Ira in the greenroom and said 'The board has decided to allow the production of *Father Murphy* to go ahead. It was a split decision; my vote swung the decision in our direction.'

No it didn't, Ira thought. It wasn't even close. Leslie's people saw to that.

Ira placed his hand on Adrian Coyle shoulder and said 'Adrian, I will always be the friend to you, that you have been to me.'

'What's Coyle up to now?' Leslie asked when the manager had left the green room.

'Inflating his ego,' Ira replied. 'It's interesting how sincere that man can be when he's telling lies.'

'Oh, stupid people always find it easy to be sincere,' Leslie replied and looked around the room. 'Ah. Richard is going to give us a song.'

Richard's beautiful singing voice circled the greenroom, wafted down the dressing room corridor and lifted Maura Sweeney's heart.

'How are you?' asked a passing May Murnane.

'Very well,' Maura replied, then to May's surprise Maura smiled. 'I'm not supposed to tell anyone yet but Cedric and I have decided to bring up the baby.'

'That's wonderful news.'

'Cedric told me he never thought he'd be a father. He wants to call the baby Jean, after my sister.' Maura drew a deep breath. She had another question for her friend. 'Do you think I'll make a good mother?'

'No, I don't think you'll make a good mother; I know you'll make a wonderful mother and Cedric will be a wonderful father.'

'He will, won't he?'

Jim watched Ira create the character of Father Murphy. He listened to the actor play with the pitch and timbre of his voice and observed how he used pauses and facial expressions to convey his character's thinking and changing moods. He watched Ira play off his fellow actors. He saw how Ira found and played with the cadences and phrasings in the text and marvelled at how the actor could do all that and still direct his fellow actors.

To comprehend why John McNabb changed from being a friend of Father Murphy to becoming his Judas, Jim read and re-read the play. He concluded that John McNabb did what he did because he was a fearful, insecure man who misread the priest's intentions and he thought that spying on the priest was the right thing to do for his country. To understand the dread and fear that John McNabb experienced every day of his life, Jim remembered the terror and fright he had felt when the Black and Tan soldier threatened to put a bullet in the head of the young woman on the street. He imagined how a fear like that could grow and devour a man until all that was left within was suppressed panic and terror. He developed a voice and a walk for the man and slowly, breath by breath, like a man emerging from a mist, John McNabb appeared and Jim started to disappear.

Cast as Lieutenant Norman, Leslie Lawrence had difficulty finding his character. While he had played military men many times he never understood Lieutenant Norman or found his soul. He tried everything he could but he couldn't find the man and so he had to rely on technique to generate a character: Leslie was not happy with his work.

The opening night of *Father Murphy* was bedlam. Over two thousand people tried to gain admission and over two hundred people were still queuing outside the theatre when the 'house full' signs went up. The Irish Transport Workers Union Brass Band that was to play at the first interval was late, Richard O'Hare's throat was sore and Fiona Whelan was detained by Black and Tans.

Minutes before curtain time the brass band arrived, a harassed Fiona Whelan rushed into her dressing room and Richard O'Hare announced that his throat had improved enough for him to perform. The theatre lights dimmed, the overture began and Ira walked over to a very nervous Jim and said softly 'If you let go, we can both soar.'

The curtain rose and Ira walked on stage. The moment Ira's foot touched the stage he transformed into Father John Murphy, parish priest of Boolavogue, and the instant Jim Brevin hit the boards he was John McNabb, the spy who would betray his priest. Every moment on stage, Ira and Jim lived and breathed their character's fears, loves, loyalties and truths, they released the characters from the text and Father Murphy and John McNabb lived.

When it came time for Jim's character to inform on the rebellious parish priest, John McNabb stood tall and delivered the information in the full knowledge that he was doing his patriotic duty. Suddenly a man in the dress circle jumped to his feet, waved his top hat in the air and remonstrated forcefully with John McNabb about his disgraceful behaviour. Jim stood, silently listened to the man and when the man resumed his seat, Jim bowed to him and the play continued. It was one of the finest moments of Jim's acting career, he knew he had created a real, living character that had burrowed into the consciousness of the audience: he knew it was a rare thing and he knew he would long remember playing John McNabb.

Standing off stage watching Father Murphy declaim his final words of forgiveness to his tormentors, Leslie turned to Jim and said 'Only a great actor can get away with a performance like that, if I tried something like that the audience would laugh me off the stage. You have to hand it to the old fellow.'

'He's not that old,' replied Jim.

'I know,' Leslie replied. 'He's not yet forty.'

The following day a glum-looking Leslie Lawrence sat in the green room reading the *Evening Herald*.

THE ACTOR

'Great show last night,' a still buoyant Jim said as he took the seat opposite Leslie.

'Not for me, it wasn't.'

'Really, I thought you gave a good performance.'

'No you don't. You know it was all technique; flat, boring and a sham.'

'I think you're being a bit hard on yourself.'

'No I'm not. It was a dreary, mechanical shell of a performance, without even a hint of honesty to it.' Leslie leaned back in his chair. 'I was never the actor Ira was and now it seems I'll never be the actor you are, but I always thought I could give a good performance.'

'You can and you do,' protested Jim. 'What's the matter Leslie; you're usually so casual about your work?'

'I may appear casual about it but I can assure you, my work is as important to me as yours is to you. I live for my work. The theatre is both my wife and my mistress.'

Leslie fell silent. Jim had never heard Leslie talk so openly and honestly about himself.

'I don't mean to pry, but you never married. Is that something to do with theatre?'

'No, I did nearly marry once, but it was my money the lady was after, not me. I loved her but ...' Leslie stopped speaking. He hadn't intended this conversation. He hadn't practiced it. He was giving away too much information. He slid on his Leslie mask and said 'I'd better get ready for tonight's show. By the way you got a good mention in the newspaper, congratulations.' He rose, handed Jim the newspaper and pointed out the theatre review, before leaving the room.

Father Murphy at the Queen's

In his new production of Father Murphy, Mr Allen expresses not one man's loss of a dream but the hopes and aspirations of a nation. Watching Ira Allen play Father Murphy is like being in the middle of a force ten gale. Mr Allen's strutting movements, his stormy frowns and his blood-chilling cries to the heavens, thrill and command the audience. In the second act when the good priest delivered his call to arms speech 'with our hearts, nerve and spirit we

THE ACTOR

will fight our foes, our courage and our God will be our strength and we will be victorious,' the moment was so true that it shocked the audience into silence. In the final horrifying scene when a Christ-like Father Murphy is stripped, flogged and tortured, the scene is so painful to watch that one wants to tear one's eyes for the spectacle. The dying priest's final words 'love them that hate you and bless them that curse you' rang around a silent Queen's Theatre like thunder on Good Friday. Mr Allen's portrayal of Father Murphy is truly a shattering thing.

Mr Brevin as John McNabb, the evil genius of the piece, was so successful in his role that at times he evoked the scorn of the audience. In the fourth act John McNabb's outbreak of rage and fury at the troublesome priest was so convincing that it stilled the audience to silence. Then almost as one the audience jumped to their feet and burst into an ovation of shouting hissing and booing so loud that the glass droplets on the chandelier vibrated.

The rest of the cast were first-rate but sadly Mr Leslie Lawrence was a little off form. A wonderful night at the theatre with two of the most powerful performances I've seen in many a year.

John Olive, critic in residence.

On Friday night, Maebh attended the play for the third time. After the show, as Jim walked her home, he couldn't stop talking about the play and acting and the theatre. When they arrived at Primrose Avenue, Maebh rested her head against the wall and smiled at her talkative Jimmy. He was still jabbering away when Maebh said 'I love you Jimmy Brevin.'

Jim stopped talking.

Maebh, shocked by her own words, pulled her head away from the wall and waited breathlessly for Jim to say something.

He cupped her face in his hands and said 'I wanted to be the first to say that.'

'Sorry, did I ruin everything?'

'Yes, now I'm going to have to find someone else to be the first to say it to.'

'No you don't. I love you and you love me. So say it.'

'You're very bossy.'

'Say it!' Jim smiled and pretended to think.

'Say it.'

'I love you Maebh Mullin. I've loved you from the first moment I saw you.'

Maebh jumped into Jim's arms.

'I suppose I better ask you to marry me, before you ask me.'

Maebh broke from Jim's embrace and in almost a whisper said 'Don't make jokes like that.'

'I'm not joking. I want you to be my wife.' Maebh eyes widened. 'Well, will you marry me or am I going to have to ask someone else?'

Maebh pulled Jim close and kissed him.

'I'm confused,' Jim said into her ear. 'Is that a yes or a no?'

'Yes, yes, yes and yes.'

37

Jim sat by the window in the back drawing room and watched black clouds approaching from the west. A storm was imminent.

'There you are,' Michael said when he entered the room. 'I want to talk to you about a few matters.'

'No time like the present,' Jim replied. He folded his newspaper and placed it on the chair that Michael was about to occupy. Michael removed the folded newspaper and cast it aside.

'You received your invitation to the wedding?'

'Yes I did, it's very fancy, very modern.'

'Glad you liked it.' Michael coughed. 'I was wondering if you'd do me a favour by not talking about your theatrical activities at the wedding. After all, you do earn most of your living in the family business.'

Jim shook his head and thought, Michael, you really are a dreadful snob.

'The second matter is a little more delicate. My future father-in-law, Augustine Wright-Moran OBE, didn't like the way your girl Maebh spoke to him at the engagement party.' When Jim cocked his head and smirked, Michael snapped, 'There's nothing funny about it. He's very annoyed and has instructed me – requested – that Maebh not be invited to the wedding.' The smirk fell from Jim's face. 'He feels she might embarrass herself again and – between you and me – she's not really suitable company for the Wright-Moran family.'

'You're incredible. Have you any idea how insulting that is?'

'Look here, the girl has no breeding, she can't even speak properly.'

'Please don't talk about Maebh like that.'

'The girl's as common as ditch water; she's an embarrassment. I make no apology for speaking my mind.'

Pain exploded in Michael's nose, he plunged backwards over his chair and by the time he hit the floor, his face was covered in his blood. It was the first Jim had hit his brother since childhood.

On Saturday night, the Ira Allen Company of Irish Players played to half-full houses in the Queen's Theatre. After the show, a subdued Ira and a pensive May were sitting in their dressing room removing their make-up when Mick popped his head around the door and said 'Mr Coyle would like a word.'

'I thought he might call,' Ira said as he pulled on his jacket. 'I don't think we'll get a second week.'

Adrian Coyle's cramped office was even more cluttered and untidy than usual. The desk top was strewn with papers, the filing cabinet drawers were half open and on the floor were three large cardboard boxes. Coyle stubbed his cigarette out in an overflowing and smouldering ashtray and motioned to Ira to sit. Ira lifted a pile of paper from the chair, placed them on the filing cabinet and sat.

'Bad news,' Coyle said rubbing his red rimmed eyes. 'I've been instructed to close your show.'

'Not really surprised,' Ira replied. 'I know that audiences …'

'The theatre is being closed.'

Ira stared in disbelief at the manager.

'For how long?'

'I don't know.'

'Is this because we staged *Father Murphy*?'

'No,' replied Adrian Coyle. 'It's because the board are afraid a bomb might go off in the theatre – and because audience numbers have been dropping for some time. I thought your show might bring them back. You had an excellent opening night; the reviews were good but the audiences never came.'

'Will the theatre reopen for the autumn season?'

'Can't say, all contracts have been cancelled, no exceptions and that includes yours truly.'

'You've lost your job? I'm sorry Adrian.'

The manager's tired eyes fell upon Ira.

'Thank you. I know you don't think much of me and my abilities as a manager. But I do love the theatre and I will continue to work in theatre.' His eyes returned to the papers on his desk and a stunned Ira sat staring at him. Then without looking up, Coyle said 'If there's nothing else, I have much to do and not much time to do it in.'

Dressed in a new sharp suit, crisp shirt and cravat, Theo Brevin stood at the drawing room door. His silver hair was freshly combed and his moustache was trimmed and waxed.

'Father you're looking dashing today,' Líla said when Theo took his seat at the head of the table.

'Thank you, I thought I should brighten myself up. I have an important wedding coming up and I don't want to be taken for anyone's grandfather.'

'You look smart, father,' Jim said.

A black-eyed Michael came into the room and took the seat opposite Jim.

'What happened to your face, Michael?' a shocked Theo asked. 'You look like you went fifteen rounds with Jack Dempsey.'

'Some thug assaulted me,' Michael replied and glanced at his brother.

'I hope you reported him to the police,' Theo said.

'I did what was necessary. Now, could we change the topic of conversation please?'

All through dinner Theo talked and chatted. Afterwards, he asked Michael to accompany him to his study.

Theo settled behind his desk and, humming to himself, slid a thick file across to Michael.

'My wedding present to you and Clara,' Theo said, leaned back in his chair and tweaked the corner of his freshly waxed moustache. 'It's not the largest of houses but it's in a good location. All your neighbours will be young professionals like yourself.'

Michael opened the file and when he read the house address, his eyes dulled and he said softly 'Thank you father. This is a generous gift.'

'I hope you and Clara will enjoy living there.'

'I'm sure we will,' Michael replied.

But Michael and Clara never lived in the house Theo gave them. Within two months Michael sold it and bought a Georgian house on Merrion Square.

The following morning Jim entered the breakfast room, poured a glass of orange juice and without looking at his sister said 'I've asked Maebh to marry me.'

Líla burst into life.

'You what?'

'You heard,' Jim replied with a smirk.

Líla jumped up and hugged her brother.

'Congratulations Jim, this is wonderful news.'

'Thank you. I don't think Michael will think it's so wonderful.'

'Since when have you cared what Michael thought?'

'I don't, but what he says can be hurtful.'

'Is that why you hit him?' Jim said nothing. 'What did he say to you?'

'He said he doesn't want Maebh at his wedding. He said she's common.'

'You were right to hit him. I'd have kicked him as well. He can be a terrible snob.'

Sitting in a private room above O'Sullivan's Tea Rooms, Ira Allen spoke to his company of actors.

'It is two months since the Queen's went dark and there is still no word on when it might re-open. Why should we stop practicing our craft simply because a few theatres have closed?'

The actors murmured their agreement.

'I have been offered a two-week residency in the trade hall in York Street; I have also been offered a week's residency in a trade hall in Cork city, and another in Galway. They requested a popular play, a crowd pleaser. However, because the venues are small, and because I have no idea how many people will come to the shows, I cannot offer you a wage. It would be impractical for me to do so. What I can offer you is a share of whatever profits are generated. What do you say ladies and gentlemen?'

Geoffrey Myers was the first to speak.

'Ira, I want to work. Count me in.'

'Thank you Geoffrey,' Ira said and looked around the table.

'I'm with Geoffrey, I'm all for work,' added Francis P.

Maura was next to speak, 'I'm in.'

'And so am I,' Fiona said.

Leslie and Richard spoke almost simultaneously. 'I'm in.'

Richard was the first to ask a question. 'What play are you proposing to perform?'

'That's something we can talk about,' Ira replied.' Do you have something in mind Richard?'

'Let me propose one,' Leslie said. 'How about *The Irish Rake?*' Turning to Richard, he added 'That's a man, not a gardening implement.'

'Rubbish play,' grunted Richard without looking at Leslie.

'I've always loved *Lady Audrey's Secret*,' said Maura.

'My favourite is *Lured to Ruin*,' offered Fiona.

'How about *The Grip of Iron?*' asked Geoffrey Myers.

'I know what play we'll perform,' Jim said looking at Ira. 'When all else fails, play *East Lynne.*'

'You read my mind, Jim,' Ira replied and the cast groaned.

The iron-rimmed wheels of a delivery cart rattled past Jim as he walked up Grafton Street on his way to the trade hall in York Street. The street was busy with shoppers, traders, street entertainers and of course, policemen.

Outside Noblett's Sweet Shop three wide eyed children gazed on the vast selection of boiled sweets, toffees and sugared fruits on display in the shop window.

'I'm going to get some Sugar Plums,' said the oldest girl.

'So am I,' said her younger sister. No, I've changed my mind I'm going to get some Peggy's Legs.'

'I want a Sherbet Fountain,' cried the little boy.

'Mommy said you can't have sherbet because you stick the sherbet up your nose – it's disgusting,' said the older girl.

THE ACTOR

The ground shook and the boom of an explosion three streets away roared through the city. The children screamed, the street went dark as dust and smoke rose high and dirt rained from the sky.

'Mary, Julie, and Vincent come here,' the young mother said as she pulled her children into the sweet shop. The street fell silent. Seconds passed, people began to whisper and then they started to talk.

'Another bomb,' a street trader said to Jim as she dusted debris from her shawl. 'I'm sick of them gougers and their fighting. I'd shoot the lot of them.'

Within minutes the explosion seemed to be forgotten and the street again returned to business as usual. Small explosions were normal in Dublin.

A pale looking May Murnane, walked briskly into the York Street Trade Hall and asked Leslie for a quiet word.

'Ira has taken ill,' May said, when she and Leslie were out of earshot of the cast. 'He wants you to take over his role and to manage the company.'

'What happened? Was there an accident?'

'No accident. He's ill, that's all I'll tell you,' May's voice was firm. 'He needs bed rest and care. I have to withdraw from the show too but I've arranged that my friend Greer Caldwell to take over the role. She's an accomplished actress and has played the part on tour in America. I'm very sorry to land this in your lap, Leslie, but I have no choice.'

Leslie put his arm around May.

'Leave everything to me. Go home and tell Ira he's in our prayers.'

Leslie did not immediately return to the rehearsal hall. He went for a walk to Whitefriar Street Church, sat in front of the giant stained glass window, and collected his thoughts. When he returned to the hall he had a long conversation with Mick and then he called a company meeting.

'How do you suggest we proceed?' Geoffrey asked when Leslie had finished explaining the situation.

'I will take over Ira's role and I will produce the show but, before anyone asks, I can't take on the direction of the play. It is simply too much for me to do. Francis P, would you consider directing the play?'

'I'm not familiar enough with the play to do that. Might I suggest Jim?'

'Good suggestion Francis,' interjected Maura Sweeney.

Jim looked in amazement at his fellow actors.

'I think you'd make a splendid director,' agreed Richard. 'Put a young person's stamp on the play. What do you say, Jim?'

'What about yourself, Maura? Why don't you direct the play? You've been in it many times,' Jim said.

'Jim, I'm still in mourning and now I have a young baby to look after,' replied Maura.

'I'm the least qualified person in the room to direct the play,' Jim said, looking around the table.

'Jim, you told me you performed the play in Cork and further back you said you performed it in Kerry, so you're very familiar with it,' Leslie said. 'And your role is not very demanding, so what's to stop you? Personally speaking, I think you'd do a splendid job.' Everyone around the table murmured their agreement. 'Will you do it?'

Jim still didn't answer.

'Silence is consent,' Leslie said. 'But a word would be nice.'

'Very well,' Jim said meekly. 'I'll give it a try.'

'Wonderful,' Fiona Whelan said. 'This is going to be very interesting.'

38

Dapper in a new lounge suit, Theo walked around the garden and stopped beneath the silver birch tree that his wife Grainne had planted when they first moved into the house. It was eight in the evening and the dying rays of the setting sun streamed through the tree's leaves and made the white bark glow like silver. He stood for a moment and recalled how his late wife had dug in the ground, then planted the tree. In the corner of his eye he saw a movement in the conservatory. He placed his hand on the tree trunk and whispered 'Goodnight love.'

Moments later he walked through the conservatory's French doors and said 'Hello Jim, you said you had some good news to tell me.'

'Yes, I do father.'

'This good news, is it something to do with someone called Maebh?' Theo asked as he settled into a wicker armchair.

'Yes it is.' Jim paused a moment. 'I've asked Maebh to marry me.'

A shaft of yellow sunlight cast the shadow of Theo's moustache across his cheekbones and Jim saw the trace of a smile break on his father's face.

'Does Maebh make you happy?'

'Yes she does.'

'Do you make her happy?'

'Yes, I think I do.'

Theo smiled broadly.

'I like Maebh, she's like your mother; a little unconventional but wonderful. Do you think she can fit into your bohemian lifestyle?'

'Yes and my life is not bohemian.'

'Compared to my life and to Michael's it is. Have you asked her father for her hand?'

'No, not yet.' Jim moved uncomfortably in his chair.

'When do you propose to marry?' Theo asked and then cringed at his unintentional pun.

'Not for a while. We'll get engaged and then think about when we'll get married. Maebh is having the devil of a time choosing an engagement ring. We've been to at least ten jewellers but she saw nothing she liked.'

Theo slipped the ring from his little finger and held it out to Jim.

'You might ask her if she would consider this ring.'

'That's mother's ring.'

'And if Maebh would like it, it could be her ring. It would be lovely to have something of your mother's at the wedding.'

After the table reading of *East Lynne,* Mick drew an outline of the set for the first act on the floor and Jim started to block the play. All was going well until Geoffrey's first entrance. When Jim gave him his entrance note the actor immediately challenged it and for the next hour Geoffrey challenged everything Jim asked him to do. At the tea break, Jim approached the contrary actor and said 'Geoffrey you can't go on challenging every direction I give you. We have only a week to rehearse the play.'

'I am an experienced actor,' Geoffrey replied. 'And I'm giving you the benefit of that experience.'

'None of the other actors feel it necessary to do that. If I am making a mistake, let me make it, it is how I will learn.'

'That would mean compromising my artistic integrity, and I simply refuse to do that.'

Jim smiled, called over Leslie and said 'Is George Brust still interested in joining the company?'

'Yes, he is,' replied Leslie. 'I was talking to him last night.'

'Didn't he play Geoffrey's role in a recent Belfast production of the play?'

Geoffrey's expression changed and his eyes danced from Jim to Leslie.

'I believe he did,' Leslie replied. 'Want me to give him a call?'

'There's no need to make that call, Leslie,' Geoffrey said in near panic. 'Jim, sorry if I was a bit over eager with my suggestions. Rest assured there will be no repetition.'

'Are you sure? I don't want to see you compromise yourself in any way.'

'No compromise at all, dear boy,' Geoffrey replied.

Rehearsal resumed and Geoffrey accepted every direction without question.

At lunchtime as Jim and Leslie walked down Great Brunswick Street to Karl's Tea Rooms, Leslie said with a wolfish grin 'Jim, when you get to heaven and St Peter asks you what you have done to deserve your place in heaven, tell him that you once directed Geoffrey Myers in *East Lynne*.'

A sunbeam shot through the green leaves of the tree and sparkled off the pond in Stephen's Green. Ducks and swans glided around the water lilies, craned their necks and gobbled the crumbs and chunks of stale bread that the children of well-to-do parents threw to them. Maebh and Jim walked over the tiny O'Connell Bridge and sat on a bench in front of the garden's west fountain. The park was teeming with people. Families lay on the grass sunbathing, couples strolled along the paths chatting and children played on the grass. A young girl gathered primroses from the carpet of flowers that surrounded the fountain and her two young brothers chased each other while their nanny kept an eye on them. Sitting on the park bench Jim removed a tiny leather box from his pocket.

'Maebh, I'd like you to look at something,' he said as he opened the box.

Maebh leaned forward and gasped.

'Oh Jimmy, it's beautiful. I love it.'

'It was my mother's ring. Want to try it on?'

'Oh, yes please.'

Jim gently lifted the ring out of the box and carefully slid it on Maebh's finger.

'It fits perfectly,' she exclaimed.

'Have we found your engagement ring?'

'Oh, yes we have,' Maebh replied and embraced Jim. 'Now all you have to do is tell me da.'

Jim closed his eyes and clenched his jaw.

On the third day of rehearsals, the cast's first day off book, Francis P called for a prompt three times during his first scene. At tea break Francis P sat on his own, his head buried in the script mumbling to himself. Jim took the seat beside him.

'Having a problem?'

'Yes,' Francis P replied. 'I don't really understand this William Levison character.'

'Levison is a tough, thankless role. I played him once.'

Francis P put down his script.

'How did you approach it?'

'The way I see it is that Levison is a man in conflict. He is a cruel and heartless man. But he has constructed a public persona that is the very opposite of his real self. Levison wants to believe he really is this public persona, but his true persona keeps breaking through, particularly when things don't go his way. Does that make sense to you?'

Francis P leaned back. 'Now that is something to think about. Levison is really two men …'

'No, not two men. Two personas.'

'I think I see what you're getting at,' said Francis P and he never asked for another line.

Jim hung his hat and coat on the hallstand of the Mullin house. Maebh straightened his tie, smoothed his hair and said to her soon-to-be-fiancée 'You'll be fine Jimmy, and don't take any messing from Da.'

'Aren't you coming in?'

'No, Da told me I had to wait in the parlour.'

Jim opened the door and the familiar smell of tea and toast

combined with the aroma of burning turf welcomed him. Mr Mullin sat at the table reading a newspaper. As Jim entered, Mrs Mullin went into the kitchen.

'Take a seat,' Mr Mullin said. 'We won't be interrupted, the children are visiting their Aunt Alice. I believe you have something to ask me.'

'Yes, I do.'

'Well spit it out man. What is it?'

Maebh listened at the living room door.

'I would like to ask for your daughter's hand in marriage,' Jim said a little formally.

'My answer is: That depends.'

Maebh gasped and Mrs Mullin dropped the spoon she was drying.

'Depends on what?' Jim asked.

'Maebh is a school teacher and brings a tidy packet of money every week into the house.'

Maebh's heart beat faster, her mouth went dry and she could hardly believe her ears.

'Mr Mullin, I don't think you understand. If I am to marry Maebh, she needs a dowry.'

'You'll be getting no dowry from me,' Mr Mullin said and slapped the table.

'Then I won't be taking her off your hands.'

Choking with indignation, Maebh crashed into the room. 'Take me off his hands? How dare you ask for a …'

Jim hands covered his mouth trying to contain his laughter. Mr Mullin slapped the table again.

'Ah Jimmy you gave the game away! We had her going, we could have kept it up for a few more minutes.'

Maebh grabbed the newspaper off the table and pounded Jim with it.

'You, you … brat. You're as bad as me father. How could you? I hate you.' Maebh then threw the paper at her father. 'You two planned this together.'

'No we didn't,' Jim protested. 'He said if I didn't go along with it, he wouldn't let us get married.'

'Da, you're just such a big child.'

Maebh plonked on a chair, folded her arms and scowled. Jim tried to embrace her but she rebuffed him.

'Jimmy Brevin, you ask me Da properly for my hand.'

'Mr Mullin, may I have your daughter's hand in matrimony?'

'Yes, you may, and we're delighted to have you join our family. I want to be serious for a moment, Jim. I know what you did for Patrick and I will never forget it. Thank you, from all my family. Now, let's get a few drinks on the table and celebrate this great occasion.'

'I have no idea why I married that husband of mine,' Dorrie Mullin said shaking her head. 'The man's a right eejit.'

The production of *East Lynne* in the trade hall in York Street was a small-scale affair. The music was played by a trio of amateur musicians. The sets were minimal; ten flats, three backdrops and a few props. The lighting was basic, just five lamps, and the interval act was a man who played the harmonica and who could juggle – though not at the same time. However on opening night, the actors and their director were as nervous as they would have been, had it been in the Queen's Theatre. Thirty minutes before curtain time when nerves were at their highest, Geoffrey Myers said to Jim 'I can't go on, my nerves are shot. Call George Brust and ask him to take over.'

Jim's escalating excitement transformed into black terror.

'I can't ask Brust to take over your role at such short notice. He hasn't rehearsed with us. He doesn't know the cuts we've made or the blocking we've devised.'

'Don't be so hasty there Jim,' a calm Leslie interjected. 'George is coming to the show tonight. I gave him a complimentary ticket. He could go on stage carrying the book and we can work around him. Why don't I fetch him while you prepare an announcement for the audience?'

'What will you say to the audience?' asked a suddenly calm Geoffrey.

'We'll have to tell the truth,' replied Leslie. 'We will tell them that you have lost your nerve.'

'If he says that, I'll never work in the theatre again.'

'That's very likely but then, the show must go on,' Leslie said, and he began to walk to the front of house.

'Wait. Wait a minute. I think I can go on,' Geoffrey said, as he squeezed his eyes shut, tightened his hands into fists and nodded his head.

'Thank God you gave George Brust a ticket for tonight's show,' Jim said when Geoffrey had left for his dressing room.

'I haven't seen George in months.'

The penny dropped. 'Geoffrey has done this before, has he?' Jim asked.

'Yes, he's a silly old sod and that's why he doesn't get much work, that and the fact that he's a tedious actor who has never produced an original performance in his life.'

The production was a success, the audience laughed and gasped, hissed and booed in all the right places and when it came time for the curtain call, all fifty of the audience cheered and applauded loudly.

'Two hundred and fifty empty seats,' Richard said as he removed his make up after the show. 'I don't think we'll be getting paid very much this week.'

'Don't imagine so,' replied Leslie.

'Pity you didn't paper the house,' Francis P said and pulled off his wig.

'I did, I gave out over two hundred complimentary tickets but only thirty of them were used.'

'You mean we only had twenty paying customers?' asked an astounded Geoffrey.

'Afraid so.'

'What about Cork and Galway?' Geoffrey asked staring into the mirror.

'If there isn't a dramatic improvement in audience numbers, we won't be going anywhere,' Leslie replied.

Leaving the trade hall that night, a tired Geoffrey said to Richard 'Glad I pulled myself together tonight. It was touch and go for a while but I was determined not to let anyone down.'

'Geoffrey, have you never wondered why you find it hard to get work?' asked Richard, as he placed his hat on his head and patted it snug.

'I don't see the relevance of your question Mr O'Hare.'

'I don't suppose you do,' Richard replied, and he and Geoffrey parted company.

Flanked by Francis P and Leslie, Jim lifted another pint of stout to his

THE ACTOR

lips and took a deep drink. It was Saturday night, the play had closed, the tour was cancelled and the trio of unemployed actors sat looking through the smoke at themselves in the stained mirror of Mooney's pub. Leslie lifted his glass of whiskey and soda and said 'I hope you know you have just drunk your wages.'

'Bit of a disaster,' Jim said and took another swallow of stout.

'Yes,' said Leslie. 'But if it's any consolation, I heard we had bigger houses all week than the Abbey Theatre. This hard old game of theatre gets harder with every passing year.'

'One good thing came out of this exercise,' Francis P said putting his arm around Jim. 'We have discovered an excellent young director.'

'Thank you Francis P, but I never wanted to be a director. I am an actor,' Jim said, climbing off the bar stool. 'Time to go home. It's been a pleasure gentlemen. Goodnight and thank you.'

Standing outside the pub, Jim waved down a passing cab, clambered into it and as the cab took off down Grafton Street, he burst into song.

39

LYING ON A SOFA IN the front drawing room with his head throbbing from his over indulgence the previous night, Jim sat up when Theo stepped into his line of sight and towered over him.

'You were the one who punched your brother.' Theo's voice was severe and his face was scowling. 'Brawling like a hoodlum. I brought you up to be better than that.'

'Could we have this conversation some other time?'

'We are not having a conversation. Apologise to your brother and don't let it happen again.'

A few hours later sitting at a corner table in the Shelbourne Hotel's elegant Lord Mayor's Lounge, Leslie Lawrence tilted a silver teapot and as the warm brew swirled around the bottom of a fine china tea cup, he said 'You look a bit under the weather, Jim.'

'Just a bit.'

Jim ordered a glass of milk and some aspirin from a passing waiter.

'Jim, you and I are very much alike, we drink to make other people interesting.'

'Spare me the wit, Leslie.'

All the conversations in the lounge ceased when three heavy-set Black and Tan officers, revolvers strapped to their thighs, tramped into the room. Two of them stood while the third officer, a tall man with arms like tree trunks, walked directly to a table by the window. Smiling at its occupants he said 'Are you finished with the table?'

'I beg your pardon?' replied the man.

The officer placed his hand on his revolver, the woman's face turned pale. The menacing silence was broken when the man at the table bowed his head and said 'Yes. Yes we were just leaving.'

'But I haven't had my cake yet,' said the man's wife.

'Never mind dear, it's time for us to go.'

'Thank you,' the officer replied and his fake smile became a sneer.

Jim, Leslie and the rest of the lounge watched in fearful silence as the man and his wife gathered their belongings and left.

'Thugs in uniform,' Leslie said under his breath.

'Be careful, Leslie,' Jim whispered and added in full voice 'What did you want to talk to me about?'

'Oh yes. I was in University College Cork the other day and someone associated with the drama society asked me to recommend a director for a student production of *The Playboy of the Western World*. It's to be entered in some drama competition. I suggested you. What do you say?'

'I say I'm an actor.'

'They don't need actors. In our business you need a few strings to your bow.'

'You're right, of course.' Jim said. 'Tell them I'd be delighted to direct the play.'

The waiter placed a long glass of milk and two aspirin tables on the tablets in front of Jim. He took the tablets, drank half the milk and watched wincing as Leslie smeared clotted cream and jam on a decapitated fruit scone and stuffed it, whole, into his mouth.

'Any word about Ira? Is he up to a visitor?'

'Ira is still in the hospital and he's not allowed visitors. You can write to him.'

'I have, he hasn't replied.'

'And he won't reply, he's not allowed.' Leslie removed a slice of Battenberg cake from the three-tier silver cake stand and cut it in three equal pieces.

'You're not going to eat that are you?' Jim asked.

'Of course I am.'

'Then I have to leave,' Jim said and as he walked across the lounge he noticed that the tables close to the Black and Tan officers had all been vacated.

The mist off the sea mingled with the scent of yellow gorse as Jim and Maebh stood on Howth Head and watched waves crash around the base of the white lighthouse.

'This work of mine in Cork is going to cause a bit of a problem,' Jim said.

'I know, I'm really going to miss you,' Maebh said, and snuggled close to him.

'And I'll miss you, Miss Mullin, but that's not the problem I was referring to. The play opens on the day of Michael's wedding, so I may not be able to go.'

'Jim, he's your brother.'

'I know that, but we were never that close.'

'Jimmy. You have to go to the wedding.'

Thirty five, noisy, and mostly dirty-faced, little girls sat in their seats while their teacher Maebh Mullin drew a map of Ireland on the blackboard. The classroom door opened and the school principal, the middle aged Mrs Jones stepped into the room.

'Miss Mullin, you have a visitor,' Mrs Jones said and patted the curls of her freshly permed hair.

'Is it a parent?'

'I don't think so. She doesn't look like she comes from around here. She said her name is Clara Wright-Moran. I'll take your class.'

'Thank you, Rose. I love your hair.'

'It's my late husband's anniversary today; I like to look special for him.' Mrs Jones looked very sad. 'I'm not being silly, am I?'

'No, you're not,' Maebh said and as she walked out of the classroom she said to her pupils 'Girls, be nice to Mrs Jones.'

Mrs Jones seemed delighted to be out of her office and teaching again.

'Now girls, who knows where Dublin is on this lovely map that Miss Mullin has drawn for us?'

THE ACTOR

'I do,' said a bright-eyed girl in the front row.

Cork City startled Jim. The centre was in ruins. Where once there were beautiful buildings now there were derelict sites piled high with rubble. Nearly every building on Patrick Street was a stark, burnt-out shell. Soldiers thronged the streets and the clatter of army lorries was constant. Outside the charred, red-bricked Carnegie Library, Jim hailed a cab and fifteen minutes later it dropped him at the campus of University College, Cork. The college campus was an oasis of beauty in a ravaged city. As Jim walked along the west wing of the gothic quadrangle, memories of his boarding school days flooded back. Sinclair Thompson, a clear-skinned, earnest young man in a collared shirt, a course corduroy jacket and trousers, met Jim at the quadrangle's main entrance.

'Mr Brevin, the drama group is waiting in room eighteen,' Sinclair said and walked briskly into the austere building.

When they reached room eighteen, Sinclair pulled open the door and the gush of musty, perspiration-laden air billowed into Jim's face. More school memories flooded back.

The four weeks of rehearsals were enjoyable and challenging for Jim. Every weekend he returned to Dublin and from the moment Maebh met him at Kingsbridge Station to the moment she returned him to his train, they never stopped talking.

On the night of the dress rehearsal Jim walked backstage in the Aula Maxima and the sounds of the theatre preparing for performance excited him. The voices of stagehands calling out last minute instructions, the flopping of backdrops as they dropped into place, the whistle of ropes being pulled through pulleys and the whizz of curtains opening and closing, thrilled him. In the dressing rooms, Jim had a word of encouragement for everybody and shook each actor's hand in turn.

Michael and Clara's wedding took place in the Church of the Assumption, in Dalkey. To Jim's eyes it was an ostentatious display, but to Maebh it was a parade of the latest fashions and style that she only ever saw in magazines. Clara and her two bridesmaid sisters, Elizabeth and Victoria wore ankle-length ivory skirts with matching bodices three-quarter length with sleeves. All the ladies wore gloves and brooches on their blouses with matching bangles on their wrists. Hair was coiffed, shoes buffed and everything was tailored to perfection. In contrast to the elaborate nature of the women's outfits, the men's attire was traditional and muted. The men wore black tail coats, white formal shirts, white bow ties and white waistcoats with top hats and white gloves. Augustine Wright-Moran OBE too was dressed in tails but across his chest he wore a red sash and pinned to the left lapel of his tailcoat was his silver Order of the British Empire medal.

Michael's face flushed red the second he glimpsed Maebh step into the drawing room of the Wright-Moran mansion on Dalkey Hill.

'She's here. I told that brother of mine not to bring her,' Michael whispered to his wife of a few hours. 'Excuse me. I'll be back in a minute.'

Clara placed her hand firmly on Michael's arm and said very softly 'Michael I invited Maebh.'

'You what? But your father said … She's an embarrassment.'

'Poppycock, she's a sweet girl. You stay here and talk to our guests while I go and welcome Maebh and your brother to my family home.'

The moment Clara left Michael's side, Augustine Wright-Moran OBE immediately positioned himself beside his new son-in-law.

'I see you invited that person into my home,' Augustine said accusingly.

'I can assure you sir, I did not invite her. Your daughter did.'

'Then you better learn to control your wife, young man,' he snapped, and left Michael standing alone in the centre of the room.

Two weeks later Jim hung Maebh's coat on the hallstand of his home.

'Why does your father want to see us?' Maebh whispered as she fingered her engagement ring.

'I told you, I don't know. All he said was that he wanted to have a little chat with us.'

When Jim opened the door to the conservatory, Theo stood and said 'Hello Maebh, how are you?'

'I'm well Mr Brevin, how are ya?'

'I'm very well, why don't we sit and have that little chat.'

Maebh glanced at Jim and the two of them sat together on the sofa opposite Theo.

'I love the ring,' Maebh said. 'But I've already told you that.'

'Indeed you have,' Theo replied. 'May I see it on your finger?'

Like a small child presenting her most precious possession, Maebh held out her hand to Theo.

'That ring hasn't sparkled like that in a long time.' Then with a glint in his eye Theo handed Jim a file that was sitting on the sofa beside him. 'That's for both of you. Go ahead, open it.'

Jim flipped open the file and lifted out an illustration of a beautiful, new, detached, four-bedroomed house. 'That's my wedding present to you.'

'It's a house.' Maebh gasped. 'A real house, oh, we couldn't accept that, could we Jim?'

'Could we accept an unreal house?' asked Jim casually.

Maebh's eyes flashed with annoyance.

'Jimmy, don't make fun of me.'

'I'm not making fun of you.' Then turning to his father said 'Thank you very much Father. We're delighted to accept your very generous gift.'

'You're very welcome. Now let's have a little drink to celebrate.'

When Theo went to get the drinks Maebh whispered to Jim 'I don't think we should accept your father's gift, it's far too much.'

'What's done is done,' Jim said and patted Maebh on the knee.

Later that evening Jim walked an unusually quiet Maebh home. When he asked her, for the third time, what was wrong she snapped 'Don't you ever speak for me again and never again patronise me.'

'Maebh, I didn't mean to patronise you. Perhaps, I should have waited and talked to you about the house, but it's done now.'

'No. It's not done,' Maebh said and slammed the front door of her home in Jim's face.

The UCC drama society's production of *The Playboy of the Western World* was not only successful, it took first prize in the Munster Festival of Drama. Jim travelled to Cork for the prize-giving ceremony and after the celebrations he congratulated the cast and crew a hundred times. He then took a cab to the Mizen Peninsula. As the cab rattled and clattered past woods, fields and heather-coloured hills, Jim thought about the two summers he spent at Mizen Cottage. The cab stopped outside the cottage, Jim stepped out of the cab and a familiar voice called out to him.

'As I live and breathe, Jim Brevin. You're a welcome surprise.'

The voice belonged to his school friend, Ciaran O'Donovan.

Sitting in a room overlooking Dunmanus Bay, Jim and Ciaran sat and reminisced about their schooldays together.

'I heard Baggy, Stewart Keogh as they call him now, went with you to King's College, Cambridge.'

'Yes, Stewart loved punting. We had many a good night in the Eagle Pub and in every other inn in Cambridge. We graduated last year and now we're both working in his family's accounting company.'

A quiet moment ensued between friends. Then Ciaran said 'I saw you once in a play in the Opera House.'

'Why didn't you come back backstage and say hello?' Jim asked.

'Why didn't you come out to Mizen Cottage?' countered Ciaran.

Both questions hung in the air and both men knew the answers to the questions.

'You're here now,' Ciaran said after a moment. 'You'll stay the night?'

'I will. Ciaran, there is a specific reason why I came to see you.'

'I thought there might be,' Ciaran replied.

'I have met someone, someone special and we are going to marry. I'd like you to be my best man?'

Ciaran jumped to his feet.

'I'd be proud and honoured. Congratulations, this is wonderful news.'

'Good, that's settled,' Jim said with a sigh. 'Now I can relax.'

'Tell me about this girl of yours?'

After dinner Ciaran finally summoned the courage to ask the question that he wanted to ask from the moment Jim arrived at the cottage.

'How is Líla?'

'Líla is well. Ciaran, I don't know what happened between you two, Líla never talked about it and I never asked.'

'When I went to Cambridge I wrote – but we grew apart.'

'Ciaran, you've been my friend for a long time, but Líla is my sister. There are things I don't care to know, things that are not my business.'

Ciaran sat back in his chair, looked out the window and watched the waves roll along the water of the bay.

Michael stood in the back drawing room on one of his infrequent visits back to his family home and said 'Father, I don't understand why you are allowing Jim marry that – Maebh girl.'

'I don't remember you asking my permission to marry Clara.'

'I didn't have to. Clara was a most suitable person to marry.'

'Maebh is a rock of sense; she'll bring a little order into Jim's life, besides I like her; she's got spirit.'

'Father, she's common and cheap.'

'Michael that comment is beneath you.'

'I'm only saying what others are thinking.'

'No, you are not.' Theo sighed. 'Michael you are turning into a frightful snob and a great bore.'

'Father, that's unfair?'

'Is it? How else does one explain the way you speak of Maebh? Or why you think the house I gifted you was not good enough for you to live in?'

The air smelled of summer flowers and the garden's lawn was covered in a sea of white apple blossoms. Theo stood in the shade of the birch tree and placed a flower in his jacket lapel. At the Brevin front door, Maebh paused a moment to compose herself before she knocked.

'He's expecting you Miss Mullin,' Mrs O'Neill said when she answered the door. 'He's in the garden. Why don't you go to him and I'll serve tea in the gazebo.'

Maebh stepped into the fragrant garden and Theo waved to her.

'Why don't we walk as we talk,' Theo said after he greeted her. 'What is this important matter you want to talk to me about?'

'I can't accept your wedding gift.'

'Don't you like it?' Theo asked.

'Oh, yes I do, it's beautiful. But I think it's too much. Jimmy accepted your gift without discussing it with me.'

'And Jim and you have talked about this, and this is a joint decision?' Maebh cast her eyes downwards. 'You're right,' Theo said. 'He should have spoken to you before he accepted the gift, but Jim was always impetuous and …'

'My father can't give us a house,' Maebh blurted out. 'So I can't accept one from you.'

'Fair enough,' Theo stopped walking. 'But let me put a hypothetical question to you. If your father could afford to give you a house, do you think he would?'

Maebh cast a sideways look at Theo.

'That's a trick question.'

'It's an honest question.'

'Very well, I'll give you an honest answer. If my father could give us a house, he would. But that's not the point.'

'Ah but it is the point. And you know it is. Now Maebh the matter is closed, let's have some tea,' Theo said, and he resumed his walk to the gazebo.

'It isn't closed,' Maebh said scurrying after Theo.

Theo stopped and took Maebh by the hands. 'Maebh, Jim is never going to earn a lot of money. This is the last opportunity I have to help him without hurting his pride. Please let me do this, for my son.'

'I think I've just lost this argument?'

'If you're as wise as I think you are, you'll let me win.'

Maebh gently kissed Theo on the cheek and whispered 'Now I know where Jim got his charm.'

'No you don't,' Theo replied. 'If you had met my wife you'd know what real charm was like.'

'Tell me about your wife? What was she like?'

'She was very bold but absolutely captivating; just like you.'

40

Sean Mullin carefully guided his right leg down the narrow-fitting, cuffed leg of the trousers of his new suit. He did the same with his left leg, pulled up the trousers and then slipped his arm through his new striped braces. He straightened his tie, put on his polished shoes, pulled on the short jacket of his new suit, combed his hair, looked into the mirror and said 'Not so bad me oul' segocia. You'd give Rudolph Valentino a good run for his money.' Sean laughed heartily at his own joke.

This was only the second time Sean Mullin had worn a new suit. The first time was on his wedding day, twenty seven years ago. Today was the day of his daughter's wedding.

'Hurry up or we'll be late, you're worse than any bride,' Dorrie Mullin called up the stairs.

Sean came down the stairs with a swagger.

'You look very smart Sean,' Dorrie said. 'Ya look like a proper gentleman.'

'And you look like a beautiful lady,' Sean said and kissed his wife on the lips.

'Will you stop that, you and your oul' palaver,' Dorrie said, as she carefully positioned her new hat on her head and stole a proud glance at her handsome husband.

Maebh's bedroom door clicked open and wearing the same lace-trimmed, ivory coloured dress that her mother wore on her wedding day she descended the stairs. Sean Mullin looked at his daughter, remembered his Dorrie on her wedding day and his eyes welled with tears.

'Ma, will you attach the veil to the headdress,' Maebh said handing Dorrie her veil.

Dorrie took her daughter's hand and said 'You look so beautiful. Does that Jimmy knows how lucky he is?'

'Maebh darling, you look wonderful,' Sean Mullin said as tears made his eyes glisten.

'Sean, stop that talk or you'll have us all in floods,' Dorrie said. Pushing Sean aside, she quickly attached the veil to Maebh's headdress and took her daughter in her arms.

Jim and his best man Ciaran waited in the front pew of St Joseph's Church, Berkley Road.

'She's late,' Jim whispered to Ciaran as he tapped his foot on the tiled floor.

'She's only ten minutes late,' Ciaran replied. Implanted

Suddenly the organ played a long note, the congregation rose and when Jim looked down the aisle, the sight of Maebh in her wedding dress was fixed into his memory forever. Mendelssohn's *Wedding March* reverberated around the church and the intensity of joy and happiness Jim experienced nearly overwhelmed him.

After the church service the wedding party, neighbours and friends gathered in the Blessington Basin for the photograph. While the neighbours were congratulating Maebh and Jim, Dorrie approached Clara and Líla and said 'Would you two ladies like to come home with me and help set the table for the wedding breakfast?'

'I beg your pardon,' asked a somewhat taken aback Clara-Wright-Moran. 'You want me to what?'

Líla nudged Clara's arm.

'We'd love to help,' Líla said, and before Clara could say another word she added 'perhaps we could help out with the cooking too.'

'Oh no,' replied a slightly miffed Dorrie. 'The neighbours are doing that. Mrs Doyle next door is cooking the sausages and the tomatoes,

Mrs Darcy across the street is frying the rashers and the black and white pudding, Mrs Walsh two doors up, is baking the scones and Mary and Rose will fry the eggs and make the toast.

'Aren't you lucky to have such helpful neighbours?' commented Líla.

'Yes I am, but I told Rose to count the sausages when Mrs Doyle brings them in. Mrs Doyle is a very nice person but she can be a bit light-fingered at times.'

'Mrs Mullin I must congratulate you on your outfit, it's gorgeous,' Líla said. 'It's beautifully made.'

'I made it myself, and I made the bridesmaids dresses too,' Dorrie volunteered.

'Everyone looks lovely, such style,' Clara added.

'Oh, you two are as bad as me husband, with all your palaver. But no matter what you say, you're still going to help set the table,' Dorrie said and laughed throatily to herself.

Sean Mullin tapped Dorrie on the shoulder and said 'We'll be off now. Won't be too long.'

Then Sean, Jim and all the men walked out of the Basin and down Blessington Street.

'Where are the men going?' Clara asked.

'Oh, they're off to the pub,' Dorrie replied. 'I won't allow drink in the house.'

'Oh,' said Clara. 'No drink.'

Sean Mullin pushed open the doors of Gallagher's Pub on Mountjoy Street and said to his guests 'Keep your money in your pockets, it's no use here today.' Sean put his arm around Theo's shoulders. 'What will you have Mr Brevin?'

'Call me Theo and I'll have a glass of porter.'

'You'll have nothing of the sort, you'll have a pint like everyone else.'

'I'll have a pint too,' Conor, Maebh's twelve-year-old brother said loudly.

'Conor, you'll have an orange mineral and like it,' Sean said and tossed his son's hair.

'Stop it, Da, I hate it when you do that.'

When everyone had a pint, Sean called for quiet and solemnly proposed a toast to his daughter and his new son-in-law and while everyone drank, Michael leaned over to Ciaran and said softly 'I wonder if the bride is like her dress, used?'

'That's completely out of order,' replied a shocked Ciaran.

'Perhaps. I only asked the question.'

'Da, give us a song,' Conor said as he sat beside his father.

'Right you are son, Jim this one is for you,' Sean said and he launched into the first verse of *I'll go with him, wherever he goes.*

Everyone laughed and when the song was over Jim, prompted Ciaran to order the second round.

'But Mr Mullin said no one is to buy a …'

'It's customary for the best man to buy the second round,' Jim said. 'And then call on me to sing.'

Ciaran ordered a round of drinks and when Michael received his drink he said to Ciaran 'The lower classes have interesting habits, don't you think?'

Without replying Ciaran walked away from Michael and resumed his seat beside Jim.

'What did Michael say to you?' Jim asked.

'Oh he was being funny – at least he thinks he's being funny.' Ciaran got to his feet and said 'I call on the groom to give us a song.'

Jim stood, bowed to Sean Mullin and sang *Molly Malone*. Sean Mullin leaned against the bar counter, loosened his tie, placed his arm around Conor and listened to Jim's singing. When the song was over Sean raised his hand in the air and announced 'We'll have one more round and then we'll go. We can't keep the ladies waiting too long.'

'I like that son of yours,' Sean said when he handed a drink to Theo. 'He's a good singer and a good fella.'

'He is, and I know he'll look after that lovely daughter of yours.'

'Well, at least he can afford to buy her a new dress,' Michael sneered to Ciaran.

The pub fell quiet. Jim jumped from his seat and lunged at Michael but Sean Mullin thrust himself between the two warring brothers. 'There will be no fighting on my daughter's wedding day. Jim, control yourself, fighting won't solve anything,' Sean Mullin turned to Michael. 'My daughter wore the dress she wanted to wear today and I'm proud and honoured she wore it.' He looked around the pub. 'I don't want

Maebh to hear a word of any of this – is that understood?'

Everyone nodded and muttered their agreement. Theo walked through the wedding party, stood in front of his eldest son and said 'The depth of your ignorance is astonishing, apologise immediately to our host.'

'Why? What did I say that was so wrong? She was wearing an old dress? Why are you being such a hypocrite father? Pretending that you're enjoying yourself. You've never been in a pub like this in your life. Look, there's even dirty sawdust on the floor, the glasses are filthy and there you are pretending you're enjoying drinking pints.' He grabbed his hat. 'I'm leaving.'

'You're going nowhere,' Theo said coldly. 'You're going to your brother's wedding breakfast and if you say another word of insult to anyone you'll regret it, and I mean regret it for the rest of your life. Do I make myself absolutely clear?'

Michael looked away.

'Apologise to Mr Mullin.'

Michael grunted an apology, sat back down and for the rest of the day hardly spoke another word.

Sean Mullin handed the bartender a five pound note and as he stood waiting for his change, Theo said to him 'I apologise for my son's behaviour.'

Sean touched Theo's arm. 'There's no need to do that. We do what we think is the best for our children and we hope they grow up to be the best people they can be.'

'That does not excuse what Michael ...'

'Theo, my own lad Patrick had to go to America. He was a rebel, God knows what he did. I tell you honestly, he didn't learn any of that stuff in my house. Enough said, let's go. I'm starving. I could murder a fry.'

After the wedding breakfast Ciaran stood, lifted his cup of tea and proposed a toast to the bride and groom. Ciaran then surprisingly called on Red's girlfriend Bridget to speak. Bridget adjusted the top of her patterned dress, stood and, visibly shaking, opened a folded piece of lined paper.

'I want to read yous a letter I got from Patrick,' Bridget said, took a deep breath and then read aloud. 'Dear Maebh and Jim, congratulations on getting hitched. I'd love to be there with you both but I can't be. Jim's a great bloke and Maebh is a brilliant sister; good luck to both of you. I think this wedding thing must be catching. Bridget is coming to America in November and we are getting married.' Everyone around the table cheered and whooped and Bridget's face went crimson. When the room was quiet, Bridget continued 'Jim, a few weeks ago I saw that film *In the Days of Saint Patrick* in the Hibernian Club in Newark, New Jersey. I never knew you had such knobbly knees. Good luck again and God Bless. Red.'

'I have a telegram to read,' Ciaran announced when Bridget resumed her seat.

'Congratulations Maebh and Jim. I wish you both a long and happy life together. Let me pass on this piece of wisdom to you. A man may be a fool and never know it; but if he's married he will be told it every day. Good luck, Leslie Lawrence.'

Maebh had changed into her going-away clothes and as she walked down the stairs Rose announced 'Mr and Mrs Allen are at the door.'

'For God's sake,' Dorrie cried out. 'Bring them in!'

'Won't stay long,' Ira said when he entered the living room. 'Maebh and Jim, we would like to congratulate you both. Maebh, I've watched you grow up, you were always a lovely girl and now you're a beautiful married lady. Jim you are a fine young man, good luck to both of you. I wish you great happiness.'

May kissed Maebh on the cheek and Ira, looking very pale, shook Jim's hand and as quickly as they had arrived the Allens departed.

Maebh hugged her mother. Sean Mullin put one arm around his wife, shook Jim's hand with the other and wished them well. At the front door, Jim embraced his father and a dour-looking Michael grunted something inaudible. The newly-wed couple stepped into the waiting cab and as they rolled away down the avenue they waved happily to their family and friends.

41

An excited Maebh sat in the first class carriage of the train as its chugged its way to Bray, Co Wicklow. She leaned out of the window and watched grey steam pulse from the engine's funnel. When she resumed her seat, she pulled her new husband's hand on to her lap and talked non-stop until they arrived at Bray station.

A uniformed, reed-thin, train porter opened the carriage door and when Maebh went to take her suitcase off the luggage rack the porter said 'Leave that to me, Miss, I'll look after that.'

'Mrs, not Miss, please,' Maebh said correcting the porter.

'Beg your pardon ma'am,' the porter replied and turning to Jim asked 'Would you like a cab, sir?'

'Yes please,' Jim replied.

The porter whisked the two new suitcases from the luggage rack, walked Maebh and Jim through the station house and placed the suitcases on the back of a waiting hansom cab.

Maebh stood in the doorway of the Bray Head Inn's bridal suite and gazed on the large brass and iron, canopied bed that dominated the room. 'It looks lovely,' she said.

In one swift movement, Jim lifted her off her feet, carried her across the threshold and placed her on the bed.

'Well, Mr Brevin, what do you propose to do now?' Maebh asked, as she ran the bed's silk curtain through her fingers.

'We could go to bed,' Jim replied and sat on the bed beside her.

'It's five o'clock in the afternoon. Let's go for a walk along the esplanade and then we'll have something to eat.'

'I think my idea was better,' Jim replied.

With their hands interlaced, Jim and Maebh walked along Bray's esplanade. In an amusement arcade at the end of the esplanade, Jim put a coin into a machine and it presented him with a small chrome ball-bearing. Jim flicked the trigger on the front of the machine, the chrome ball shot around the circular maize and fell into a no-win slot. Maebh laughed and pulled Jim over to the Madam Zorb fortune-telling machine. She inserted a coin, lights flashed, the machine rattled and whizzed and coughed out a small rectangular card with the words *Madam Zorb predicts you will meet a tall dark man who will sweep you off your feet.*

'Too late, Madame Zorb,' Maebh said, tittering while carefully placing the card in her handbag.

The sun was disappearing into the sea when Jim and Maebh returned to their hotel. At the foot of the hotel's staircase Maebh placed her hands on Jim's arm and said 'You stay here and in twenty minutes come to the room.'

'Twenty minutes,' Jim protested softly.

'Yes and no longer.'

Jim strolled into the hotel's Victorian lounge, sat by the fireside and time seemed to stop. He ordered a drink. A minute passed. The waiter placed the drink on the mahogany table beside him. Another three minutes passed. Jim finished his drink. Seven minutes had passed. He wandered around the lounge looked at the various pieces of art. Nine minutes had passed. He walked to the hotel's front door and watched as the moonlight danced on the sea. Eleven minutes had passed. He had another drink. Seventeen minutes had passed. He walked up the hotel stairs and knocked on the bedroom door. Exactly twenty minutes had elapsed.

'Come in,' Maebh's small voice called out.

Jim entered the room. Maebh was sitting on the bed wearing a white silk nightgown. She looked at her husband of eight hours and beamed a smile that was the brightest Jim had ever seen. She looked adorable. He turned down the gaslight and sat on the bed beside her and kissed her.

'Why don't you get undressed?' Maebh said and patted the pyjamas she had laid out for him.

In the near darkness, Jim undressed and when he climbed into the bed. Maebh whispered 'I'm a little nervous.'

'Don't be,' Jim replied and slid his arm around her slim waist. 'I love you, Maebh.'

I love you too,' she sighed, they kissed and the gentle sounds of their lovemaking floated around the room.

When Jim fell back against the pillow, Maebh placed her head on his chest and whispered 'Jimmy Brevin you're a sexy man.'

'And you're a sexy woman.'

Maebh leaned up on her elbows and in a show of modesty held the sheet against her breasts.

'I am, aren't I? I'm a sexy woman.'

'Yes you are.' Jim closed his eyes and leaned back on the pillow.

'You're not going to sleep are you, Jimmy?'

'No, I'm not,' he replied; he pulled her close and kissed her ear, her eyes and her nose her lips and her breasts.

The next morning when Jim awoke, Maebh's body was curled into his. Jim lay motionless and listened to the sound of his young wife breathing. He was at peace. Maebh's body moved and like a child awakening from a deep sleep, she rubbed her eyes drowsily with her fist.

'Good morning,' he whispered and kissed her on the forehead.

Maebh's eye fluttered open and as she stretched she brushed her slim body against Jim's.

'Good morning,' she said mischievously.

'Maebh, you're being very bold?'

'Am I?'

'Yes you are.'

'And what are you going to do about it?' Maebh asked, and she wrapped her arms around Jim. 'Oh, I think you're a naughty man Jimmy Brevin.'

THE ACTOR

'And I think you are a very perceptive woman Maebh Brevin.'
Maebh threw back her head and laughed her beautiful throaty laugh.

42

In the summer of 1921 a truce was signed between the IRA and the British authorities. Suddenly the war was over. The fighting stopped; the hated Black and Tans vanished from the streets. The British military ended their raids and the curfew was lifted. The IRA ceased all operations and peace fell like a gentle blanket of calm over the island of Ireland. The markets reopened, lorries and carts moved freely about the city, food supplies returned to shops and people begun to attend dances, picture halls, theatres and football matches and very quickly a near normality returned to everyday life.

With jotter and tape measure in hand, Maebh Brevin visited every room in her new home. She measured the windows, doorways and mantelpieces and wrote each measurement in her jotter. Then sitting on an orange box in the centre of the living room, she thought how she would like to decorate each room. She imagined the colour of the room, the floor covering and the curtains and then she decided where she would place each of the eight pieces of furniture her grandmother had left her. She wrote everything in her jotter and when Jim returned home that evening, she presented him with her day's work.

'Very nice,' he said, when she had finished explaining her plans for their home. 'And who is going to do all this work?'

'I am,' Maebh replied. 'And so are you.'

'Oh, am I?'

'Oh yes, you're my live-in handyman.'

'And how are you going to pay this live-in handyman?'

Maebh bit her lip and looked up at Jim.

'We'll do a trade.'

'That sounds interesting. What will we trade?'

'Use your imagination.'

'Mrs Brevin! You're shameless.'

'I am, aren't I?' Maebh replied, and laughed her delicious laugh.

The following day Maebh and Jim set about decorating their home. They started in the back bedroom and proceeded slowly and painstakingly through the house. Over the next few months they bought curtains, curtain rails, a kitchen table and chairs, a brown sofa, two wooden armchairs and a printed carpet.

In early August, Leslie pulled open the heavy door of his Georgian home and greeted his friend and colleague Ira Allen.

'Come in, glad you could make it,' Leslie said, as he walked Ira down the high ceilinged hall. 'You're looking well, you've even got some colour in your cheeks.'

Sitting in the spacious drawing room, the two friends talked about theatre and theatre gossip. After a while, Leslie asked if Ira had heard anything from the Queen's Theatre.

'Before I answer that, let me tell you the true position of my health. I'm not fully recovered, I'm not near as strong as I used to be and the doctors have told me to take things easy. Leslie, would you consider taking on some of the acting company's day-to-day management responsibilities?'

'I'd be delighted to,' Leslie replied.

'Good. Vincent Finnie is the new Queen's manager. He's told me that the theatre is to reopen in September and he has offered me my usual October slot.'

'That's wonderful news.' Leslie's eyes were alive with interest. 'Have you chosen the plays yet?'

'No, I wanted to talk to you about that.'

'Don't want to remind people of the war, they've had enough,' Leslie replied. 'What about comedies?'

'That's my thinking too,' Ira replied, beaming a knowing smile. 'How about *A Noble Brother* and *Arrah-Na-Pogue?*'

'They would fit the bill beautifully,' Leslie said and he lit a cigarette, inhaled deeply, and for the next two hours the two men planned the forthcoming productions.

On the 10 September, 1921, the Queen's Theatre re-opened its doors to the public. The lower part of Great Brunswick Street was cordoned off, the Lord Edward Brass Band played on the footpath opposite the theatre and the Alice Fielding's Troupe of Irish Dancers danced on a temporary stage on the road. The opening play was *The Cattle Thief; A Tale of the Cattle Country* with George A Street, the play's author, performing the lead role of Mardo.

The following day the Ira Allen Company of Irish Players began re-rehearsing *A Noble Brother*. Ira used the same cast as in the previous production and a larger more spectacular waterfall was imported from London for the production. Once again, Mick reminded Richard not to interfere with the waterfall machine.

'I have no interest in the blasted contraption,' Richard replied, and this time he was as good as his word.

On opening night while hundreds of people streamed into the theatre, Maebh and Líla took their seats in the front row of the dress circle. Maebh had not seen her husband play a villain in a melodrama before. At first, she found it difficult to believe that Jim could act so cruelly to another person, but as the play progressed she got caught up in the drama, and by the end of the second act she was booing and hissing her husband's dastardly acts as enthusiastically as everyone else in the theatre.

On the 6 December, 1921, the British and Irish Governments signed the Treaty that created the Irish Free State. The reaction of most people was one of relief that the fighting was now permanently over, however that sentiment was not shared by all Irish politicians. When the Dáil, the new Irish Parliament, met in the Dublin's Mansion House, the Treaty was accepted, but by only a small majority. The Dáil split. Those who supported the Treaty aligned themselves with the newly-formed regular army – the Free State Army – and those who opposed the Treaty aligned themselves with the IRA and became known as The Irregulars.

It was the evening of Ira Allen's fortieth birthday, and his wife, May, organised a surprise dinner party for her husband in the Trocadero restaurant. After the meal Richard O'Hare stood, made a toast to Ira and called on him to make a speech.

To the applause of those present, Ira rose and said:

> 'First let me say a big thank you to my most wonderful wife for organising this evening.' Ira leaned down and kissed May's hand. 'I would also like to thank you, my good friends, and my two sons, for coming along here tonight. Now, you'd like a speech, so let me recount to you a story from my amateur days in theatre.'
> Everyone around the table relaxed, sat back in their chairs and Ira slipped almost imperceptibly into performance mode.
> 'As you all know I have very little knowledge of firearms but one day as I passed an old curio shop in Capel Street, I saw an old-fashioned muzzle-loading pistol. I was so taken with this beautiful article that I bought it and brought it home. I cleaned and oiled it and I learned that to fire it, you filled the muzzle with gunpowder, rammed it home with a wad of paper, then you placed an ignition cap on the touch-hole pivot and you pulled the trigger.
> Now the question was, what was the correct quantity of powder necessary to give a good report? I took no risks. I filled it. I later learned that one-third of this quantity would have been sufficient. I rammed home the paper wad and then placed the cap in position.
> That night I was to perform in a melodrama in a local temperance hall. As usual, I was "the villain of the piece"

and in the library of a large mansion, I had to stab an old man through the heart.'
Ira lowered his voice conspiratorially. 'Now, I thought I would spring a little surprise on the old man. I would shoot him with my muzzle-loader pistol.'
Ira's voice became big again. 'The stage was small, the lights were low, murder in melodrama invariably happens in the dark. I enter through the French window to creepy music, forced open the safe; it's wonderful how easy it is to force open a safe in a melodrama. I am rifling through the contents of the safe when I am discovered by the old man. He seizes me by the throat and exclaims "Ah villain! Now I have you!"
'Curse you, let me go' I cry, and in the struggle I throw the old man from me; he staggers back. I draw my muzzle-loader and raise it. He rushes into the line of fire. Bang!'
All eyes were fixed on Ira.
'The audience is dumbfounded. The stage set is rocking to and fro, plaster dust is falling from the ceiling and the stage and frontmost rows are filled with smoke.
'Curse you, you made me do it,' I cry triumphantly and kneeling down I whisper 'Are you hurt Shaun?' No answer. I shake the old man. He doesn't move. The bold, bad villain is now meek as the mildest of milk.
'Then the "dead man" spoke. "Is the curtain down?" he asks. I nod.
'I help him to his feet but what a changed face he had. The blazing gun-powder had caught him full in the face and had transformed his face to black. We took him to a nearby chemist who said "My God, man, you've been shot."
'"No," says Shaun. "Mr Allen bought me too much porter".'

As his audience laughed, Ira bowed, and after a hearty round of applause he resumed his seat.
It was nearly midnight when the Allen party left the restaurant and as Francis P was putting on his coat, Ira said to him 'You were

unusually quiet tonight, everything all right?'

'Family matters. My eldest boy, Rory, has joined the Irish Free State Army and Eamon, my youngest is with the Irregulars. Mealtime in our house is one long argument. The sooner the politicians sort this mess out the better.'

In the summer of 1922, the anti-Treaty Irregulars occupied and set up headquarters in Dublin's Four Courts. The building's columned atrium was barricaded and armed guards stood on all entrances and exits. Inside the building, Private Eamon Pierce was cleaning his weapon when he was informed that he was wanted at the building's main entrance. When the puzzled private walked into the barricaded atrium his father, Francis P, was standing on the other side of the barricade.

'What are you doing here, Da?' Eamon whispered.

'What are you doing here?' Francis P whispered back. 'I thought we agreed you'd give up this nonsense?'

'No we didn't agree. You told me to stay at home but I'm doing what I know is right for Ireland.'

'I don't want to argue son, I want you to come home.' Francis P pointed across the River Liffey to field guns being unhitched from lorries. 'That's the Free State Army over there. Your brother Rory is in charge of one of those blooming guns and they are preparing to shell this building. Come home, your mother and your sisters are distraught with worry.'

'Who's in charge here?' bellowed an imposing officer standing beside Francis P.

'Do you mind,' Francis P said to the officer. 'I'm trying to talk some sense into my son's head. I want him to come home with me before he gets himself killed.'

The officer glared at Francis P. 'I was talking to the soldier,' replied the officer. 'Although, going home would be a sensible thing to do, young fellow.'

'No sir, I'm here to defend the Irish Republic,' replied Eamon.

'Jesus Christ,' the officer said and he rolled his eyes to the heavens. 'Young fellow, you can either go home with your father now or you can go back in there and tell your commander, Rory O'Connor, that General Michael Collins, Commander-in-Chief of the Army of the Irish Free State wants a word with him.'

'Sorry Da, I have to go. I have my duty to do.'

Private Pierce snapped to attention, saluted the general and marched back into the building.

Those twelve words were the last words Francis P ever heard from either of his sons. The following day, when the Free State Army's artillery bombardment of the neoclassical building commenced, Private Eamon Pierce was one of the first to be killed. Two days later Francis P's other son, Rory, was killed in a shootout with anti-Treaty forces in Sackville Street.

A new war, a civil war had begun; this war divided families and friends, pitted father against son, and brother against brother. It was a bitter war that wreaked havoc on the county, the economy and every citizen.

Michael sat as Theo, Jim and Líla came into the boardroom room and took their seats.

'Twice this week our vans have been stopped and looted,' Michael said, as if he was a military commander. 'It is an intolerable situation and it is costing the company a fortune. I suggest that we suspend all deliveries for the foreseeable future.'

'And how would our customers get their supplies?' Líla asked.

'They'd come and fetch them,' replied Michael. 'That's what our competitors are doing.'

'That's not the way we do business,' said Theo.

'There is another way,' Jim said, and leaned on the table. 'We could put an armed guard on each delivery van.'

'I don't know if that's legal,' said Theo.

'It would be very expensive,' remarked Michael.

'I don't like the idea of guns. It sounds very dangerous,' added Líla.

Jim replied calmly. 'First, it is legal. Yesterday I saw an armed guard on a bread lorry. Second, yes, there is a cost, but the cost of employing two armed guards is far less than the sales or stock we'd lose. Third, guns are dangerous but these are dangerous times and the men we will hire will be familiar with firearms.'

THE ACTOR

After more discussion, Theo, Michael and Líla agreed to a trial period of three months. Líla suggested that Jim organise, hire and schedule the armed guards. Jim agreed and then informed the board that in two months' time he was going on a national tour with the Ira Allen Company but he gave an assurance that the armed guards would be operational before he left.

When the meeting was over, Theo asked Jim to stay behind. When they were alone he said 'I didn't want to bring it up at the board meeting but there is something that is causing me some concern. Twenty years ago Myles Keogh, an old school friend, asked me to invest in a new company that planned to import tea and other products from India. I invested a tidy sum of the company's money in the venture, and over the years I got an excellent return. However, last month I was looking through the company's books and I was surprised to find no mention of the Keogh Trading Company. I asked Michael about it, and he got a little flustered and told me a few years ago the Keogh Trading Company's shares dropped in value and that he'd sold them on behalf of the company. I thought no more about it until I read in *The Times* that the Keogh Trading Company has posted record profits this year and have being doing so for the past five years.'

'What do you think is going on?' Jim asked.'

'I don't know. But as you're going to Cork, I want you to call on the company's offices and talk to Myles about it. Be discreet. Don't let him know we're concerned about anything.'

43

Cork was the last stop on the Ira Allen Company of Irish Players' ten-venue tour.

The country's second city was filled with Free State soldiers and the mood sombre. A week earlier, Free State forces had arrived by sea and taken the city by force from The Irregulars. While the city was now peaceful, the hinterlands of Munster were in the grip of a guerrilla war.

After the opening night performance, Jim's old friend Ciaran O'Donovan arrived back stage. The two friends sat in the green room and enjoyed the singing and merriment of the cast and their friends. The only person not present was Francis P. The death of his sons had changed him utterly. He was withdrawn and seldom socialised.

In Cork, Jim took the opportunity to contact the Keogh Trading Company as his father had requested. Myles Keogh, chairman of the company, was a tall man who had an uncanny knack of putting someone at their ease and making them feel they were the most important person in the world.

'Mr Keogh, my father asked me to drop by, to say hello, and hopefully, to get some advice on a business venture we are contemplating.'

'If I can be of help, I certainly will,' Myles replied and guided Jim into his office. 'How is your father?'

'Father is well. He sends his regards,' Jim said, as he took a seat in the leather chair that faced the large mahogany desk. 'On the train journey from Limerick Junction I saw a skirmish between Free Staters and Irregulars.'

'Yes, the last few weeks have been most awful; all the fighting and shooting. It's amazing we manage to turn a profit at all.'

Jim feigned a puzzled look. 'Really? I was looking over our company books recently and didn't notice any dividend from the Keogh Trading Company.'

'That's very odd – hold on a minute …' Myles lifted the telephone which stood on his desk and spoke into it. 'Young Dillon in accounts will get back to me in a few minutes,' he said, as he replaced the earpiece. 'But that's not why you're here. You said you had something you wanted to run by me?'

'I did. Our company is thinking of expanding into Cork. Father was wondering if you'd have any thoughts on the matter.'

'That's retail, I'm afraid, not really my area. I could have a discrete word with some friends, see what they think?'

The phone on the desk rang. Myles lifted the earpiece, listened awhile, nodded his head several times and hung up. 'Yes, I thought so. Two years ago your brother, Michael, informed us that Brevin and Sons had transferred ownership of the shares to your subsidiary company in Cork. So you have already been working on this planned expansion?'

'Pardon? Oh yes.' Jim forced a smile. 'The Cork Company, of course. Well that explains everything.' Jim rose to leave. 'I think I've taken up enough of your time.'

'Not at all. I believe you're appearing in the Opera house this week? Mrs Keogh does so enjoy the theatre.'

'Yes, yes I am,' Jim replied, still trying to come to terms with what he had just learned.

Myles Keogh was positively beaming at him.

'Oh. How stupid of me,' Jim said. 'Could I interest you in some tickets for tonight's show?'

'That would be lovely,' Myles said and relaxed his smile.

THE ACTOR

'I'll leave two tickets at the box office in your name, and again, thank you for your time.'

'Think nothing of it and give all my best to your father. Over the next few days I'll talk to a few people and let you know their thoughts on your next step with the Cork Company.'

A whistle shrieked and clouds of grey-black smoke billowed into the blue sky as the three thirty from Dublin steamed into Cork station. Carriage doors clattered open and men, women and children poured out of the train. Jim's eyes searched the milling crowd and when he saw Maebh step out of a carriage his heart leapt. Dodging people, perambulators and trolley-pushing porters he made his way down the platform. When he reached Maebh, he took her in his arms and kissed her.

'I missed you so much,' he said, his face buried in her hair.

'I missed you too,' she replied and held him close.

'Hello Jim,' a smiling Líla said when Jim finally released Maebh.

'Líla, I didn't know you were coming!'

'I wanted to surprise Ciaran. I hope I don't shock him.'

'He won't be shocked,' Jim said and kissed his sister on the cheek. 'He'll be delighted.'

'Are those flowers for me?' Líla asked, grinning at Jim.

'No they are not, cheeky girl, they're for my wife,' Jim said and presented the flowers to Maebh.

'You two love birds,' Líla said with mock exasperation. 'I had to listen to "Jim this" and "Jim that" all the way from Dublin and now all this hugging and kissing. It's just too much.'

'You're just jealous,' Jim said, as he linked the two most important ladies in his life and escorted them out of the station.

That night, halfway through the Act Two, to the audience's great surprise the theatre's main curtain was lowered, the auditorium lights burst into life and a grim-faced theatre manager walked on stage.

'Ladies and gentlemen. I have the most tragic news to impart to you.' The manager's voice was grave, and cracked as he spoke. 'It is with great sadness that I have to inform you that General Michael Collins has been shot and killed at Beal na mBlath this evening.'

A wave of shock rolled over the audience, some people gasped, some sat speechless, and some burst into tears.

'This is an outrage,' shouted one man in the stalls.

'Those blasted Irregulars, they did this!' cried a woman in the grand circle.

But one woman sitting in the stalls leaned over to her husband and whispered 'Isn't it great news, Paddy.'

The theatre manager raised his hands and the audience quietened. 'I ask everyone to remain calm. Out of respect for the deceased I have cancelled tonight's performance. Good night and take care on your way home.'

Some members of the audience left the theatre, but many remained in their seats. Backstage, Francis P sat in his dressing room and for the first time in two months, he spoke of his loss. 'Eamon. Rory. How many more people have to die before we will have peace in this wretched country of ours?'

After the death of General Collins the civil war escalated. The Free State Government passed the Public Safety Bill which empowered military tribunals to impose life imprisonment or execution on any citizen found in possession of firearms or ammunition. The new laws caused consternation and panic. Thirteen thousand republicans were jailed and seventy-seven anti-Treaty republicans were executed by firing squad.

On the same day as the passing of the Public Safety Bill, Michael called an emergency board meeting. The armed guard initiative was immediately terminated and each guard was instructed to surrender his gun and all ammunition to the police. On that same day Ira Allen walked into Mountjoy Police Station and surrendered his beloved muzzle-loading pistol.

At the end of the board meeting, when Michael asked for any other business, Theo said 'There is something I'd like to discuss.'

'And what is that?' asked Michael as he gathered up his papers.

Theo placed two Keogh Trading Company's annual reports on the table, Michael's eyes flashed with shock and he resumed his seat.

'Michael, tell me again why we are not receiving a dividend from the Keogh Trading Company?'

'As I recall, the company was not doing so well and I cashed in the shares.'

'And can you explain why there is no mention of that transaction in the company accounts? Can you also explain why a substantial dividend from those shares is being sent to an account in your name at a bank in Cork?'

The blood drained from Michael's face.

'I'm waiting for your answer.'

'There is no mention of the transaction because …' Michael's eyes darkened and his brow furrowed. 'I gave up a promising rugby career, I gave up a university education and I invested my life in this company. And what did I get in return? I got a sick father to look after, a silly sister to rear and a dreamer of a brother to support. Oh yes, I'm the chairman of the board but I don't earn enough to live the life I want.'

'You stole from the company.' Theo's face was white.

Michael slammed his hand on the table. 'I only took what was due to me.'

'You're an embezzler and a fraudster. Jim, call the police.'

'Father, please, let's not act in haste,' Jim said. 'Let's take a moment to think about how we should proceed with this matter.'

'There's nothing to think about.' Theo's voice was righteous and determined.

'Father, for God's sake …'

'You stole from the company.' Theo stood to leave. 'Jim, if you do not notify the police, I will.'

'Father, please sit down,' Líla said. 'This is a board meeting. The board should talk before involving the authorities.'

Her interjection made Theo pause. He resumed his seat before he spoke again. 'All right. But before we talk further, I want Michael to resign from the board.' He impaled Michael with an icy look.

'You have no authority to do that,' said Michael flatly.

'We have every authority,' his father snapped. 'Resign now or without further discussion I notify the police. The choice is yours.'

'Very well, I resign.'

'Leave the room please,' Theo said without looking at Michael. 'You have no place here.'

A dejected Michael walked silently out of the boardroom. Jim and Líla were shocked by their father's threat but it was clear Theo was so angry that there was no point at that moment in talking further.

Michael spent that afternoon and most of the evening drinking in the snug in Doyle's pub. The thought of telling his wife about what he had done terrified him. But shortly before nine o'clock he left the pub. He was attempting for the third time to insert the key in the front door of his home when Siobhan, the downstairs maid, opened the door and Michael stumbled into the hall. He grunted something incomprehensible to the maid, steadied himself, and swayed into the dining room where he grabbed a glass and a decanter of whiskey from the drinks cabinet.

'Fetch the lady of the house,' he barked at the still shocked maid, as he spilt whiskey from the cut glass decanter into his glass.

'What's the matter with you Michael?' Clara said, hurrying into the room a few moments later. 'You've frightened poor Siobhan.'

'Send the servants home,' slurred Michael.

'Don't be ridiculous. We haven't eaten yet.'

Glassy-eyed, Michael shouted 'Did you not hear me?'

Startled, Clara left the room. He half-heard her hurried footsteps up the stairs. Then a lot of rushing about, then more footsteps on the stairs; the hall door opened and closed.

'What's happened?' a stern-faced Clara asked when she returned to the dining room. 'Why are you in this condition?'

Michael placed the glass and the decanter of whiskey on the table and stared at his reflection in the polished table.

'What happened, Michael?'

'I've done a terrible thing.'

Clara took a deep breath. 'What terrible thing have you done?'

'I've embezzled money from the company.'

She slowly sank back in her chair. 'Why would you do something as foolish as that?'

'I did it for you. I wanted to give you nice things, this house, good furniture, fashionable clothes, everything.' Michael's speech slurred. 'I wanted to impress you. I wanted to impress your father. I wanted to provide for you in the way he provided.'

'How much money did you embezzle?' Clara asked and stroked her cheek with her fingertips.

'Enough to buy the house and everything in it.'

Clara covered her face with her hands, her shoulders shook and Michael poured himself another glass of whiskey.

The following day when Jim arrived home a distraught Clara was sitting in living room waiting for him.

'Please don't let your father inform the police about Michael,' Clara pleaded. 'If he goes to prison he won't survive. Jim, you always knew what you wanted. But Michael never did. All he ever wanted was to be as good as everyone else. If he goes to prison, the shame will kill him. Jim, I beg you to talk to your father.'

'Clara, both Líla and I have talked to father and pleaded with him not to involve the police. But Father is so angry with Michael. He feels so betrayed by him, he won't listen to reason. Perhaps if you talked to him yourself?'

'I have tried, but he won't see me,' Clara replied; she pressed her lace-trimmed handkerchief to her red, swollen eyes and wept.

Ira Allen and his wife were in the parlour of their home in Primrose Avenue. 'Vincent Finnie, the new manager of the Queen's, has asked me to meet with him,' Ira said. 'I wonder why?'

'It's probably to confirm your slot in new season schedule,' May replied taking a seat at the piano.

'I can't quite put my finger on it,' he said, 'but there was something odd about the way he asked for the meeting.'

'What play did you propose to him?'

'*Father Murphy*. I do so much enjoy playing the part.'

'It's always a crowd pleaser and Lord knows we need the money. Young Florence needs a new school uniform and the boys need shoes,' May said, opening some sheet music.

'May, the children are out for the day with your sister, let's not talk about them. Play me a Chopin nocturne.'

'Certainly dear,' May replied, and her thin fingers fell on the first notes of Chopin's Nocturne in E flat.

The sun was setting and the evening was drenched in yellow autumnal light when Maebh approached Theo in the garden gazebo.

'Should we go inside?' Theo asked, watching as the brown leaves swirled about her feet.

'No, not yet. I like the light chill of an autumn evening, it makes me feel alive,' Maebh said as she sat beside Theo.

'I suppose you're here to talk about Michael too?'

'Yes. Are you really going to involve the police?'

'Michael has broken God's law and the law of the land,' Theo replied without looking at Maebh. 'He stole from me, he lied to me and he took me for a fool. His own father.'

'Just because you can do something, doesn't mean you should do it,' Maebh said and pulled her cardigan around her. 'I don't think you should involve the police.'

'He stole; he must be punished.'

'He hurt your pride. Are you going to let your pride send your son to prison?'

'It's not my pride,' Theo replied sharply.

'Very well, if you say so, it's not your pride. But you and I both know it *is* your pride.' Maebh's voice was very soft. 'You're a stubborn man, Theo Brevin. Don't involve the police. Let me repeat to you some words a man once said to me. If you're as wise as I think you are, you'll let me win this argument.'

Theo's hand went to his face and he rubbed his eyes and after a long silence he said 'It hurts, Maebh. It hurts so much.'

'And it would hurt even more if Michael went to jail.'

Theo gazed around the garden as if he was looking for someone.

'Very well Maebh, you can tell Michael I won't go to the authorities but I want him to repay every penny he stole.'

'Mr Brevin, you're Michael's father, you must tell him that.'

'Will that end the matter?'

'No, the matter will not end until you forgive your son.'

'I can't do that, not now. Never.'

'Never is a very long time,' Maebh replied; she slipped her arm into Theo's and they walked into the warmth of the house.

Ira Allen entered the Queen's Theatre to meet the new manager as arranged. Vincent Finnie was a wiry man with a pencil-thin moustache. He had four wisps of hair which he combed over his bald pate. Dressed in an inexpensive suit and a colourful bow tie, he said cheerily '*Father Murphy*, love the play, saw it many times and always enjoyed it.'

Ira leaned back in the small uncomfortable chair and said 'It's a crowd pleaser.'

Mr Finnie unconsciously patted his four strands of comb-over hair and said 'Are you aware that J B Burke's *When Wexford Rose* played to poor houses last month?'

'Yes, I heard something of the sort.'

'Mr Burke lost money on the show and so did the theatre. The board was not pleased. In fact they concluded that the political melodramas are out of touch with the mood of the country.'

Ira sat bolt upright. He started to protest but Finnie raised his hand to silence him.

'Audiences need to be entertained; they need to be taken away from the misery and the suffering of war. Why don't you think about another play, perhaps a comedy?'

Then he said something that froze Ira's blood. 'Personally I think the future of the Queen's Theatre is in cine-variety. You know, a motion picture with an accompanying musical revue? A number of theatres are experimenting with that format. What do you think?'

Ira did not answer Mr Finnie's question, but a month later his company presented a new production of *The Colleen Bawn* on the Queen's stage. It too was a crowd pleaser.

When Michael was told of his father's change of heart he collapsed into a chair. 'Father you have no idea how relieved I am. Thank you.'

'I want you to repay every penny you stole from the company.'

'I have no money,' Michael said, shrugging his shoulders. 'You can't get blood from a stone.'

'You have your house.'

'You can't ask me to sell my home?'

'You will sell your house and you will hand over the proceeds of the sale to the company. You won't be homeless, as the company will provide you with an appropriate home. You will close the Cork bank account and transfer the money to the company's Dublin account. Then we will make arrangements to have money deducted from your salary until every penny is repaid.'

'I'll be penniless,' Michael protested. 'This is so unfair.'

'It is not unfair. Stealing and deceit is unfair,' Theo snapped and left Michael sitting alone in the room.

On the 30 April, 1923, the IRA leadership declared a ceasefire; the civil war ended but a harsh bitterness continued to divide the country.

44

On a beautiful, late summer afternoon in 1924 Jim was pruning the rose bushes in the small back garden when the back door flew open and Maebh rushed out.

'Maebh, what's the matter?' Jim asked as he guided her to a small garden seat.

'Nothing's the matter. I've just been to the doctor.'

'You never said you were going to the doctor. Are you unwell?'

'No, I'm well.' Maebh touched Jim's hand and her eyes sparkled. 'We're both well.'

A moment passed. Maebh kept smiling at Jim. He looked sideways at her.

'Are you?'

Maebh silently mouthed the words 'Yes, I'm pregnant.' Then she added in full voice 'We're going to have a baby.'

Maebh delighted in her pregnancy. She weighed herself daily, read every book she could get on the subject and talked endlessly to her mother about birthing and babies. When she was three months pregnant she decided to transform the back bedroom into baby Brevin's nursery. She scoured Dublin markets for baby furniture and toys. In one market she bought an antique Italian baby cradle and in another she bought a rocking chair.

The pregnancy brought a new intimacy to Maebh and Jim's life. She loved to watch Jim turning the spare room into a nursery. She would sit on the window ledge with her shoe dangling from her foot and chat endlessly to him. Every so often he would steal a glance at her. When something occurred to her that she had not previously considered, her brow would wrinkle and she would call out 'What do you think Jimmy?'

He would stop painting, or whatever it was he was doing, and look at her.

'You have no idea what I'm talking about, do you?'

'No,' he would reply and she would laugh her throaty laugh and say 'Ah, you men.'

Whenever Jim talked seriously about baby Brevin, his voice would take on an earnest tone and he would announce, as if he was the all-knowing father of ten, the conclusion or decision he had just settled upon. The day Jim announced that 'young Theo or Dorrie will not be sent to boarding school' Maebh smiled her agreement and thought to herself, Jimmy Brevin, no matter what you would have decided I'd never be parted from one of my children.

While Jim was out of the house, working in the theatre or with the Brevin Company, Maebh only had to think of her handsome husband and her face would light up with a smile. When he came home she'd flirt with him and in bed at night, when he'd kissed the gentle swelling of her stomach, she'd fold her arms around him and they would make love.

Six months into Maebh's pregnancy they got the first indication that all was not well. On one of the coldest nights of the year, Maebh woke Jim and told him she didn't feel well. He lit the gas light and was shaken when he saw Maebh's appearance. Her skin was sallow, dark circles ringed her eyes and her hair was matted across her forehead.

'What's the matter?' he asked, taking hold of her clammy hand.

'I'm hot and thirsty, could you get me a glass of water.'

Jim bounced out of bed, dashed down the stairs and when he returned with the water Maebh was asleep.

The following morning, Maebh, looking drawn, visited the doctor. Dr Moore senior had retired and his son Declan, an equally gentle and courteous man, had taken over the practice.

'Everything seems all right,' the young doctor said after he examined Maebh. 'Your temperature is normal and your blood pressure is good. Your colour is a little worrying – we'll have to keep a careful eye on that. If you experience another episode like last night, call me immediately, day or night, and I'll come to you. In the meantime get lots of rest and drink plenty of liquids.'

Two nights later Maebh awoke at three. Her breathing was rapid, she was drenched in perspiration and she had a spiking fever. She patted her hand on Jim's arm and he awoke. When she spoke, her voice was so weak that Jim had to put his ear to her mouth to hear her.

'I feel awful. I'm so thirsty.'

Jim lifted a glass of water to her lips, she took a few sips and fell back on her pillow.

'Maebh, I'm going for the doctor. I won't be long.'

Jim pulled on his clothes and raced down the stairs. When he opened the front door, a freezing wind blew snow into his face. He thrust himself into the howling wind and holding the railings made his way along the snow-covered, slippery path to the doctor's home. He pulled on the bell of the doctor's house and waited for what seemed forever for the door to open. The moment the bleary-eyed young Dr Moore opened the door, Jim stepped into the hall.

'Maebh is sick again, she's hot and sweating.'

'Go to her, Jim. I'll join you in a few minutes, leave your front door on the latch for me. I want you to get Maebh to drink some water.'

The doctor dressed, grabbed his leather bag and drove the short distance up the road. Maebh was holding her stomach and writhing in pain when the doctor entered the bedroom. Her face was yellow, her eyes were closed and she was babbling incoherently. Dr Moore pulled back the bedcovers; Maebh's nightdress and legs were covered in blood

'Jesus, what's happening?' Jim asked, his eyes wide in horror.

'She's haemorrhaging. She's losing the baby. We have to get her to the hospital.' The doctor grabbed a blanket from the bottom of the bed and wrapped Maebh in it. 'We can't wait for an ambulance. Jim, carry Maebh to my automobile and I'll drive her to the hospital.'

An icy wind howled and swirled snow around Jim as he carried

Maebh out to the automobile. He placed her in the back seat, climbed in beside her and cradled her head in his lap. The car engine burst into life and the vehicle slipped away from the kerb.

Travelling at twenty miles an hour the car crept along the snow-covered North Circular Road. Thanks be to heavens the roads are deserted, the doctor thought, as the car turned onto Berkley Road.

In the hospital Maebh was placed on a trolley and she, Dr Moore and a nurse quickly disappeared down a long white corridor. A porter walked Jim to a small, empty waiting room and time seemed to come to a standstill as he paced and worried and waited.

Then Dr Moore came back. 'Maebh is comfortable now, they're giving her some fluids and she's responding.'

'Thank God she's all right!' Jim leaned his head against the waiting room's white- tiled wall. 'How is the baby?'

'Jim, I didn't say Maebh was all right. She is losing the baby. The hospital is doing all it can but the signs are not good. The baby's heartbeat is very faint.'

'Oh God … Oh God … Poor Maebh. Can I see her?'

'Yes, she's about to be taken to theatre,' Dr Moore said and walked Jim down the white corridor that seemed to go on forever.

At the door of St Mary's ward, the doctor put his hand on Jim's shoulder and said 'Maebh hasn't been told about the baby's condition. If the child is to have any chance of surviving it's vital that Maebh remains strong. And Jim, you need to be strong too, for Maebh and the baby's sake.' Dr Moore opened the door and Jim entered the ward.

Maebh was lying on her back, her eyes were closed, her hair was plastered to her forehead. Her arms were covered in bruise marks. Startled by her appearance, Jim looked to Dr Moore but the doctor's eyes told him to ignore his wife's appearance and talk to her.

'Hello Maebh,' Jim whispered and kissed her damp forehead.

Her eyes flickered.

'Hello love,' she murmured and managed a faint smile. 'Is the baby all right?'

'The baby's fine.'

'Oh that's wonderful. I had such dreadful thoughts.'

'Don't think things like that. Just concentrate on getting better.'

THE ACTOR

The ward door burst open and a doctor followed by nurse in a stiff white uniform and a nun, marched into the room.

The doctor took Jim aside. 'Mr Brevin, my name is Dr Brogan, your wife is now under my care. We are taking her to the operating theatre and we'll do everything possible to save the baby.'

The nun held open the door, the nurse pushed the bed through the open door and they were gone.

Dr Moore said goodbye to Jim and left him to wait.

Hours later, when Dr Brogan returned, the look on his face offered Jim no consolation. 'I'm afraid your wife has lost your baby boy.'

Jim reached out his hand and leaned on the wall. He was aware that Dr Brogan was still talking but the doctor's voice sounded muffled and far away, like he was underwater. Then he heard the doctor say 'Mr Brevin your wife is still in great danger' and felt a terrible squeeze of panic in his chest. 'What's wrong with her?'

'She has a blood infection.' The doctor paused a moment. 'It's very serious. It could, potentially, be fatal.'

'Can't you help her, can't you do something, give her something?'

'We've done all we can. We have to rely on her body's natural defences to destroy the infection.'

'And what if that doesn't happen?'

'The next few hours are critical,' Dr Brogan said.

'Doctor, Maebh is only twenty-six years old, she'll be twenty-seven in two weeks. How can this happen?'

'I have no answer to your question. Some things are beyond our knowledge,' the doctor replied, clearly uncomfortable with confessing his ignorance.

'May I see her?'

'Yes, I'll have the ward sister bring you to her. I'm very sorry I can't be more positive.'

Dr Brogan left the waiting room and the screaming inside Jim's head started.

The nun returned to walk Jim to Maebh's ward. 'Mr Brevin, try to get your wife to sleep, she really needs to rest,' she said.

Maebh's appearance had deteriorated. She seemed to have shrunk; her skin was yellow and clammy, her eyes were blood-shot and her beautiful shiny hair was matted and damp.

'I lost the baby. Baby Theo is gone,' Maebh murmured and tears streamed down her yellow cheeks. 'I'm so sorry, Jimmy.'

'I'm sorry too, my love. But try not to think about that now.' Jim took his wife's hand and she looked at him and said 'Am I going to die too?'

'No. You are not,' Jim replied forcefully and he squeezed her hand gently.

'I don't want to leave you. I want to grow old with you.'

'And you will, we'll have a wonderful life together. Maebh you need to rest. I'll sit here now and you rest.'

'My baby is gone, my baby is gone,' Maebh repeated to herself until exhaustion closed her eyes and she slept.

Jim remained at her bedside, held her hand and tried not to listen to the screaming inside his head.

Every moment Maebh was in hospital, Jim was by her side or in the waiting room. Theo and Líla were the first to arrive. Líla embraced her distraught brother, sat beside him and held his hand. Theo's heart broke for his son and the memory of his own marriage cruelly cut short came flooding back.

Later that morning Jim was stroking Maebh's hair when Sean and Dorrie Mullin came into the ward. Dorrie leaned down and kissed her daughter on the forehead.

'My darling daughter, what's happened to you?' Dorrie said somewhere in the back of her throat.

Sean Mullin put his arms around his wife and the heartbroken couple stood gazing at their sleeping child.

'What happened?' Dorrie asked looking at Jim.

'That doctor said...'

'I know what the doctor said. Everything was all right a few days ago. I talked to her, she was so well and so happy,' Dorrie said pleading for an explanation.

'It all started in the middle of the night,' Jim replied and talked the distraught parents through everything that had happened.

When Jim finished talking Dorrie walked over to him, embraced him and said 'Pray to God she'll be all right. The doctor told us not to stay long. We'll be in the waiting room if you need us.'

Sean Mullen took his daughter's limp hand, lifted it to his lips and kissed it.

'Get better darlin'. We love you.'

Jim was with Michael and Clara in the waiting room when the grey-haired Dr Brogan entered the room.

'Maebh's condition has deteriorated,' the doctor began. 'I'm sorry Mr Brevin your wife is losing her battle, there is no more the hospital can do,' Jim staggered as if he'd been struck. 'Would you like to be present as she receives the last sacrament?'

Jim tried desperately to comprehend what the doctor had said.

'Jim, go with the doctor,' Clara said. 'Go to Maebh.'

Jim followed the doctor.

'In the name of the Father, Son and Holy Ghost,' the priest began. When he finished the prayers, he nodded to Jim and quietly left the room. Jim looked at his beautiful wife and thought she looked peaceful. He sat at her bedside, took her hand and whispered 'Please don't leave me Maebh. I love you so much.'

Maebh half opened her eyes.

'Hello Jimmy, I love you,' Maebh said in little gasps.

Jim leaned over, kissed Maebh gently on the lips and held her in his arms. Then he sat and took her hand. An hour later Maebh's body slackened, her breathing stopped and Jim's heart screamed.

The following morning when he awoke, he turned his head and when he saw her empty pillow the agony of his loss shot through him. He called out Maebh's name, softly at first then louder and louder until he was screaming at the top of his voice.

A numbing nothingness descended on Jim and all he remembered of the following days were fragments of moments drenched in grief and pain. He remembered seeing Theo, Líla, Michael and Clara in the mortuary chapel, he remembered putting his arm around Sean and Dorrie Mullin as they entered St Peter's Church, and he remembered standing in the front pew of the church and the overpowering smell of incense and fresh flowers. He remembered seeing his school friend Ciaran talking to Líla and he remembered embracing Theo outside the church and sadness, so much sadness. He remembered the snow clinging to the tops of the tombstones and he remembered standing at the open grave and holding Líla's hand. He remembered looking at Maebh's brother and sisters across the grave and he remembered the tears that burned his eyes and the howling of the wind as Maebh's coffin was lowered into the ground. He remembered picking up a handful of clay and dropping it on the wooden casket and he remembered the chilling sound of the clay as it bounced off the coffin. He remembered stiffening his spine and walking out of the cemetery and he remembered walking up the slush covered path to his empty house.

45

Jim walked into his silent house and everywhere there were memories and shadows of Maebh. He locked the nursery door, went to his bedroom and placed the key in Maebh's jewellery box. He opened the wardrobe, hung up his jacket and ran his fingers along Maebh's clothes. He removed one of Maebh's blouses, sat on the bed and waves of pain and sadness washed over him. Never again would he see Maebh's cheeky smile, or her shining hair, never again would he hold her hand or touch the curve of her back. Jim buried his face in her blouse and wept.

The following morning as he awoke – still fully dressed – he reached out to touch his beloved Maebh and the awfulness of her absence exploded anew in his brain. Instantly his grief rushed in and filled his soul. She was gone and so was his unborn child. He sat up and gasped; he was alone.

An hour later Jim was making tea in the kitchen when the doorbell rang.

'Hello,' Líla said, when a dishevelled Jim opened the door.'Thought I'd drop by on my way to work and see how you're doing?'

'You don't have to check on me,' Jim said as Líla stepped into the hall.

'I'm not checking on you.'

'Yes you are. I'm making tea, would you like some?'

'No thanks, I've had breakfast.' Líla noticed the dark circles under Jim's eyes. 'You look like you didn't sleep last night?'

'Does that surprise you?' Jim replied and walked into the kitchen.

'The reason I stopped by is, father asked if you'd care to join us for dinner this evening.'

'Not this evening. I think I'd rather be alone.'

'I don't think that would be good for you Jim.'

'How the hell would you know what's good for me? And stop giving me that pitying look.'

'Sorry Jim, I don't mean to upset you,' Líla said and fiddled with her hair.

Jim sat and placed his head in his hands. 'Sorry Líla, I didn't mean to pick on you.'

'That's all right,' Líla said and embraced her brother.

'I miss her so much.'

Jim was returning to the kitchen after saying goodbye to Líla when he saw Maebh standing at the sink.

'Hello Jimmy,' Maebh said and smiled at him.

Jim took a step backwards, lifted his coat off the rack and walked out of his house. When he returned the cold tea cup was still sitting on the kitchen table.

Two nights later, after a dinner in his family home of which Jim ate little, Líla said 'Would you like to hear some good news?'

'I would,' he replied. 'Good news would be welcome.'

'Ciaran has asked me to marry him.'

'Congratulations! My little sister getting married?' Jim kissed his sister and hugged her. 'Maebh would have loved to have heard your news.'

'She did hear it,' Líla said looking into her brother's sad eyes. 'I told her before she …' Líla stopped speaking, she almost saw the memories flood into Jim's mind.

'She never said anything to me.'

'I asked her not to tell you. I wanted to tell you myself but then …'

'When will this wedding of yours take place?'

THE ACTOR

'Probably spring twelve months,' Líla replied but she knew Jim was not thinking of her wedding.

In the middle of the night, Jim's eyes snapped open, he looked into the darkness and sudden terror grabbed him; he couldn't remember Maebh's face. He ran down to the living room, rummaged through a photograph scrapbook, found a picture of her and stared at it. Then, as he did almost every night, he roamed the tomb of remembrances that was his house. Some nights he thought he felt Maebh's presence and it both reassured him and disturbed him.

'What can I do to stop the pain?' Jim asked his father one evening as they sat in the back drawing room.

'There's not much you can do but let time pass.'

'Will time ease the pain?'

'No, nothing will ease the pain, but you will learn to live with it, at least I did.'

On the night of Maebh's twenty-seventh birthday Jim was alone in his house pouring himself a glass of wine when a line from Ira Allen's play *The Bailiff of Ballyfoyle*, floated into his mind. 'There is nothing in my future but nothingness.' The words almost paralysed him. He prised himself out of his chair and with a tremendous effort took a single step, then he walked the room, and then he walked the house.

It was one month and one day after Maebh's death when Jim suddenly exploded in a fit of uncontrollable rage and anger. He was in the kitchen cutting bread when he knocked the bread and the knife onto the floor. He was suddenly overcome. 'Damnation!' he cried surprised by his own anger. Then it just took over and he let rip. 'Why did you leave me? Why did you have to go? I loved you and you left me. You said you loved me Maebh and you do this to me? Damn you, bloody damn you.' And in one violent movement he swept everything on the kitchen table on to the floor.

An hour later, calmer, in the bedroom, he opened the wardrobe and ran his fingers along the line of Maebh's clothes. He whispered softly 'I'm sorry, Maebh, I know you didn't want to leave me. I just miss you so much.'

THE ACTOR

*

'It's time I returned to work,' Jim told Theo one evening as Líla brought a tray of coffee into the back drawing room.

'Jim there is no rush,' Theo replied, helping Líla with the cups.

'Father, I think it would be good for me to work, it would stop me thinking so much.'

'If that's what you want?' Theo replied.

'I think it's great news,' Líla said. 'And good timing too, Michael is going away on a wine purchasing trip and we'll be short in the office.'

With forced enthusiasm, Jim returned to work. Due to the troubles, mass unemployment and ever increasing emigration, business had steadily declined so Jim set himself the challenge of improving the company's turnover. First he reviewed all the company's activities and business practices. He spoke to customers, the company accountant, the office staff, the two van drivers and everyone connected with the business. He noted customer buying behaviour and began to devise a strategy for the company's future.

Jim was standing at the foot of Maebh's grave when Sean and Dorrie Mullin approached. Dorrie's eyes were dull and she was carrying a small bunch of flowers.

'Sorry to intrude on your time with Maebh,' Dorrie said. 'We usually come on a Saturday but Sean had a union meeting and I don't like to come alone. Hope you don't mind?'

'Of course I don't mind,' Jim replied. 'How are you?'

Dorrie forced a smile and as she placed her bunch of flowers on the grave said 'I miss her, she was always my helper.'

'Patrick and Bridget are coming home from America,' Sean said putting his arm around his wife.

'That's good,' Jim replied.

'But it's not all good news,' Dorrie said and glanced at her husband. 'Sean might be losing his job.'

'Woman, would you stop bothering the man,' Sean said and squeezed his wife's shoulder. 'Jim has enough concerns without having to listen to our woes. How are you, Jim?'

'Sorry to hear about your job, Mr Mullin.'

THE ACTOR

'It's not gone yet,' Sean replied unconvincingly.

After Sean and Dorrie left the cemetery, Jim remained at the graveside. As he stood looking at the mound of earth that was his wife's grave, flashes of images and sounds from their life together assailed him.

A month after resuming work Jim presented his strategy for the Brevin Company to the board. He proposed that the van drivers be trained as salesmen and sent on wine appreciation and salesmanship courses. He proposed they expand into selling wine associated merchandise; silver plated wine buckets and stands, a range of hand cut glasses, decanters and silver-plated wine screws. He proposed to redesign and upgrade the delivery vans and the purchase of new business machines for the office. After much discussion, Theo and Líla agreed to implement Jim's plan and within a short time wine sales improved and the office was running more smoothly and efficiently. But away from the office Jim's life didn't change; he thought about Maebh almost all the time and he missed her every second of every day. It was a sharp physical pain that deadened his body and haunted his mind and it never stopped. On the nights he slept and dreamt about his wife he woke up happy; it was the only way he could experience his Maebh.

One evening after dinner, a very serious looking Ciaran and a happy Líla followed Jim into the back drawing room of his father's home. Líla sat on Jim's right and Ciaran sat on his left.

'Is this some sort of an ambush,' Jim asked looking from Líla to Ciaran.

'Jim, it would mean an awful lot to us if you'd consent to be the best man at our wedding,' Ciaran said and waited for a reply.

'Thank you for the honour but I feel I must decline. I'm happy for you both but it's only been five months since Maebh's passing. I really don't think it would be right for me to do it.'

'Jim, the wedding won't be for nine months. Please say you'll think about it?' Líla pleaded.

'That's all we ask,' Ciaran said. 'Just think about it.'

'I'll think about it,' Jim said.

*

'I fear the plan to diversify into wine merchandise was not one of my better ideas,' Jim confessed to Theo when they were looking over the latest sales figures. They hardly registered on the ledger and a lot of money was tied up in the stock.

'It's only been a few months,' his father replied. 'A new departure like this needs time. Perhaps we need a different approach. Delivery men may not be the best sales people.'

'I think I have an idea of how I can make the merchandise move a little faster,' Jim said.

'Very well, let's give it another six months,' Theo said. 'If the merchandise is not selling and making a profit by then we will have to consider our options.'

With the passage of time Jim's torment abated a little. Some days he could go an hour or two without thinking of his beautiful ghost but a glimpse of one of her cardigans, a shoe or any one of a thousand things would remind him of her and his grief would again overwhelm him.

Jim sat in the living room of the Mullin home and handed Dorrie the photograph she had asked him to bring to her.

'Thanks, I always loved this photograph of Maebh,' Dorrie said as she inserted it into a small frame. 'How are you bearing up Jim?'

'Up and down. It's been a long six months.'

Maebh's two younger sisters thundered down the stairs. 'Ma, can we talk to you?' Mary, the slimmer of the girls, said to her mother.

'Can't you see I'm talking to Jimmy?' Dorrie replied.

'Sorry, Ma, this is very important, Jimmy doesn't mind; do you Jimmy?'

'Er, no,' Jim said and looked apologetically at Dorrie.

Dorrie's eyes rolled upwards. 'Into the kitchen, girls, and if this isn't important I'll kill the both of yis.'

Sitting alone in the small living room Jim tried not to listen to the conversation in the kitchen but there was so much vitality and life in the voices of the girls he couldn't stop himself listening.

'Patrick will be home in a month and we would both like to have new dresses for the party,' Mary said without taking a breath.

'Is that what you dragged me into the kitchen to tell me?' Dorrie asked.

'Yes,' the girls replied in unison.

Dorrie drew a breath.

'Girls, you know your father has lost his job. We can't afford a party and we certainly can't afford to buy you dresses. Now back to your rooms and don't interrupt me again.'

Annoyed at being dismissed the girls stormed out of the kitchen and clattered up the stairs.

'Mary, Rose may I have a word?' Jim called after the girls.

'Wha?' replied the two girls abruptly.

'Mind your manners, girls,' Dorrie said. 'Now come down and talk to the man.'

'Sorry,' Mary and Rose muttered and slouched back down the stairs.

'I was wondering if Maebh's clothes could be of use to you,' Jim said. But the instant he made the offer he regretted it.

The two girls looked at each other, then Rose looked at her mother and said 'Do ya think that would be all right Ma?'

'Are you sure you want to do this Jim?' Dorrie asked.

Jim steeled himself. 'I'm sure.'

'I'd like to have her yellow dress, the one she wore at Christmas,' Rose said and added tentatively 'If that's all right, Jimmy?'

'I'd like to have her green stripy dress,' said Mary.

'I think you misunderstand me, girls. I'd like you to have all her clothes.

The girls' eyes lit up. 'I'd love them, we'd love them,' Rose said, correcting herself.

'I'll bring them down in a few days,' Jim said. 'If you can't use all the dresses and things perhaps you could give them to someone else.'

'We could,' said Mary.

'But we won't,' added Rose and the two girls scurried up the stairs.

'Thank you, Jim. I think Maebh would have loved the girls to have her things,' Dorrie said as the sound of a bicycle clattering in the hall signalled the arrival of Sean.

'How are ya Jim? Good to see ya.'

Sean pulled the bicycle clips from the bottom of his trousers. 'Jim, young Florence Allen stopped me in the avenue and told me her father would like a word with you.'

'Thanks. I'll drop over in a while. How are you Mr Mullin?'

'I'm sick and tired and weary of looking for a job,' Sean said and plonked himself at the table. 'Is there tea in that pot Dorrie?'

'I'll get you a mug,' Dorrie said and disappeared into the kitchen.

'There's something I want to talk to you about,' Jim said.

'Go on, I'm all ears.'

'The company bought a line of merchandise, silver-plated wine buckets and stands and other items like that. The plan was to have the van drivers sell them to wine shops and off-licences, but it didn't work out. I think the merchandise needs a dedicated salesman. Would you like to give it a try, Sean? You would be paid a wage while in training but the pay would decrease when you go on the road. Then you'd be on commission.'

Sean Mullin rubbed his nose. 'Are you offering me a job as a salesman? I'm a baker; I've never sold anything in my life.'

'You're an unemployed baker,' interjected Dorrie placing a mug in front of Sean and pouring tea into it. 'You're a great spoofer. You'll make a great salesman.'

'Hush woman.' Sean sipped the tea. 'Is this a charity job, Jim?'

'No. If you don't take it I'll have to get someone else, but whoever gets the job, if the merchandise doesn't move, he'll be out of a job in six months. What do you say?'

Sean looked at his wife and then at Jim.

'I'll give it a try. When do I start?'

'I believe there is still a lot of interest in political melodramas,' a pale Ira Allen said to Jim as they sat in the semi dark parlour of 5, Primrose Avenue. 'So much so that I have taken a lease on the Rotunda Theatre for three months. I plan to mount three productions *Father Murphy*, *Tara's Halls* and *The Eviction*. Other companies, possibly O'Grady or Burke will take the second month and the third month will revert back to me. I would like you to join the company. What do you say, Leslie, May and Francis P are all on board?'

'I appreciate the offer but I don't think I'm ready for a return to the theatre, not yet.'

'Jim, I have no idea of the loss or the pain you experienced, but the theatre could be a consolation to you. Francis P told me that without his theatre work he could not have dealt with the loss of his sons. He said, for a few hours every night the theatre let him be someone else. He said it dulled his pain, perhaps it might do the same for you?'

'Let me think about it,' Jim replied.

That evening in the back drawing room after dinner, Jim asked Líla if she'd help him pack Maebh's clothes for the Mullin sisters.

'That's a very kind thing to do,' Líla said. 'I'll drop by tomorrow.'

'Good. I was talking to Ira Allen and he offered me some theatre work.'

'And what did you say?' Theo asked from the doorway.

'I told him I didn't think I was ready to return to the theatre.'

Theo sat on the sofa beside his son. 'Son, it's all too easy to live in the ghostly world of the dead. God knows, I did it long enough. Living with the living is hard but it's something you have to do. You lost your wife and your child, don't lose your theatre too. Maebh would have wanted you to go on acting.' He ran his aging fingers along his grey moustache. 'Go back to the theatre Jim, it's where you belong.'

46

By 1926, most Irish people in the twenty six counties had accepted the concept and the reality of a Free State, partitioned from the remaining six counties in the North. The Four Courts and many other iconic buildings had been rebuilt. The new and unarmed police force, An Garda Siochana – the Civic Guard – had restored law and order and the country had returned to a sort-of normality.

But life for the poor had not changed. One of every four Dublin tenement dwellers were still unemployed, disease was rife and the mortality rate was still one of the highest in Europe. However, the shops on Grafton Street were again filled with luxury goods, Jammet's fine restaurant had a three-week waiting list, and the fashionable ladies of Dublin promenaded around Stephen's Green wearing the latest boldly-patterned coats and smart cloche hats.

Jim placed his hand on the door of the rehearsal room and wondered if his return to action was an insult to Maebh. How could you think about going back to the theatre and your wife barely cold in her grave? He was about to go home when Maura Sweeney said to him 'When my sister died I thought I had no right to be alive and no right to do things that made me feel alive. But I knew my sister and I knew she would have wanted me to get on with my life.'

Most of the cast was already in the hall. Ira Allen, looking gaunt, was sitting at the long table, deep in conversation with Leslie, May was talking to an animated Fiona in the kitchenette and Richard and Francis P were glaring at each other in disagreement over heavens knows what. When Jim entered the room, all eyes turned to him.

'Come and sit with me,' Ira Allen called out to him. 'Welcome back.'

'Wouldn't be the same without you,' called out Richard. Fiona waved and Leslie raised his cup of tea in salute to Jim.

Jim shook Ira's hand and after exchanging greetings took the seat beside his mentor. May sat on the other side of Jim and said 'I know all the cast have given you their personal condolences. But we know what a private person you are, so Ira and I have asked the cast and crew to be mindful of that fact and not to invade your privacy. If we are being too protective, please forgive us.'

'I appreciate that,' Jim replied. 'Thank you.'

'Now I have something to ask of you.' May glanced at her husband and then whispered to Jim. 'Ira is still recovering from his recent illness – would you be so kind as to keep an eye on him and help him whenever you can?'

'Of course,' Jim replied. 'How is he?'

'He's improving.' But May's eyes dulled. 'I'd rather not talk about his illness. I'm sure you'll understand.'

Leslie called the company to the long table and when everyone was settled, Ira spoke. 'The stage in the Rotunda, or the Roto or the Roxy as locals call it, is a little wider than and not as deep as the Queen's Theatre stage, so we will have to adjust the blocking of each play to take account of that fact. This week we will rehearse *Father Murphy* and have the evenings to ourselves. The following weeks we will all have to work a little harder.'

A collective theatrical sigh resounded around the table. Ira smiled. 'We will rehearse *For Ireland's Sake* in the mornings and play *Father Murphy* in the evenings. During the run of *For Ireland's Sake* we will rehearse *The Eviction*. It will be hard going for a few weeks but we've all been around the block a few times, so we know what to expect.' Heads nodded around the table. 'Mick is, as usual, our stage manager, Grainne

Murphy is our costumer and Rena Brady is joining us as props mistress.' Everyone waved at Rena. 'We have all worked together in the past so there is no need for introductions. We will rehearse here for three days and then we'll move into the Rotunda. A quick word about my health. I am well, not a hundred per cent, but I am well enough and if I take things a little easy, then I will be fine. All I ask is that you not fuss about me.' May cast a glance at Jim. 'We had better get started; we open in one week.'

At the tea break, an unusually serious Leslie approached Jim and said 'May would like you and Ira to switch roles in *For Ireland's Sake*.' Jim's mouth fell open. 'Will you do it?'

'Ira's role is the lead role and mine is no more than …'

'A cough and a spit, I know,' Leslie replied. 'Jim, this is Ira's decision. To play Father Murphy he needs to conserve his energy; he can't rehearse by day and then perform at night, it would be too much for him. However he is contractually obliged to appear in every production and this will fulfil that obligation. Will you do it?'

'Of course I will. It would be an honour.'

To Jim's surprise, May took the rehearsal and Leslie liaised with the stage manager and the printers and dealt with all production questions and problems. During rehearsals May directed the actors and every so often Ira would have a quiet word with her. Ira rehearsed each of his own scenes only once. If for any reason the scene had to be repeated, Francis P or Richard took Ira's place.

During the morning tea break, Richard O'Hara approached Leslie and said 'What's this I hear about Jim playing the lead in *For Ireland's Sake*? That part should be mine. I'm the right age and I have seniority in the company.'

Leslie removed his monocle, cleaned it with a white handkerchief and said 'Richard, seniority is no substitute for talent.'

'I beg your pardon?' huffed an indignant Richard. 'This is no time for levity.'

'Richard, it was Ira's decision. Take it up with Ira if you must but before you do, let me tell you Geoffrey was in yesterday sniffing around looking for a job.'

THE ACTOR

'What?' Fear flashed in Richard's eyes and Leslie could almost see Richard change his mind. 'If that's what Ira wants, who am I to disagree?'

When May called an end to the rehearsal, a very tired Ira called Jim to his side.

'Captain Gowan is one of my better creations,' Ira said with a weary smile. 'It's a good part, you will look after it for me?'

'I will sir, I'll do my best.'

'How ill is he?' Jim asked Leslie when Ira and May had left the theatre.

'More ill, I fear than we're led to believe,' replied a concerned Leslie.

The air was damp, the breeze was cold and dark clouds filled the sky as Jim passed the Rotunda Hospital on his way to the theatre. Suddenly images of Maebh's death swarmed in his mind. He saw her covered in blood, her frightened face, their dead child and then he saw her bruised trembling body fall back in the bed. He lost his breath and gasping for air he grabbed hold of the hospital railing.

'Are you unwell?' asked a concerned elderly passer-by. 'Can I be of assistance?'

'I'm just a little light headed,' Jim replied, still holding on to the railings. 'I'll take a moment and I'll be on my way. Thank you for your concern.'

Leslie Lawrence stood in the back of the seven hundred and thirty-six seater Rotunda Theatre and watched the workmen remove the screen that was used for motion picture screenings.

'Let's hope this theatre never uses that thing again,' Leslie said when Jim joined him in the back of the stalls. 'Jim, you're perspiring, are you unwell?'

'It's nothing,' then deliberately changing the conversation, he asked 'Why does a maternity hospital have a theatre in its grounds?'

'The hospital is a charitable institution and in order to raise funds it has several public function rooms. The theatre is one of their public rooms.'

That night Maebh visited Jim. He saw her through a mist. She was holding baby Theo in her arms. He reached to touch her, but she and the boy dissolved in the mist.

*

The sale of silver buckets and other associated wine merchandise was not going well for Sean Mullin. After two months all he had sold were four buckets and two stands. He was carefully placing two returned buckets into the back of his van when a very tall and strangely dressed man walked out of a jeweller's shop and approached him.

'What have you got there?'

'Wine buckets.'

'Are they silver?'

'No, silver plated.'

'May I have a look at one of them?'

Sean handed the man a bucket and looked quizzically at the man's strange clothes and flat hat.

'I might have a customer for one of these. Could you let me have a bucket and stand on sale or return?'

'Mr Jacob is it?' Sean asked reading the name above the jeweller's. The tall man nodded. 'Mr Jacob, you can have as many buckets as you like, sale or return.'

'Just leave me one bucket and please, call me Saul.'

'And you can call me Sean.'

A nervous May Murnane sat with her husband in the dressing room on the opening night of *Fr Murphy*. Ira coughed and May cast a worried glance at him.

'It's nothing, just a little cough,' Ira replied to May's unasked question.

'It's not just a cough,' May replied. 'I know what it is.'

'The doctor said it was a very mild case. When the season is over, if I need to convalesce I will.'

A sharp knock on the dressing room door ended their conversation. Without opening the door Mick called out 'Miss Murnane, they're ready for your speech and Mr Allen, beginning in five minutes please.'

Wearing an Elsa Schiaparelli evening gown, which she had borrowed from her sister, May strolled on the stage. A limelight flared into life and the audience burst into applause. When the applause died down May spoke. 'Ladies and gentlemen, may I say what a very handsome audience you are.' A titter of laughter rippled through the auditorium. 'Thank you for coming here tonight and supporting the work of the National Association for the Prevention of the Spread of Tuberculosis. The Irish census records tells us that in 1841 over 135,000 deaths were a result of TB. Today, eighty five years later, TB is still the biggest single killer in Ireland. Twelve years ago, when the association started its work, it was recognised that the great and immediate need was to tackle the general public's ignorance of the disease. I can report to you that the association now has educational programmes in every county of Ireland.' Gentle applause. 'Some people think that tuberculosis is a disease that only affects the poor but that is not so. There is not a family in Ireland that has not been touched in some way by this crippling disease.' May's voice cracked but she continued her speech. 'The war against tuberculosis is a long way from won but, with your continued support, we will win the fight against this most terrible disease. Again, thank you for your support.'

The moment May stopped speaking the audience leapt to their feet and as May left the stage her eyes welled with tears.

The curtain parted and the play began.

In his early scenes, Ira was alert, energised and in total control, but as the play progressed Jim noticed Ira's voice weakened, his movements slowed and his eyes lost their focus. Every moment off stage, Ira sat in an armchair and drank sugared water. May never left his side and at the interval, she walked him to his dressing room.

By the end of the play, Ira's appearance mirrored that of his stage character; weary, exhausted and troubled. On stage, as Jim delivered his final speech, he glanced off-stage and saw the fatigued figure of Ira Allen lift himself out of his chair and, to Jim's amazement, he saw the ashen-faced actor walk on to the stage and transform into the proud and tortured Father John Murphy.

The production was an overwhelming success. The audience loved it and the critics were rapturous in their praise. They marvelled at Ira's performance: *The performance of a lifetime ... A sensational show not to be missed ... A marvellous performance ...* read the review headlines. Jim's performance too was well received. *A truly wonderful portrait of a spine-chilling character ...*

THE ACTOR

Life for Jim became suddenly busy. His days were filled rehearsing *For Ireland's Sake* and his evenings with performing in *Father Murphy*. But at night alone in his house he thought about Maebh. He thought about their special moments, the first time he saw her, their first embrace, their first kiss and the first time they made love. Sometimes he heard Maebh call out to him and then he knew that he would see her in his dreams.

The rehearsals *For Ireland's Sake* went very smoothly. May directed the play, Leslie produced and Jim took the lead role. Ira only attended the first rehearsal and as he was leaving the rehearsal room, Jim asked him for advice about playing Captain Gowan. Ira answered 'When in the prologue the narrator says *go search the pages of the past and from your history take the gallant deeds of men who fought and died for Ireland's sake*, the narrator is telling us that we need heroes, they help us make sense of our world. Play Captain Gowan as a gallant man, a hero who sacrifices his life for the life of his friends and for Ireland.'

With May's direction and Ira's words in mind, Jim went about creating the gallant Captain Gowan. Jim first developed a military walk for the captain, then he developed an internal monologue for the character and by the end of the week Jim was Captain Gowan.

On the last night of the run of *Father Murphy*, Jim was walking back to his dressing room when he saw two figures approaching. One was a dapper young man and the other a very oddly-dressed young woman.

'How are you Jim?' the man called.

'Red, when did you get back?' Jim asked as he shook his brother-in-law's hand.

'We got back yesterday,' a sombre Red replied. Jim looked at Red and his eyes were filled with tears. 'I'm so sorry about Maebh and the baby. I don't know what else to say.'

Red's shoulders shook, Jim put his arm around his brother-in-law and all three walked to the dressing room.

The opening night's audience of *For Ireland's Sake* was delighted with the show and gave the cast an enthusiastic five curtain calls. The newspaper reviews too were very positive; one reviewer questioned why Ira had taken such a small role but praised the production, others singled out Jim's performance and all agreed the production was most entertaining.

On the third night of the run Jim was standing in the wings waiting to make his first entrance when Ira said to him 'You're not enjoying performing, are you Jim?'

'Yes I am,' Jim replied defensively. 'My reviews were good and audiences are enjoying the show.'

'Yes, that is so. But your performance lacks soul. When I look into your eyes on stage, you are not there. You're thinking of your late wife, aren't you?'

'She won't let me go.'

'Or you won't let her go. Jim, letting go of her is not the same as forgetting her. Being the actor she'd want you to be requires your full concentration.'

Jim heard his cue, walked briskly on stage and felt a current of fire flow through him. He was a man lost in his craft and his performance had a conviction and a vitality that was exhilarating and thrilling for him and for the audience. It was the performance of his life and he gave it to an audience of one hundred and twenty three people.

On Sunday evening, as the last rays of the setting sun were streaming orange light through the back drawing room windows, Líla and Ciaran walked into the conservatory.

'Father was so right to encourage you to return to the theatre,' Líla bubbled as she plopped herself on a couch opposite Jim. 'I think it's one of your best roles.'

'I agree, you were really good, never better,' Ciaran said taking Líla's hand. 'Now, you said you had something to tell us.'

'Oh, yes. I've reached a decision about your wedding. I'd like to be your best man; that is if you still want me?'

Of course we want you,' Ciaran replied and Líla jumped up and hugged her brother.

When Theo arrived he took one look at Líla's face and said 'Jim, I see you told your sister the good news.'

*

Because of the weather, because of the venue or because the public no longer had an appetite for political melodramas, *The Eviction* failed to draw audiences. On the Wednesday evening forty minutes before the show, Ira and Leslie were summoned to the office of Mr Donal McNeala, the Rotunda's theatre manager.

Sitting behind his desk, Mr McNeala removed his steel-rimmed glasses, placed them on the desk and wearily rubbed his eyes.

'Mr Allen, Mr Lawrence I believe you have not yet contracted a company to perform here next month.'

'Not exactly true,' Leslie replied. 'We are still in negotiations.'

'Really, that's not what I heard.' Leslie frowned and Mr McNeala glanced at the open ledger on the desk. 'The box office receipts for the last week were poor and bookings for this weekend are equally weak.' Ira's face remained expressionless. 'I'm sure your company has lost money.'

'That's a triumph of deduction,' said Leslie.

'This is not a time for sarcasm, Mr Lawrence,' the manager's voice was cold but polite.

'You're right, Mr McNeala,' Ira said and glanced disapprovingly at Leslie. 'But I do believe we have met all our contractual obligations.'

'That is true to a point, Mr Allen.'

Ira nodded, aware that Donal McNeala had not asked for the guaranteed minimum financial return the venue was entitled to.

'However the contract does state that either party can withdraw at the end of the first month. This is the twenty first day of the first month and I am invoking that clause.'

Leslie sat bolt upright in his chair.

'But that's ...'

'I'm sorry, Mr Lawrence, but the theatre is reverting to a picture palace at the end of the month. Our little experiment, noble as it was, is no more.'

'You've hardly given it a fair chance,' protested Leslie.

'The venue must make a profit,' the manager said firmly. 'Lives depend on it.'

Leslie was about to protest further when Ira raised his hand. 'I think Mr McNeala is being very fair.' He rose and held out his hand.

'Thank you sir, you're a gentleman.'

'Thank you, Mr Allen, you are the finest actor I've had ever had the pleasure of working with,' Donal McNeala said and shook Ira's hand.

Later, when Ira told May how the meeting went, she blessed herself and said 'Thank God, oh thank God.'

47

Elizabeth Wright-Moran, Michael's sister-in-law, was a privileged young woman who thought taking a job as junior clerk in the Brevin and Sons company office was a major act of independence. On her second day of work, she sat at a desk and slowly and carefully dipped the nib of her pen into the inkwell. She was about to make an entry in the sales ledger when the phone on her desk rang and startled her. Elizabeth dropped the pen, it bounced off the desk and splattered black ink across the front of her new, high-necked, white lace blouse.

'Oh goodness,' she muttered and as she watched the ink stain spread. 'Blast and double blast.'

'The phone, Elizabeth,' Líla said and glared at the ringing phone. Elizabeth snapped the phone off its hook and barked 'Hello?' Then, after a moment, she said 'I've no idea what you're talking about. We don't sell buckets and we don't have anyone called Sean working in this office.'

Elizabeth was about to replace the earpiece on its tall stand when Líla took it from her. 'Hello,' Líla said in a friendly voice. 'I'm afraid Sean is out of the office. Can I take a message?' Líla listened, nodded twice and smiled. 'Sean will deliver ten buckets and stands to you tomorrow sir. Could I have your name? Thank you, Mr Jacob.'

Líla hung up the phone. 'Elizabeth, you'll have to learn to be polite to our customers.'

'Why?' asked a bewildered Elizabeth. 'I don't think I like being an independent person. Perhaps Daddy was right, perhaps I'm not cut out for this sort of thing. I think I'll go home. Líla, would you be so good as to bring me my coat?'

'You'll find your coat on the rack in the hall,' Líla replied.

The following day, Sean Mullin delivered ten silver buckets and stands to Mr Saul Jacob, Camden Street, and when Saul asked Sean to drop off the merchandise to the Fielding Hotel, it set him thinking. An hour later he talked to the manager of the Central Hotel in Wicklow Street, showed him his merchandise and got an order for four buckets and stands. Over the next six months, Sean visited every hotel in Dublin and every day he made sales.

Leslie Lawrence asked Jim to meet him in the lounge of the Shelburne Hotel and after ordering tea and scones Leslie said to him 'Ira has been admitted to hospital again.'

'I know, Francis P phoned me. How is he?'

'May said he's doing well. He doesn't want visitors.'

'He's getting worse, isn't he?'

'I'll put it this way, there'll be no Allen productions for the foreseeable future.'

Jim bowed his head and although he didn't really believe in a God, he said a prayer for Ira.

The day was bright and the people's garden in the Phoenix Park was filled with families taking the sun. Bridget spread a tartan blanket on the grass, opened a small wicker basket and removed three jam sandwiches and a bottle of milk.

'So, what did Jim say about your American Steak House idea? Will he put up the money?'

'Not all of it,' Red replied. 'He said he'd put up half the money, if we'd put up the other half. He said I'd be the manager and would run the restaurant, but that he would run the office, and we'd get a fifty per cent share of the profits.'

'Do we have enough money?' Bridget asked.

'Yea, if we use every penny we saved in America.' Red said and rubbed his chin. 'But there's something else.'

'What something else?'

'Sorry Bridget, but I told Jim about the fortune teller.'

'You what?' Bridget's eyes shot wide open. 'I told you not to tell anyone about the gypsy!'

'I know, but it just slipped out and now Jim says he won't give us the money unless you tell him what the gypsy told you.'

'I can't do that. I know you, this is another of your schemes to get me to talk to people when I only like to talk to you and me mother and me sister Irene.'

'Then how are you going to talk to the people in the restaurant?'

'That's different. I'll get you for this Patrick Mullin,' Bridget said. And with that, she put the sandwiches and milk back in her basket and marched out of the park.

'What about the picnic?' Red called after Bridget but she ignored him and walked to the tram.

The following day Bridget, Red and Jim sat at a table in McKeon's Tea Rooms in Dorset Street. When the waitress finished taking their order Jim placed his hands on the table and said 'Well Bridget, tell me what the fortune teller told you?'

Like a spoiled child, Bridget pouted, folded her arms across her chest and stared straight ahead.

'Bridget, tell Jim what the gypsy told you?' Red said. 'It's very interesting.'

'If it's so interesting why don't you tell it to Jim?'

'Come on, tell us,' Red pleaded.

Bridget inhaled deeply, looked around the café, waited for the couple at the next table to leave and began her story.

'I'm not going to tell yous everything the gypsy told me. Me and me sister Irene went down to Gloucester Street and when we couldn't find the gypsy caravan, we asked a woman that was standing at a corner if she knew where the gypsy was.' Bridget lowered her voice. 'I think the woman was one of them women, you know?'

'One of what?' Jim asked.

'You know,' Bridget said, jerking her head.

'A whore?' asked Red.

Bridget's hand jumped to her mouth.

'Oh, a prostitute?' said Jim.'

'Jesus, Mary and Joseph,' Bridget said, her face flushed as red as a ripe tomato. 'Oh God! I wouldn't call anyone that.'

'What did the whore say to you?' whispered Red.

'Don't call her that. The woman said, "I don't need to be a fortune teller to know I won't be making money out of you, but at least you're not one of that Frank Duff crowd." Then she laughed and pointed down a side road. "The gypsy's caravan is down there, love. Tell her Honour Bright told you where she lived."' Bridget stopped talking when the waitress placed the tray of tea on the oilcloth-covered table.

Jim poured the tea. 'What did the gypsy woman look like?'

Bridget waited until the waitress was out of earshot and said 'Oh, she was lovely, very foreign looking. She had long, coal-black hair with a big red flower stuck over her ear. She wore a long red dress that swished when she moved. She had a silk shawl, oh, and she had huge half-moon earrings.'

'What did the inside of the caravan look like?' asked Red.

'It was like being in a big barrel, all dark and mysterious. There was hardly any furniture, only a glass case, a small table, three chairs and a crystal ball. "My name is Tasaria," the gypsy said. "I am a Romany gypsy. I'm the seventh daughter of a seventh daughter." "Can you really tell the future?" me sister asked out straight. "I am a clairvoyant, I see everything because everything is predestined." Irene looked at me and we both wondered, what the hell the gypsy was talking about. "I see things before they happen," the gypsy said, like she was annoyed at us for not understanding her. "I read tarot cards, tea leaves, the waters and I read me crystal ball." "Which is best?" Irene asked.

"The crystal ball never lies."

Read your crystal ball, I said and took Irene's hand.

"I don't like upsetting people but I always tell the truth," the gypsy said looking me straight in the eye. Then she held out her hand and said "Cross my palm with silver." I put a sixpence in her hand. She closed her fist, pulled her shawl around her and said "Place your hands on the table dear."

I did, and she looked in her crystal ball and told me ... lots of things.'

Bridget sat back in her chair and folded her arms.

'So, what did she tell you?' Jim asked after a long pause.

'Private things. I'm not going to tell you everything.'

'You haven't told us anything, yet,' complained Red.

'All right.' She leaned forward and unfolded her arms.

'The gypsy said, "I see a new beginning. I see a room full of people eating. I see lots of happy faces and I hear the chink of money." Then the gypsy grabbed my hand and said something that nearly knocked me off the chair.'

Jim and Red leaned forward.

'"Bridget, you'll have a daughter in five months' time."'

'You never told me she said that to you,' Red said, reeling.

'Well, I know you want a son. I didn't mean to tell you that bit about the daughter but I got all caught up telling the story and it just slipped out.' Bridget averted her eyes and smirked.

'Is that all the gypsy told you?' Jim asked.

'Ya,' Bridget replied, still looking away but no longer smiling.

'She told you something else, didn't she?' Jim insisted.

'All right. She gave me a message for you. She said to tell you that your wife is at rest …' She stopped again.'

'And she told you something else?' Jim asked

'You don't want to know.'

'Tell me.'

Bridget sighed. 'She said you should prepare for another sadness.'

In November 1926, Red opened his American Steak House in Wicklow Street. It was an immediate success and a month later Bridget gave birth to a son.

Low thunder rumbled and dark clouds emptied heavy rain on Leslie as he pulled furiously on the bell. Jim opened the door and Leslie walked into the hall, pale, his shoulders slumped. He said 'Ira is dead. He died this morning.'

Jim, speechless, took Leslie's soaking coat and hung it on the hallstand.

'He was my closest friend, a great colleague and the finest man I ever knew,' Leslie said as Jim handed him a glass of whiskey. 'The man was only forty three years old with a family of five children. Ira had great plans for the future and now he's gone.'

THE ACTOR

Jim sat and a great darkness again descended on him.

The rain lashed down and wind howled across the front of the small chapel in Glasnevin cemetery as four weary gravediggers in moleskin trousers, heavy overcoats and boots, lifted the wooden casket on to a long trolley. Floral wreaths were placed on top of the casket and a lone gravedigger dragged the trolley to the graveside. Dressed completely in black, with a veil covering her face, May Murnane walked with their five children behind the trolley; in complete silence, family members, friends from the theatre and members of the public followed after her to the graveside.

Jim wasn't aware of the rain, or the wind or the hundreds of people in the cemetery; all he was aware of was, that he had lost a great friend and mentor and that he would never again meet the likes of Ira Allen.

At the graveside, the four gravediggers lowered the wooden casket into the deep hole. After a few words from the Reverend Falls, straw was dropped on the wooden casket; the four gravediggers lifted their shovels and plunged them into the mound of earth beside the grave.

Jim shuddered when the clay thumped off the coffin.

48

During the interval of Verdi's opera *Rigoletto* at the Gaiety Theatre, Jim was having a drink in the circle bar when he met Francis P and his wife Maureen. As they had little time for a conversation, Jim and Francis P agreed to meet in Maher's Pub the following day.

'What are you up to?' Jim asked after he had ordered two pints.

'I've been busy with accountancy work. Next week, I start directing an amateur production of an O'Casey play.'

'I thought you didn't like O'Casey's plays.'

'Don't be daft. O'Casey is a great writer. Besides, his roots are in melodrama.'

Jim looked sceptically at Francis P.

'Jim, I love Ira's plays, but his plays were for yesterday. Ira's plays spoke to the heart but O'Casey's plays speak to the soul. People say O'Casey's plays are realistic but his characters are no more real than Ira's. They may sound like they are pulled from the streets of Dublin but they are not, they are highly crafted characters that speak like poets. Jim, if you are to survive in theatre you have learn to play this new kind of drama.'

After Ira's death, May worked with the J P Burke and the J F Mackey companies. Leslie performed with the Frank Delany and H

J Condron's company and Jim spent a lot of time in Cork with the O'Donovan Company.

To learn more about the new style of theatre, Jim accepted work with amateur companies and performed in new plays by Irish, European and American playwrights. Gradually, he learned to appreciate the more realistic style of play writing and the more restrained, less affected, style of acting it required.

In the spring Ciaran moved to Dublin, having accepted a post with the Woods Accountancy Firm. He purchased a house on the North Circular Road close to where Theo lived. On the 9 March, Líla and Ciaran married in St Peter's Church. Jim was best man and Ciaran's sister Julie was bridesmaid. Six months later, and to her great delight, Líla became pregnant. Líla told Theo and Jim that she planned to resign from the Brevin Company board. She also suggested that Michael be reinstated as a board member. After a lot of persuasion from both Líla and Jim, Theo agreed and Michael was once again on the board. In early February, after Líla and Ciaran's baby was born, Jim became baby Grainne's godfather.

One foggy morning in November, amid a sea of bicycles, horse-drawn carts and automobiles, an electric tram navigated its way around College Green. When the tram juddered to a stop in Dame Street, Jim alighted and started his search for the office of the newly-formed Actors' Repertory Company. He pushed on the door of 64 Dame Street, mounted the creaking stairs and when he reached the first floor landing he saw Leslie Lawrence sitting in the office of the Scally Property Company.

'Leslie, how are you?' Jim said delighted to see a familiar face. 'Haven't seen you in ages.'

'I'm well. Are you here for an interview?'

'Yes I am,' Jim replied softly and stepped into the property company's office. 'What do you know about this Actors' Repertory Company?'

'There's not much to know. They're a new company, only starting up.'

'That explains why I've never heard of them,' Jim said and removed his hat. 'Líla took the call, they said they wanted to talk to me about more than an acting engagement. What do you think they meant?'

Leslie leaned forward and mimicking Jim's quiet tones said 'I believe they're looking for a good wine supplier.'

'Leslie, be serious.'

'Very well,' Leslie replied and tilted his head in a way that gave no real clue to his thinking. 'They're going to offer you the artistic directorship of the company.'

Jim looked askance at Leslie. 'I asked you to be serious.'

'That's the word on the street. They said to ask you to wait in the office.'

Jim rapped on the door of the Actors' Repertory Company's office and opened it. The room was small and contained an old wooden desk, two rickety chairs and a filing cabinet that had seen better days. He sat in the chair facing the desk and waited. He heard shuffling in the adjoining office, the connecting door swung open and a grinning Leslie swanned into the room.

'Well Jim, how's that for an entrance?'

Jim laughed. 'What is going on?'

'I've told you most of it already,' Leslie said and sat in the chair behind the desk. 'We want you to be the ARC's first artistic director. What do you say?'

'Who's we?'

'Right now there is only me, and possibly you.'

'What's wrong with you being artistic director?'

'Not my cup of tea. Besides, you're young, you've got ideas and you can direct.' Leslie's face lost its grin. 'Jim, the theatre is changing and we have to change with it, otherwise we get left behind. Ira had the right idea. If you want things to happen, you have to make them happen. You will choose the plays, act in them and direct as many or as few as you please. I will put up the finance and will act in every production; not always in a main role but always a decent one. What do you say?'

Jim leaned back in his chair and the enormity of the task and the opportunity were clear to him. It was a flattering offer, but how much control was Leslie really ready to hand over?

'Can I bring Francis P on board?'

'As artistic director you are free to employ whomever you choose.

Francis P would be a great addition to the company.'

'And Richard O'Hare?'

Leslie removed his monocle and gave a hesitant, somewhat uncomfortable, 'Yes.'

Jim smiled and said 'Leslie, why are you sitting in my chair?'

Leslie and Jim continued to talk and before the meeting was over, they had agreed that the ARC's first production would be O'Casey's *Juno and the Paycock*. Leslie would play Captain Boyle; Jim, Joxer Daly; May Murnane, Juno; and Maura Sweeney would play Maisie Madigan. Francis P would direct and the venue would be the Father Matthew Hall.

The following day Francis P, Leslie and Jim sat in the company office and talked about their forthcoming production.

'What are your thoughts on how I should play Joxer Daly?' Jim asked Francis P.

Francis P lit a cigarette. As he watched smoke rise in the air and drift out the window he said 'Most of O'Casey's characters are tenement dwellers. What do you know of tenement life?'

'I know nothing of tenement life,' Jim replied, surprised that Francis P would even ask the question.

'You've never been in a tenement building?'

'Certainly not.'

'One of the major themes of *Juno* is how the poverty of tenement life dehumanises and destroys people and families.' Francis P fixed his eyes on Jim. 'How do you hope to portray the effects the extreme poverty of such a life without having even stepped inside a tenement?'

'I'm an actor,' Jim retorted. 'I've played murderers, yet I've never murdered anyone.'

'You've played murderers in melodramas,' Francis P shot back. 'O'Casey's characters are flesh and blood human beings. To play them, you have to know them, know how they live, what they eat, what they drink and even how they sleep.'

Irritated, Jim glanced at Francis P.

Francis P held his gaze and said firmly 'The character of Joxer Daly is one of Irish drama's great creations. I won't let you play him as a stereotype, prancing about the stage like some character out of

Boucicault. He has to be real. He needs to be a believable human being and for that you need to anchor him in tenement life. I want you to visit a tenement and talk to a man who live there.'

'What? I have no intention of ever going into a tenement building. That's taking things too far.'

'No. It's not. Not if you want to play the part properly.'

'Francis, you're forgetting I'm the company's artistic director.'

'Is that so?' replied Francis P, as he sat back in his chair.

Jim's finger tapped on the table.

'Who is this man you want me to talk to?'

'His name is Paddy Walsh, and he lives in Dominic Street.'

'Dominic Street?' Jim snapped. Francis P shrugged his shoulders. 'And how do you know this Paddy Walsh?'

'I do voluntary work with the St Vincent de Paul. He's on my visitation list.'

'If you insist. I suppose I could accompany you.'

'No, you must go alone.' When Jim stiffened, he added 'You'll be perfectly safe. Just don't wear your best clothes, wear your worst clothes. They'll still think you're a toff but …'

'Why would this man talk to me?'

'Because I'll ask him to, and because you'll bring him a bottle of whiskey,' Francis P said matter of factly.

Then, suddenly softening his tone, he said 'Jim, a lot of hard-working, decent people live in tenement buildings. They won't eat you.'

It was like something Maebh might have said, Jim thought.

'Very well. I'll go, I don't want to, but if you think it will help, I'll go.'

'Good,' Francis P said and deliberately neglected to tell Jim that Paddy Walsh was anything but a decent man.

'That settles it,' Leslie interjected, smiling mockingly at Jim.

'Leslie, I have someone in mind for you to visit,' Francis P said turning to him. 'He lives in Henrietta Street, he's a bit of a drunk but he's not violent.'

'I know enough drunks. I have no need to go a tenement building to meet another one.'

'If you want to play Captain Boyle, you will. Right, Jim?'

'Most certainly, Francis,' Jim said, and tried hard to hide his smirk.

THE ACTOR

*

Jim stood at the top of Dominic Street and looked fearfully down the row of once glorious Georgian houses. Over the years, the buildings' spacious rooms had been divided and sub-divided. Now each room was home to two and three families. Soiled, striped mattresses jutted from windows and washed rags hung from drooping make-shift clothes lines.

Jim started his walk down the litter-strewn street. Barefoot children in rags played hopscotch, crippled men with undersized bodies and hard faces sat on steps or leaned against railings, and poorly dressed young mothers, babes in their arms, stood in doorways and smoked as they gossiped. A yellow-faced man, propped up against a railing, coughed and splattered spittle on the ground in front of Jim's highly polished left shoe.

'Sorry there, mister,' the man said apologetically.

Jim kept walking. As he moved down the street, people standing in the doorways or sitting on steps stopped talking and looked suspiciously at the well-dressed intruder.

Nineteen families lived in 43 Dominic Street. Among the inhabitants were charwomen, hawkers, labourers, prostitutes, unemployed men, many malnourished children, and one Paddy Walsh. Jim entered through the building's open door and recoiled at the smell of dried urine, damp and decay. The backdoor was open and through it Jim glimpsed a child drinking water from the tenement's only tap.

'Who are you looking for mister?' asked a coarse little voice.

Jim's eyes struggled to adjust to the dim light of the hallway.

'I'm looking for Mr Paddy Walsh,' Jim said to a filthy, barefoot boy standing in front of a half-open door.

'Don't know him,' replied the boy as he scratched a rash on his arm.

Jim held a ha'penny out to the boy. The child grabbed the coin and shouted to the half-open door 'Ma, do you know where Paddy Walsh lives?'

'That's Gimpy the informer,' came a shouted reply from inside. 'He's up at the top of the house.'

Up the stairwell the air was filled with the smell of boiling cabbage, stale urine, boiling tripe, damp and a heady mix of the odours that wafted up from the piggery in the yard. Jim's stomach churned as he climbed the dark, filthy staircase. The door to Paddy Walsh's room was open. Jim held his fingers to his nose and called out 'Mr Walsh?'

The flat was empty, except for a mattress covered in rags and an upturned wooden box. The rags on the mattress moved. Startled, Jim took a step backwards. A filthy, skeletal thin, almost naked man appeared from under the rags. The man's head was large, his teeth were yellow and broken and his skin was the colour of wax.

'Who's there?' The man's voice was gruff and filled with suspicion.

'Are you Patrick Walsh? I'm Jim Brevin. Francis Pearse said that you'd talk to me.'

The man grabbed a small cardboard box of personal belongings that sat on the bare floorboards beside his mattress and after checking its contents, he said 'Surely. Mr Pearse is a decent man, God bless him. He said you'd bring whiskey?'

'I have,' Jim replied, taking a bottle of Power's whiskey from its paper bag and holding it aloft.

At the sight of the whiskey, Paddy's mood changed, He sat up, leaned his back against the distempered wall and said 'There's a couple of jam jars on the mantelpiece, bring them over to me and we'll have a drop.'

Jim looked at the two jam jars on the mantelpiece but didn't move.

Paddy grinned. 'Don't worry, I had the woman downstairs rinse them out for me.'

Jim poured whiskey into each of the jars and handed one to Paddy. He downed it quickly and held out his jar for more. Again Jim poured and again Paddy downed the whiskey but this time he coughed and continued coughing until his face was beetroot red.

'Ah that's gorgeous,' he said when the coughing subsided. 'And it cleared me cough too, beautiful. Sit down there on that box, mister, and tell me what you want me to talk about?'

Jim placed a handkerchief on the box and sat on it.

'I'd like you to tell me about your life.'

'My life? Now that's a wonderful thing to be talking about,' Paddy said with a cackle. 'But so long as you keep pouring that whiskey, I'll keep talking. Right?' He smiled up at Jim. 'Now, me jar is empty.'

Jim poured.

THE ACTOR

'I'm forty nine years old. My mother was born in Queen Street and father was born not far away in King Street. Smithfield people always married Smithfield people. Me mother, Lord have mercy on her, was no good. There was no love or nurturing in her. Me father was different. He looked after me.'

Jim was suddenly aware of scratching under the floorboard. Paddy banged on the floor with his fist and the scratching stopped for a moment. 'Don't worry about them creatures, they never come into the room during the day.'

Jim shuddered.

'Me mother threw me, and me father, out of the flat. We had to come here to live with me aunt Biddy, that's me father's sister. There was twelve of us here, nine children, me father, me aunt and me uncle, all living in the one room. We didn't have mattresses to sleep on, so we slept on the floor.'

Jim looked around the room anew as he struggled to imagine twelve people in the squalor being described.

'Do you think I'm lying to you?' Paddy asked, his voice raising in annoyance.

'No,' Jim replied. But he was regretting even more that he had set foot in the place. It bothered his conscience too that he had been so dismissive of Maebh's concern for the city's poor. While he had often listened to her in earnest, he had never really taken what she had said to heart.

Paddy gulped down his whiskey. He coughed so hard this time that Jim thought he might do himself an injury.

When he recovered, Paddy went on. 'I never starved,' he said. 'Do you know why?' Jim shook his head. 'The fruit market. It's only down the road. There was always good pickings there, oul' grapes, damaged apples and pears – and stray potatoes. On me own, I'd go to some waste ground, light a fire and cook the potatoes. Lovely baked, they were. You see, I used me wits and that's what kept me going all me life, me wits!' He spoke triumphantly – the whiskey had returned some light to his eyes.

'So you lived here in this room all your life?'

'Oh no. When me father died, me uncle sent me down the country to me other aunt. But she didn't like me. She said I was sneaky and useless, so she sent me to another relation and they sent me to another relation and when I was fourteen I said, feck them all and came back to Dublin. Me uncle and aunt Biddy were dead, and so were four of the children – the whooping cough got all o' them. I moved back in here with me four cousins and I've lived here ever since.'

Paddy held out his empty jam jar and Jim poured.

'Where are your cousins now?'

'They're all dead. But I always had friends, lots of friends. The McCaffrey boys were me best friends, hard chaws they were. Sure, didn't they become top men in the IRA. I remember when we were sixteen we use to break into the cellar of Maher's pub. It was a very dangerous thing to do.' Paddy's emaciated face grew severe. 'If oul Maher had caught us he'd a killed us. You see, oul 'Mr McCaffrey was a carpenter and the boys used to borrow his gimlet. We'd break into the pub's cellar and they'd bore a hole in a barrel of beer. And after we got our fill, they'd hammer a wooden peg into the hole, rub a bit of dirt on it and oul' Maher never knew that the barrel had been touched.'

'Where did you work?'

'I never worked – and I was never a scab. I don't know what Mr Pearse told you, but I was never a scab – nor an informer.' Paddy suddenly became aggravated and shook his finger in Jim's face. 'That was a lie, put about by them Metcalf brothers. They are the ones that wrecked me foot.' His eyes became intense and he started to scratch his head, tearing at the scalp so hard that it bled. 'The Metcalfs said I was an informer. They tied me to the railings downstairs and took a hammer to me ankles, that's what the Metcalfs did to me, them fucking bastards.'

Alarmed at the malevolence in Paddy's voice, Jim got to his feet.

'Don't go mister, I haven't talked to a living soul in days. Pour us another drop of your whiskey.'

Jim resumed his seat and poured. 'How did you manage after that?'

'I did the best I could. I used to hobble down to the brewery and sell newspapers. That's when they started to call me Gimpy.' Paddy's eyes went glassy and he began to slur his words. 'Did a bit of stealing but I was never good at it. I couldn't run fast enough.'

THE ACTOR

Paddy laughed and closed his eyes. After a moment, his eyes shot open and he started to cough.

'How do you manage for food now?' Jim asked when he thought Paddy was ready to continue.

'Mr Pearse or someone like that comes and gives me food, some of the neighbours are all right too. But them children across the landing have me demented. They stand at the door, throw rubbish and stones at me and shout "Gimpy the informer" at me. The other day they brought a pig up from the yard and set it loose in me room. The fucking pig ate me bleedin bread.'

Paddy's voice went quiet, and he lay down on the filthy mistress.

'I didn't tell the Tans anything about then McCaffrey boys,' he murmured. He sat up. 'Sure I didn't know they were even in the IRA.'

Paddy slumped back on the mattress, closed his eyes and fell asleep. Jim placed his untouched jar of whiskey and the half empty whiskey bottle on the mantelpiece and quietly left the room.

White light cut through the darkness of the Father Mathew Hall stage, as Jim and the rest of the cast took their final curtain call.

The reaction of the opening night audience was euphoric and the critic's reviews were unanimous. One critic wrote *'May Murnane was magnificent and Leslie Lawrence, cast against type gave one of the best performances of his distinguished career.'* But the critics reserved their highest praise for Jim. *'Mr Brevin's portrayal of Joxer Daly was so authentic that it seemed like the man had just walked out of a tenement and on to the Dublin stage. Mr Brevin did not recite O'Casey's words; rather the words were reborn within him; it was a truly great performance.'* Another critic wrote *'Full of great comic timing, Mr Brevin slowly exposed layer after layer of the man's obnoxious character'.* The review ended with the words *'Mr Brevin's Joxer is a hypocritical opportunist, yet somehow the actor showed us the human being beneath the fawning, ingratiating man.'*

Night after night the theatre was full to capacity. The run was twice extended and when it finally closed its doors, it transferred to Wexford, Limerick and Cork. Every night as Jim walked on stage to take his curtain call, he wished Maebh had been there to share it.

49

On the third night of the run of *Juno and the Paycock* at Cork's Opera House, a young woman in an expensively tailored coat and black velvet hat approached Jim as he left by the stage door. Smiling brightly, the fashionably dressed young woman thrust a leather-bound autograph book and a silver fountain pen into Jim's gloved hands and said 'Mr Brevin, may I have your autograph, please?'

Jim removed his gloves, flicked open the book and asked somewhat formally 'May I ask your name?'

'Andréa Newman,' the young woman replied, looking confidently into his eyes. 'I hope you're going to write something nice?'

Andréa Newman wasn't a conventionally pretty person but she had a sensitive, arresting face and she could be bewitching when she wanted to be. Tonight, she wanted to be bewitching.

'So you're delighted I enjoyed the show,' Andréa said when she read what Jim had written in her book. 'I never said I enjoyed the show.' Jim's forehead creased and Andréa's bright blue, angelic eyes shot wide open.

'I'm only joshing you,' she said, with a giggle. 'Let me show you my most treasured autograph.' She flipped to a page at front of the autograph book and Jim instantly recognised Ira Allen's familiar scrawl. 'He was a fabulous actor. I first saw him in a play right here in the Opera House many years ago.'

'Really!' Jim was intrigued. 'What was the play?'

'*A Noble Brother*, it was very funny.'

'I was in that production.'

'You were?' Andréa gasped, her hand to her mouth. 'What part did you play?'

'I believe I was some sort of a servant.'

She giggled again. 'Yes, I think I remember you. Did a woman servant chase you around the stage and try to kiss you?'

'Yes, I believe so.' This time, his smile was genuine.

'Then I've seen you many times at the Opera House.' She lowered her voice. 'It's wonderful to finally meet you.'

'Thank you,' he replied, tipping his hat. 'Now, I must be off.'

Andréa placed her hand gently on his arm. 'Daddy had to rush away but I wanted so much to get your autograph that I told him I'd make my own way home. Would be so good as to walk me to the front of the theatre and hail me a cab?'

'Certainly, I'd be delighted.'

Jim and Andréa walked along the side of the theatre and, as they passed a side door, two very large women wearing bucket hats, short skirts and high heels clip-clopped out of the theatre, swaying like drunken sailors. Andréa giggled and Jim tried to look serious. However when one of the women said very loudly in a slurred voice 'That was a dreadful play. Who wants to spend a night watching poor people do terrible things to each other?' he lost his battle and had to smile.

'There doesn't seem to be any cabs about,' he said, looking up and down the empty street. 'What do you live? Perhaps I might walk you home.'

'Oh, that would be lovely. I live in Youghal.'

'I don't think we should walk that far. It might rain.'

'You're right, but I'm not going home to-night. Daddy and I are staying in the Metropole Hotel on MacCurtain Street.'

'That far, I can walk,' Jim replied, and they began their journey through the glimmering gas-lit streets of Cork city.

'How often do you go the theatre?' he asked, stealing an admiring glance at the woman on his arm.

'As often as I can,' Andréa said, and she did not stop talking until they reached the hotel, where she paused and looked up into his eyes. 'I've talked too much, haven't I? I'm sorry; you must think I'm a very self-absorbed person. I feel a right fool for running on so much.'

'You're not a fool and you didn't talk too much. You are very charming young woman.'

'You're very kind,' she murmured with a smile, and walked away into the hotel.

In the autumn of 1933, the extremely confident Tony Tanner, the new assistant stage manager, knocked on Jim and Leslie's dressing room door in the Gaiety Theatre and said in his affected English accent 'Jim there's a young lady looking for you at the stage door. She says she knows you from Cork. Not a bad looker.'

'Must be Patricia O'Donovan. I haven't seen her since spring,' Jim said and wiped the cold cream and make-up from his face.

'Surely Patricia would come back backstage and say hello,' Leslie commented.

'Perhaps she doesn't care to meet you again after the scalding remarks you made about Cork actors.'

'All I said was that a Cork actor is considered great if he can keep his audience from coughing.'

'*That's* what I mean.'

'There are one too many people in this room and that one is you, Jim, so please leave,' Leslie said with mock annoyance.

Jim slid his sticks of greasepaint in his make-up box and pulled on his jacket.

'So Patricia is your lady-love?' asked Tony Tanner, running his fingers down the frayed lapels of his old overcoat, like a character from a Dickens' novel.

'No, she is not my lady-love, she's an old friend,' Jim replied and went out to meet her.

But when he stepped out of the warm theatre, flipping up the collar of his coat against the damp, blustery autumnal night, it was Andréa

Newman who was standing at the stage door. 'Hello Mr Brevin! A very good show tonight,' she cried as she slipped her arm into his. 'Let me take you to dinner and this time I promise not to talk too much.'

He was delighted – and then a sudden rush of guilt caught him unawares, making him wish she wasn't there. 'I've already eaten, I'm afraid. And besides, I have a meeting with my business partner in the restaurant trade.'

'Oh, don't be so stuffy. Talking of restaurants, Daddy has booked a table in Jammet's and I'm famished. I've spent the whole day shopping and it would be so lovely to spend some time with you. It won't cost you a penny. Come on, Jimmy.'

Confused by his own feelings, he answered coldly 'Do not call me Jimmy. I decide when I take a lady to dinner and when I do, I am well able to pay for it. Thank you for your invitation, but I must refuse. Would you like me to call a taxi for you?'

Andréa's smiling face dissolved into incomprehension. 'I'm very sorry. I didn't mean to impose myself on you.'

He remained stony-faced.

Flustered, she brushed away tiny drops of rain that had gathered on the lapels of her coat. 'Yes, I would be obliged if you'd call me a taxi. I'm staying at the Gresham.'

A bitter wind blew freezing rain into their faces as they waited in agonising silence for a cab to come down South King Street. When one eventually arrived, Jim promptly opened its door and, without a word, Andréa stepped into the cab and they parted.

Jim swung open the door of Flanagan's pub and the smell of smoke, sweat and last night's porter wafted into his face. Flanagan's was a dock bar and that night the pub was filled with men who had spent their day unloading coal boats. Jim looked across a sea of black faces with white eyes, white teeth and red lips. A docker standing at the bar coughed and spat into a spittoon; the man's spittle was black. Jim looked around the smoky room and saw a lone white-faced figure sitting in booth at the rear of the pub.

'I was about to leave,' Red said when Jim slid into the booth. 'Did the show run late?'

'No, I was delayed by someone.'

'A female someone?'

'Yes, if you must know.'

'Was she good looking?' Red teased but Jim didn't respond. 'Did you like her?'

'Enough about the woman. Why did you choose here to discuss our business? It seems like a rough place.'

'It is, it's an old IRA haunt of mine. I needed to talk to an old friend, get some information. I'm bringing Bridget to see your show tomorrow night.'

'You live a life of leisure, Mr Mullin,' Jim replied and lifted the pint a bartender had placed in front of him.

'Very funny, Jim. Bridget and I haven't been out in three months. That's what being a restaurant owner has done for my life.'

'Are you complaining?'

'Not in the least. The restaurant is booming and my plans for the second one are nearly done. I've found a location and last week I went to London to look at some new kitchen equipment. Hey, I met an old friend of yours there.'

But while Jim listened to Red his mind wandered. He had been in the office the day before, checking through the books and noticed something.

'Remember you said you thought there was something amiss with the books? Jim said interrupting Red. 'Well, I think I've spotted what it is.'

Red's face registered great interest.

'According to the books we buy in approximately six hundred steaks each week but we've receipts for only five hundred. That's a hundred stakes unaccounted for. Every week. Is it possible that we have that much wastage?'

'Absolutely not. We might give a few complimentary meals during the week, and we might get a few returns, but nothing like the number you're talking about.'

'So how do we account for the shortfall? Is the butcher leaving us short?'

'No, I count all incoming meat and it's always correct. So, someone must be stealing from us. And I think I know who it might be.'

'We'd better call the police.'

'No. No police.' Red's face turned to stone. 'Leave it to me to sort out.'

'You're not going to do anything illegal are you?'

He held Jim's gaze for a moment, then his expression changed and he grinned. 'Don't you want to know who I met in London?'

'Yes. Tell me.' He didn't take his eyes off Red's face. 'Who did you meet?'

'Shamus McGovern. He said you were his one true friend.'

Jim sat up straight. 'We were friends, once. How'd you meet him?'

'He's a down and out, poor bastard. He was begging outside a theatre. I bought him some food and he talked about you. He was staying in some hostel, you should go and see him.'

'We weren't really on the best of terms when we last saw each other.'

'Does that matter?'

'I suppose not. When the play finishes I'll go to London, see if I can do anything for him.'

'Good, it might stop you feeling sorry for yourself.'

'I don't feel sorry for myself, besides if I do, I have good reason to do so. Have you forgotten I've lost my wife and child?'

'Sometimes, Jim, you can be a right shite. You're not the only one who loved Maebh, have you forgotten, she was my sister?'

He winced. 'I'm so sorry. That was a stupid thing to say.'

'Yes it was, but forget about it.' Red's voice softened. 'Jim, you've mourned Maebh long enough. It's not what she would have wanted.'

'How would you know what she would have wanted?'

'I know my sister, she would have wanted you to get on with your life.'

'I am getting on with my life.'

'No you're not. You're wallowing in your misery. You're afraid even to think about another woman.'

'There is no other woman for me, there is no replacement for Maebh, there is no substitute and I have no interest is looking for one. And in future please keep your nose out of my personal life.'

'I didn't mean to …' but before Red could finish, Jim was on his feet and halfway out of the pub.

*

THE ACTOR

At midnight in Red's American Steak House, Phil Byrne, the skinny, dark-haired grill chef, locked the meat locker, picked up his laundry bag and turned out the kitchen lights. Passing the steel kitchen sink, he saw something move in the shadows.

'Who's there?' he called out.

'What's in the bag, Phil?' Red's voice was slow and calm.

'Is it yourself Red?' No answer. 'It's me kitchen clothes.' The chef's tone was edgy. 'You know how I like to wear clean clothes every day.'

'That's very hygienic of you.' Red stepped out of the shadows. Phil looked shiftily at his employer. 'You gave me your word you'd be straight with me.'

'What do you mean?' Phil asked and he licked his drying lips.

Red lunged forward, grabbed the laundry bag, shook it and ten sirloin steaks plopped on to the floor.

'We're having a little party and ...'

'You don't throw parties, Phil, you're so mean you can peel an orange in your pocket.' Red took a step forward. 'Phil, you were always a useless little pillock, but for old time's sake I gave you a chance, and how do you thank me? You steal from me.' He took another step forward, the kitchen knife in his hand shimmering in the half light.

'Now wait a minute ...' Sweating, the chef stepped back against the kitchen wall.

Red placed the tip of the knife to his chef's throat, pricking it gently.

'I was in Mahoney's Pub the other night,' he said very softly. 'And I was told you were supplying meat to the restaurant. I know exactly how many steaks you stole.' He stroked the tip of the knife across the man's skinny neck. 'You've twenty four hours to pay me the three hundred pounds you owe me.'

'I don't have that kind of money!' Phil was squirming against the wall.

Red pushed harder on the knife and broke the skin; blood streamed down the chef's dirty shirt.

'Twenty four hours and then I come after you. And *you* know what I can do to people.'

The following day Phil Byrne skulked into the kitchen and handed Red a brown paper bag. Red counted the money, then fired the chef.

Sitting alone in the small kitchen office, Red sat and listened to the pounding of his heart. He shuddered. The demon was out and Red cursed Phil for releasing it. He knew if the chef hadn't come up with the money, he would have killed him.

Jim walked past the red-brick terraced homes of Primrose Avenue. When he got to Number 27, he stopped and knocked on the door. He was still looking across the street at Number 5, when a smiling Dorrie Mullin opened the door and welcomed him into the house.

'Jimmy, come in and we'll have a cup of tea. I've just made some soda bread.' In the living room, she placed the fresh loaf of soda bread on the table. 'Is everything all right?'

Jim answered her softly. 'Red ... I mean, Patrick and I had a few words the other night and I just came to apologise to him. Is he about?'

'He's not here but he told me what you said.'

Jim bowed his head.

Dorrie sat beside him, resting her hands on her lap. 'We're family, Jimmy. Patrick understands. We all do. We all have terrible things to deal with in our lives. Jimmy, you're still a young man and being interested in someone is a natural thing and it's not betraying Maebh.' Then, to hide her gathering tears, she rose and went into the kitchen to make the tea.

Standing at the reception desk of the Gresham Hotel, Jim asked the receptionist if Miss Andréa Newman was still staying in the hotel. The receptionist consulted the hotel register, lifted the internal phone and after a mumbled conversation said 'Miss Newman will meet you in the lounge in ten minutes.'

Fifteen minutes later, a beautifully-dressed Andréa strolled into the hotel lounge as if she hadn't a care in the world. Jim, who had stood up as soon as she appeared, shifted uncomfortably from foot to foot. 'Hello Miss Newman, thank you for seeing me,' he said when she came within hearing distance. Without answering, she pointed to two armchairs in an alcove. They sat. 'Miss Newman, I have come to apologise for the way I spoke to you the last time we met. I hope you can forgive my rudeness.'

She looked at him. A long moment passed then she slowly smiled, her eyes lit up and she said 'You really are stuffy and old-fashioned, aren't you?'

Encouraged, he answered 'I don't think of myself as stuffy, but perhaps from your point of view, I am. I was hoping we could begin again, as if we'd never met before?'

'Do you indeed?' she said. 'I don't usually talk to men I haven't met. And you haven't even introduced yourself.'

'I do apologise. My name is Jim Brevin.'

'And mine is Andréa Newman. May I call you Jim?'

'You may. And may I call you Andréa?'

'Yes, you may.'

'And how often do you come to Dublin, Andréa?'

'Jim, you look devilishly handsome when you smile,' she said, and laughed when he blushed. 'I come to Dublin four or five times a year. Daddy loves horses, so we always come for the Horse Show. We also come for the opera season and we always come just before Christmas. Most of the girls I went to boarding school with live in Dublin or have a house here, so I sometimes come up to see them. I love shopping in Dublin. Daddy says I have too many clothes and shoes, but how could anyone have too many clothes and shoes?'

She talked and talked, and before they parted, they made an arrangement to meet again on his return from London.

50

Jim walked past the red telephone box outside Charing Cross Police Station, through an iron-studded door and into the station's bleak but functional reception area.

'The desk sergeant will call your name when he's ready to talk to you,' the young constable said politely when Jim tried to explain the reason for his visit.

Sitting on the wooden benches that ran along the drab walls of the reception area were a youngish woman with a bloodied face, two wild-looking youths and an older man in soiled clothes who continually shook his head and muttered to himself. The desk sergeant, a tall, broad-shouldered, older man came out of an inner room. He looked into the daybook and called out 'Lizzy Hepburn?'

The youngish woman pulled a soiled, red-chequered shawl around her shoulders and sauntered up to the chest-high reception desk. 'I want to make a complaint.'

'Lizzy, were you soliciting again?' the desk sergeant asked in the rasping tones that served him well when he was dealing with criminals, or "ne'er-do-wells", as he called them. 'You know the law; you can't solicit on the streets around here, you have to go to Soho to do that.'

She ignored the question. 'He has no right to hit me.'

'Who hit you Lizzy?' the sergeant asked, spreading his hands wide on the counter.

'Some gent, I don't know his name but he hit me and he never paid me.'

'Lizzy, if you can't identify who hit you, how can I arrest him?'

The woman continued to talk and argue her case until the sergeant grew tired of her and said firmly 'Lizzy I told you, if you can't give me the gent's name there is nothing I can do for you and if you continue to waste police time I'm going to have to lock you up.'

'Bloody useless coppers,' Lizzy muttered as she cupped her hand gently to her swollen cheek and wandered out of the police station.

The sergeant shook his head, looked into the daybook and called out 'Jim Brevin.'

When Jim explained to the desk sergeant that he was looking for a friend who was down on his luck, drinking too much and probably homeless, the sergeant took a deep breath and said 'Sir. Is your friend a reported missing person?'

'Not that I know of,' Jim replied meekly.

'Then there is nothing the Metropolitan Police can do for you, sir.'

'Could you suggest how I might go about looking for him?'

'You might ask in charity hostels or workhouses,' the sergeant said and stroked his moustache. 'Or you might find he is sleeping rough. But a word of warning, sir – if you go looking for your friend among the down-and-outs, you'll be putting yourself among villains and thieves.'

'My friend was never a thief or a villain.'

'He may not have been, but life on the streets can change a man.'

'Thank you, sergeant. Could you give me the address of the nearest hostel?'

'That I can do sir, the closest one is the Rowton House in King's Cross.'

That afternoon Jim visited three Rowton House Hostels and two workhouses in and around London's West End, all without success. The sun was disappearing behind the Houses of Parliament when Jim exited the third hostel. The porter screeched the bolt of the gate closed just as a weather-beaten older man in tattered clothes ran up to the gate and demanded entry.

THE ACTOR

'You're late, Joseph, we're full for the night,' the porter said and closed the workhouse's heavy wooden door.

'Jesus, another bloody night under the stars,' grumbled the man as he pulled a bottle of cider from inside his coat. 'Another freezing night on a bench.'

'Where will you find a bench to sleep on?' Jim asked him.

'What's it to you?' the troubled man replied and took a long drink from his bottle of cider.

Jim held out a shilling; the man snatched the coin from his hand. 'I usually get a bench along the embankments,' the man replied and pointed to the newspaper in Jim's hand. 'Can I have that?'

'Certainly,' Jim replied, handing it to him. 'Are you interested in the news?'

'I put it around my legs and tie it with a bit of string. They say it keeps out the cold. But, don't matter what you do, the cold gets ya. It's cruel.'

'I see. Do you know a man named Shamus McGovern?'

'Never heard of him. But then no one on the streets has a name,' the man replied and shuffled off into the growing darkness.

The small opening in the hostel's wooden door slammed open and startled Jim.

'Sir, if you intend looking for your friend on the embankments,' the porter said, 'get yourself a sturdy cane and be prepared to defend yourself with it.'

London that night was a city of thick fog and shadows. With a newly purchased, metal-topped Malacca cane gripped firmly in his hand, Jim walked the Victoria and Chelsea embankments. He had to press a handkerchief to his nose to mask the smell of raw sewage and other foul secretions from the tanneries and factories that emptied their effluent into the river. Most of the men Jim encountered on the benches stank of cheap drink or vomit and when he disturbed them they answered with a grunt, or a curse or a threat. One man was so cold and stiff that Jim thought him dead. All through the freezing night, derelict men and women rambled through the fog – some begged for money, but most of them passed him by like ghosts, expressionless and silent, looking for rest or solace. Twice during the night he was approached by aggressive drunken men but when he raised his cane to defend himself, the men disappeared back into the fog. Enshrouded in gloom and mist, Jim continued to edge his way along the embankment; only when dawn broke and the bench inhabitants disappeared into soup kitchens or day houses, did he end his search and return to his hotel.

Seagulls were screeching for their late afternoon feed when Jim began his second night's search for his one-time friend. Even though the evening was clear, he barely noticed the new electric lamps that illuminated the south bank of the river. The night was so cold that every time he stopped at a bench or a doorway, he had to stamp his feet to keep his circulation going. By the time a red dawn was breaking over the sleeping, freezing city, he had looked into the faces of countless dirt-encrusted homeless men and women. As he retraced his steps, he still occasionally stopped to gaze down on another unconscious body. Stirred from sleep, one man half opened his eyes and sleepily scratched the rash on his face. Jim was moving on when the man croaked 'Jim!' He hurried back. It was Shamus, only a much older-looking Shamus. His clothes were filthy, he stank of stale perspiration and vomit and his eyes housed the look of the defeated. When the once successful actor tried to speak again, only foul air hissed through his dry, cracked lips.

'I'll get you to a hospital!' He gazed around the foggy embankment; footsteps were approaching through the rosy mist. 'I need some help! Please, over here!'

Three hulking figures in torn clothes and flat caps appeared. 'Sure, we'll help you. That's a nice topcoat you're wearing,' grunted the largest of them.

Jim's heart beat furiously and he tightened his grip on his cane. 'Go about your business. I am helping a friend.'

'We all need help, how about you giving us some help?' sneered the second figure. 'I like your hat.'

'Keep your distance,' Jim shouted and raised his cane in the air.

The first man lunged forward. Jim stepped aside and smashed the cane against the small of the man's back and he crumpled to the ground. The second man rushed at Jim and Jim quickly raised his foot and kicked him in the groin. The man clutched at himself, howling, as Jim lashed him across the face with his cane. The first was staggering to his feet, shaking his head, but Jim cracked the metal-topped cane handle across his skull. He staggered against the embankment wall, then followed the others as they slunk away into the rosy morning mist.

Jim helped Shamus to his feet and, lurching like two drunks, they made their way to the roadside. Jim stopped a passing cab and over the protests of the driver, pushed Shamus into the vehicle and laid him across the dimpled leather seats. 'Where's the nearest hospital?'

'St Thomas's 'ospital, Westminster Bridge Road,' the cab driver replied sourly.

'Take us there and hurry!' He placed his overcoat over a shivering Shamus. The horse's hooves clattered loudly on the cobblestoned streets and within ten minutes the cab pulled up in front of St Thomas's Hospital. After much discussion and argument, Shamus was admitted into the hospital. An hour later, a doctor informed Jim that his strange companion was suffering from exposure, hypothermia and pneumonia.

Shamus survived three days in the hospital. Most of the time he slept but in his semi-waking hours he muttered wildly and incoherently about the theatre, or recited lines from parts he once played, as though he was once more in front of an audience. But the doctors could not save him.

The sun was rising over the city when a sad and despondent Jim stepped out of the hospital and wandered down to the river. Standing on the embankment, peering aimlessly along the Thames, Jim thought about his one-time friend and wondered why things had turned out the way they had. Then he returned to his hotel and later that day he began his journey back to Dublin.

51

Life in Dublin continued as if Shamus McGovern had never lived. Each day the city came to life and at night, it returned to sleep. Every day men and women went about their work, children played, singers sang and dancers danced.

On a cold grey November morning, Jim sat in the small office of the Actors' Repertory Company in Dame Street and waited for Leslie.

'Sorry I'm late,' an excited Leslie cried, as he bounded into the office. 'I was chatting to the manager of the Gaiety Theatre and he told me they have a cancellation and have offered us the two-week slot.' He plumped down in the chair facing Jim. 'What do you say to that?'

Jim leaned back in his own chair and rubbed his forehead.

'Will we have enough time to pull a new show together?'

'Oh yes, plenty of time!' Leslie fixed his monocle to his eye. 'Jim, our last two productions were artistic successes but financial disasters. We need to make a little money. I was thinking about *East Lynne*?' And when Jim mimed hitting his head off the desk, he said, 'I know, I know, it's been done to death but it does bring in the punters.'

'Not *East Lynne*. There was a touring production of it in the Olympia just a few months back.' Jim thought a moment and decided to have a little fun at Leslie's expense. 'What about an improvised play? I know

Francis P would like to get his teeth into something like that?'

'Improvised plays are nothing but the blathering of gobshites,' Leslie replied hotly and then realised Jim was grinning. 'Well, you may think this is funny, but we need a play that will make us some money.'

'When I was in London a while back I saw a revival of *Hobson's Choice*. How do you think that would play here?'

'Now that's something worth considering.' Leslie tapped his long fingers on the desk. '*Hobson's Choice* fits in well with the times.'

'Why do you say that?'

'*Hobson's Choice* is about a changing order, much like what's happening here in Ireland. It's a great mix of *Cinderella* and *King Lear* – deceased mother, three daughters, two of whom are pretty, but frivolous, and a third daughter who is smart and hardworking. It's even got a fairy godmother in it. Is it available?'

'It is indeed.'

'Good, all we need now is a theatre!'

'But don't we have a theatre?'

Leslie looked confused. 'What theatre?'

'Come on, didn't you just tell me that the Gaiety is available?' Jim waited, smiling, for Leslie to laugh at his own joke.

But Leslie blinked as if he still didn't quite understand. Then his face cleared. 'Oh, of course, the Gaiety! Sorry. I completely forgot.'

The opening of Red's second American Steak House Restaurant was as exciting to Red as any theatre opening had been to Jim. With his hair carefully oiled and wearing a dress suit, Red stood proudly at the head waiter's desk and personally greeted every customer. He showed them to their tables, exchanged a few pleasant words with them and wished them an enjoyable meal. By eight o'clock the restaurant was buzzing, and waiters were busily taking orders and serving tables. A piano player played ragtime music and customers chatted. Bridget took over seating duties and Red went from table to table and talked to customers. He was opening a bottle of Châteauneuf-du-Pape at Jim's table when Bridget showed Andréa to her seat.

'Sorry I'm late, I had a few things to do,' Andréa said as she handed Bridget her coat. 'Hello Líla and Ciaran, nice to see you again.'

'Andréa, I'd like you to meet the proud owners of this fine new establishment,' Jim said. 'Meet Patrick Mullin and his good wife Bridget.'

'How do you do Mr and Mrs Mullin?' Andréa said indifferently. 'This is a very fine establishment. Good luck with your new endeavour.'

'Nice to meet you, Andréa,' Red replied.

On hearing Red address her by her first name, Andréa turned to Líla and said 'I love your dress.'

Bridget stormed off to the cloak room. Red paused to touch Jim on the arm. 'Jim, we need to chat. There is something I need to run past you.'

'Certainly, come on over when things quieten down,' Jim said and resumed his seat.

'That waiter is very familiar with you,' Andréa said as she lifted her serviette and placed it on her lap. 'He's seems such a common chap.'

The table fell quiet and all eyes went to her.

'Did I say something wrong?'

'Red is my brother-in-law,' Jim replied coolly. 'He is one of my closest and dearest friends, and he is the business partner I told you about when we first met.'

'He's your brother-in-law? And partner?' Her expression of disbelief mutated into an embarrassed smile. 'These days it's hard to know who's who, isn't it?'

'I don't like Jim's new girl,' Red whispered to Bridget when he returned to the head waiter's station. 'And you were right, she does have an invisible moustache.'

'I never said that?'

'Didn't you?' he replied with a smirk. 'It must have been someone else.'

Sitting in Bewley's café, Jim carefully placed his coffee cup back on its saucer and said 'Leslie, why won't you play the role of Henry Hobson? One of the reasons I suggested that we put on the play was that it had choice roles for the both of us.'

'I know, but I'd rather give it a miss this time. Give it to Richard?'

'Richard doesn't have the stage presence to make the part work.

Besides, he lacks comic timing. Leslie, the part is perfect for you.'

'Jim, please find someone else, that's my final word on it.'

Jim approached Barry Fitzgerald, Jimmy O'Dea, P J Burke and Breffni O'Rourke to play the part of Hobson but all were busy or unavailable and one week before rehearsal an almost desperate Jim asked Leslie to reconsider his decision. Reluctantly, he agreed to play the part.

Rehearsals did not go well. A concerned Francis P asked Jim for a word in private.

'Please don't complain to me about Leslie?' Jim begged, when they were seated together in the tiny office in the back of the rehearsal room.

'I don't want to, but I have been asked by the cast to speak to you. Leslie should be well off book by now. All his stopping and starting and calling for lines; it impossible to get the rhythm of a scene.'

'I know it's difficult. But I can assure you Leslie is not doing it on purpose.'

'I know that, but it is affecting everyone's performance and the production is suffering.'

'I'll have a word with him and see what can be done.'

'How are you feeling?' Jim asked a tired-looking Leslie at the end of the day's rehearsal.

'I know people are upset with me but the words don't seem to want to stick in my memory,' Leslie sighed. 'My sister Grace is over from England. Last night when I ran the lines with her I never missed a cue. Then I come in here and there are large chunks I can't remember. I don't understand it. It's most annoying and more than a little embarrassing.'

'The worst thing you can do is to start to worry about it,' Jim said, and he placed his hand on Leslie's shoulder. 'We're rehearsing Act Two tomorrow, will you be all right?'

'I'll be fine. I only have one or two short scenes in Act Two,' Leslie replied. The following day he never once called for a line.

Wearing a new drape-cut suit and a fedora hat tipped down over one eye, Jim pulled open the doors of the Gresham Hotel's elegant private dining room and beamed his brightest smile.

'Who the hell are you?' growled the short man with an enormous stomach who was sitting at a table devouring the last of a plate of sandwiches.

'Jim Brevin, sir, am I addressing Mr George Newman? I do believe we have an appointment for afternoon tea.'

'Do we?' asked the fat man as he took a savage bite of the large slice of walnut cake.

'Never mind, Daddy,' a flustered Andréa said getting to her feet. 'You're early, Jim. Daddy, this is my friend Jim Brevin. I told you he would be joining us.'

'I don't remember you mentioning that.' George Newman looked questioningly at Jim. 'Do I know you?'

'No sir, I'm Jim Brevin. I'm an actor.'

George Newman's face changed from surprise to annoyance.

'Never liked theatre people. Never saw the point of it.'

Jim looked to Andréa and she shook her head as if to say don't pursue the conversation.

'Jim's family is in the wine importation business, Daddy. Jim manages the company, and also is a partner in two restaurants.'

'So acting is your *hobby*. Now I understand. Good business the wine business – we always need wine. Now if you'll excuse me, I have an appointment in the Australian Consulate.'

'You're not staying for tea?' Jim asked.

'I've had my tea. Andréa? A quick word.' George Newman glared at Jim. 'In private.'

'Please excuse me.' Jim stepped out into the hall, closing the door behind him. He didn't intend to eavesdrop but Newman's voice was so loud that it was impossible not to hear the man.

'That person is not a suitable person for you to be socialising with. He's practically a tradesperson.'

Andréa's voice was too low to carry, so a silence followed. Then the man spoke again 'I might have known something like that. You're being a Good Samaritan.' More silence then George Newman's booming voice said 'Andréa I do wish you'd stop calling me Daddy in public: makes me feel old. You may be a Good Samaritan, but in many ways you are an incorrigible young woman.'

The private dining room door swung open, George Newman

marched into the corridor, turned on his heels and kissed Andréa on the mouth. Then, without acknowledging Jim presence, he paraded down the corridor and into the lift.

'What was that all about?' Jim asked, barely concealing his annoyance.

Andréa returned to the dining room, resumed her seat and said in a voice filled with sadness 'I must apologise for Daddy, sometimes he says and does inappropriate things.'

'Andréa, I want you to make it clear to your father that my primary profession is acting. I am a professional actor and proud to be so.'

'Jim, I know how important the theatre is to you and I'm sorry if I spoke out of turn, but Daddy will need a little time to get used to that idea.'

On the opening night of *Hobson's Choice*, the illuminated facade of the Gaiety Theatre shone like a beacon of excitement in a city of gloom. A tin whistle tooted merry tunes, as hundreds of chattering men and woman flowed through the Gaiety's tall glass doors. Men and women swarmed into the stalls and jostling crowds crushed and clambered up the staircases and stairwells to the second and third balconies. People waved and smiled to each other, older men checked their glasses, and ladies preened and patted their hair while young men purchased programmes and chocolates for their ladies. Excitement and expectation buzzed around the auditorium. Andréa, Líla, Ciaran, Clara and Theo took their seats in the front row of the grand circle, while Michael stood and opened a large box of chocolates which he passed down the row.

The stage crew made their last minute adjustments to the set and Tony Tanner, the assistant stage manager, checked the prompt book and made his final check of the prop table. Leslie rushed into the wings, placed a play script on each side of the stage and, as he returned to his dressing room, he passed the prop table, stopped and said to Tony Tanner, 'Where's my top hat?'

The young stage manager smiled at Leslie.

'Are you deaf?' The veins in Leslie's forehead started to pump and his face glowed red with aggravation. 'Where's my hat?'

'Steady on there,' Mick, the stage manager, said. 'Lower your voice. What's the matter?'

'I asked this young man for my hat and he laughed at me. The curtain is about to rise and I haven't got my hat.'

'Leslie,' Mick replied calmly. 'Your hat is sitting on your head.'

Leslie hands shot to his head.

'Oh my God, I apologise Tony, I'm so sorry.' Leslie's eyes shot from Tony to Mick. 'First night nerves.' Leslie patted Tony on the shoulder and, looking shocked and confused, took up his entrance position, stage left.

The house lights dimmed, the curtain rose and the stage lights burst into life. Towards the end of first act, Jim was standing backstage awaiting his entrance when he heard the ruffle of paper. He craned his neck, Leslie was peering into a script and mouthing words. When Jim approached him, Leslie closed the script and whispered a comment about how well the show was going. Jim heard his cue and walked on stage.

Leslie was right, the play was going well – very well. The audience loved Leslie's drunken scenes, particularly the one where he was trying to step on the reflection of the moon in a puddle of rain water. However, midway through the second act, Leslie took a sudden and unrehearsed pause. Immediately Richard realised that Leslie had forgotten his lines. What he didn't know was that Leslie's mind had collapsed and that not only did Leslie not know his next line, he had no idea what play in was in. All Leslie realised was that he was in a theatre and a sea of shadowy faces were staring at him.

Without hesitation Richard turned upstage, and unseen and unheard by the audience, whispered Leslie his line. Leslie heard the line, picked up on it and played the rest of the scene without further incident.

'Thank you Richard,' Leslie said, the moment he and Richard walked off stage. 'I will never forget your kindness.'

'We all dry from time to time,' Richard said with a wave of his hand. 'Think nothing of it.'

But Leslie did think about it. He thought about it all the following day and all during the following night's performances, but fortunately, and to his great relief, the incident never re-occurred.

At the curtain call, raucous cries and whistles rained down from the second and third balconies and enthusiastic applause rose up from

THE ACTOR

the stalls. Audiences and critics loved the production and every night the actors were greeted with a tidal wave of cheering, whistling and applause, but the loudest volleys of applause was always reserved for Jim and Leslie.

'How are you feeling tonight, Leslie?' Richard asked as they as they prepared for the performance on the second week of the run.

'I'm well thank you. I seem to have gotten over my little problem,' Leslie replied but Richard noticed that on three occasions during the performance Leslie consulted the scripts he had placed in the wings.

To celebrate the play's great success, Jim took Andréa to dinner in Jammet's Restaurant in Saint Andrew's Street. Sitting in the spacious restaurant in front of the Bossini's mural of *The Four Seasons*, Andréa told Jim stories about growing up in Youghal. Her face came alive when she talked of her brother Harry and how they spent their days playing on the estate. She spoke of her love of horse riding and the great pleasure she and her brother took in looking after their animals. But when Jim asked why he had never met Harry, her face darkened.

'Harry died in a car accident five years ago.'

'I'm sorry,' Jim replied very softly and placed his hand on hers. 'We both have lost someone very dear and important to us. I know how difficult it can be.'

'No you don't,' Andréa said and her eyes welled with tears. 'I was driving the car when the accident happened.'

'It must have been horrible for you.'

'It was worse for Harry, he lost his …' Andréa bowed her head and after a while she said with a forced a smile 'In a few weeks' time, when your play comes to Cork would you like me to come and visit you?'

'That would be nice,' Jim replied and squeezed her hand.

Two weeks later, when the three o'clock Youghal train puffed and hissed its way into Cork Station, Jim was standing on Platform One. With a thunderous hiss the train came to a halt and when the pall of steam cleared Jim saw Andréa alight from her first-class carriage. He rushed along the crowded platform and to his surprise he kissed her on the lips.

'I've booked us into the Metropole Hotel,' he said. Then, blushing furiously, he added 'Separate rooms, on different floors, of course.'

'Of course,' Andréa repeated quietly.

After checking into the hotel, Andréa and Jim walked along the banks of the Lee and up Patrick Street. Later they had dinner in the hotel and when it came time to retire, Jim walked Andréa to the wrought-iron lift, kissed her goodnight and returned to the lounge for a brandy before sleep.

Thirty minutes later as he sat on the bed removing his shoes, he heard a gentle knock on the connecting door in his room. He placed his ear against the door and bolted upright when a second more urgent thump rattled the wood.

'Jim, open the door please!' a female voice called out.

Jim cautiously opened the door. Andréa was standing on the other side, dressed in a sheer nightdress, holding a bottle of champagne and two glasses. 'Aren't you going to invite me in?' she asked brazenly.

'I ... I booked a room for you on the floor below,' a startled Jim stuttered.

'I know. I changed the room,' Andréa replied. She walked past him into his room, sat on the bed and, holding up the champagne bottle, said firmly 'Jim. Be a dear and open the champagne.'

52

When Hobson's Choice opened in Belfast's Grand Opera House, Andréa joined Jim and they spent six nights together in the glorious grandeur of the Victorian Merchant Hotel. On sunny days, they visited Queen's University, took a trip on the river Lagan or strolled around the Botanical Gardens. On inclement days, they explored the Linen Hall Library, Stormont Castle and the Ulster Hall. Every evening Andréa attended the play and every night they made love.

During the three-month tour of *Hobson's Choice*, Leslie's personality changed. He now spent most of his time alone. Each evening, he arrived at the theatre two hours before performance, checked that his two scripts were in the wings and then went to his dressing room, changed into his costume and sat mumbling his lines.

'Try that, and let me know what you think,' Michael said as he handed his wife a glass of Nuits-Saint-Georges Premier Cru. 'It's from a new supplier.' He stood at the window of his art deco drawing room and held his glass up to the light. Clara swirled the ruby liquid in the glass and inhaled its rich bouquet.

'Good nose, good colour.' Clara sipped the wine. 'It's fruity, spicy with a lovely aftertaste. It's a very elegant wine, Michael.'

'My thoughts exactly.' He sat in his chair by the window. 'Clara, you said you had something important to tell me.'

'Oh, yes and it's a little awkward.' Clara rested her glass on the tic-tac side table. 'I was talking to Thérèse Nolan yesterday and she told me the oddest thing, she said the Newmans of Youghal are childless.'

'The Newmans of Youghal? Is that's Jim's girlfriend's people?' Clara nodded.

'But that's impossible, it would mean that Andréa is not who she says she is.'

'Yes. Are you going to mention it to Jim?'

Michael looked thoughtful. 'I don't think so. Thérèse is a bit of a gossip and besides I'm still trying to regain Jim's confidence. Any talk like that from me could re-open old wounds.'

'There may be a simple explanation,' Clara replied.

'Yes, let's hope so. But if it's true, who is Andréa?'

Shortly after the national tour of *Hobson's Choice*, Leslie asked Jim if he would like to visit him in his home. As they were sitting in the conservatory, Leslie at first was chatting away; then his demeanour changed. He grew uncomfortable, stood up and paced the room and then sat down again.

'Jim,' he said, an urgent tone in his voice, 'I'm telling you this in absolute confidence. Of late I'm having great difficulty remembering things, particularly new things.'

'That's nothing to worry about,' Jim said. 'It happens to everyone from time to time.

'But I am worried about it. It's happening to me all the time. I sometimes get confused and I can't think properly and I can get very irritable. The tour was horrific for me. You have no idea how terrified I was before each performance. I had such great difficulty remembering my lines. I would get very nervous, so nervous I would shake and sometimes I got physically ill.' Leslie bowed his head and buried his face in his hands and when he lifted his head again his eyes were filled with terror. 'I think I'm losing my mind.'

'Leslie, don't be silly, you're not losing your mind.'

'Don't call me silly,' Leslie said, raising his voice. 'I've been to my doctor and he has referred me to a specialist in Harley Street.' His voice quietened. 'In two weeks I have an appointment with a psychiatrist in London.' His voice cracked. 'Would you accompany me, please?'

Jim said sadly, 'I will, Leslie. Of course I will.'

Michael and Clara were in the Wright-Moran mansion for a formal dinner when Elizabeth, Clara's younger sister, blurted out across the table 'Clara, I was telling my friend Linda from Youghal that your brother-in-law was seeing one of the Newman children. She informed me that the Newman family are childless. What do you make of that?'

Before Clara could reply, the hard-of-hearing Dr Veale said 'This economic war with Britain over land annuities is getting very serious. How is it all going to end?'

Once politics was introduced into the conversation, Elizabeth's question about Andréa was forgotten by everyone, except Michael and Clara.

It took Michael a further week of thought before he decided to tell Jim what he had heard. Twice he left his office with the intention of telling his brother, but each time he lost his nerve.

He was approaching Jim's office for the third time when Jim opened the door and nearly walked into him.

'Sorry Michael. Were you coming to see me?'

'I was, as a matter of fact. It has to do with family and it's somewhat awkward,' Michael replied.

'Come on in.' Jim sat behind his desk and Michael carefully closed the office door. 'Sounds ominous.'

'Jim, I don't want to jeopardise our growing confidence in each other but I have heard something that I feel I must pass on to you.'

'Michael, what are you talking about?'

'I'll come straight to the point. I have learned that Andréa Newman may not be who she says she is.'

'I see,' Jim replied with a slight smile.

'Clara told me that the Newman's of Youghal are childless.'

'I see. And how did Clara come across this information?'

'Thérèse Nolan told her.'

'Thérèse Nolan is the biggest gossip in the city.'

'I know, but she also heard it from her sister Elizabeth.'

'Is this the Elizabeth that worked in the office for a few days and decided that an independent life was not for her?' Jim asked with a grin. 'Well then, I'd better take her seriously, she is such a great fortress of insight and knowledge.'

'It's not a laughing matter,' snapped Michael, now thoroughly annoyed. 'I've done my duty. I've passed on the information to you. What you do with it is your concern.' And he stormed out of the office.

Jim and Leslie walked past the fine terraced houses of Harley Street until they came to Number 93. An apprehensive Leslie gazed doubtfully at the doorbell; Jim noticed his hesitation and promptly pressed it.

A plump, uniformed nurse opened the door, took Leslie's name and showed them to a waiting room. As Jim sat on an elegant chaise longue, Leslie paced the room. Five minutes ticked slowly by, the nurse returned to the waiting room and escorted them to Mr Anthony Leaver's consulting room.

'Take a seat, gentlemen,' the tall, smartly dressed Mr Leaver said. 'Now, Mr Lawrence, what can I do for you?'

'Mr Leaver this is my friend and colleague Mr Jim Brevin. I would like him to be present during the consultation.'

'Perfectly understandable,' replied the doctor. 'Mr Lawrence, I have received a letter from your GP explaining your condition. But I would like you to tell me in your own words why you've come to see me?'

Leslie removed his monocle, placed it in the pocket of his waistcoat and told his story. The doctor listened attentively and asked a few questions to clarify a detail or two. When Leslie had finished talking, the doctor called in the nurse. Then, for the next hour and a half, they administered a series of memory tests to Leslie.

At the completion of the tests the doctor spoke to Leslie.

'We have accomplished all we can today. Tomorrow morning we'll continue with some more tests and then we'll talk.'

'What do you think is wrong with me, doctor?' Leslie asked, as he stood to leave.

'Far too early to say. I need time to review the tests we've taken today and I'll need to look at the tests you will take tomorrow, then I hope to arrive at a preliminary diagnosis. Make an early appointment with the nurse. Tomorrow afternoon we'll talk again. But I must stress they will be only be preliminary results.'

The following morning in Mr Leaver's consulting rooms, Leslie was given a battery of cognitive tests, which he found difficult and tiring. After some lunch Leslie and Jim returned hoping for some answers.

'Well doctor, am I a lunatic or am I just losing my mind?'

'You're not a lunatic, Mr Lawrence, and I would never refer to my patients as such. I've reviewed your tests and I have made a preliminary diagnosis.' The doctor opened a green file on his desk. 'I'm afraid I don't have good news for you.'

Leslie's face tightened and he sat back in his chair.

'I don't suppose you've heard of a Dr Alois Alzheimer?'

Leslie shook his head.

'Dr Alzheimer was a doctor who specialised in treating patients who were experiencing difficulty with memory, who experienced confusion and cognitive deficiencies, people much like yourself.'

'So I'm not alone?' Leslie asked, relieved that at least that his condition had been diagnosed.

'No, you are most certainly not alone.'

'So, what's to be done? What's the cure?'

'I'm sorry to tell you, there is no cure.'

Leslie's hands gripped the armrests on his chair.

'Current treatments can help with the symptoms of the disease but there is no treatment that will stop or reverse its progression. Some doctors maintain that mental stimulation and a balanced diet can delay the disease's progress, but there is no conclusive evidence to support those theories.'

'What's going to happen to me?' Leslie asked, his knuckles white from gripping the armrests so tightly.

'Forgive me being so blunt but it's important that you understand your condition. As the disease advances, you will experience greater confusion, irritability, aggression, trouble with language, short-term memory loss and, eventually, your long-term memory will be affected too.'

'How long will all this take?' Leslie asked, his eyes riveted on the doctor.

'The deterioration will be gradual, and of course it varies from patient to patient. Average life expectancy is approximately seven years but I've known some sufferers to live more than fourteen, fifteen years.'

'What do you suggest I do?'

'I'll suggest some possible treatments, some medication. But you must try to live your life in a manner as free from stress as possible. Stress is the great enemy. Later, much later, you will have to consider care. There are some wonderful care homes. But for now, live your life as you like. I'm sorry to be so blunt but there is nothing to be gained in offering you false hope.'

Leslie did not return to Dublin with Jim; instead he journeyed to Stow-on-the-Wold, Gloucestershire, and informed his sister Grace of his condition.

'What are you going to do?' Grace asked, her bright eyes blinking rapidly.

'I'm going to fight this. It may beat me, but I'm going to go down fighting.'

'Of course you are. Leslie, I would like you to consider coming to live in Gloucestershire with Derek and me.'

'Thank you Grace, but no. I'm going to return to Dublin. I have some very good friends there. In time I will go live in a care home. Perhaps there's a good one nearby in Gloucestershire? Would you look into that for me?'

'Of course I will,' Grace said, and she placed her hand gently on Leslie's. 'How are you coping, Leslie?'

'I don't know yet, it's all so very new to me, but as a great man once said, life is a comedy to those who think and a tragedy to those that feel. Thankfully I'm a thinker.'

'And a wonderful man too,' added his sister.

It was a hot summer's day. Children were sticking twigs into the blistering tar on the roadway outside Kingsbridge railway station, when the train from Cork chugged in. The moment Andréa saw Jim her face broke into a bright smile, and they hurried to each other. After a flurry of greetings and kisses, Jim carried Andréa's hand-made bags to his new gleaming, six-cylinder Wolseley Hornet Special Tourer, and they set off for Brittas Bay.

'I just love your new car,' Andréa said, as a warm breeze fluttered her short hair around her face. Travelling through the picturesque garden county they chatted and laughed, and when Jim asked her why she was so happy, she replied 'I'm with you, and that makes me happy.'

Two hours later, they arrived at the Bel-Air Hotel. After they checked into their rooms, they went for a walk along the bay's three-mile stretch of powdery white sand. Giddy as children, they frolicked on the shoreline, and when Andréa splashed water on Jim, he chased after her. When he caught her, he pulled her close and they kissed again and again.

Later, as they lay on the warm sand looking up into a cloudless blue sky, Andréa asked Jim what he was thinking about. He rolled on his side, looked into her small round face and said 'I was wondering, do you ever wear the same clothes twice?'

'Of course I do.'

'That's a new outfit you're wearing today,' Jim said, eyeing Andréa's new red and white printed chiffon dress.

'That's because it's our special time.'

Jim jumped to his feet. 'How about a dip?'

'I don't have a swimsuit?'

'I do, I put it on in the bathroom.' Jim quickly removed his blue-striped blazer, white trousers and shirt, and ran straight into the sea.

After lunch, they visited an equestrian centre, where Andréa, to no avail, attempted to teach Jim the fundamentals of horse riding.

After dinner they sat on the hotel's veranda and watched a gleaming silver crescent moon disappear and re-appear behind fast moving clouds. Jim quietly reached into his jacket pocket, removed a long, slender, soft leather case and presented it to Andréa. Bright-eyed as a child on Christmas morning, she opened the case and the look of joyous surprise on her face thrilled him.

'It's beautiful,' she said, as she removed a golden necklace and placed it around her neck. 'I'll never take it off, it will stay on my neck forever.'

'And that's where it should stay.'

'Jim, it's so beautiful, I love it. Thank you ever so much,' she said, and kissed him. 'Are you going to miss me next week when Daddy and I are away?'

'Of course I will. I'll miss you every day. Oh, and I must tell you the amusing gossip Clara told Michael the other day.'

'What did she say?'

'She said that she'd heard the Newmans of Youghal were childless.'

Andréa went silent; her eyes darkened but her face smiled.

She said lightly, 'That's not a rumour, that's the truth. The Newmans of Youghal are childless. Uncle Roger, my father's younger brother and his wife Sally live in Youghal town and they are childless. Daddy and I live in Newman House in the hinterlands of Youghal.'

'Well that explains that! Why don't we drive to Youghal tomorrow, and I might be able to convince your father that the theatre has value?'

Andréa hesitated a moment, looked out to sea and fingered her new necklace. 'Yes,' she said quietly. 'Let's do that tomorrow.'

Lying on the bed, Jim plotted the route to Youghal while Andréa sat and read. After a while he asked 'You're very quiet. Is everything all right?'

'Sometimes I like to be quiet. Besides, I'm a little tired. We had a busy day. Can we have an early night?'

Andréa hardly spoke through dinner but that night her lovemaking was passionate and, Jim felt, somewhat desperate.

When Jim awoke he was alone in his bed. The phone rang and when he answered it, a joyous Andréa said 'Get up sleepy-head. I'm already packed and ready to go.'

'I'll be down in ten minutes and don't have breakfast without me.'

Over breakfast, Andréa was her usual flirtatious self and, as they left the dining room, she took Jim's hand and said 'Let's go for a walk on the beach.'

'I thought you were in a hurry to leave?'

'I am, but we have time for a short walk.' Andréa tugged on his hand. 'The beach is so lovely.'

The sun was shining, waves were rippling onto the sand and the morning air had a salty tang to it. Jim and Andréa strolled hand in hand along the almost empty beach. About half a mile down the beach, Andréa let go of his hand and stepped away from him. Her face lost its flirtations half smile and she turned and looked at Jim coldly.

'What's the matter?' Jim asked.

'I'm ending our affair,' Andréa said brusquely. 'It's over.'

Jim blinked, not sure if he had heard right. 'What are you talking about? I don't understand, I …'

'There is nothing to understand. Jim, I was your lover, for a while, your personal whore if you like. Now I'm tired of playing that part.'

The strange remoteness of her voice astounded Jim no less than her words.

'What are you saying? I never thought of you as anything like that! And I don't like you using that word.'

'I know. But I liked being your whore, at least for a while. Jim, you are not the man for me. You're a dreamer, a ridiculous man with absurd ambitions.'

'Why are you talking like this? Andrea, what are you saying? You said you thought my life was exciting?'

'I did say that, didn't I? But then I said a lot of things I didn't mean. I suppose I thought it was exciting at the time, but it's actually quite a silly way to live.'

'Andréa, why are you talking to me like this? Don't do this to me, I love you!'

A momentary warmth flickered in Andréa's eyes; then the coldness returned.

'Sorry Jim. You were a passing fancy. It was only an inconsequential fling.'

'It was never that to me.'

'Well, whatever it was, it's over.' She placed a cold kiss on Jim's cheek and before she turned away she said, 'It's for the best and someday you'll thank me.'

He was lost, marooned. He felt physically sick. As he stood and watched Andréa walk up the beach, seawater fizzed around his shoes and disappeared into the soft sand.

53

On his return to Dublin, Jim wrote to Andréa at Newman House. When his letter was returned with the words *Unknown at this address* scribbled across the front of it, he was furious. The following day he drove to Youghal, pushed open the gate to the Newman estate and drove through the woodland of spruce, native oak and beech. A quarter of a mile beyond the wood stood the three-storey Newman House. The huge windows were shuttered, the main entrance was locked and the building looked uninhabited.

Jim parked his car close to the columned entrance porch, walked briskly to the granite building's front door and pulled on the bell chain. Somewhere deep within the house the bell rang. Jim was looking around the grounds when a scowling, burly man carrying a shotgun under his arm strode towards to him.

'You're trespassing,' the man said with barely suppressed aggression. 'Clear off. No one is home.'

'I'm here to talk to Mr Newman.'

'I told you nobody is home.'

'When will he return?'

'I'm the gamekeeper,' the man said as he hooked his finger around the trigger of his shotgun. 'We get a lot of poachers around here and when I see them, I shoot them.'

'I'm not a poacher.'

'How would I know that?'

Jim stared a moment at the gamekeeper and then returned to his car.

Back in Youghal, he parked his car near the Clock Gate and walked into the police station.

'All I know is that a week ago, the couple informed us that they were leaving. They told us that the house was all locked up and that Henry Darcy, the gamekeeper, had been left in charge of the estate,' the constable told Jim when he had inquired the whereabouts of the Newmans.

'Did their daughter leave with them?'

The constable scratched the greasy hair above his left ear.

'The Newmans don't have a daughter, they never had any children.'

'But what about their son, the young man that was killed in an automobile accident?'

The constable shook his head. 'I'm living here twenty years or more and I've never heard anything about that.'

'Could you at least tell me where Mr Roger Newman lives?' Jim asked. Then, when the constable returned his question with a vacant stare, added impatiently 'He's George Newman's brother.'

'You've been misinformed, sir. Mr Newman doesn't have a brother, at least not one that lives around here.'

Three months after Leslie Lawrence's illness had been diagnosed, Jim persuaded him to take a small role in an Actors' Repertory Company's studio production of Licel Ellan's new naturalistic play *Transcendence*. On the first day of rehearsal the table reading went well; however on the third day, the day when everyone was to be off book, Leslie was unable to remember his few lines.

Jim suggested that Leslie take a rest. But Leslie replied 'I'm not tired, I've been resting all morning waiting on this blasted scene.'

'Leslie,' Jim said, 'Please, take a seat and we'll pick up your scene later.'

A dejected Leslie sat and watched the cast continue the rehearsal.

THE ACTOR

Jim called the lunch break and as the actors were chatting, Leslie stood and announced 'I want to apologise for my behaviour this morning. You are all professionals and you deserve to be treated better. I'm sorry.' Then he turned to Jim. 'I'm leaving the show. I'm sorry for any inconvenience.'

Stunned, the group watched is silence as Leslie gathered his things and walked out of the room. When Jim went to follow, Richard stopped him.

'Leave Leslie to me,' Richard said. 'It's the old dog for the hard road.'

Leslie was standing staring idly into the still water of the Royal Canal, when Richard caught him up.

'Don't say anything,' Leslie said without looking at his colleague.

'It's a free country, or do you not remember the revolution?' Richard said and leaned against the arm of the canal's lock gate.

'Wit was never your strong suit, Richard.'

'You're right, I was always more of a lover than a wit.'

The corners of Leslie's mouth curled in a slight smile.

Richard lit a cigarette, drew on it and, savouring a lungful, exhaled. 'You're not the only one living in a prison. We all live in a prison of one sort or another.' He cast his eyes over to the high walls of Mountjoy Jail. 'The men in there have no option but to accept their prison, but you do. You can escape, at least for a little time. And you have friends who'd like to help.'

Thirty minutes later, Leslie and Richard strolled back into the rehearsal room. Richard took a seat near the door and Leslie walked to Jim and said 'I'm so sorry for my outburst. I'm ready to resume rehearsals – that is, if you still want me.'

Before Leslie had even finished speaking, the cast and crew stood and applauded their colleague.

For the run of *Transcendence*, Leslie had his twelve lines written on small cards which he carried around in a silver cigarette box in his breast pocket. He never had to use his cards or call upon his friends for assistance. Every night, when the show finished, he beamed with delight at his little victory over his disease. In the following months, he featured in two other ARC productions. His fellow actors, particularly Richard and Maura, kept a close eye on him.

But Leslie's illness did progress, and in February 1934, he finally announced his retirement from the stage. It was a bereavement for Leslie. The stage had been his life for so long and now that part of his life was over. After his last performance, the cast and crew went to the Trocadero Restaurant. May, Richard and Jim paid glowing tributes to their friend and colleague. A month later, Leslie went to Stow-on-the-Wold to live with his sister. Six months after that, he moved into a nearby rest home. During the following year, long after Leslie ceased to be able to recognise them, Jim and Richard continued to visit their friend in the Cotswolds rest home and on the 5 June, 1936, Leslie Lawrence passed away peacefully in his sleep.

Ireland of the 1930s was a bleak place to live. The newly-emerging nation was still learning to govern itself and the ghosts of the civil war continued to haunt and divide the people. Most country dwellers depended on subsistence farming while the mass of people in the cities lived with great unemployment and crippling strikes. The government paid little attention to emigration and the general welfare of the people. The battle against typhoid and diphteria showed some success but the number of infant deaths increased. In July 1937, the Irish Government introduced a new constitution which made Ireland a fully independent country and renamed it the Free State 'Eire'. When the Second World War began in Europe, the Irish Government declared Ireland neutral, but that didn't stop thousands of young unemployed Irishmen and Irishwomen joining the British armed forces or going to England to work in armament factories.

In July 1936, Jim was driving home from a visit to the Opera House, Cork when he decided to stop in the walled town of Youghal and see if he could learn something about Andréa or the Newmans. The gates of the Newman Estate were wide open but the house was shuttered and locked, the gardens neglected and the grounds deserted. When Jim stopped for lunch in O'Keefe's Inn in the town, he asked the innkeeper about the family.

'They weren't the worst, they put a lot of money into the town,' Phyllis O'Keefe replied. 'They're sadly missed. They bought a lot of my fish, the good stuff, the expensive stuff, sole, crab and lobster and they bought a fair amount of drink too, I can tell you.'

'Where are they now?'

'I heard they're in Australia,' replied the innkeeper as she wiped the bar counter in front of Jim. 'But I don't know.'

'When will they be back?'

'Don't know that either. Old Newman might have looked as trustworthy as a fox in a henhouse but he paid his debts, so good luck to him.'

On the night of the 31 May, 1941, Francis P and his family were asleep in their small house on Charleville Avenue when the silence of the night was shattered by an enormous explosion. The house shook and every window was smashed into smithereens.

'Jesus, Mary and Joseph,' Francis P shouted as he jumped out of bed and watched a wardrobe fall across the bed. Maureen, his wife, was already at the window and calling out to her neighbour 'Dee, what in God's name was that?'

'Get down from the window,' Francis P called across the room.

'Will you look at that, the roof of the Beirne's house is blown off,' Maureen said in amazement. 'You can see Dee lying in her bed, she's half naked.'

'Is she all right?'

'Yes, I think so, she's getting out of the bed.'

Thirty four people were killed that night, ninety people were injured and three hundred houses were damaged or destroyed. A Luftwaffe aircraft had dropped four high-explosive bombs on the North Strand Road area of Dublin.

The Actors' Repertory Company continued to produce modern Irish and European plays. Francis P took on the main responsibility as director, while Jim acted and produced the shows. Jim also worked with other companies, and over the years he performed in every theatre in Dublin and most of the theatres in Ireland, North and South of the border. He was highly regarded as an actor of intelligence and integrity.

*

THE ACTOR

In the spring of 1943, six long winters after Leslie's death, Jim was performing in a production of George Bernard Shaw's *The Devil's Disciple* in the Olympia Theatre, when a scented letter was left for him at the stage door.

In his dressing room after the show, Jim opened the letter. The writer requested a meeting with him at noon the following day in the lounge of the Gresham Hotel. The letter finished with the melodramatic phrase 'I have something important to tell you.' Jim smiled but when he saw the signature it was if a rusty knife had been plunged into his heart.

It was Andréa Newman's.

Bright morning sunlight shimmered on the rain-drenched footpaths of O'Connell Street as a man with a sandwich board ambled past the Gresham. Jim, dressed in a blue pinstriped suit and homburg hat, stepped out of his car and hurried up the hotel's three granite steps. He crossed the bright foyer, stood in the doorway of the Wintergarden Lounge and removed his homburg as he perused the room.

A white-haired woman in a prim grey suit with a small child were sitting in the back of the lounge, to Jim's right was an elderly couple drinking tea, to his left were two military officers deep in conversation. He walked in and there, sitting on a large couch in an alcove near the residents' lounge, was Andréa. To his surprise he still found her beautiful and vulnerable. Then he remembered how she had treated him and felt his anger rise.

Andréa saw him. Still slim and petite, her genial acknowledgment of him unleashed a torrent of emotion in him. Each step he took towards her, he relived the pain of her rejection and betrayal so that by the time he reached her, his feelings were as raw as the day she had abandoned him on the beach.

Andréa, immaculately dressed, offered him a slight smile. The necklace he had given her on their last night together was around her neck.

'Hello Jim,' she said.

'You said you had something to tell me?' Jim's voice was as cold and as impersonal as he could make it.

'Why don't you sit down?'

She patted the sofa she was sitting on.

'I prefer to stand.'

'I'd prefer if you sat. I don't want you towering over me like Nelson's Pillar.'

Jim sat on the sofa opposite.

'How have you been, Jim?'

'I've been fine. Where have you been?'

'That's no concern of yours.'

'You said you had something important to tell me?'

'I have a child.'

'Really,' Jim replied in a tone as empty as a theatre an hour after performance. 'Well, that's of no concern to me either.'

'It should be. Jim, the child is yours.'

He swallowed hard. 'That's absurd.'

'It is not absurd. I was pregnant when we parted.'

There was a moment's hesitation. 'Why should I believe you? Truth was the only thing you ever economised on.'

'Now, don't be nasty. When you see the child – that is, if I allow it – any doubt will be dispelled. Let's try to be civilised about this.'

'Why are you telling me this, why now? Why didn't you tell me at the time?'

'You would have wanted to do the right thing,' Andréa smiled. 'It's part of your charm. You would have wanted to marry me, wouldn't you?'

'I don't see that as a fault.'

'No you wouldn't. But I couldn't marry you.'

'You made that perfectly clear to me at the time.'

'Jim, I *couldn't* marry you. I was already married.' Andréa's confession thumped into Jim's head. 'Daddy and I were married six years before you and I met. I always wanted to be a mother; at least I thought I wanted to be, but ironically Daddy was unable to father a child. I should have guessed it. He and his first wife were childless. So I had to find someone who could – deliver the goods, if you pardon the expression.' Andréa smiled coquettishly. 'When you told me you had had a child I knew you were the one.'

Jim's face flushed with anger. 'You're disgusting and shameless.'

'Don't get all upset. That's why I never told you about our own child.'

'Then why are you telling me now?'

'Unfortunately, Daddy died last year …'

'So, you're looking for money?'

'Do I look like I need money?' Andréa cocked her head to one side, condescendingly. 'I spend more on clothes in a month than you live on in a year. No, the truth is motherhood has turned out to be a disappointment to me. It's quite boring and frankly the child is needy and can be tiresome.'

'Let me see if I understand this correctly. You asked me here today to tell me you have an annoying child and that you're tired of motherhood.'

'I said nothing of the sort,' Andréa said with an impatient gesture of her hand.

'If you don't want my money, what do you want from me?'

'I don't want anything from you. However I am offering you the opportunity to be a part of your son's life.'

'My supposed son.'

She glared at him and said nothing.

He sighed. 'What did you name the boy?'

'I called him James.' Jim's jaw tightened. 'I thought that might get a reaction. If you want to meet James you have to agree to a condition.'

'Really? And what might that be?'

'There's no need for sarcasm.' Her tone was terse and imperious. 'The condition is this: You must never tell or even imply to James that you are his father.'

Jim's face registered his bewildered amusement.

'I want my son to inherit the Newman fortune. The father's name on his birth certificate is George Newman. If you say or do anything that challenges that, I will take the boy out of the country and you will never see him again.' Her voice lightened. 'But I will allow him to refer to you as Uncle Jim and you could visit him regularly. Whenever you like.'

'That's very good of you.'

'Thank you.' She ignored the sarcasm.

"And where is my … the boy now?'

'Ah, I have piqued your interest. Before I can tell you where James is I need your word that you will never divulge to him what we have discussed today.'

'You have my word,' Jim replied, more to hear what preposterous lie

Andréa might reveal next, than out of true interest.

'Our son is in boarding school in Middleton College, in County Cork. You can visit him any time you like. I'm taking a very long, much needed holiday and I won't be back until this time next year.'

'You're leaving your son in a boarding school for a full year? What about Christmas and summer holidays?'

'It won't be the first time the boy has spent holidays in the school. There are other boys there. The school has all the necessary permissions for doctors and so on. I'm going to tell James that I'm not well and that I'll be away chasing some treatment or other.'

He stood up, towering over her. 'I've had enough of this nonsense. You're a preposterous woman. I do not believe a word you've told me.' He settled his homburg on his head and added by way of farewell 'The day I met you was the sorriest day of my life.'

Some days later Líla was playing with her children and their nanny in the garden when Jim came out on to the patio.

'Hello Uncle Jim!' young Jamie called out and held up his toy dinosaur for his uncle to admire.

'Hello Jamie,' Jim said, taking the boy in his arms. 'What's your dinosaur's name?'

'Dinosaurs don't have names.'

'I see,' Jim replied and waved to his niece Chloé .

'Hello Uncle Jim,' Chloé called, and she waved as she raced up the garden.

'Jim, this is an unexpected pleasure,' his sister said. 'Come sit beside me.'

Jim remained standing. Líla read the look on her brother's face. 'Marie,' she called out to the nanny, 'keep the children entertained. Jim and I are going inside.'

'I met Andréa Newman the other day,' Jim said the moment he and his sister were seated in the drawing room. 'Remember her?'

'Good God. That's a surprise. What did you say to each other?'

'We exchanged … unpleasantries.'

'Don't be flip, Jim. It doesn't suit you.'

'She told me she has a son. She said that I'm the child's father.'

'Good God,' Líla sat upright. 'You're full of surprises, Jim. Do you believe her?'

'No.'

'What are you going to do?'

'I'm not going to do anything. It's not my child.'

'How can you be so sure?'

'It turns out that Andréa was married all the time we having our … affair.'

'Good God! I don't believe what I'm hearing.'

'Would you stop saying "Good God"? It's repetitive.'

'Sorry.'

'Andréa is the most manipulative person I have ever met. She's up to something – and before you ask, I don't know what it is she's up to.'

'Are you going to meet the boy?'

'Why should I? I've told you the child's not mine.'

Líla placed her hand on her brother's arm.

'If you really believed that, you wouldn't be here telling me about him. When are you going to visit the boy?'

Jim stood to leave. 'I have no interest in the child.

'You'll visit the boy and Andrea knows that too. Let me make some tea.'

Jim sat down.

54

Jim parked his car outside Middleton College. It was impressive; the main building was limestone, probably seventeenth century. He walked up the gravel path and knocked on the heavy oak door.

A gaunt uniformed maid answered the door. She led him through the high-ceilinged vestibule, ushered him to the door of an austere, wood-panelled room and said 'Please wait here. The headmaster will be with you in a few minutes.'

Too nervous to sit, Jim walked the room. He was still pacing when the Rev Michael Morris, a jolly man with red cheeks and enormous white moustache, bounded into the room.

'Mr Brevin,' he boomed. 'So good of you to come,' and he vigorously shook Jim's hand. 'Please, take a seat.'

The Reverend sat in a high-backed chair and opened the green file he had carried with him.

'I have the letter here from Mrs Newman,' the headmaster said as he stroked his moustache and re-read the letter. 'I am instructed to give you access to James Newman whenever you request it, with the sole proviso that James is agreeable to it.' The headmaster lifted up the letter to catch the light from the window. 'In a footnote Mrs

Newman refers to you as the child's uncle, yet in the body of the letter she says you are a family friend? Is that significant?'

'I am a family friend,' Jim replied. 'How is young James?'

'He's a fine, healthy lad. Miss O'Grady is fetching him now, he should be along presently.' Jim's heartbeat quickened. 'Is this your first visit to Middleton College?'

'It is.'

There was a knock on the door and the headmaster called out 'Come in.'

Jim took a deep breath. The door knob turned. Jim's hands began to sweat. The lock clicked and the door opened and a small boy wearing a blue blazer, white shirt, school tie, grey shorts, knee high socks and black shoes walked confidently into the room. Jim's mouth went dry and he almost gasped. He was looking at himself when he was nine years old.

'Master James, I'd like you to meet Mr Jim Brevin,' the Rev Michael Morris said.

'How do you do, sir?' the boy said and fully extended his right arm for a handshake.

Jim took the boy's soft hand and emotion erupted within him.

'I'm very well, James. And I'm very pleased to meet you.'

The boy smiled and his little cheeks creased into dimples.

'Why don't you show Mr Brevin around the school?' the Rev interjected. 'I think there's a cricket match in the south field?'

'Yes sir,' James replied and again flashed a dimpled smile.

There was a late-spring chill in the air and sun dodged in and out of the clouds as Jim and James strolled through the school's orchard on their way to the sports grounds.

'Do you play cricket?' Jim asked.

'Yes sir, I do, and rugby too. Did you play cricket when you were a boy, sir?'

'A little,' Jim replied with a smile.

Conversation flowed easily between father and son. James talked about school and about his two best friends, Ian and Roddy. When Jim told James he was an actor the boy looked into Jim's face and said 'I've been to the theatre, I liked it, but mummy said it was silly.'

As Jim watched the confident child walking along beside him, inexplicably he felt a great surge of protectiveness course through him.

Two of the cricket players were pulling the stumps out of the ground and the rest of the teams were strolling back to the school when Jim and James arrived at the cricket field.

'We've missed the match sir,' James said, as he waved to a wicket-keeper who was removing his face guard. 'Do you have children, sir?'

'No, I did once have a little boy, but he died. But that was a long time ago.'

'Do you still miss him?'

'Yes I do. I think about him and his mother every day.'

'I think about my father every day. He's dead too, sir.'

Jim and James fell quiet for a moment then James said 'Mummy said I should call you uncle.'

'Yes, if you wish, you can call me uncle.'

'What do uncles do?'

'Well, that's something we'll have to discover together.'

'I nearly had an uncle.'

'What do you mean?'

'Before I was born, mummy's brother Harry was killed in an accident. So I nearly had an uncle.'

'Well, now you really do have an uncle. If you want one, that is?'

'Yes. I'd like to have an uncle,' James said, and the honesty and openness in the boy's eyes won Jim's heart.

'I want to hear everything,' Líla said, as she ushered her brother to the drawing room sofa. 'What's he like?'

'What's who like?'

'Don't tease me!' she cried, her eyes wide with interest and excitement.

'I never thought I'd say this …' Jim grew serious. 'He's my son. I couldn't deny him, there's such a family resemblance.'

'Good God, Jim! You have a child.'

'I have,' Jim replied and smiled in a way he hadn't smiled since Maebh's death.

'You like him?'

THE ACTOR

'I like him. I'd never thought I could feel this way again about another human being. I think I'll go and see him again next week.'

'Jim, don't rush this. Take things slowly. Let him discover you. He needs time and so do you.'

Jim took Líla's advice and decided on a twice-monthly visit to Middleton College. On each visit he learned a little more about his son and James learned a little more about the man he called Uncle Jim. On the days they spent together, Jim usually took James to visit some nearby place of interest or to a sports event. James was a happy child, but on Jim's fourth visit, he was unusually quiet and responded to Jim's questions with one-word answers or a shake of his head.

'I don't want to go to the rugby match,' James said when he sat in Jim's car.

'Very, well. What would you like to do?'

'I'd like to go home to Youghal.'

'You know your mother's not there and the house is closed?'

'I know, but Darcy the gamekeeper will be there. I'd just want to see my room.'

During the sixteen miles to Youghal, James remained silent. He was still scowling when Jim pushed open the gates of the Newman estate and it was only when the boy caught a glimpse of the grey house he called home that his mood changed. It was as if the house energised him and lifted his spirits. Jim stopped the car close to the front entrance.

'Hello there, Master James!' the shotgun-carrying gamekeeper called out as he strolled across the front garden.

'Hello Mr Darcy!' James cried as he ran to the bearded man and embraced him. 'Can you let us into the house, please?' Darcy looked at Jim quizzically. 'This is my Uncle Jim.'

'We've met before, haven't we sir?'

Jim nodded, briefly.

'I have instructions not to let anyone into the property, but seeing as you're the master of the house …' The gamekeeper smiled at James. 'I have to take my orders from you, don't I?' He pulled a ring of keys from under his coat, placed a key in the lock, turned it and pushed open the door. 'Let me know when you're going. I'll need to lock up the house again.'

'Thank you Mr Darcy,' James said. 'Come on Uncle Jim and I'll show you my room.'

The entrance hall of Newman House was dark and quiet. The hall's furniture, fittings and paintings were draped in dust sheets like floating ghosts.

'This way,' James said.

He took Jim's hand and pulled him across the hall. With their clattering footsteps echoing off the barrel-vaulted ceiling, James took Jim through an arch and up a carpeted cantilevered staircase. On the half-landing Jim released a catch on the wooden shutter that shielded a bay window, and folded it back. Shafts of sunlight beamed into the stairwell illuminating the motes of dust that floated aimlessly in the air.

'That's better,' Jim said.

'This way Uncle Jim,' James called out tugging on Jim's hand.

On the first landing, James let go of Jim's hand, ran down the wood-panelled corridor and disappeared into a room. When Jim followed James into his bedroom the boy was sitting on his bed looking at a framed picture of his mother.

'I want to take this picture back to school with me,' James said without taking his eyes off the photograph.

'If that's what you want to do, that's what we'll do,' Jim said as he opened the shutters on the bedroom. 'You miss your mother, don't you?'

The boy's face darkened, his eyes welled up and he started to sob.

Jim sat down on the bed beside him. 'Why, what's the matter?'

The child pulled a folded letter from the top pocket of his blazer and held it out; he put his hand on Jim's arm, almost as if he was demanding an explanation. 'Mummy's not coming home for a long time. She said she won't be home this summer.' Tears gathered in the child's eyes and his small fingers gripped Jim's sleeve. Jim slowly freed his arm and draped it around his son's shoulders. The child wept, and Jim rocked him gently as he sobbed.

After a while, he offered 'You could come and stay with me for the summer, if you like.'

'I don't want to go with you.' James shook off Jim's arm. 'I want my mummy.'

'Of course you do.'

When James seemed a little more composed, Jim said 'Why don't you show me your toys?'

Eyelashes still wet from crying, James slipped off the bed and opened a large leather trunk under the window. 'I'll show you my favourites.' He leaned so far into the trunk that he nearly tumbled into it, and pulled out a wooden box of painted lead soldiers. 'I have tanks and trees and jeeps too,' James said and handed Jim the box. 'I have lots of other toys too.' He again almost disappeared into the trunk. 'Look,' he said and held up two board games. 'I have model airplanes and I have a cricket bat and ball.'

Half an hour later, as Jim went to close the shutters on the windows in James' bedroom he said 'You have spent summer holidays in school in the past, haven't you?'

'No, I haven't,' the boy replied, appalled at the suggestion. 'I always spend holidays with mummy.'

'Oh, I thought otherwise,' Jim replied. 'I know it's not the same as being with your mother, but I would like you to think about spending the summer with me. I have a brother and sister and they have children your age and as you call me uncle you could call them cousins. My brother's boy Robert plays cricket, you could play with him.'

James held the framed photograph of his mother against his chest. 'Will you take me back to school now?'

On his next visit to Middleton College, James informed Jim that he would like to spend his summer in Dublin.

The arrival of James in Dublin was as exciting for Jim as it was for his son. Jim fitted out a bedroom for his young guest. He placed a train set in one corner and a bookcase filled with classic boy's books in another. Opposite the window, he positioned a bed and a dressing table on which he placed a model airplane kit, a small bottle of liquid glue and a photograph of Andréa.

When James saw the photograph of his mother, he picked it up.

'I've never seen this photograph of mummy, is it new?'

'No,' Jim replied. 'It's from a long time ago.'

'You knew my mummy a long time ago?'

'I did,' Jim replied softly. 'She's a nice lady.'

THE ACTOR

The doorbell rang and Jim was glad of the interruption.

Michael and his ten-year-old son Robert strolled into the drawing room. James was impressed by his new older cousin and, that afternoon, all four went to the Phoenix Park and watched a cricket match. After the match, the foursome visited Líla's home and from the moment James met Chloé they were instant friends. The following day, when Chloé and Líla visited Jim's home, James showed Chloé his room and when he showed her the photograph of his mother, Chloé said she thought she looked like a beautiful princess.

In a cricket match the following day, Michael's son Robert was sub, and because a few boys didn't show up they asked James to play to help make up the team. Within weeks James was a regular on the team. Jim took the two boys and Chloé to the theatre, to the concert hall, to museums and to all sorts of events. James greatly enjoyed the summer, but the time he enjoyed the most was when he and Jim talked about his mother.

When it came time for James to return to Middleton, he didn't want to leave his new cousins or his new room.

That November, the Middleton College head, the Rev Morris, phoned Jim to tell him that James had become unsettled. He had gotten into fights, and in one he had broken the nose of another boy. Jim drove immediately to the school.

'This sort of behaviour is most unacceptable,' the Rev Michael Morris said as they walked into the infirmary. 'However, as it turns out, the other's boy's nose is not broken, so there is no lasting damage.' Then dropping his voice to a whisper, he added 'I don't understand it. James is usually such a mild-mannered child. I'll leave it with you. But please impress on him that this sort of behaviour is not acceptable.'

'What happened, James?' Jim asked after an awkward silence.

'I got a letter from mummy,' he said sullenly. 'She said she won't be coming home for Christmas. She says she's really sick. She will get better, won't she Uncle Jim?'

'I'm sure she will,' he replied. But silently he cursed Andréa for her lies. Perhaps you'd think about spending Christmas with me. I get lonely

at Christmas and it would be nice to share it with someone.'
'Will I be able to see Chloé and Robert?'
Jim nodded and half-smiled.
'Ok, Uncle Jim. I'll spend Christmas with you.'

On James' first night in the Dublin, Jim brought him to the pantomime in the Queen's Theatre and the boy loved it. The next day, Líla and her children stopped by and James and Chloé talked and talked and played happily together with young Jamie. On Christmas Eve, Jim took all the children to the zoo, and later they went to the carol service in church. Sitting in the church alongside his son listening to the carols, Jim was at peace with himself and his world. Christmas Day was spent in Líla and Ciaran's home and sitting around the table were James's new extended family of Theo, Michael and Clara and their son Robert, Líla, Ciaran, Chloé, Jamie and Jim.

'This is the best Christmas ever,' James said as he skipped happily along the path on his way home that night. 'If mummy was here, it would be perfect.'

55

Every day at noon, the Middleton College boarders would stand in rows in front of the stage in the school hall and the bookish Miss Scally, the history teacher, would call out the name of a boy who had received post or even better, a parcel. The boy would come forward and the Rev Michael Morris would present the boy with his letter or package. On the first Tuesday in March, James's name was called. He jumped out of his row, raced past the other boys and up the steps of the stage.

'There's no need to run,' the quiet-spoken Miss Scally said seconds before the Rev Michael Morris handed James his letter.

Ten minutes later, sitting on his bed, James opened the letter. When he had finished reading the familiar scrawny handwriting, his face broke out in a bright smile. Jim too had received a letter with the same scrawny handwriting, but he did not smile.

'Mummy will be home next week,' James announced excitedly to Jim the following Saturday when he arrived at Middleton College.

'Yes, I heard. I'm sure you're delighted.'

'Oh yes I am,' James replied as he hopped and tripped through the college grounds, completely unaware of the apprehension that his Uncle Jim was feeling.

Jim drove his four-cylinder Rover Ten through the gates of the Newman estate and as he journeyed through the woodland, the butterflies in his stomach fluttered like new leaves in a breeze. The grey house loomed into view and with a crunch the car came to a stop on the pebbled driveway. He took a moment to compose himself then walked to the front door and pulled on the bell.

'Jim Brevin to see Andréa Newman,' Jim said to the maid at the door.

The maid stepped back and Jim walked through the portico and into a much changed entrance hall. Bright, airy sunlight streamed into the vestibule. The walls were freshly painted, the furniture was polished and the austere uncovered portraits of the Newman family ancestors looked unsmilingly down from their heavy frames.

'Follow me sir,' the maid said as she walked across the hall and turned down a corridor. With a glance at Jim, the maid stopped, took a deep breath and opened the door to the morning room. The rush of hot, fetid air that blasted into Jim's face made him almost gag. The arid air stank of disinfectant, medicine and stale perspiration. Jim entered the sweltering room. Two enormous log fires, one north and one south of the room, pumped even more hot air into an already sweltering room. Sitting on a gilt couch with her back to Jim was a grey-haired older woman. Jim was about to remind the maid that he was here to see Andréa Newman, when the woman said 'Good morning Jim.'

'Good morning,' Jim said as he walked past a small table filled with an array small brown and blue bottles. When he rounded the corner of the couch he saw that the woman was Andréa. He stopped and couldn't speak. Andréa's skin was almost translucent, her eyes were sunken, her lips were purple and she was skin and bone.

'Thanks Colleen, put a few more logs on the fire,' Andréa said with a slight gesture of her hand. Jim swallowed hard. 'It's rude to stare.'

'Sorry,' Jim said, finding his voice. 'You're unwell?'

Andréa waited for the maid to leave.

'You have made a great impression on our son. I knew you would like him. Take a seat.' James sat opposite Andréa but as far from the fire as he could. She said 'I apologise for the heat. This meeting will be short.'

'As you wish,' Jim replied. 'Andréa you look unwell.'
'That's not your business.'
'What then is my business?'
'James is your business.'

His body and mind tensed. 'I'm not here to play games Andréa. So if you'd just say what you have to say I'll be off.'

'I'm not playing games.' Her voice was frail but firm.

'Then what are you doing?'

Andréa remained silent.

'Very well, you refuse to answer my inquiries after your health. Last time we met you lied to me and misled me. James never spent a holiday in the Middleton College, although you said he did. You also said you had little interest in him, yet apparently you welcomed him home every weekend and every night he spent in Newman House, you put him to bed you told him you loved him. You said he was tiresome, yet James told me you visited him regularly in school. Then you did the unforgivable. You deserted him. How could you do that? He's your child and he loves everything about you.'

Andréa removed a linen handkerchief from a small mother of pearl handbag on her lap and gently patted her damp forehead.

'I love my son, more than I have loved anyone in the world.' Andréa's voice was so frail, Jim had to lean forward to hear her. 'I lied to you because I thought you wouldn't believe me if I told you the truth. I knew if you thought I was a bad mother you'd be particularly drawn to the boy. And the reason I spent a precious year away from my beautiful James is that I was searching for a cure for my cancer. As you can see I've been unsuccessful. The doctors have told me I have only a few months left.'

Jim stared into Andréa's emaciated face. 'I'm sorry ...'

Andréa stopped him with a scowl. 'I brought you into James' life because neither my husband nor I have any living relatives. I want my son to be loved, to be cared for.' Andréa took a shallow breath, her concentration faltered and Jim glimpsed her terror. 'You will look after James, won't you?'

'I will,' he replied unhesitatingly.

'Thank you. I will make you his legal guardian. You'll be his father in everything but name."

'No, I want James to be known as my son.'

Andréa inhaled deeply, straightened her back and gathering all her strength said 'You gave me your word. You promised me he would always keep the Newman name.'

'That was before …'

'You gave me your word. I have set up a trust fund for James's and when he reaches twenty one he will inherit the house, the estate and the Newman family fortune. Until then you will be his guardian and the executor of the trust fund.' She coughed and her frail body shuddered.

Jim looked at the shrunken, sickly woman sitting in front of him and could not reconcile her with the healthy vivacious, young woman he met ten years earlier. 'I will be there for my son and I will abide by my word,' he said, when Andréa's eyes focused on him.

'Thank you.' Her face creased into a tired smile. 'One last thing. I would like you to consider living in Newman House. It's James' home and he was always happy here.'

'That's something I'd have to think about.'

Andréa inclined her head as if to say, as you wish. Her eyelids closed, her mouth twitched and she dropped her head to hide the convulsing of her jaws.

'I need to rest. Think about living here and try not to fill James's head with too much theatre nonsense.'

Jim stood and buttoned his jacket. 'Andréa, did you ever feel anything for me?'

She did not reply but turned her head and looked out on to the terrace garden. When Jim leaned down to her to kiss her goodbye, she raised her hand and, looking straight through him, said 'I don't want your pity.'

'It isn't pity, Andréa. I loved you once. And for the briefest time, I thought you were returning my love. Goodbye.' As he closed the door behind him, she quietly echoed his farewell and tears welled in her eyes.

Líla and Jim sat quietly in the conservatory of his home and watched the stars flicker and shimmer in the night sky.

Jim broke the easy silence between them. 'Andréa has suggested I live in Newman House after … She said the familiar surroundings of the house would be a comfort to James.'

'She has a point. But what about you? If you go and live in Youghal, what will happen to your career?'

'Theatre was always the most important thing in my life,' Jim said without taking his eyes from the stars. 'But when I look back on my life, the only thing I regret is that I didn't spend more time with Maebh. I've already lost nine years of James's life. I can't get that time back but I can have the next ten years and if giving up theatre is the price I have to pay, then so be it.'

Líla did not respond. She knew Jim had thought long and hard about his decision, she knew he was sacrificing his dream for his son, and she was proud of him for doing it.

56

When Andréa died, James was devastated. The funeral was horrendously difficult for him and the weeks that followed were even worse. To help his grieving son, Jim took up residence in Newman House.

A month after his mother's death, James returned to Middleton College. His friends Ian and Roger were delighted to see him and their company was good for him. The school routine gave structure to James's days and, in time, he began to enjoy his school and his school friends again. He resumed playing cricket and learned that he was good at track and field sports. Jim attended all the school sports events and welcomed James's friends to Newman House. In the months following, James became ever closer to the extended Brevin family. He enjoyed his visits, particularly the days he spent with Chloe and Jim's father Theo. James often spoke of Andréa and Jim always spoke well of her.

Jim's weekdays were spent in Dublin working with Brevin and Sons and Red's Steak Houses, but each weekend he returned to Youghal to be with his son. He refused all offers of theatre work and, after a time, the offers stopped coming.

The years passed and Jim nursed James through measles, mumps, a broken leg, a dislocated shoulder and colds without number. Father and son regularly attended music recitals, exhibitions and sports events. In time, James came to love his new life. Jim too was happy but every time he attended the theatre he envied the actors.

In the spring of 1950 Jim was surprised to receive a phone call from Tony Tanner, the onetime stage manager of the long defunct Actors' Repertory Company. When Tony suggested they meet for coffee in the Shelbourne Hotel, Jim readily agreed. The moment Jim walked through the hotel's revolving doors, an excited Tony ushered him to a quiet corner of the hotel's lounge.

'You're late,' said the overweight Tony as he wiped his brow with a handkerchief. 'I was beginning to think you weren't coming.'

'Sorry, a meeting ran on. If you're pushed for time, we can have our coffee another time.'

'Another time? This is not a social call, Jim.' A waiter padded up to the table but Tony dismissed him with an impatient flick of his hand. 'I couldn't tell you on the phone but you are about to be offered the role of your career.'

'Tony, I'm not available for theatrical work.'

'What?' Tanner's eyes bulged with incredulity. 'Don't be ridiculous, I never heard the likes.' Tony shook his head and blew his nose into his damp handkerchief. 'Jim, let me fill you in on the situation and then you can make your decision. An American motion picture producer contacted me specifically to locate you and to arrange a meeting. He has you in mind for a major role in his film.'

Jim cast a wary eye at his one-time stage manager

'The film's producer is Mr Paul Kavanagh,' Tony added. 'He said he knows you.'

Jim thought a moment. 'I don't know anyone of that name?'

'Well he knows you, he speaks very highly of you, and he wants to see you.'

'This is all very odd.'

'It might be odd to you but it's very real to me.' Tony glanced at his watch and sighed. 'Look at the time. We better go. Mr Kavanagh doesn't like to be kept waiting. He's a bit of an odd fish like that.'

'He's not the only one,' Jim replied but Tony was already halfway to the lift.

THE ACTOR

When the elevator stopped on the second floor, Tony swept open the concertinaed door, marched briskly to the O'Carolan suite, and knocked.

'Come in,' a harsh American voice called out.

With a great flourish Tony opened the door and said 'Mr Kavanagh, Mr Jim Brevin.'

Jim entered the suite, Tony remained at the door, swung his left foot backwards and closed the door before him.

'Jim Brevin, by God it's good to see you again,' said a dapperly dressed, slender older man. Smiling broadly, he hobbled across the suite, leaning on the silver handle of his walking stick. 'How have you been, Jim?'

'I'm, er, well, thank you,' Jim replied, taken aback by the earnestness and sincerity in the man's voice.

After shaking hands, the man leaned on his walking stick, caressed his pencil-thin moustache and said 'By God, you do look well.'

'Thank you,' Jim replied, embarrassed by the openness in the man's eyes. 'Should we sit?'

'Yes, we should,' the man replied. 'Where would you like to sit?'

'Perhaps by the window?'

'Excellent choice, by the window, how very appropriate. I should have thought of that,' the man said and clapped him on the back.

Jim sat and the man took the chair opposite him.

'Mr Kavanagh ...'

'Call me Paul, please.'

'Paul, I think ... you may have mistaken me for someone else?'

Kavanagh slapped his knee and released a hearty laugh.

'So, that explains your odd behaviour. You don't remember me?' Kavanagh rested his chin on the silver handle of his cane. 'Well! I'll be damned.'

'To tell you the truth, I have no idea who you are, Mr Kavanagh.'

'Let me see if I can jog your memory.' Kavanagh rapped on the window with his cane. 'Out there in Stephen's Green, Easter 1916, I was shot in the ankle and you carried me across the street to the College of Surgeons and what's more, the following day you drove me to a doctor in Wicklow.'

'Ah yes! Of course, I remember. So that's who you are! I took you and another man to Roundwood. What happened to the other man?'

'Sadly he didn't make it.' Kavanagh fell quiet and looked out the window.

After a while, Jim asked quietly, 'And you went to America?'

'I had to go. I was a wanted man.'

'And you went into the film business?'

'Yes, among other things. Let's talk business and get it out of the way. I'm one of the producers of a movie that we're going to make in Ireland. I remembered that you said you were an actor, so I made a few inquiries about you. Word came back that you're pretty good. So I put your name down for a substantial role.'

'Mr Kavanagh, I'm afraid I haven't acted in years.'

'Is that so?' Kavanagh frowned and again rested his chin on the handle of his walking stick. 'I don't mean to pry, but why did you give up acting? I wouldn't have thought of you as a quitter.'

'I have responsibilities that require that I have my weekends for myself. However in a few years' time I'll be in a position to return to the stage.'

'So, you need to have your weekends free?' Kavanagh paused, considered, and then nodded to himself. 'How about if we shoot your scenes during the week?'

'You can do that?' And for the first time in years Jim's mind was fired with the excitement of performance.

'Certainly, I can do that. I'm one of the producers aren't I? We never shoot on a Sunday and I can make sure that you're not scheduled for any Saturday work.'

'I don't know what to say!' His heart pounded so fast, he thought it might jump out of his chest.

'Well, for a start, you could say you'll do it,' Kavanagh replied.

'Oh, I'll do it. Thank you so very much. When will you be holding auditions?'

'Jim, you don't have to audition. The role is yours.'

Jim's eyes glistened, and he was speechless.

'Enough about the movie. There's something else I want to talk about. That day, back in Stephen's Green. There was a uniformed soldier that gave cover as you helped me across the road. I think you called him Red. You wouldn't know what happened to him?'

With his head still buzzing with excitement Jim just about heard Kavanagh's question.

'Yes, I do. He's still called Red and he's a very good friend of mine.'

'I'd like to meet him and personally thank him for what he did that day. Do you think you could arrange that?'

Delighted to be in a position to reciprocate so quickly, Jim stood and said 'Mr Kavanagh … Paul, let's go, you have a man to meet right now.'

The following day, a large black limousine stopped outside Jim's house. A liveried chauffeur stepped out of the car, opened the rear passenger door and removed a white package. When Jim answered the door the chauffeur handed him the package and asked him to sign a receipt for it.

Jim sat in his study and placed the package on his desk. He carefully opened it and read the handwritten note that was attached to the front of the film script.

Dear Jim,
Your role is the character called Mick Melvin. I know you will be excellent in the part and I hope it will hasten your return to the stage. I will always be in your debt.
Yours sincerely
Paul Kavanagh.

Jim opened the manuscript and when he saw his name in the cast list he felt a surge of excitement. A minute later he was lost in the screenplay. Two hours later, when he had finished reading, he was in shock. It was more than "a substantial role", it was the second lead. His character appeared throughout the film and he was going to share many scenes with the best of British and Irish actors and ten scenes with the great Hollywood legend, James Cagney, in the film *Shake Hands with the Devil*.

Six weeks later, when Jim arrived at Ardmore Studios, Bray, he was met by Tony Byrne, a long-haired first assistant director, who walked him to Sound Stage One. In the middle of the huge, empty, sound stage was a long table around which sat the actors Dana Wynter, Glynis Johns, Sybil Thorndike, Michael Redgrave, Richard Harris, Noel Purcell, Cyril Cusack, Harry Brogan and Christopher Cassin. The assistant director introduced Jim to each actor and, amid a hail of hellos, Jim took the vacant seat at the end of the table.

Two minutes later the studio door flew open and the sharply-dressed, charismatic, five-foot six-inch James Cagney and a much taller man breezed into the room. With a quick smile for everyone, James Cagney walked around the table and shook everyone's hand. When the film actor took his seat at the table, the tall man stood and said 'My name is Michael Anderson, I'm the director of the motion picture we are about to make. But before we begin, Mr Cagney would like to say a few words.'

'Hello everybody,' James Cagney said, leaning his forearms on the table. 'All I want to say for now is this. I'm not here to make another *Quiet Man* movie. That was a great movie, but not the kind of movie I make. I believe in this script, it's a good script with a serious message that violence inevitably leads to more violence. Now I've said my piece and as we song and dance men say, let the singing and dancing begin.'

After the script read-through, Jim was outside the studio stretching his legs and trying to calm his excitement when James Cagney walked up to him and said 'Hello, Jim Brevin isn't it?'

Jim nodded and James Cagney lowered his voice. 'My good friend Paul Kavanagh told me you're the man to talk to, to get inside information about the IRA.'

'Mr Cagney, I can assure you my involvement with the IRA was purely accidental.'

'That's not what Paul Kavanagh told me. He said you saved his life carrying him across a street under fire. And stop calling me Mr Cagney. My friends call me Jimmy.'

'Mr Cagney, Jimmy, I was never a member of the IRA. However I do know a man who was.'

'I'd like to meet this man. Can you set up a meeting?'

'I can, but there is a condition.'

THE ACTOR

James Cagney took a step back, looked Jim straight in the eyes and said 'Go on, what's the condition?'

'Mr Cagney, I'm a stage actor. I'd like your help with my screen acting.'

'I like your style, Jim,' Cagney replied. 'Screen acting is simple. All you have to do is hit your mark, look the other fella in the eye and mean everything you say.'

'I think there's a little more to it than that, Jimmy?'

'Ok, how about this?' Cagney said with a wink. 'I'll watch out for your screen acting if you'll watch out for my screen accent.'

'Now that sounds like a good deal to me,' Jim said and both men laughed.

Inside the snug of Doyle's Pub on Phibsboro Road, a quiet Red watched the heavy rain wash down the outside of the frosted glass window. He lit a cigarette. Suddenly the snug door burst open and a very wet Jim and James Cagney clattered into the snug.

Shaking the rain off Jim introduced the two men.

'I've been looking forward to meeting you,' James Cagney said. 'Thank you for coming along.'

Red stared at the man he had seen on the giant screen of the Savoy Cinema two nights previously.

Jim asked, 'What are you drinking Red?'

'I'll have a pint please.'

'I'll have a pint too,' Cagney replied.

'I'll get the drinks,' Jim said and knocked on the snug's service hatch.

'Everybody thinks I'm a tough guy,' Cagney said unravelling the scarf from around his neck. 'But they'd sure change their minds if they knew that my first job in the business was as a chorus line dancer in a vaudeville show.' Cagney slapped his knee. 'I guess we all have to start somewhere, ain't that so Red?'

By the time the drinks arrived, Red and James Cagney were deep in conversation about American football.

'It's not a football game at all. It's a game of stops and starts,' Red said with a dismissive wave of his hand.

'I love this guy,' Cagney said. 'Red, Jim, I bet you didn't know that my father was Irish? He used to say to me, go to Ireland, it's a beautiful land, full of good-looking men and women.'

'You know what, Mr Cagney?' Red said raising his glass. 'You didn't kiss the Blarney Stone, you swallowed it.'

Conversation between the three men flowed easily and fluidly. But when the famous actor asked questions about the IRA, Red's face darkened and he gave short answers to the actor's questions.

'Red, I'm not trying to pry sensitive information out of you,' Cagney said softly. 'What I'm trying to do is get some understanding of how people deal with violence when it becomes a constant thing in their life.'

Red's face closed like a clenched fist; he sat back in his seat and in a calm, pain-filled voice said 'I've spent most of my life trying not to think about the things you want me to talk about. I don't have answers for you. I was a soldier. I did what I was ordered to do. I'm not ashamed of anything I did, but I'm not proud of it either.' Red's eyes focused on the snug's stained table. 'I know this much, violence releases a monster inside you and that monster never leaves you, ever. You try to control it, and you do, but sometimes, it slips its leash and, well, it shames you, and that shame never leaves you either.'

The three men sat in pensive silence.

Red felt relieved that he had finally spoken of his pain.

Jim felt sad that he had not realised what his friend had to live with and James Cagney knew he had just been given the key to portraying Sean Lenihan in *Shake Hands with the Devil*.

57

The early morning sun glinted on the sea, as Jim and his son walked along the beach at Rush, Co Dublin. A light breeze blew a small cloud of sand along the surface of the strand and around the feet of the film crew as they set up for the first shot of the day.

'When Ian and Roger heard I was going to meet James Cagney they were really jealous,' a smiling James said as Jim steered him towards the row of caravans near the base of the sand dunes.

'You could have brought them along.'

'No, I wanted to meet him on my own.'

'You dirty rat,' Jim said, doing his best Cagney impersonation.

Tony Byrne, the assistant director, waved to Jim and placed his index finger to his lips.

'They're about to shoot a scene,' Jim whispered. 'We'd better be quiet.'

'Roll camera,' shouted Tony; the crew fell quiet and gathered around the stands of the huge outdoor film lights. The boom operator held the microphone high in the air and ten seconds later the director called 'Action!'

James Cagney, looking upset, appeared over the top of a sand dunes and marched briskly towards the camera. Then an angry Don Murray ran after Cagney, grabbed him by the shoulder, spun him around and spoke angrily to him. When they had done the scene three times, the director called 'Got it, take three's a keeper, print it. Thanks James and Don. Why don't you get a cup of coffee and Tony will come and get you when we're ready to shoot the close-ups.'

James was engrossed in watching the assistant camera operator reloading the film camera when James Cagney tapped him on the shoulder.

'Hello, do you know you have a great first name?'

Dumbstruck, young James stared at the famous actor.

'Hello Mr Cagney, nice work,' Jim said, putting his arm around his son's shoulders.

'Hi Jim, how about some breakfast?' Cagney smiled.

Standing by the catering trailer, Jim and the two James ate hot crispy bacon rolls and drank steaming hot coffee. Young James found his voice and in minutes, he and the film star were deep in conversation about gangsters and gangster films.

'Mr Cagney we're ready for you now,' the assistant director said interrupting the conversation.

'Thanks, Tony. James, would you like to be in the movie?'

'Yes sir, I would,' James beamed. 'Uncle Jim, is that all right?'

'Of course it's all right.'

'Tony, can you find a place for this young fellow in the crowd scene this afternoon?'

'Certainly, consider it done,' Tony replied.

'Great!' Then, turning to Jim, the film star said 'We'll have lunch in my trailer. I need some help with the pronunciation of a few words.'

Half an hour later, the assistant director took James to the costume tent where Miss Karen Keeley, wardrobe mistress, a waif-like creature who the cast and crew called Miss Pin, dressed James in frayed short trousers, a threadbare jacket and a tattered cap.

'You haven't given me any shoes,' James said when the wardrobe mistress told him she had finished dressing him.

'Your character is poor, he wouldn't have shoes. You can wear your own shoes until you're called to the set, then make sure you take them off and put some dirt on your feet.'

THE ACTOR

James was enthralled with the film-making process and how the actors and the crew went about their work. He watched how the lighting director liaised with the camera operator, how the camera operator worked closely with the director. He watched the assistant director's work with the crew and props people. He watched the grips prepare the set and the sound engineer and the boom operator test the sound equipment and plan the placement of the boom. Just before each shot he observed how the director and the actors talked and planned every action and gesture. Then in a blast of energy, he watched the director blend the skill, craft and talents of the cast and crew into a seamless filmed sequence.

At the end of the day as everyone was packing up to leave, James Cagney handed young James a large envelope.

'There are three signed photographs in there. One is for you and the other two are for your friends Ian and Roger. Tell them I said hello.'

James stared at the envelope and his face broke into a huge smile.

'Kid! Make sure you get paid for your work today and, I got to tell you, your uncle here is one hell of an actor.' James Cagney shook young James's hand and a very happy and proud father and son went home.

The following day they filmed the first of Jim's big scenes with James Cagney. In the scene, Jim's character realises that Cagney's character is not a patriot, but a violent brute who is out of control. After the first take, Jim asked Cagney to comment on his acting.

'What you are doing is good, but it's too much,' Jim Cagney replied. 'Your reactions are telling the audience how to react. That's not a good idea; you got to let the audience figure things out for themselves, let them do a little of the work. Just think your character's thoughts and then trust your eyes. This is your close up, the only thing the audience is seeing is your face. Let them figure out what your character's thinking, don't tell them, just give them a hint. The director will tell you if you're doing too little.'

Nine months after filming had finished, Jim received an urgent phone call from a breathless Tony Tanner.

'Jim it's huge, the critics are saying it's Cagney's best performance in years. And Jim, they're talking about your performance too. They're saying you're a great find and they want you to go to New York for the East Coast premiere of the film.'

'Are you talking about *Shake Hands with the Devil?*' Jim said down the 'phone.

'Of course that's what I'm talking about. How many films have you made? I've already had four enquiries about your availability. The premiere is on the 26th in New York, that's three weeks from now. Leave everything to me, I'll organise flights, hotels everything. Jim! You're on your way to Hollywood.'

Two days before Jim was to leave for New York, James, Ian and Roger and four other students from the Middleton College Walking Group stepped off a bus in Adrigole Harbour, West Cork. After tea and biscuits the noisy group of boys and a teacher set off up the Hungry Hill Mountains. On a precipice, near the top of the mountain, the group took a break before tackling the steepest part of the climb. As they rested James decided to take a picture with his new box camera. He asked his friends Ian and Roger to pose in front of the great waterfall. To get a better shot James took a step backwards, stepped on a loose rock, lost his footing and careered head over heels down the mountainside. Ian and Roger watched in horror as their friend rolled over rocks, crashed into trees and came to a halt when he smashed into a giant jagged boulder.

The ringing telephone tore through the silence of Newman House.

'Mr Brevin, James has had an accident,' Rev Michael Chimmery said when Jim answered the phone. 'He's in St Joseph's Ward in Middleton Hospital. Come quickly.'

'How is he?' Jim said to the school principal the moment he arrived at the hospital.

'Mr Brevin I must apologise for this unfortunate accident. I can assure you that a teacher was with the boy and promptly took the appropriate actions.'

'How is he?' Jim repeated his question; his eyes bored into the school principal's face.

'Sorry, James is serious but stable.'

'What does that mean?'

THE ACTOR

'It means – I don't really know, but Dr Joe Brennan will be with us shortly and he will explain everything.'

'James had a very nasty fall,' the bearded Dr Brennan said when he talked to Jim on leaving the operating theatre. 'His right arm and left leg were broken. We've set them. He had many cuts and bruises which we've dressed and he had a deep gash in his back that needed twenty sutures. He is breathing well – but he has a head injury and he's in a coma.'

Jim felt physically sick.

'Later today we will transfer James to the Mercy Hospital in Cork.'

'How serious is the head injury?'

'I know no more than I've told you,' the doctor said and stroked his beard. 'You'll have to wait for a report from the specialists in head trauma in The Mercy.'

Twelve long hours after being admitted to the Mercy Hospital in Cork, a severe-looking Dr Shields looked at Jim over the thin-rimmed spectacles that were perched halfway down his narrow nose and said 'Mr Brevin, most head injuries are benign and require no treatment beyond pain killers and close monitoring. However, a coma does complicate matters. If a patient remains in a coma for more than forty eight hours it becomes a cause of concern.'

'James is going to be all right?' Jim asked, his eyes pleading for a positive response.

'I cannot say that. We'll have to wait and see.'

Ten hours later a very groggy James opened his eyes on to a blurred world. He saw fuzzy white figures moving around his bed.

'Hello James, you've had a nasty fall,' Jim said softly to his confused son.

James turned his head and when he saw the shadowy image of a man sitting at his bedside, he groaned. 'Who are you? I don't know you. Where's my mother? I want my mother.'

'The news is good,' Dr Shields said after he examined James. 'It doesn't appear that there is permanent brain damage.'

'But he doesn't know who I am – he has lost his memory!'

'Amnesia is not unusual in cases like this,' the doctor said. 'It is most likely temporary. But James will probably experience memory problems from time to time. He may also experience occasional dizziness and much tiredness. He will need convalescing and physiotherapy, but he's young and he should make a full recovery.'

'What are you going to do about the trip to New York?' Líla asked Jim as she sipped coffee in the hospital canteen.

'I'm going to be here for my son,' Jim replied and later that day he called Tony Tanner and told him he wasn't going to New York.

Gradually James regained his memory, learned to walk again and with a lot of physiotherapy he resumed his track and field activities. In the weeks and months that it took James to recover, Jim turned down four offers of film work in the US and the UK.

The years passed and when it came time for James to go to university, he chose to read Art History in St John's College, Cambridge. Three days after James left for Cambridge, Jim began rehearsals for Arthur Miller's play *The Crucible* at the Gate Theatre. This was followed by a play at the Gaiety Theatre and another in the Opera House, Cork.

On the 23 September 1955, the last day of Jim's fifty seven years of life, he rose early. He was sitting at the breakfast table and reading a letter from James, recounting a night he spent in the Eagle public house, Cambridge, when he experienced a mild discomfort in the centre of the chest. The discomfort lasted less than ten seconds and when it had passed, Jim thought no more of it. Later, in his office at Brevin and Sons, he experienced an uncomfortable pressure in his chest. But it too passed. After a cup of tea, Jim felt his old self again. He had an early evening meal in the Central Hotel and made his way to the Olympia Theatre, where he was playing the role of the narrator in Thornton Wilder's *Our Town*. The show went well and as Jim took the curtain call he experienced mild shooting pains in his left arm. On his way to his dressing room he exercised his arm and the sensation left him. Then, as he was removing his make-up, Jim felt very hot and began to sweat profusely. He reached for a tissue, the room swirled around him and he crashed to the floor.

Looking up at the ceiling of his dressing room in the final seconds of his life, Jim saw three images. He saw his mother smiling at him and he smiled back at her. Then, in a river of light, he saw Ira Allen and himself in the final scene from *Fr Murphy*. Then he saw Maebh move through a mist. He saw her beautiful smile and her gleaming eyes. She had baby Theo in her arms. He reached out to take the baby and the world faded to black.

Epilogue

When the young man in the leather hat and coat was halfway down the church aisle, the organist began playing music arranged from Dvorak's 9th Symphony. Suddenly there was a clambering and a shuffling, Red clambered out of a pew and embraced the young man.

'He was a great friend and a great man,' Red said as he wiped his eyes with the back of his hand. 'He was my best friend.'

'Thank you, Red,' the young man said. 'Thank you for saying that.'

Red resumed his seat and the young man continued his sad walk down the church aisle. When he reached the altar he placed his hand on the coffin. Chloé stepped out of the front pew and embraced the young man.

'I'm glad you got here in time,' she whispered in his ear. 'I'm so sorry, I loved Uncle Jim. I'm going to miss him very much.'

'So am I,' whispered the young man.

Líla was next to embrace the young man, Michael extended his hand and after they shook hands, the young man stood beside a heartbroken Theo.

'Glad you're here son,' Theo said in a very tired voice as he placed his hand on the young man's hand.

The sacristy door opened, a priest walked to the altar and the

THE ACTOR

frumpish woman standing behind the young man tapped him on the shoulder and said 'Who are you?
   'My name is James and like my father I'm an actor.'

Acknowledgements

My first thanks goes to my grandfather Ira Allen, a man who dedicated his life to theatre and a man I would have dearly loved to have met.

My next thanks goes to two fine actors, the late Jim Reid and the late Jim Mooney, both of whom provided me with great insights into acting and who shared many theatrical stories. Thanks to Brendan Beirne for designing the book's cover and his endless interest in the developing novel. I would also like to thank Godfrey Smeaton for his watercolour painting of the Queen's Theatre used for the book's cover. I thank the 'real' Leslie Laurence for graciously allowing me to use his name.

Thanks goes to John Swords, Treasa Brogan, Mary and Joe Brennan, Michael Fielding and Al Valentine for reading early drafts of the book and for their encouragement and insights. I would like to thank Jimmy McGlone for generously loaning me Ira Allen's original manuscripts.

I sincerely thank my editors Derek and Helen Falconer for their sensitive editing which brought great clarity of meaning and continuity to the book. My thanks to Gerry O'Hara for his input on all things historical, if there are any historical inaccuracies in the book, the blame is mine, not his. I would like to thank my eagle eyed proof-readers Mary Kiely and Miriam O'Hara for their thorough work on the novel. Thanks to Vanessa O' Loughlin for her advice and help through the years.

A very special thanks to my family Paul, Mark, Therese, Chloe and Jamie for their indulgence, help and support. But nobody deserves more thanks than my wife Julie for her endless patience and encouragement.

This book is available as a paperback and an e-book from
Amazon.com

My website can be found at www.cecilallen.com
You can e-mail me at theactor@cecilallen.com

Printed in Great Britain
by Amazon.co.uk, Ltd.,
Marston Gate.